Lords of Kerballa

VOLUME ONE

of

MORDUC: A MODERN ROMANCE

Lords of Kerballa

Volume One

of

MORDUC: A MODERN ROMANCE

John H. Underhill

To order additional copies of this book, contact:
Xlibris LLC
1-888-795-4274
www.Xlibris.com
Orders@Xlibris.com
623034

CONTENTS

Dedicated to John and Kyp, who loved Morduc

CHAPTER 1

The Awakening

John lay face up on the stone floor of the King of Time's banqueting hall. Black briars bound his hands and feet. High above him in the rafters dozed the Lady Topalak, her blind serpent snout resting on her chin spider legs.

John tried to shake his mind free from its inner darkness. Far off, a blue-white star appeared. *At last*, he thought, *rescue*. He began to twist and thrash as the star floated slowly toward him. The SpiderSnake stirred, her eyelids lifting on empty eye sockets. The heat-detecting membranes of the two red pits on her snout quivered. Somewhere below was living flesh in which she could lay her eggs. She began flowing around the beam like a brook of black oil, drooping her head into the shadowy air of the banqueting hall.

John opened his eyes—and screamed. Instead of a floating blue-white star, he saw the huge blind snout of the SpiderSnake, her hairy chin-legs palpating the air. He hunched and scrunched away from the snake, leaving white spur marks on the slates. The SpiderSnake arrested her descent. From far away came a flutelike whistling. The bell at the door jangled. No steps ran to answer it.

One huge leaf of the door banged open. A figure as tall as a three-year-old maple sapling stood silhouetted in the morning sunlight. "Is there no one here to offer me breakfast?" said the figure in a loud voice as he strode into the dark hall, kicking cups out of the way.

"Gardez en haut," rasped John's voice from the darkness.

The figure looked up and saw the snake's huge head swaying in the dark air. In a single motion, he drew an arrow from his quiver, fitted it to his bow, and let it fly into the SpiderSnake's abdomen. She crashed to the floor, the arrow throbbing in her belly. She lunged toward the bowman on her chin spider legs. He sent a second arrow straight into her open hissing mouth and then a third into her empty right eye socket, straight through to her brain. She collapsed at the bowman's feet in a writhing bloody coil.

The bowman waited until the snake lay still and then, carefully stepping around the slippery red mound, said, "Many thanks, oh bodiless voice."

"Grhwff," came a muffled sound from the shadows. On the floor, among the tipped-over tabletops and trestles, the bowman saw a stocky, red-haired youth encased in red-steel armor, his hands and feet bound with black briars.

"Who are you?" asked the bowman, approaching the trussed-up youth cautiously.

"John," croaked the young man. "Will you cut off these cuffs before the thorns bleed me to death?"

The bowman drew a small green knife from his belt sheath and deftly slit the briars binding John's wrists. The thorn cords slithered eyelessly away, slipping into the cracks between the flagstones.

"What have we here," chuckled the bowman, "a nest of briar constrictors?"

"Joke later, please," coughed the youth.

The bowman slit the young knight's ankle bonds. They too scuttled away into the cracks between the flagstones. "My, my," he said, resheathing his knife. "You've been up against some *thorny* company and lost, by the looks of it. A wild wonder it is, red-carapaced one, you aren't dead."

"'Tis indeed," said the red-haired knight, slowly sitting up. "Would a bin paralyzed'n planted. Haaaaaaagh. Thanks, li'l savior. Is it chance or Drefon's Dee? Oooooooooglahxxxx. You have my gratitude even if ye seek the princess yourself. Grrrrraaoughf."

The bowman looked puzzled but said only, "For my arrival, no doubt it is Drefon's Desire, oh red-haired and red-armored one, but for the rest, it was only fair return for your warning. Anything less would have been ungreen ingratitude, and we of the green are never ungrateful."

The red knight waved his hand self-deprecatingly. "That SpiderSnake was only interested in me. You could have run. Yet you deserved a warning just the same. I didn't want her to get you too, little one."

Who does he think I am? mused the bowman. *The day I can't kill a SpiderSnake, especially an old blinder like that, will never dawn.* But aloud he said only, "Strong red knight, I could do with a little less of your 'small' and 'little' and 'young.' Since you don't speak as if your wits are as thewy as your thighs, I excuse the diminutories, but pray cease them. I am older than I look. May I ask what brought you under attack?"

"Sorry, young . . . I mean old . . . I mean . . . sharp-aiming . . . sir. I apologize. I've been lying on these stones for how many days and nights now, I don't know."

"At least a beard's worth," observed the bowman.

John rubbed his cheeks and chin, which were covered with a short growth of red beard. "The cold stone slates chilled my very spine bone, and then that SpiderSnake wanted my brawn for her babies' breakfast and would have gotten it too but for . . ."

"Ah, *breakfast*!" broke in the bowman. "What a marvelous . . ."

But John kept right on talking. "You came just in time to prevent the bite and the burying. I'm sorry I spoke in a way that offended you."

"Apology accepted, but you just mentioned breakfa—," said the bowman as John interrupted again.

"I don't suppose, ah, young, ah, I mean, well, however old you are, that you've got something about you that would wash these cinders out of my throat? Haaaaak. A bit of wine or water, perhaps?"

"I've got one and will get the other," said the bowman.

He picked up a fallen cup, exited the hall, and, after some creakings of a well winch in the courtyard, came back with the cup full of cold water. From a green leather bottle by his side, he added a splash of glowing red wine. He swirled the two together and handed the cup to John, who, propping himself up on an elbow, sipped the mixture meditatively, letting its healing balm slip slowly down his throat.

When the cup was empty, he said, "That restores me. What is it? Never drank wine and water like that before."

"It's pomegranate wine from my father's garden," said the bowman. "I carry it with me wherever I go."

"Never heard of any wine made from granite, little fel . . . Ooops."

"Not granite, stone mind," replied the cupbearer. "*Pom*egranate. It's a fruit, bigger than an apple, with a tough red rind, but within, twinkling ruby-jewel seeds, sweet almost as life itself. You most of all should know the virtue of that color."

"Why?" said John.

"Because you yourself have a tough red rind. But what's inside? Unless the fruit be ripe, it can be bitter as sin."

"Well, I suppose so," said John, wondering whether his new acquaintance were entirely sane.

"Never mind," laughed the bowman, seeing the skeptical look on John's face. "Don't worry about it. I'll explain later if you wish. For the present, Red John—if you don't mind my calling you that—it would be enough to get you standing."

"Good idea," said John. John sat up. Morduc shoved a chair behind him, and John hoisted himself up by the chair's arms until he was sitting in it. After a short rest, he pushed himself up from the chair and stood teetering on his red-steel-shod feet. Holding on to the smaller figure's shoulder, John clankingly shook out his legs one after the other. "That's better," he said as the blood began to tingle again in his toes. When John finally felt steady on his feet, he said, "Thankee, stranger. Thankee much."

John was looking down at a boy-sized but full-grown man, with smooth leathery cheeks, a hawk-beak nose, and a pointed chin. His skin was green.

His hair and eyebrows were a nearly black shade of green. His eyes glowed like dark emeralds lit from within. He was dressed in seventy times seven shades of green, from his pointed cap with an iridescent green feather to his green-black leather boots. He had on a light-green shirt under a medium-green jerkin over dark-green leggings, all belted with a green leather ceinture. By his waist, in a green, tooled-leather scabbard, hung the knife with which he had cut John's bonds. On his back was a mottled green quiver full of green arrows, fletched with feathers of the same hue as the one in his hat. His bow and bowstring were green as well. "You know *my* name," said John, "and you have even added to it. Now I'd like to know yours."

"My name is Morduc," said the figure in green.

"Funny name," said John.

"Funny fellow," replied Morduc sharply.

"Sorry, sorry. Didn't mean to speak offendingly again."

"Don't worry. I'm getting used to it. Candor is no crime. 'Only the dishonest the honest detest,' my father says."

John was silent for a long moment, mastering an inner pain. Finally, he said, "Thank you for that. I have an uncle whose sentiments are the same, though they haven't brought him peace or happiness."

"Truth is not the food of peace, my big Red John. Any fool knows that."

"But it *should* be," said John, striking his fist vehemently on a tabletop. Morduc took a step back. John went on, "If truth isn't light, water, bread, and love, then what is life for?"

Morduc said nothing. John lapsed into head-hanging silence as he walked this way and that among the disarranged tables. When he spoke again, he said, "What kind of a name is Morduc? I don't recognize its nation or language."

"It's an elvish name. I've been traveling since sunup. I had hoped to find some breakfast and welcome at this castle, but I find no one outside and only you within."

"'Ellish name?" said Red John, rubbing the back of his neck.

"You push me too far," replied Morduc.

"What?" said John, looking up. "What did I do now? I have no intent except to show you the utmost respect . . . and . . . and . . . gratitude for saving me from the SpiderSnake."

"Then why did you say my name was hellish?"

"Oh no, no, no, Morduc. My throat is still dry and my lips numb. *Elfish.* I understood." And then John smiled the most radiant, warm, friendly smile that Morduc had ever seen.

Morduc laughed in delight. What was the use of being angry with this intense, bumbling ox?

Morduc resumed, "Once more then. Elvish it is, and actually, East Elvish at that, and furthermore, it's a contraction. My full name is so long that even if I told it to you, you wouldn't be able to remember it. It goes on for days and days in your time."

"My time?" said John, looking up. "Isn't time just time, wherever you go?"

"No, my naive red-armored knight. There's *your* time, human time, you know—birth, growth, grief, and death. I'm a visitor *in* your time, but I don't live *by* your time. Elves live forever, or almost. That is . . . unless they're killed in battle or . . . SpiderSnake attacks. At least, I don't know any who have died any other way. The longest human life is no more than a seventh of a seventieth of a seventeenth of a second of a May morning—just like this one—in elves' lives. *This* morning I've come out for a walk. I'm strolling about the world to see what it's like, and so far I don't like what I've seen. Thick, hairy SpiderSnakes, blind scuttling briars, and empty, joyless halls. *And* I'm still hungry. I've been trudging since birdsong, and you know that doesn't fill a belly. What did you do to them? There's not a living person in the house as far as I can tell, not a horse, cow, donkey, dog, rat, or cat, though I do think I heard some renegade chickens clucking somewhere. Why don't you go look for some eggs while I rummage in the pantry?" said Morduc over his shoulder as he disappeared down a narrow stairway.

No horses? thought John to himself as he walked out to the yard and found the chicken house. *Where is RedFire then?* He searched in the straw under the protesting hens and found five large eggs. Then he filled a bucket at the well and returned to the banqueting hall. Morduc reappeared from the stairway with several small, round loaves in his hands.

"Mice didn't get these," he said, "But the kitchen looks like a whirlwind hit it and lifted everyone out, all at once. Bowls left every which way, spoons and knives scattered. Some terrible tumult went through this place. What happened?"

"I'll tell you while we eat," said Red John.

Morduc went over to the hearth, filled a small black kettle with water from the bucket, put the eggs in it, and swung it over the cold, dark ashes. Then he arranged some tinder grass in a small pile beneath the pot, stuck his hand into it, and snapped his fingers. Immediately a thin curl of blue smoke sprang up.

John's eyes opened wide. "Talk about getting a fire going in a snap," he said.

"It's just my spark-ling personality," said Morduc over his shoulder.

Red John groaned. "You have a pun-ishing wit."

Smiling to himself, Morduc took twigs from a pile by the side of the hearth and added them to the burning grass. He added larger and larger sticks until he had a brisk fire going under the kettle.

After the five eggs had boiled hard, they sat down to eat. John tossed a hot egg from one hand to the other, and as he cracked it on his cuisse piece and peeled off the shell, he said, "Do you know what place this is, Morduc?"

CHAPTER 2

How Red John Came to the Castle

"I had hoped you would tell me," Morduc replied. "I can read the words carved over the door in the sandstone, but I can't tell what they mean. They say: 'Land Castle of the King of Stone, King of the Wind, King of the Moon, King of Space, King of Time.' Does that mean anything to you, Red John?"

"It does," said John. "Many weeks ago, there came riders past our farm proclaiming that the King of Time's daughter had a riddle and a quest and that whosoever answered the riddle and performed the quest would marry her and become the Prince of Time, and when the king her father died, her husband would be King of Time and she would be his queen, and they would reign together over stone and wind and light and love. I was fired at the thought. I had heard of the red-gold princess, Aleth Trealthweow, her justness of soul, her intelligence, her liveliness of spirit, her beauty, but at my practices with wooden sword and lance or riding bareback on my favorite plow horse through the hill forests, I had not thought such as I could ever actually win so high a bride. My father had been a true knight, but he died before I ever really knew him, so I never learned the ways of war, the world, and how to speak to men in council and highborn women in court. All he left me was his armor. Not even the rocky farm where I grew up was mine, but rather my mother's for life, and her brother, my uncle's after that. So I had nothing—no wealth, no patrimony, no education, hardly even a name. I grew up on that apple-and-oat farm with my mother and my young sister, Anyalysia, and my mother's brother, Yedward. The education I received consisted of but handfuls of half-told tales from my one-armed uncle as he sat long nights by the fire after cider and supper and cider, and more cider, and on the few mornings when he was sober, some short lessons in fighting and riding. He had fought side by side with my father in a great battle to the north, where he had lost his arm and my father his life. He crept home to heal, but he wouldn't talk about that battle at all, just cried and cried and drank and drank, merely saying over and over that my father had fought bravely but had gone underground.

"What he loved to tell most were tales of the times when he and my father had been young and had gone off adventuring in the service of one lord or another and had brought home plunder aplenty, and had gone to great feasts in the halls of kings and mingled with noble warriors and counselors and beautiful wise women, and visited many a nation. 'Lost, all lost,' he would sigh, weeping. Then for an instant, a fierce fire would kindle in his eyes, and he would say to me, '*You* can get it back, lad.' He'd teach me ward and thrust and slash and all the tactics of battle. But when he would begin to try to explain strategy to me over the chess board, he'd lapse into his cider-dark winter mood again, and I would have to await return of the spring of his spirit to learn more."

"It doesn't sound like all that spotty an education," said Morduc. "You're well spoken, if one excuses a little impulsive candor, and you seem right-minded and kindhearted, ready of courage, and loving of justice. What else need a knight know? What did your mother tell you about your father?"

"Nothing. She never spoke ill of him, but that's because she never spoke of him at all. Whenever my uncle's face would fill with the light of the adventures of their youth, she'd merely say, 'Teach him of apples and oats and honey, Yedward. In the end we'll all be the better for it, until my Orra returns.'"

"Orra?"

"My father."

"*Your* father? Orra? Orra StrongThews?"

"Orra is all I know," said Red John, gnawing on a piece of dry bread. "I never heard he had any name or fame. He's just dead. A nameless, meaningless dead knight. A nothing. You can't really have heard of him, can you?"

"Possibly I have," said Morduc. "If you are the son of Orra StrongThews, you come from a lineage known favorably even in the furthest forests of elfland."

"Really?" said Red John, looking up. "That's hard to imagine, but I like thinking it might be so. Sometimes I feel it must be so, but what's a feeling? A nothing. It comes. It goes. It means nothing."

"Is that what you think of feelings?" said Morduc.

"Of course. What else is there to think? Where'd *you* study philosophy?"

"Where did I . . . ? See here, my strong but naïve Red John, I have studied philosophy with the greatest masters of mind in Drefon's Shadow, and I was taught that, among mortals, feelings make facts. Your father's feeling for your mother, for instance."

"Oh, well *that* isn't a feeling. That *is* a fact. A man's true love for a woman is as . . . well . . . solid . . . as . . . as . . . eternity. And after all, I am here as proof of it."

"I see," said Morduc with a small smile. "You were mentioning your father, named Orra. Possibly Orra StrongThews. Have you ever heard of any other Orras?"

"I haven't, Morduc. Perhaps there's really hope for me after all. What else have *you* heard?"

"What I have heard, my sad and lonely Red John, is that he has indeed gone underearth. And yet you say your mother expected him to return?"

"Yes, she always said, 'Until my Orra returns,' and that would send my uncle off into another one of his fits of grief and weeping."

"And your mother did not encourage your battle exercises?"

"She didn't forbid them, but when she read to me, it was always stories of young men who became priests of Drefon. I always asked for stories of wars, but she refused to read me any. I finally had to teach myself to read the books in my uncle's big wooden chest in order to learn about the wars to the south and the wars to the north and the wars to the east."

"No wars to the west?" asked Morduc.

"Not that I know of. To the west is the ocean, isn't it, and across that Argusturia, the floating world?"

"So I have heard," said Morduc. "Well, say on. You were mentioning a princess."

"Right. When I heard there would be a contest for the hand of the princess, I declared to my mother that I would put on my father's armor and find out where the King of Time kept his court and see how I might win this princess and a proper kingdom for myself."

"You had your father's armor? How strange."

"Why strange, Morduc?"

"Well, if he died in battle, the knight who defeated him would have taken his armor as a prize."

"I don't know anything about that sort of battle. What does it mean?"

"I'm not sure myself," said Morduc thoughtfully. "What did your mother say when you wanted to go a questing?"

"She gave me a sad, pained look, kissed me on my forehead, and said, 'If you will go, you will go.' I asked her what she meant, but she refused to discuss it with me. That night she packed me two great saddlebags of provisions. In the morning, she took me down to the storeroom under the house, to which only she had the key, and opened up a great red wooden chest. In it lay my father's armor. When I first saw it, I thought it had rusted, and I was angry with her. But when I tried to wipe the rust off, I saw that the color was in the steel. I held it up to me, and though it was a little big, I saw it would do."

"We carried it upstairs, and my uncle put me into it, showing me how the buckles and straps went. He had tears of pride shining in his eyes when he saw me fully accoutered. My mother stood at the door as I mounted, trying hard not to let me see her fear and appall. My sister was looking up in awe at me from behind my mother's skirts. Although my horse was but a plow horse, I had raised him from a colt, and he carried me easily on his red back."

"A red horse too?" asked Morduc.

"Yes, when I saw him foaled, I knew he was mine for life. Everyone on the farm just called him the redlich, but I whispered in his ear that his true name was really RedFire, the steed of a knight. If the farm workers had known what I said to him, they would have thought I was insane, a poor farm boy imagining adventures on a plow horse. Well, I've plowed fields with him, and he's smart, and he's strong, and he wanted adventures too, and I've loved him and cared for him, and in return he's carried me with stamina and steadfastness, with his ears always forward."

"I can see he would do so, particularly if he had the same spirit of adventure in him that you have. He told you that he wanted adventure? How could you know?"

"You understand it exactly. Just because we started without station in life didn't mean we were *never* to go anywhere or see anything or become someone. I loved the farm and my mother and my uncle and even my little sister, annoying though she could be, but I always wanted to see more of the world, whatever the risks, and to be more than a nameless farm boy. When the proclamation about the princess came, I thought it was my moment. You see that, don't you?"

"Of course," said Morduc, without irony.

"I set out riding westward. I rode for several weeks, asking along the way for the route to the King of Time's castle, and what people knew of the princess. Most did not care to talk about the matter. They were content with their milk, and bees, and pears, but since they saw I was friendly, some invited me to stay with them. Once I even fought in a minor skirmish against some cattle raiders alongside a king called Clifford of the Rocks. I saved his life. He knighted me on the battlefield, which was really just a rocky cow pasture, but he made me swear the knight's oath, flattened his sword on my shoulders, one after the other, and then embraced me hard with his fierce, strong arms. He took me home to his court—that is his large stone farmhouse. I stayed with him for a whole month. He taught me much about war, and he let me practice proper behavior in hall among the wise and graceful women there, namely his wife and sister and daughter. He ground off some of my rough edges and told me he wanted me to stay and marry his daughter. Since the day of the contest for the princess was fast approaching, I respectfully declined. Besides, I had talked with the girl and discovered that she, Alana the Swift, was in love with a handsome shepherd. She would have run away to the mountains if I had proposed to her as her father wanted. King Clifford bid me good-bye with tears in his eyes. 'Dear boy, I shall always remember you. You are ever welcome here.'"

"'I shall remember you too, my foster father, and first kind king. I hope I shall prove worthy of your love.'" I jumped up on RedFire and pressed on until I finally came to this castle."

"Clifford of the *Rocks*?" interrupted Morduc with amusement. "That must have been some grand castle."

"It was only a good, stout stone farmhouse but with ten miles on a side of rich pasture," said John. "He treated me kindly and well. He was more a father to me than my own, and I loved him for it. I will hear naught said against him."

"Very well," said Morduc, suppressing a laugh. "Carry on, my stony-field knight. You arrived at this castle."

CHAPTER 3

The First Night of the Riddle

"The yard was filled," resumed John, "with other knights and their horses and squires. I was received courteously enough, I suppose, since I was taken into the great hall and seated at a table for dinner along with the other knights. I spoke to several and found that they too had come in response to the same proclamation I had heard. I had not thought there would be so many to compete against."

"Was it in this very hall, then, you were?" asked Morduc.

"Yes. Right here. Dinner had been served, and afterward, large bowls of salted sunflower seeds had been set out, and a wonderful sweet, dark wine poured out to each in his own cup. The whole feast had been presided over so far only by the seneschal. Neither the king nor his daughter had appeared. Then, as we were sitting over the thick, purple wine, we heard drums and trumpets and nakirs in a fanfare, and the seneschal called for us all to stand. A door in the far corner of the hall opened. A number of lords entered in procession, filing in to stand behind the head table, and in the center was the king with the princess on his arm. When the king and princess were in front of the two thrones on the dais, they stopped, and along with the lords on each side of them, surveyed the knights standing at the tables filling the room.

"I had never seen a woman of such beauty in all my life, Morduc. She wore a white gown shimmering with millions of silver droplets, and the light from her unbound red-gold hair lit up the entire hall. She had dark eyebrows, and huge green eyes, and a strong nose. She looked at us with so searching a glance that each one of us felt as if he alone mattered to her. Suddenly we all grew jealous of each other, each wanting to possess that magical face for himself alone, each wanting forever to be the sole object of that gaze, to see the lips smile at us and to kiss them. The king and the princess seated themselves, and the seneschal motioned for the rest of us to be seated as well.

"The king began to speak in low measured tones, in a brogue of the north. I could hardly understand what he was saying at first. Eventually I was able to make out his meaning. He was welcoming us and inviting each of us to advance and give our names and where we came from before he announced the conditions of the quest and posed the riddle. When my turn came, I did as the others had. I went up to the space before the thrones, bowed, and stated who I was, who my father and mother were, and where I came from. The princess looked at me piercingly, and then, surprisingly, leaned toward her father and behind her cupped hand murmured something to him that I could not hear.

"The king turned and gave her an angry look and then turned back and welcomed me, repeating my name and parentage and place and then nodded for me to return to my seat. When all of the other aspirants had likewise given their names, the seneschal called out, 'Are there any others who would present themselves to the king for the hand of the princess?' There was a scuffle and a stir at the back of the hall, and in stalked a gigantic knight dressed in black armor, with a plume of slick black feathers on his helmet. He had a long black sword by his side, the hilt stone of which was a huge single black diamond, shining and brilliant yet opaque at the same time.

"That's hardly possible," interjected Morduc as he broke off a piece of bread.

"I know," replied John, "but that is not the least of the impossibles of that knight."

"Indeed," said Morduc, stopping with the bread halfway to his mouth and lifting an eyebrow. "Well, say on, then."

"The sparkle of that hilt stone was not a reflection, but a swallowing of light. What we saw were the mere foamy flecks tossed off as its facets gulped down the beams of light around it into a whirlpool of darkness. My heart stirred in anxiety. I did not like to look at it for fear it would drink the very light out of my eyes." John shuddered and fell silent.

"Drink the light out of your eyes?" said Morduc gently but incredulously. "My dear Red John, forgive me, but I don't think that's possible!"

"Don't laugh at me," said John, suddenly angry. "You weren't there!"

Morduc looked with astonishment at the thick young knight. Was he a fool or just an innocent? A wed-to-his-own-words half cock, or merely a good-hearted, if inexperienced, idealistic young man? *Well*, thought Morduc, *perhaps there is really no difference.*

Finally, Morduc spoke gently into the cavernous silence of the banqueting hall. "I'm sorry. We elves, you know. Fearlessness and logic and all that. We sometimes forget. Please go on. Who was this so-called knight with the light-swallowing hilt stone?"

John continued, "The black knight named himself to the king, but I was so fascinated by the hilt stone that I didn't catch it. The king seemed highly agitated, and when he stood up to speak, he was even harder to understand than ever. He said something like, 'You have all come here to win the hand of my daughter. To do this, you must fulfill a quest, but to win the quest, you must first discover what the object of that quest is. What you are to seek will be described in a riddle. Those who claim they understand the riddle may present their answers, one by one. Each will have but one chance to answer. The first knight to answer correctly wins the quest. If he is then successful in the quest, returning here with its object in a year and a day, that knight wins the princess and all our kingdoms forever.' Here the king paused for a moment and then went on more slowly and with great emphasis. 'If, on the other hand, your answer is incorrect, I charge you on your honor as a knight, first to leave this realm immediately and never to disclose the riddle. Second, if you fail to correctly answer the riddle, you are never again to seek a mortal woman in marriage. Is that understood?'

"There was a general uproar in the hall with many loud voices protesting the conditions. 'All that distance, and then to learn *this*?' shouted one.

"An extremely handsome young knight stood up and called out angrily, 'We may breed, is it, but only bastards?'

"A voice from the back of the hall called out, 'You'll breed bastards anyway, won't you, ye young cockerel,' and the rest of the knights laughed, and the handsome speaker sat down red faced.

"Through it all, the king stood impassively, waiting for silence. He finally raised his hand, and the room became silent again.

"'You may leave if you are not satisfied with the terms,' said the king slowly, making sure his words were clear. 'This is a voluntary game.'

"'Easy for you to say, when the prize is so great and you're not competing,' called out a voice. 'It's an outrageous oath.'

"'Silence,' called out the seneschal. 'We will have order and decorum here.'

"The room quieted again. The king said, 'If you wish to remain, you must swear.'

"One of the knights who was sitting close to the head table got up and addressed the king. 'How may we know whether we have answered correctly? In a matter of such weight and with such a penalty, who can judge? I urge you not to make the cost of error so extreme. Never to marry? That which all the world wishes?' The room was filled with murmurs of assent.

"The king waited again for silence. 'You shall all hear the answers. The RiddleMaster shall judge, and you shall judge him.' The king signaled with his hand. A long-bearded old man whose mouth worked constantly, opening and closing like a fish's, shuffled forward. One eye was dead white but the other had a wild pale-blue light in it. The knights looked long and hard at the old man. As they looked, he grinned toothlessly, his lips opening and closing, while a dribble of spittle rolled out of the corner of his mouth and down his dirty-white beard.

"The knight who had protested said disgustedly, 'I'll not be judged by a madman,' and stalked out of the hall.

"'That man understands himself well,' continued the king. 'I advise any others who lack the courage for such a contest to leave now. For, you see, gentlemen, the conditions are proper to this choice. It is no slight matter that I put before you, this riddle and marriage quest. The winning is priceless, but the cost of failure is only slightly less than all. Think well, then, before you enter its hazard.'

"He waited for any others to stir. When none did, he lifted his hand and said, 'Before I propose the riddle, all who remain to hear it must swear.'

"'Propose the oath then,' came a mumbled voice.

"'Do you swear, on your oath and honor as a knight, to tell no one else this riddle, to depart in peace if you attempt and fail to answer it, and to defend to the death the honor of the man who is successful in it?'

"There were a few who mumbled, 'I swear.' Suddenly the king roared in a voice like an angry whirlwind, '*Rise and swear!*' At that, every knight in the room stood up, and they said together in loud chorus, '*I swear.*'

"The voice of the king dropped back to its customary level and said, 'Good. I approve the oath. Hear now the end of your searches.'

"At a nod from the king, the RiddleMaster tilted his head back and chanted in a high, thin voice:

'Swiftest and most slow,
Above and then below,
Beauty's best
In shadow's show.'

"Here he paused, fixing the whole assembly with his one good eye and then snapped out the last line:

'Mind me, find me, bind me.'

"There was absolute silence as each of us tried to think of an answer. Suddenly the wizened figure let out a high cackle and looked triumphantly over the hall full of tall, brawny men in full armor. He seemed about to say something more, but the king raised his hand again, and the chanter stepped back.

"Except for the sound of breathing, and the flaring of the torches, and the soft puffing in and out of the RiddleMaster's lips," continued John, "the hall remained silent while the multitude of knights turned over in their minds what the verses could mean. I searched my memory too, trying to remember all my mother had told me, all I had read in the tall leather-bound books I had found in the chest in my uncle's room, and all I had heard from the old women as they sat spinning in the sun, singing ancient songs and asking riddling rhymes of the children. But no answer flew into my head, and I began to despair that I would fail even before I had begun."

"What did the king do then?" asked Morduc. "That riddle is almost elfin in difficulty. Did anyone figure it out?"

"One tall, slim young knight, with dark flowing hair and dark eyes, stood up confidently and strode to the cleared space in front of the thrones. 'Your Majesty,' he said. 'I am Count Alexisander of the Olavé Islands, and I believe I have the right answer and thus deserve to be awarded the quest, but if my answer is correct, I have some difficulty in seeing how I can achieve its object.'

"'I know your family well,' replied the king. 'You have always abided by your oaths. If you have doubts, you need not answer, but if you choose to hazard, tell your answer to the RiddleMaster. Remember, however, that you have agreed never to marry if your answer is wrong. Do you so declare?'

"The knight hesitated for a moment and then said, 'I so declare.'

"'Give your answer, then, oh Alexisander of the Islands, and may it fare well with you,' replied the king.

"'My answer,' said the knight, 'as to what is swiftest and most slow, above and then below, beauty's best in shadow's show, is—the stars.'

"A murmur of respectful approval rippled around the room. 'Not bad,' said one voice. 'Ingenious', said another. The old man with the long beard who had proposed the riddle danced with glee beside the king, hopping from one foot to the other. He stretched his scrawny neck forward and croaked excitedly,

"'Explain, explain,
Receive your pain.'

"'Clearly,' said the knight, 'the stars are swiftest because they revolve around us once every day and night, but they also take twenty-six millennia to come round to their original rising positions at dawn. They are above us and below us and surely in shadow's show, the night, they are what is most beauteous.'

"'Ah, yes. I see it,' said a voice in the crowd of knights. 'Surely, a winner,' said another. 'Good show, Alex,' said a third. The wizened old man looked long and hard at the knight and then said with an ugly sneering smile,

'Wrong, wrong,
Is your song.
Thou'st not the knack;
Step back, step back.'"

John stopped speaking and took up another egg, cracked its shell, peeled it, and then began to eat silently, as if he had completely forgotten the story he was telling Morduc.

"And then . . . ?" asked Morduc gently.

"Yes," John replied, looking up in surprise with his mouth open.

"Why did you stop the story?"

"Did I stop?"

"Most assuredly."

"I was even now seeing in my mind's eye what happened next."

"Well, tell *me*, silent visionary. I can't read your mind, you know!"

"Of course, Morduc, of course," replied the red-haired knight, smiling. "I sometimes drift off like that. Sorry."

"All right, then. What happened?"

"Well, the knight did not step back. He stood there calmly, as if he were in a polite conversation and had not just lost all his hopes for happiness in life.

"'Surely your judgment cannot be right, RiddleMaster,' said the knight calmly. 'I declare my answer is the true one, or if not the true one, surely as good as any other. How can you show I am wrong? Your riddle, I suspect, has infinite correct answers. I demand either to be given the quest or to be given a clear explanation of why my answer is wrong. If you cannot do this, RiddleMaster, I believe that you yourself would then owe a forfeit, perhaps even your life, for posing ambiguous and foolish riddles. Do you not agree, oh king?'

"'The implied threat under your smooth speech does not do credit to your noble name,' said the king sternly. 'I urge you not to disgrace yourself with violence but to depart in peace as you have agreed and to observe your oath strictly. Can you deny that it was freely spoken?'

"'I do not deny it, King, and, when appropriate, I shall depart, but I would prefer it to be after this RiddleMaster's head has been severed from his Adam's apple so the wind whistles differently in that scrawny weasand of his.'"

"Oh, ho," said Morduc. "That was a vivid threat. What happened?"

"The old RiddleMaster wasn't in the least intimidated. He stepped toward the knight, jabbed a long, bony finger under his nose, and then chanted in his singsong:
'Oh, an answer good, an answer fine
But not the answer that is mine.
Quest, if you wish, to reach a star.
No girl you win; it is too far.
And the trouble too you clearly saw.
Now you're killed by riddle's claw.
No doubt a handsome, gracious knight;
Too bad you're just not very bright.
Brain, like body, is soft and slack;
Forever wife now shall you lack.
Oh, fool, be gone! Step back, step back.'

"You could see in the knight's eyes that he knew he was defeated, but he was angry at having been made a fool of and said loudly, 'I demand another chance. It is not fair to be set riddles that have impossible answers. Answers that are impossible should not be accepted. It is only too clear that no one can reach the stars. Such answers are neither right nor wrong—they are simply not answers. Therefore, I claim another turn. I will not step back. Ask again, old man.' And at this, he began to draw his sword, but all the other knights rose in their places, and one even put a foot up on a tabletop, ready to leap at him."

"'You've had your chance,' growled a voice in the crowd. 'Get out while you still have your pretty face and can walk.' The count stopped, looked around him, and then dropped his sword back into its scabbard. Turning, he walked sulkily down the hall as the knights opened a way for him. The whole room stood silently watching him go.

"When he finally reached the outer door, he turned and addressed the room, smiling languidly. 'Ah, but what does it matter? I still have the sun, the air, good food and wine, and the night will ever be the time of satisfied desire. It is of so little importance, these marrying matters. I urge you all, come back with me to the islands. There I will feast every one of you, and provide you as well with companions to your taste. My ship will stay for you. What do you say?'

"No one answered and no one moved. After a long, long moment, he gave a deep sigh and a small wave of his hand. 'Ah, well,' he said as he turned and went out, 'So be it. The more's the pity.'

"The rest of us all turned back to the princess. Although each remaining knight was eager to try his luck, each wondered whether he, too, would meet a similar fate, first ridiculed by that crazy old man and then dismissed to an unmarried life forever."

"What happened then?" asked Morduc, cracking an egg on his knee.

"We all sat down again, no one speaking, no one getting up, with only the sound of feet scraping the floor, or the occasional sound of wine being poured from flagon into cup. Finally, the king rose, and the princess with him, and said, 'If there are no others who wish to try to answer the riddle tonight, I invite you all to return tomorrow to try again.' Then he disappeared with the princess and all the attendant lords into the recesses of the castle. The rest of us got up, stretched, and exchanged words to the effect of 'I thought he had it for sure,' and 'I can't, off hand, think of a better answer,' and 'Are *you* going to stay and try tomorrow?'

"Some appeared to be getting ready to leave immediately. Those of us who were staying were led off one by one to a bedroom. Mine was small, shaped like a segment of a circle, high up in one of the turrets. A bent old woman carrying a light showed me the way. She was courteous and serviceable but would not talk about the king or the princess or the wild wizard who had posed the riddle.

"The small chamber was simply furnished with a bed, a chair, and a table. I lay awake a good while turning the riddle over in my mind, gazing out through the small slit of a window at the slow silent stars revolving across the night. 'Stars.' That answer had been rejected. Yet it made sense except for the finding and binding. How could one reach the stars, let alone bind them? I turned a number of other possible answers over in my mind but could not come up with one of which I felt sure. Finally, the embracing firmness of the bed and the warmth of the covers brought me sleep in spite of myself."

CHAPTER 4

The Second Night of the Riddle

"It was full light when I was awakened by the scolding of a small red-gold squirrel perched on my windowsill."

"A golden-red squirrel?" interrupted Morduc.

"Yes," replied John. "Just a common red tree squirrel, with maybe a little bit or a good bit more gold in the red than usual."

"Indeed," replied Morduc. "How strange."

"Yes," said John. "She did turn out to be quite strange after all."

"*She?*" said Morduc loudly, looking up. "How did you know it was a she?"

John blushed so deeply that his ruddy cheeks nearly matched his beard.

"I suppose I don't really know absolutely, but I have my reasons for thinking so. She wasn't that strange a beast, really, once you got to know her."

"There are many strange beasts in the world," said Morduc, looking thoughtfully at John and the red gold of his burgeoning beard. "But go on, John. What happened next?"

"I spoke to her. 'What do you say there?' I asked. But all she did was chitter and flick her tail up and down over her back as she perched on the narrow in-sloping window ledge. 'I have nothing for you,' I said as I jumped out of bed and dressed. 'But I pledge to you, oh bright omen of the morning, that if I am in this room another night, I will bring something for you, if you chose to return.'

"She seemed to approve of that because she flicked her tail twice, turned, and scampered off down the ivy on the turret wall. I put my head out of the narrow opening into the sunlight to see where she had gone, but she had disappeared. When I looked down, I saw there was a great bustle in the castle yard below. I ran down the stairs. I saw knight after knight mounting and leaving by the great gate, abandoning the competition. I never for a moment thought of going myself. After my first sight of the princess, seeing the intelligence in her eyes, and her capacity for love, and presuming the justice in her heart which her outward beauty promised, I had determined that I would marry only her or never marry at all, so the strict conditions meant nothing to me."

"You mean, just at one sight of her, you fell so in love with her that no other woman would *ever* do?"

"That's right," said John simply.

Morduc marveled at the ways of mortals, still so new to him. "What happened then, oh Red John?"

"I made sure RedFire was fed, and curried him myself, and arranged with a groom for his exercise, and then I went inside again for a bit of bread and cheese and coffee and fruit. For the rest of the day I wandered around the castle and its grounds, thinking and thinking and thinking about that riddle. Swift *and* slow. Above and *then* below . . . I couldn't puzzle it out. What do you think it means, Morduc?"

Morduc stopped with an egg halfway to his mouth. "Why do you ask me what I think it means, John? Didn't someone eventually answer the riddle correctly?"

"Well . . . in a sense . . . someone possibly did . . . but I'm not sure it was the right answer." John leaned forward. "Please tell me your answer, Morduc. It might be worth something, well . . . how shall I say . . . someday."

"Stop now, stop now, my evasive red-bearded friend," said Morduc, putting up his hand. "Why could you want to know now? You don't think you are still in the running do you? You didn't answer the riddle, obviously."

"Well, that's the problem. I'm not sure whether I did or not."

"*Not sure!*" said Morduc in amazement. "Then you'd better count your toes to make sure no one's stolen any. How can you be '*not sure*' whether you answered correctly? If you had, you'd be hot on the quest, not oversleeping in a lazy stone bed. But if you failed, then I can understand the way I found you. *You* are a riddle yourself, Red John."

"That is exactly what I answered," said John excitedly, "and I'm not sure whether it was right or not."

For the second time that morning, Morduc stopped with food halfway to his mouth and looked in utter amazement at this strange, intense young mortal. Finally he said, "I admit I have heard a somewhat similar riddle in elf lore, but how that old wizard got hold of it, I don't know. I can't imagine any elf teaching him Elf-Fang."

"Tell me, Morduc, please tell me your answer."

"Finish your story first. Then I may indeed be able to help you."

"Very well. When we assembled again in the great hall that evening, there were still enough aspirants left to almost fill it. Again after dinner, the king came in with the princess on his arm, the two of them marching in the center of that line of lords. As I looked at the procession, it suddenly struck me that the lords were acting more like guards than attendants. I wondered whether the king was in charge of his own castle. I looked at the princess closely. Her singularly direct gaze that had excited the fire of desire in me the night before swept the hall again. As it came to rest on me for a fleeting second, I instantly came to believe that I had read it utterly wrongly the night before."

"You had read her gaze wrongly?" said Morduc.

"Yes, Morduc. It wasn't coquetry designed to excite us to competition for her. She was searching our souls. She was looking for some lost jewel in the depths of each of our hearts."

"Some lost jewel?" said Morduc, suddenly alert.

"The jewel of loving justice, Morduc. Don't you see? She was being forced to marry. She was too courageous to be frightened and too noble to be contemptuous of us and too proud to be rebellious, but she was looking into our souls to see whether there was a single good and true heart among us, among all those bold men and knights who sought her hand in marriage."

"You are making quite an assumption there, Red John. But nevertheless, say on."

"In that moment, as her gaze, which was life itself to me, rested on my face, all selfish thoughts of winning a kingdom went completely out of my mind. Now I longed only to serve her, to see her truly smile, to smile at receiving from me the respect and comfort and justice that, it was now clear, all others, perhaps even her own father, were denying her. I could feel the others responding to her gaze, not as I just had but as we all had the night before, as straw to flame. Suddenly, I realized that to serve her I had to save her. I *had* to answer the riddle now, not to win her, but to free her, and the puzzle and bafflement of how to do so began to make my head ache.

"You did truly set yourself a difficult task," replied Morduc. "What happened next?"

"The old riddle maker shuffled along at the end of the line, his eyes, or rather eye, gleaming with wicked delight at the prospect of foiling another brave young knight.

"Just as he had on the preceding night, the king called on the wizard to chant out the verse and then invited anyone to try to answer it. At first no one stood up. Then a pockmarked, balding, corpulent knight with a patch over one eye, wearing a dull brown ridged suit of armor, arose and moved slowly up to the dais. He seemed nearly as broad as he was tall, clearly immensely strong, and with a certain look of crafty intelligence about him, but coarse faced and ugly.

"'Give your name,' said the king.

"'I am known as Otto the Squat,' said the knight, bowing as well as he could. 'I hold the Rock Passes of Ice in the Land of AllNoneSun.'

"'Your name and kingdom are known to us. Do you wish to answer the riddle?'

"'I do,' replied the knight, and leering in the direction of the princess continued, 'and I fully expect to repeat those same two words at another time.'

"Although she maintained her outward composure, I felt an inward shudder of disgust pass through the princess. I became more determined than ever to preserve her from such assaults.

"'It may possibly be that you will get a chance to use those words again in a ceremony of marriage,' said the king, 'or you may not. All things may be, nothing is written but in the hearts of men. Your character is your destiny. But first, here in this hall, you must answer the riddle.'

"At a sign from the king, the RiddleMaster chanted out the verse a second time that evening.

'Swiftest and most slow,
Above and then below,
Beauty's best
In shadow's show.
Mind me, find me, bind me.'

"The fat knight replied immediately, 'I believe what is swiftest and most slow, both above and then below, beauty's best in death shadow's show can only be the oceans, and by that answer, I claim the quest.'

"An excited buzz ran round the hall, for everyone recognized that it was a clever answer. The RiddleMaster trembled with malevolent excitement, like a dried leaf rattling on a limb in a winter wind. At a nod from the king, he stepped forward and chanted,

'Both beautiful and deadly is the sea,
In clouds above, and then below we see,
So too, most slow sapping let it be,
But such, such is *not* my decree.'

"The RiddleMaster cackled and stepped back into line.

"'I challenge the decision of the umpire,' said the thick knight stolidly. 'The sea can be found, we can be mindful of it and its danger, and when I conquer all the globe, *that* will bind it. I am prepared to begin the task this very moment if you will guarantee me my reward.' There was a scattering of applause.

"The RiddleMaster stepped forward and shouted angrily at the top of his voice at the knight:

'But swiftness belongs to neither it nor thee.
The King rejects your shallow plea.
Wifeless as witless shall you ever be.'

"And then he put his driveling, scraggly face up to the squat knight's and snarled sneeringly:

'All beauties shall you ever lack:
Your own or Princess's. Step back, step back.'

"With the last words, some of the spittle that so far had merely dribbled down the old man's beard flew into the face of the knight. He turned red with rage and seemed to grow thicker and shorter until he looked like an immense armored toad. Fuming, he turned and stalked down the hall without any courtesy of departure. At the door he turned and shouted, 'You have not heard the last of me. Otto the Squat will be bound by no enforced oaths. I depart—for now—but not in peace.' With that, he thrust out, slamming the hall door shut with a thunderous clang."

"Did he ever come back?" asked Morduc, "this King Toad?"

"Not while I was there . . . and awake," replied John.

"Well," said Morduc. "Go on. What happened next?"

"What was most amazing," continued John, "was that throughout all this, the princess had retained her composure, as if she could really have borne to be bound to such a beast if he had indeed solved the riddle and had been granted the quest and then had succeeded in it and had won her. Nevertheless, I felt her relax within herself when he left, and from where I sat at the far side of the hall, I smiled at her. As her somber and serious eyes met mine, I thought I saw a recognition in them of my sympathy for her sufferings and then gratitude for that sympathy."

"And was she grateful for your sympathy?"

"That's the strange thing," replied John. "The knight next to me nudged me and whispered, 'See, she's looking at me. She has picked me to love. I know it.' I turned in astonishment to him but said nothing. As I looked around the hall, many of the other knights were rustling in pleasure, as if they too had been the recipients of her glance.

"And did *each* of you," asked Morduc, interrupting again, "think that she had looked at you alone?"

John paused, and hung his head dejectedly. "It would seem so," he said in a low voice.

"And *is* it so, my youthful, red-haired, wet-behind-the ears friend? If she did not give you her look of recognition—how shall we put it—exclusively, would it matter to you?" said Morduc as he handed John the last egg.

John thought about that for a quite a while as he ate. Then he finally said, "No, it would not matter. All I desired was her happiness. Many, perhaps, thought the gift of her gaze was for him alone, but in fact, it was only for me. Of this I am sure because I am sure that I was the only one who understood the complexity and depth of her pain as she experienced it. And even if her glance were not for me alone, that would not alter my love for her and my desire to serve her. It was clear to me that she was in desperate trouble. I was simply the only one who really wished to help her out of it. The rest wanted her for themselves. I merely wanted to restore freedom to her." Here he paused for a moment, and then went on, "Ah, but what a queen she would make! Such a mind. Such courage. Such self-control." He lapsed into silence.

"And the beauty?" asked Morduc. "I think you mentioned beauty before as well."

"Oh, of course," said John. "The beauty. She *is* very beautiful, but beauty like that is merely gold on dung without a noble soul. Surely you know that, Morduc."

"Indeed," said Morduc, looking in wonderment at John and thinking to himself that perhaps there was more to this red calf than his youthful looks suggested.

John continued enthusiastically, "A man could never fear for his kingdom with a partner like that beside him. She would love justice equally with him and would understand without instruction how each thing partook of good and how it did not, and . . ." His voice trailed off.

Morduc waited a while and then spoke again. "And then what happened? Did you finally have a go at the riddle yourself?"

"Not then," said John. "After the disgrace and departure of the toad knight, no others arose. The king proclaimed a third and final trial for the night following and then withdrew with the princess. Some of the other knights were standing around discussing the second answer, but I had no taste for doing so. I pocketed a handful of the salted sunflower seeds from the table in case the squirrel returned and finally was again shown by the same crone as the night before to my small turret room. Again I lay awake trying to sound the depths of the riddle. Was the answer wind? But then how to find and bind it? Was it knowledge? But then, why above and then below? Eventually, as I had the night before, I fell asleep, and because I had been awake so late, the sleep was very, very deep.

CHAPTER 5

The Third Night of the Riddle

"Toward morning I began to hear what I thought was someone speaking in my ear in a small, raucous voice. I only half awoke and saw the same red-gold squirrel from the previous morning perched on the turret window edge, flicking her tail up and down to keep her balance. In my half-awake state, suddenly I thought I began to understand what the squirrel was saying, and I thought she told me how to go about getting an answer to the riddle. It didn't sound all that sensible, but since I had no answer anyway, I felt as if I had nothing to lose by doing what she said."

"And what did she say?" asked Morduc in astonishment.

"She said, just stand up, say I had the answer, and she would bring it to me."

"That is a very strange instruction," said Morduc. "What happened then?"

John continued. "I awoke fully at that point, sprang out of bed, found the handful of seeds from dinner, and put them on the table. The squirrel jumped from the window to the floor and then scrambled up a leg of the table. She cracked and shelled one of the sunflower seeds and, though still alert for flight, nibbled it happily on the table, flicking her tail all the while. Then she packed her cheeks full of seeds, leapt from the table back to the window in one bound, and disappeared, leaving only the sound of rustling ivy behind her.

"I could hardly wait for the day to pass. That night's questioning would either make me or finish me. I went to the stables twice to check on RedFire, but all was well with him. Another group of knights was in the process of leaving. I looked for the knight with the black-diamond-hilted sword, but he was nowhere to be seen.

"Evening finally came. A third banquet was set before the remaining knights. Even with the diminished number, the hall was still hot and noisy, and in my excitement, I fear I drank somewhat more wine than was good for me. My face became flushed, and the music of the viols and the oboes ran round in my head. Just as on the two previous nights, after the dessert had been cleared and the bowls of seeds set on the tables along with the decanters of sweet black wine, we heard in the far distance the harsh music of the drums and trumpets and nakirs. Slowly and solemnly into the hall came the princess, escorted both before and after by the line of nobles, including that scrawny, driveling old wizard. The hall fell silent. Again, at a sign from the king, the old man stepped forward and chanted the riddle in his wild voice:

'Swiftest and most slow
Above and then below
Beauty's best
In shadow's show.
Mind me, find me, bind me.'

"And as before, the king once again invited any who wished to attempt the riddle to come forward and present themselves. All were craning their necks to see who would stand up and go forward. Amidst all that bustle and movement in the room, I felt as if I would burst if I didn't say something. I jumped up and called out over the tables, 'I have the answer.' A bare second after I had jumped up, the dark knight I had seen on the first evening, in a voice sounding as if it came from dark caves filled with black ocean-washed stones, called out, "I too have an answer."

I was so shocked to hear opposition that I stumbled, nearly tripping over my sword as I struggled forward to claim my chance. The black knight strode forward too. We both reached the space before the thrones at the same moment and simultaneously made our obeisances to the king and the princess. She gave me a long, grave, searching look as I bowed. Yet she seemed to look in a similar fashion at the black knight too. This rather cast me down. However, then, she did something quite extraordinary, which overjoyed me and gave me a wild hope.

"And what was that?" asked Morduc, continuing to gnaw on a leathery piece of gray bread.

"She took a few sunflower seeds out of an invisible pocket in her glittering white gown, and putting one between her teeth cracked its shell."

"A *sun*flower seed?!" said Morduc, stopping in midbite. "She was eating seeds? Cracking them open with her own teeth? And during the asking of the riddle? I don't believe it. How could she do such a thing at such a solemn moment? It's grotesque."

"No, no, no. Don't you see, Morduc," said John excitedly. "It was a signal that she had sent the squirrel to me. That *she* was going to give me the answer, right then."

"Humph," said Morduc. "Or she *was* the squirrel, you mean. How well do you really know this princess? I should have thought perhaps you might not have wanted to answer the riddle after that."

"How ridiculous you are, Morduc. It was a sign from her that she was accepting my help. Don't you see?"

"No," said Morduc. "I do not see. But I do think she is a very strange personage. *Did* she give you the answer?"

John looked silently off into a far dark corner of the hall. Finally, he turned back to Morduc and replied awkwardly, "Well, not exactly. She both did and didn't, to be precise about it."

"Now what do you mean by that, O Red John? The logic of contradiction says that being and not being cannot coexist. What in Drefon's name happened?"

"Well, I was standing there with my heart on fire with love, watching her nibble the sunflower seed, waiting for her to slip me the answer, when I heard the black knight begin to speak.

"'Oh King of Time,' the knight said. 'I must be allowed to answer first, being senior in rank and no doubt in valor to this stripling bumpkin here. I demand it as my right.'

"He spoke with such a heavy menace that it chilled my bones, and I saw he was intending to intimidate not only the king, but me as well.

"Perhaps because of the wine, or perhaps because of my passionate nature, I became indignant and spoke up. 'I spoke first, King, and, therefore, I deserve the right to answer first.'

"I heard the black knight draw in his breath between his teeth in hissing disapproval, but I thought I saw a flash of respect and interest in the eyes of the king. His face became grave, and he said, 'Do you really wish to risk it, young man? If you fail to answer correctly, then the Master of Darkness here will have the advantage of your answer by which to guide his own, whereas if you accept second position, you will have the advantage of knowing his answer to adjust your own. Let me advise you to let your elders precede you. It would show wisdom as well as re—'

"'Most clearly, sire,' I said, breaking in, 'that is true, but now is not the time for false deference. How, if he answers correctly, am I then to win the princess, for surely she is not two, but one?'

"At my response, there was a shuffling and a murmur of approval from the other knights in the room. 'The lad speaks well. Let him answer.' When it had died down, the king went on, 'You refuse to give way, then?'

"I could feel the Master of Darkness beside me becoming heavier and heavier and colder and colder with anger while I became more and more heated by my indignation. Trying to keep the anger and irony out of my voice, I responded as courteously as I could, 'With no disrespect to this obviously great champion by my side, Lord King, I do refuse and ask, in justice, to be allowed to give my answer first.'

"'Very well, young knight, answer on, then,' said the king. 'Master of Darkness, you will have to wait your turn.'

"That Master of Darkness, or whatever he called himself, turned away from the king and, as he passed behind me, said in a low voice colder and more cruel than the black depths of the ocean, 'In my own time I will have my turn, little red knight, and then I will give you such an answer as will rattle your teeth.'

"I had no chance to answer this insult because the scraggly wizard shuffled forward and jabbed his dirty-nailed finger in my face and croaked out,

'Well, whippersnapper, what is it? Swift, slow, above, below, beauteous show? Mind, bind. What is it? Don't know, do ye? Can't tell, can ye? Didn't think so! Ha, ha, ha . . .' His crazed, contemptuous laughter rang through the rafters as he turned his back on me. I began to panic. I had followed the squirrel's instructions and was waiting for some sign from the princess, but none came. Perhaps the squirrel herself would bring an answer. I turned my head this way and that, up and down, looking first into the rafters and then under the tables, but the squirrel was not there. I turned quickly back to the princess as the wizard's mocking laughter filled the room. I looked hard at her trying to catch her eye, to understand what I was to do, but she merely continued to look at me profoundly with her infinitely deep, intelligent dark-green eyes. Had I been wrong? I thought. Was this just a plot to disqualify me? I began to stammer.

"'I . . . I . . . I . . .' Suddenly the wizard's high, harsh crazy laugh strangled in his wrinkled throat and he stopped short. He spun around and looked at me fiercely, fixing me with his one watery pale-blue eye.

"'*What?*' he screamed. '*What* did you say?'

"I had no choice but to go on, though this was not what I had expected from what the squirrel had said."

"What you *thought* the squirrel had said," corrected Morduc, "if the squirrel really said it and if you were not merely dreaming."

John looked up at Morduc with troubled surprise on his face. "Do you really think that's all it was?" he said.

"Stranger dreams have been recorded as truth," said Morduc lightly.

John hung his head dejectedly.

"And of course," Morduc continued, "Equally great truths have been dismissed as dreams. Say on. After all, *something* happened after that. Perhaps I just don't understand it yet."

John revived a bit and continued, "Well, I knew that the RiddleMaster would ask me next to explain how I, myself, Red John, was the answer to the riddle, and yet I had no idea whatsoever. So, wine flushed and as defiant as I was innocent of an explanation, I just yelled it out again, as loudly as I could. 'I, I, I am the answer. Make of it what you will. Is it right or wrong? I demand judgment, or Drefon drown you.'

"There was an animated buzz among the other knights. Out of one corner of my eye I saw the princess for the first time smiling, a small, pleased, and brief smile of relief. As she did so, she brushed the seed shells from her lap, as if to say 'Well, That settles *that*. Now we can move on.' Perhaps I really had succeeded in answering the riddle in spite of myself, but if so, what did my answer mean? I didn't have time to ask.

"Suddenly, directly in front of me, all the bony aggressiveness went out of the old wizard. He just drooped and hung on himself like a marionette on a peg. He looked around wobbly headed and idiotic at the king, and then back to me. As his gaze went past me, his face became filled with terror.

"The king stood up by his throne and spoke as loudly as when he had administered the oath. '*Declare, RiddleMaster. I charge you, declare your judgment immediately!*' From behind me I heard the Master of Darkness muttering in a low voice, 'I thought you told me no one could . . .' and then louder, he said, 'You lie RiddleMaster. I challenge the young knight's answer. A black stone rose is the true answer. It is my emblem, and I claim the victory.'

"Then I heard a roar like a great sea storm and I turned to find the Master of Darkness drawing his sword. My eyes were fixed on the black diamond hilt swirling with a darkness that flowed into it like a swallowing black fog. The room began to spin around me in dizzy agony. He stepped past me to the dais and, with one swing of his black-bladed sword, severed the head of the RiddleMaster from his shoulders. The head, its face still filled with terror and surprise, and its beard now darkened with blood as well as spittle, bounced down the steps of the dais and rolled among the feet of the knights at the tables surrounding the hall, who kicked it away from each other like a hairy, bloody, blind soccer ball.

I began to draw my own sword as the Master of Darkness turned toward me. The sea storm roaring in my ears became deafening. The room spun faster. I felt as if I were being rolled up inside a huge, thick carpet, spinning around faster and faster, with light diminishing to a smaller and smaller dot above my head. I began to fall . . . and . . . and . . ." John became silent.

"Yes?" said Morduc after a moment.

"And that's all I remember until I woke up here where you found me, looking up into the blind, black face of the SpiderSnake above me."

Morduc sat silently, turning over the scene in his mind. Finally he stood up and began pacing back and forth. "Most puzzling indeed," he said. "And when you woke up, everyone was gone? And you were here, bound so you could hardly move? And then I came in? Is that all of it, my strong young Red John who had too much of too thick a wine? Are you sure that the whole thing is not some vagabond drunkard's dream?"

A look of shocked injury passed over John's face. He spoke slowly. "You speak to me with a contempt very much like that of the Master of Darkness himself. If you plan to insult me and do me injury of spirit, I do not need your company. I suppose you'll be telling me next that I bound myself with those cruel hooked briars just to make the story look good."

Morduc laughed in acknowledgment, and said immediately, "Well. You do have a point, Red John. A number of points. A fact is a fact. Excuse me for doubting you. We elves are not much experienced in mortal things."

"Good dream or bad," continued John, "real or not, she it is I love and will seek to help, come life or death, she and no other."

Chapter 6

A Quest for a Quest

John stood up and went over to the fireplace and leaned his head against the stone mantel.

After a while Morduc said, "In truth, Red John, I am glad to hear you say so. Dedication of any lesser fervor would hardly serve the purpose, would it, oh newly bearded one. Where, then, do you plan to seek her?"

John pondered and spoke without turning. "That is a very good question . . . but I don't have any answer."

"Indeed," said Morduc. "Very much like the riddle. Then let me ask you a slightly different question. If you were the Master of Darkness, where would you go?"

"But I'm not the Master of Darkness. I'm Red John."

"I *know* that, but it appears to me—correct me if I am wrong—that *he* may have been left standing after you fell. Does that suggest anything to you?"

"It means if I could find him, I could ask him where the princess is."

"Aha!" said Morduc. "Now you're getting somewhere. I agree that you should seek him, though carefully, since he seems no friend to you. Where does he live?"

"I don't know," exploded John. "What do all these questions mean? Where *does* he live?"

"Oh Drefon! By all the little pink peppers in the Palan's garden, this is not a school lesson. Why do you think I know? I thought *you* loved the girl."

"I do," said John, turning from the fireplace and coming over to Morduc. "But what does that have to do with it?"

"Love is more than a mere yearning desire, even a desire to serve. There's a practical side to it as well. You have to have some wit and strength, and you have to use your common sense too. Don't you understand that *you* have to figure all this out, John?"

"I thought you said elves didn't understand mortal matters," said John, with a wry smile.

"They don't, and yet they seem to understand them better than you do," said Morduc. "Are you ready to really think now?"

John drew up a bench and sat down. "I'm ready."

"Well, then. What else do you know about this Master of Darkness?"

John scratched his new red beard thoughtfully. "All I really know is that his voice sounded like stones clacking in the depths of the sea."

Morduc threw up his hands in exasperation. "Is that what you call *knowledge*, Red John? I am amazed at what passes for thinking in mortals' minds. Don't you have *any* other clues?"

John searched his brain. Finally he said, "No. None."

"Well, John," said Morduc. "Suppose you had decided to start looking for him. Where would you start?" Morduc put up his hand as John opened his mouth to speak. "This time don't answer me until you *have* an answer. Don't rush. Stop. Stop! *Stop!* Don't say anything until you can say it in one arrow shot."

"But . . .," John protested.

"No, *no, no!*" insisted Morduc. "Don't say to me, 'I don't know,' or 'You tell me.' You must wait to speak until you have your complete *whereiswhat* arranged in your mind. Wait and think. Breathe. Innnnnnn two, three. Out, three two, one. Breathe again, and only then say your say. Now in what direction would you go to find your enemy and, possibly through him, the princess?"

John lowered his jaw onto his chest, the short growth of sandy beard whispering on the red-steel armor as he turned his head from side to side in thought. Morduc clasped his hands behind him and began walking back and forth in the hall. He stopped at the body of the SpiderSnake. He coiled the ungainly beast like a black hawser, bound it with its own silk, and dragged it into the cold ashes of the hearth. He then went about tipping the trestles upright. Just as he was about to burst out in a stone-shattering, wood-cleaving, ear-deafening, silver-sword-elven scream of frustration, suddenly, without warning, in a low voice, John said, "*Sea.*"

"See what?" asked Morduc, spinning around, scanning the empty room. "What do you see?"

"No," murmured John gently. "I mean the sea, the ocean, saltwater, wet. You know about that, don't you? Elves get their feet wet sometimes, don't they?" said the broad young knight in an expressionless voice.

"Yes, they do, sometimes," said Morduc, giving John a quizzical look, wondering whether this hitherto literal-minded youth was teasing him for the first time. "But very rarely, and never willingly," continued Morduc, keeping his own voice as flat as he could. John continued to sit in silence. Finally, Morduc spoke again. "Now how do we see the sea? Are you saying we should head in the direction of the sea?"

"We?" said John, lifting his head.

Morduc stopped. He had in fact said "we." Why had he said "we"? What was John to him or he to John? Slowly, thoughtfully, he said, "If you would accept my companionship, Red John, I would just as soon go with you as go wherever I was going, which was . . . hmmm, nowhere. No, that's not what I meant to say. I mean, it seems to me that you could use someone at your back if you got into a fight. And you *do* need cheering up now and then too, don't you, in spite of your broad shoulders and strong neck? What do you say?"

"It's true. I do slip under a dark cloud from time to time," replied Red John. "Sometimes I lose hope so completely I can hardly move. No one has ever seen that in me before." John lifted his face to look at the slim, green figure, gathering all of him into his dark-brown eyes. Then he held out his huge hand saying, "Yes. And most gratefully welcome. Comrades."

Morduc took the large hand and shook it. "Comrades."

Nothing more, nothing less, mused Morduc. Yea or nay, forever and a day, and all heart behind it. What astonishing beings these mortals were. Of the earth, with the weight of earth. No more length of life or freedom of motion than . . . well . . . than a beetle, he thought, looking at John encased in his red-steel carapace. Can the Greater Powers be friends with an insect, with a buzzing, hopping piece of wing, with a red frog at the bottom of an air-blue pond, and a rather shallow pond at that? So serious, they are, he thought. Well, one could hardly expect frogs to have a sense of humor, any gaiety or lightness, sunk in the mud of ignorance as they were. He would let himself be dragged along this foggy road by a froggy toad, toady to a toad. Not *quite* that, he mused. He would help this hairy toad catch his pretty lady toad so they could, yes, it must be admitted, breed a brood of toadlets. Was that fit and fair faring for one such as he, an elf prince of the Moon Mountain forests? Perhaps not fit, but surely, surely, no harm in it, no harm to the red hairy toad, no harm to himself.

It was less than a minute of a morning of a day in his ever-long life, Morduc thought to himself. It would be amusing to see what this beefy boy did with his strong mortality. *Afterward*, thought Morduc, *I can go back to the Blessed Trees, to the fluting green-silver sounds of moon-thought songs, to my home, where I will perhaps wring this adventure into a bright brushed flower-light song. A soft day's diversion this, and perhaps in its course, I can teach this rough young ox a little about reality.*

But what astonishments these mortals hold. What *can* this muscle-bound toad see in that cow-toad, or she in him, *if* she does see anything. That incident of the squirrel was curious though. Perhaps there is more under the sun and stars than even agile elf can understand. Unlikely, of course. Yet. He would see. Well then, to work, he thought.

"Now then, Red John, what do you say to our heading in the direction of the sea?"

"I say fine, but what direction is that?"

"A most excellent question, my fine Red John, and that bit of geography will have to be the first order of business, if we can find a first-order geographer. Are you a first-order geographer?"

John looked at Morduc. "Why do you always speak so lightly? This matter concerns the life of the princess. 'Twill not last forever, as it will for thee."

Morduc stared at John and then gently replied, "My apologies, friend. Yet I must ask again, where would you suppose the sea to be?"

John was about to say, "I don't know," when Morduc held up his hand again, and John remembered to think first and speak second. He considered the matter for a minute and then said, "Sun."

"Sun? Sun? Do you say so?" chortled Morduc, jumping up and down. "Now why sayest thou sun, ye of the red case?"

"Well, in the west, you know, the sea, the sun, down, into," said John.

"Your coherence leaves a bit to be desired, oh Red John, but I think I *see* your point and concur. I too have heard that the sun goes down into the sea, and if we follow its rays, we might reach a shore. We can start out in the direction of the setting sun, and we can ask the first knowledgeable spirits we meet whether we are going in the right direction. Will that, so to speak, re-a-shore us?"

"Your wit is wretched wet," said John, smiling a small smile in spite of himself.

"A-pun my word, the man has humor in his heart after all," said Morduc. "If we start west, I do hope we won't have to retrace our steps, and I have a certain confidence we will not. In this whole matter so little is known, that almost any direction we go will tell us more than we know now. Shall we be off?"

The sun was almost directly overhead as they started across the causeway from the castle. The sky was blue, the leaves and flowers fully out. The water in the lake around the castle reflected the sky and the sun within it as well as the two figures who moved down the road curving beside it. The smaller one in green whistled his high lilting song, striding along with his bow across his back and a bulging bag over his shoulder. Master John, the Red, walked by his side. In his armor he looked like a red-steel pin, not to be broken or bent by any force. After a while, to Morduc's whistling random song, John added another deeper sound, likewise without words but punctuating the high melody with zooms of booming, like a drum able to hold its note yet change its pitch. The two sounds circled around each other, moving on together as Morduc and John walked improbably into the west to meet, to conquer, and to accept their fates.

CHAPTER 7

Two Travelers Meet Three Dogs

As they walked along in the deepening afternoon, Morduc and John saw wisps of smoke curling up into the blue sky.

"Farmhouses?" asked Morduc, gesturing toward the swirls.

"Probably," replied John.

"Dinnertime?" asked Morduc hopefully.

"Not yet," said John doggedly.

They trudged on, the sun shining more and more fully in their faces, igniting John's red-steel armor and red-brown hair and beard until he seemed like a walking flame followed by the long black scorch of his shadow. Morduc shimmered beside him in his seventy times seven shades of green.

At one point, their west-wending road intersected another well-traveled track going to the north. They looked as far up the road to their right as they could but saw no one and then shading their eyes against the sun, as far forward westward as they could, with identical results. "Which way do you suppose they went?" asked John.

"They might have gone either way," answered Morduc. "Or neither," he added cryptically.

John went a few steps up the north road, paused, turned, and came back. Then, after another pause, he pointed the way due west, and they continued straight on. Far, far in front of them a low line of darkness on the horizon emitted occasional bright flashes of light as the sun dropped slowly toward it.

"What do you suppose those lights are, Morduc?" asked John.

"Can't be sure. Might be ice on mountains."

"What?" said John, stopping in the road. "Are there mountains between here and the sea?"

"It wouldn't surprise *me* if there were," said Morduc.

"Aren't there monsters in mountains?"

"Sometimes," said Morduc.

"Stone-scaled snakes with icicle fangs and red-lightning eyes?"

"So I've heard."

"Wouldn't it be better to go around them then?" said John. "Maybe we should go back and take that other road after all."

"Seriously, Red John, you must decide whether you really want what you want or whether you want an easy time of it. I thought you had already decided what you wanted."

"Well, I do want the riddle, and the quest, and the princess, and . . . and . . . all that, of course, but mountains and monsters! I have fought men before and fought well, and I have fought beasts in the forest too, bear, and boar even, and the wily wolverine, but monsters are something else."

"So am I something else," said Morduc. "Easy road is no road, you know, and I will back you."

"You'll back me, even against monsters?"

"*Especially* against monsters," said Morduc. "It's the mortals I fear."

"And I fear no mortal," said John laughing.

"Then between the two of us," said Morduc, laughing in his turn, "there shouldn't be any entity living or loutish that together we can't face."

"Yes," said Red John, beaming at Morduc. "That would be the case."

"Is it direct on then?" asked Morduc.

"Yes, direct on," replied John, "come mountain, monster, or malefacting mortal."

"Perhaps we can find out about them where we stay tonight, *if* we can find a place to stay."

"About the monsters?" asked John.

"No. About the mountains. We may have to leave this road and seek lodging at one of the farmhouses hereabouts." The sun continued to drop toward the horizon like a huge red-golden plate sliding slowly down a blue wall. As they continued walking, leading their lengthening shadows, they suddenly saw by the side of the road a large yellow flowerpot smashed to pieces. On the ground around it amid the spilled dirt were the wilted remains of a large red flowering plant. A small bird flew down from a tree, perched on the edge of one of the fragments of the pot, and began scolding them.

"Does he think we did it?" said Morduc laughing.

"Whoever did was brimful angry," said John.

About a hundred yards further along down the road, they encountered a dark-green bush which had originally been carefully pruned to the shape of a teacup and then surrounded with a disk of white stones at its base for a saucer. A great gaping hole had been hacked out of the bush, and the saucer stones nearest the road had been kicked into disorder.

"Where's the rest of the tea service?" said Morduc, looking around. Sure enough, a few feet further on, a larger bush had been pruned into the squat round shape of a teapot, but here too damage had been done. The spout and handle had been viciously lopped off. "Does this tell us your Master of Darkness has been on this road, John?"

"If so, he had a sharp spoon," replied John grimly.

"And was mightily stirred," replied Morduc.

"How can we joke about it?" said John.

"How can we not?" said Morduc. "Courage always laughs at danger."

"Really," said John drolly.

"Of course," replied Morduc. "It's part of the heroic ideal."

"And who among us claims to be an ideal hero?"

"Not I," said Morduc lightly.

"You're trying to teach me something," said John with a sideways ironic smile at Morduc. They trudged on in silence.

As the sun's bottom edge touched the tops of the faraway mountains, the travelers came around a bend in the road to see at some distance ahead of them a large stone farmhouse, the window frames of which were painted a phosphorescent purple. Designs in the same color—stars, circles, moons, and triangles—had been painted on the whitewashed stones of the house walls. Off to the left and up a little rise was the farm's well house, and above its small, round, whitewashed stone base, both the crank frame and well roof, though not the bucket sitting on the rim, had been painted the same gaudy purple.

"I propose we see about putting up for the night here," said John.

"I agree," said Morduc, "but they must be strange who live here." The dusty wagon track leading off the road to the gate was lined with more discs of white stones, in the midst of which had been growing three-foot-high rosebushes. But every bush on both sides of the gate had been shredded to the ground. White moonflower and blue morning glory vines had been torn from the stone gateposts and were lying tangled, limp, and lifeless in the grass. The heavy wooden gate was painted the same luminous purple as the window frames of the house, but the bars were gashed splintery. The gate was chained shut. Behind the house they saw a huge barn with an earthen ramp leading up to double sliding doors. The lower level of the barn was the stable. Clouds of swallows flew back and forth over the empty yard.

"Farm food," said Morduc in eager anticipation, "but they may be hostile to travelers after what was done to their plants and pots. Do you still want to try here?"

"I do," said John, "less for the belly than for the information, but even I wouldn't mind making friends with a bit of bread and cheese about now."

"Well, in I go," said Morduc, as he slipped swiftly and easily between the two bottom bars.

John, more awkwardly, with clankings and creakings, began climbing the gate like a ladder. Behind the house, a furious barking began.

The barking increased as three large dogs came bounding around the far corner of the house, charging toward the gate. In the lead was a gray barrel of a beast with upright triangular ears on a wolflike head. A short, bushy tail curled up over his back. Following the gray dog were two others, one huge and sandy with enormous paws and head, the other a smaller, sleeker black water hunter. The three had covered about half the distance to them as John touched earth on the inner side of the gate.

Morduc abruptly dropped down in the dust. "Sit down," hissed Morduc.

"What?" said John, bracing himself and putting his hand on his sword as the dogs drew nearer.

"Sit *down*," said Morduc again, this time kicking John's feet out from under him so that he fell in a rattling pile of armor in the dust beside him.

The dogs came to a skidding halt right in front of the two travelers. The look on the face of the lead dog had changed from snarling challenge to silent laughter at the two ridiculous creatures slumped in the dust, one big and red, the other small and green.

The gray dog now sat down, cocked his head, and inspected John with relaxed interest. He yawned. The other two dogs remained standing with dopey expressions on their faces. John stirred and began to get to his feet. The gray dog stood up and growled. John let himself fall back. The dog sat down again.

"Now, dog," said Morduc, "is that any way to treat weary travelers? You must invite us in." From where he sat, the gray dog simply opened his mouth in a silent laugh and wagged his head back and forth. "Listen, dog," Morduc continued. "I'm an elf, of sorts, and I've come a long way. We've been walking since noon from the Land Castle of the King of Time. We are tired. We are hungry. We are looking for a place to sleep and eat. If you and your friends would let us by, we would like to knock at the door of your farmhouse to see if your masters will put us up for the night. What do you say, dog? Will that satisfy you?"

At that point the gray dog twisted his head in a half circle back past his shoulder and barked twice. The huge sandy dog came slowly forward, sniffing. John and Morduc sat there while the dog advanced warily with its quivering black muzzle outstretched. First he sniffed John from his toes to his beard, snuffling and dribbling on him. Then he did the same to Morduc. When he reached Morduc's head, he suddenly opened his mouth and, with his great tongue, knocked off Morduc's hat and then gamboled back to his place.

"Hey, now, big dog!" said Morduc, irritated, "what do you think you're doing?" John laughed and laughed. Morduc picked up his green hat from the dust, slapped it carefully against his arm so as not to damage the feather, and set it back in place on his head. Morduc continued. "I see we have a practical joker to contend with. Look, gray dog. You seem to be in charge here. What can we do to induce you to let us through? You don't look as if you could be bribed with bits of bread, and you seem too self-possessed to fall for flattery and pats on the head. What do you want us to do, tell you silly stories about King Dog of Dogland, or should we give you a formal account of where we've come from and what adventures we have in prospect?"

At this the gray dog jumped up and began wagging not just his tail, but all of himself eagerly from side to side, from his shoulders on back past his rump to his gray-black tail tip.

"That dog is smiling, Morduc, if ever a dog could smile," said John. The other two dogs flopped down in the dust and seemed to exchange looks of bored disgust. The gray dog danced sideways over to Morduc and looked into his eyes with eager interest.

"Do you really understand what I'm saying?" said Morduc, putting out his hand slowly and beginning to scratch behind the dog's ears.

The dog wagged wildly. The other two drooped their heads resignedly on their paws.

"This dog seems more interested in talk than in table scraps," observed John. "It's ridiculous. A tale for a tail!"

The gray dog gave a little moan amid the wagging.

"He seems to appreciate your pun too," said Morduc with a laugh, "bad though it is."

"With puns, badder is gooder," said John, "but it isn't a real pun, it's just a homonymic play on words. Do you seriously think he can understand?" asked John.

"As seriously as I think your squirrel could," said Morduc, glancing sideways at John. "Have you a better idea?"

John did not answer. He looked back through the gate at the road. He looked up into the darkening blue sky of early evening. He looked past the dogs toward the white stone farmhouse, from whose chimney arose a faint curl of smoke, carrying to them the faint aroma of baking bread. He looked at the great gray dog and slowly put his hand on its head again and scratched behind its ears thoughtfully. Finally, he said,

"I admit I haven't a better idea."

"Very, well. I'll try him," said Morduc. "Now, dog, as I said before, I am Morduc the Elf. This is my comrade, the young knight, Red John, whose home is under a hill many a day's march to the east. We have come from the castle of the King of Time, and we are looking for the Master of Darkness." At that name, the other two dogs abruptly stood up and growled. The gray dog stopped wagging and withdrew his head from beneath the hands of Morduc and John. "We want to find out what happened to the Princess of Time and to the rest of the court. We have started out westward, believing the Master of Darkness to live near the sea. We need to know if this road is indeed one that will take us there. Can you help?" The dog stood still for a moment, then made a small, sharp whine in his throat, turned, and started for the house. The other two dogs trotted after him.

CHAPTER 8

An Invitation to Supper

Morduc and John remained sprawled by the gate, unsure whether to get up and follow the dogs or not. About halfway across the broad yard, the dogs stopped, and the gray dog turned his head, barked twice, and waited. Morduc and John scrambled up out of the dust and walked briskly until they came up to the dogs, who promptly trotted off again in the direction of the farmhouse door. John and Morduc followed. When they reached the door, the gray dog barked again twice, at which a voice from inside said loudly,

"Yes, Anga, what is it?"

The door was opened by a large woman with blond hair wound in two braided coils about her head. She was wiping her hands on a broad white apron. Beneath the apron, she wore a black bodice whose laces strained to confine her body. A long red skirt with small yellow flowers on it covered her broad hips and reached to the ground. Her large arms were bare to the elbow and at the moment were white with flour. She was tall enough so that she could easily look down on the two travelers.

"Who do we have here?" she said. "Two hungry boys, by the looks of it. We don't much like knights around here though," said the woman, glancing at John's armor, "but you have a good face, and if you have gotten past Anga there, the chances are that you have a good heart as well. And you, little one in green. You look as if you've never had enough to eat in your whole life."

"Good wife," said John, "my name is Red John, and this is my comrade, Morduc. We are travelers in need of food and lodging and seek your hospitality and will do you no harm and will help you in any way we can."

"It is not the likes of you," she replied, "that can do *me* much harm, I think, and as for help, only fools refuse to take it or give it. You speak courteously, and it is a kind offer, and so I welcome you. My husband and sons will have to take counsel as to whether you may stay the night, but I'll see you get some supper. Come in. My name is Willa, wife of Hubert de Wain, or as he likes to style himself, Hubert the Gardener."

John and Morduc exchanged looks.

They entered a large room that was both kitchen and dining room. A fireplace occupied all of one end. A narrow plank table set for six occupied the center of the room. Gleaming pots and pans hung on the inner wall. The space above the rafters was filled with onions on strings, bundles of roots, fruits, and drying spices, and hung hams and ropes of sausage.

"Sit there on the bench, by the door," said Willa. "I'll get you something to drink." Then she called out so loudly that both John and Morduc jumped, "Illanna!"

From far inside the house a young voice replied, "Coming, Mother." Presently a tall young girl came into the room. She had blond hair the same color as Willa's but braided in a single thick rope hanging down her back. She started when she saw the two visitors and blushed so deeply that the red covered her chest and neck and went up her cheeks and temples into the roots of her hair.

"We have two visitors for supper, Illanna. They have been walking all afternoon on the dusty road and are no doubt thirsty. See that they have something to drink, and give them some cheese as well. You, young man!" she said, turning to John, who had stood up when the girl had entered, "You go with her to the well and carry the pitchers for her. And you," she said, turning to Morduc, "you come here and cut carrots. No work, no food on this farm."

Illanna took two large pitchers from hooks by the door and led the way outside. Her long braid of yellow hair swung behind her as she walked with vigorous strides ahead of the knight up across the yard toward the well house. Illanna set the pitchers on the stone well rim and then dropped the leather bucket down until it hit the water. She tilted it, filled it, and then stepped aside so John could turn the crank. John raised the bucket swiftly, drew it to the well rim, and filled both pitchers from it. He put his hand on the handle of one and was about to start back toward the house when Illanna put her hand on his and stopped him. She spoke to him in a low, urgent murmur. John raised his arm and pointed off down the road in the direction from which he and Morduc had come and then in the other direction westward.

As they stood there, they heard a huge clattering and rattling behind the barn. A large flat wagon came into view, driven by a huge grizzled man wearing a domed, flat-brimmed straw hat standing at the forward edge of the wagon like a chariot driver. Three younger men stood on the wagon bed, holding on to the side poles as the wagon jounced along. Two had bright blond hair like Willa's, but the third had jet-black hair, with a jagged white streak in it that ran from front to back like a bolt of lightning on a dark night. He was the first to catch sight of the figures by the well and hit the larger of the blond boys on the shoulder and pointed in John's direction.

As the wagon came to a halt by the barn in a cloud of dusty creakings, Illanna removed her hand from John's and the two started back toward the house, each carrying one of the heavy pitchers. The three young men jumped down and ran to John and Illanna, forming a menacing circle around them. Willa came out of the house, wiping her hands on her apron, and called out in the same astonishingly loud voice that John and Morduc had heard before. "Ingmar! Brockbear! Steingar! He is our guest!"

The large grizzled man now came up and looked long and hard at John before extending his huge hand. "I am Hubert de Wain. For the moment, welcome. My sons are very protective of their sister. We will do you no harm if you mean none to us. We have just recently had some . . . well . . . trouble, you might call it, with knights, or their look-alikes, and so my sons do not take kindly to such as yourself who are dressed in the suit of such fighters, unhorsed though you may be. I cannot say I have ever seen such armor as you wear. It is gray, like good steel, yet it is red at the same time. Welcome."

John took the extended hand. The grip was strong but not hostile, and John returned it with warmth.

Now the dark-haired, white-streak-headed brother stepped up and clamped his left hand on the pitcher John was holding in his left and then, crossing over it, extended his right to John, saying, "I am Steingar. Give me the pitcher." From Steingar, however, the handshake was not friendly, but cold, viselike, and deadly. John returned the pressure of the hand in equal measure as the two stood toe to toe, hands crossed. Just as bones were about to crunch, John released the pitcher to Steingar. The other two brothers crowded around, extending their hands, thereby ending the secret struggle between Steingar and John.

Steingar followed Illanna into the house. Both Ingmar and Brockbear shook John's hand with an unfeigned friendliness and good nature that put the young knight more at ease. Brockbear returned to the horses and unhitched them from the wagon and led them off toward the stable under the barn while Ingmar and Hubert escorted John back to the house.

After they had washed and had a long drink of water, the two blond boys and their father sat in the far end of the kitchen near the fire along with John and Morduc, waiting for supper to be spread. Willa and Illanna moved about swiftly, putting two more plates and cups on the table as well as cutlery and serving spoons. Steingar sat back in the shadows beside the chimney.

Brockbear suggested that John might be more comfortable out of his armor and helped him out of the cuirass, the greaves, and the cuisses and piled them by the fireplace along with his shield.

"I'll keep the sword, if you don't mind," said John, rebuckling the baldric over his byrnie.

"No need, by gar," said Brockbear in a friendly tone. "But suits you yourself. We be none here to harm. Right, Ingo?"

"Ya," said Ingmar.

Steingar, deep in the shadows, said nothing.

Presently supper was ready and they pulled benches up to the table. Hubert sat at one end and Willa at the other. Across from Illanna, who had taken a place next to John, sat Steingar, glum, silent, and glowering.

Hubert said a grace to the effect that all good things came from gardens and that he was grateful to be steward of this one, that he would tend it properly and pass it on to others as well kept as when he had received it.

Hot ham and beef accompanied by huge dishes of beans and potatoes and corn and squash and carrots filled the table along with baskets of thick, brown bread and plates of cheese. There was fresh and preserved fruit, butter, honey, and pickles as well as tall pitchers of milk. When all had set aside their hunger, Hubert drew out his pipe and a pouch of fragrant cut weeds, filled the pipe, and lit it with a slim stick from the fire. Settling down comfortably, he spoke to John.

"It would not be amiss now, young man, if you would tell us your business in these parts. You seem like a good fellow, well set up, and courteous, but we farmers have little love for the usual knights we see go by. They are supposed to protect us, but they don't protect and sometimes plunder and sometimes even kill. Favor us then with an explanation of who you are, where you are from, and where you are going."

"My name is John, son to the knight Orra, whom I never knew, brought up by Bluthor . . ." As John began speaking, there came a scratching at the door. Illanna got up silently and let the gray dog, Anga, into the room. He went under the table with a slight clicking of his nails on the stone floor and lay down next to John's feet. "Bluthor, my mother's brother, on a small, rocky farm with only my mother and sister."

"Ha, ha," said Hubert, interrupting excitedly and slapping his thigh, "A farm boy after all. I knew ye looked well. But you say you had no father in the house?"

"When I was at home on the farm," John continued, ignoring the question, "I defended it against wolf, bear, fox, and mountain lion. I sought out every opportunity to show my valor further, but none fell in my way until I heard that the King of Time was setting a quest for the hand of his daughter. I rode westward many days. On my way to the King of Time's castle I helped a small-hold king, Clifford of the Rocks, to repel cattle raiders from the north. I was lucky enough to save King Clifford's life in battle, the Battle of Pleasance. He knighted me then and there for valor even though I was only a farm boy dressed in my father's armor and riding a plow horse.

"I finally came to the castle and was admitted to the riddle competition for the hand of the princess. On the third day, I managed to offer an answer to the riddle, but before it could be judged, a strange event occurred, having to do with the Master of Darkness. He overcame me in some way I still do not understand, and I fell to the stone floor senseless."

"By gar, dat Master is a nasty vun," said Ingmar who had been listening openmouthed.

"Ssh," said Hubert.

"I awoke in the hall with a severe ache in my head and joints. All were gone, the castle deserted, and I was bound in living black briars. That is when Morduc found me. He cut me free, revived me, and we set out westward to see if we could find out what happened to the princess. This is our first day on the road, and that not a full one. And now we are arrived here."

"Well," said Hubert, "I will tell you, O John, son of Orra, something strange that happened three nights ago and may likely be part of your own story. We had all gone to bed and had been sleeping for some time. I heard a great rumbling in the distance, like thunder on a summer night. I got up and looked out my bedroom window. There were no clouds, and the moon was full and bathed in white light everything in the yard. Still the thunder continued and grew louder. Our gates are stout, but since I did not know what might be coming, I awakened my sons. We dressed quickly and ran with pitchforks and a chain to the gate. We looped the chain—you must have seen it—over the gatepost and through the gate, and then lay down in the ditch grass, hidden, to see what was coming. First we saw a troop of armed men on horseback riding along at a quick walk. Following them came a large black-armored knight on a huge black horse pacing along in front of a wagon. Behind the wagon came a band of men and women on foot guarded by a second troop of armed riders. From time to time, the large black-armored knight rode up and down the line, waving his strange sword with a black blade and a huge shining black jewel in its hilt."

John shuddered and looked at Morduc.

"He kept urging along the slackers and stragglers in a roaring, angry voice like nothing I've ever heard before. Two cloaked and hooded figures were riding bound on the wagon. The entire line took perhaps a quarter of an hour to pass. One of the walking prisoners, poor wretch, tried to drop down unnoticed on the road and roll into the ditch, but one of the guards saw him and yelled. The prisoner got up and bolted for our gate and was just scrambling over the rails when that black knight came riding back furiously and cut off his head just as he had swung his legs over the top bar. The poor man's body fell off the gate in two parts. The head rolled back into the road outside the gate, and the body sprawled chest down on the dust inside. That huge black knight was so angry, I thought he was going to whittle my gate to kindling. When it held and he could not easily get at that poor man's body to hack it any further, he started cutting my bushes to pieces, all my pretty little welcomers. He even galloped further back down the road, where I heard him chopping at some of the plants I'd spent years pruning and shaping. I still can't think of it without . . ." He stopped in his story and puffed furiously on his pipe. Finally, he collected himself and continued.

"When he had finished his slashing and cutting, he came galloping back up to the gate and yelled at us, 'I know you're there, hiding in the dark. Enjoy your fanciful gardening for now, but this is what I will do to you if you oppose me when I return,' and with that he just whirled that black sword like a hundred scythes and cut the open white moonflower blossoms and the closed blue morning glory trumpets growin' on the gatepost off at the roots and rode on."

"Let him come back!" growled Brockbear. "We'll teach him a lesson, and anyone who sides with him too."

"All my pretty little roses!" said Hubert, weeping into his white beard. "What had the innocent shrubs done to him?"

There was silence in the room.

After a while Morduc gently asked, "What happened then?"

Hubert sighed deeply and continued, "We waited until the noise of the column faded into the distance, and then we stood up and gathered the head and trunk of that poor man who had sought shelter within our gates and gave him a decent burial."

"That surely was the Master of Darkness," said John grimly. "And he seems to have kidnapped the entire population of the castle. No doubt it was the king and the princess on the wagon. Tell me, good Hubert, did you see in the train any great red thick-ankled plow horse?"

"Even though the moon was out, it was still fairly dark, of course, and we stayed down in the grass behind the wall, so I can't say I saw a horse such as you describe, though I think none of the black knight's men were on such a steed, for I would surely have noticed."

"Good," said John. "If they were merely leading him, less harm is likely than if they were trying to ride RedFire. I do not think he would stand for it. He might be killed."

"We know then," said Morduc, "that we are at least on the same road the Master of Darkness took. Tell us, Hubert, do you know anything of the way to the west and how far we might be from the sea, or even where this Master of Darkness dwells?"

Hubert puffed on his pipe and then answered carefully, "When I was young, I made a three-week journey to the west, but I returned before I reached the foot of the mountains" (John moved suddenly, exclaiming "Ah!" disturbing the dog reclining almost on his feet), "and I never saw the sea nor smelled its saltness as was reported to us by someone . . . we once knew." Here Steingar growled in the corner, and Illanna and her two other brothers stirred uneasily at the mention of the unnamed person. "This road goes west quite straightly, but it branches south off to the left about eight days from here toward a thick woods. The main track continues westward rising gently until it comes to the mountains. I went as far as a barren flint plain that led up to the foot of the towering peaks. The road continued on, but whether it crossed the mountains by going over them or whether there is a pass, or"—he hesitated—"caverns, I cannot tell. Between here and where the two roads diverge is a rich, fertile country, well farmed by good, solid folk, though they are independent and none too eager to see strangers. There is also a deep river you must cross. A stout log bridge spanned it when I made my journey, but that was many years ago."

"We are most grateful indeed," said Morduc, "for this information. But have there been no travelers from the west coming this way, someone that might have told you something of the coast?" There was suddenly another awkward silence. Illanna abruptly got up and left the room. The brothers scowled, scraped their feet, and shifted in their chairs. Hubert leaned forward and looked intently at Morduc, who, somewhat disconcerted, glanced from face to face, trying to discover what in his questions had provoked the sudden reaction.

"What is it?" he said. "I meant no harm. Tell me."

"I'll tell you, I will," said Steingar bursting from his dark corner. He stood with clenched fists directly opposite Morduc, looming over the small green elf like a black thundercloud. "There was a visitor, not over a month ago, a sailor, he called himself, and he came this way from the western water. He came up to our gate very much like you two, young, footloose, and cheery, with a big bright smile on that broad brown face of his. We invited him in, just as we have you, and he stayed with us, telling us fancy stories about the world to the west beyond the mountains, of green sea and white sand and salt tang in the air, of ships, and of goings from harbors and comings into, of the great lord there, and of a rich castle on a huge rock, and how the crews of the ships when they got home would feast by firelight on the beach under the stars in the inky velvet sky. All these things he told us, and he spoke in a strange language to us and told us of countries even beyond the sea where it was spoken.

"He worked with us in the fields for a bit, to see if he liked the feel of it, and since he seemed to like Illanna, and since she was altogether taken with him—altogether, do you understand—we thought he might give up his roving days and settle down here with us. We thought he would, but two days ago, the morning after this Master passed, perhaps it was *his* master, he was gone, vanished into thin air, and all he left behind where he slept in the barn was a shark's tooth with his name on it, L'Orka. *That* was L'Orka the Sailor, who put pain, and dishonor, and deception on our house and sister, and I mean to kill him if I ever find him, and I will do the like to anyone else who does the same."

All this time he had been looking fixedly at Morduc with only an occasional swift stab of a glance in the direction of John, but as he finished his story, he turned his gaze to look straightly and steadily at the knight, who bore the hostile stare with calm imperturbability. After a short silence, John spoke. "Steingar, you need not fear me. I am on a quest to win the hand of the Princess of Time. My entire soul is devoted to her. I think of no other. It is not in my thought to disturb with more pain the quiet of your family. I neither trifle with other women nor care to dally on the roadway which leads to my own true love, whom I will win or die, for no other woman has significance for me."

"Such grand talk is all very well," said Steingar, "but I know what evil is at the heart of men, and I warn you I will not be tricked again."

"You may know what evil is in your own heart . . .," John said as he rose in his seat but was interrupted by Morduc.

"If we are not welcome here," said Morduc, "perhaps it were best to be on our way now, with thanks for this filling meal."

"Im*poss*ible," said the old man, standing up abruptly himself, "that guests should be turned away. We know enough yet of the old ways to treat travelers properly. Steingar, these are our guests and under my personal protection. You must rein in your mad horse of anger. We do not know that L'Orka is one of the Master's men, and if he is, it were better he were gone."

Then, turning to Morduc and John, he said, "Nevertheless, rather than within the house, we will lodge you in the hay barn above the stables. I hope you will not object and all will sleep easier. Then we will see you off in the morning with a good breakfast in your belly and good luck wishes for your quest. Will that do?"

"Most well it will do, Hubert de Wain," said Morduc.

CHAPTER 9

A Knight in a Barn

John gathered his armor while Morduc took their two scrips. Hubert led them out the front door, around the side of the house, and up the broad earth ramp to the large sliding doors of the barn. Through the large opening they could see that there were two levels beneath the high roof peak. The upper was filled with hay while the lower storage rooms were still empty. Below the barn floor at the far end, the horses and cows could be heard stomping quietly in their stalls. Hubert agilely ascended a fixed ladder into the hayloft and tossed down several large pitchforkfuls of the sweet, dry grass on to the barn floor.

"There you are, Red John and Morduc. That ought to be comfortable for you. We are up well ahead of dawn around here, and breakfast is soon after. I'll see you before you are off in the morning. Is there anything else you need?"

"I think not, kind Hubert. You have been most hospitable, and we will always have cause to thank you. Good night."

Hubert went out, sliding the barn doors together until only a tall thin line of the lighter darkness outside could be seen. A star or two shone pointedly through it.

The two travelers lay back on the hay, adjusting it with soft rustlings under them until they were comfortable. They inhaled the aroma of the dry grass and listened to the noises around them, the breathing of the horses and cows at the far end of the barn beneath them, the rustling of leaves outside, the faint distant noises of movement in the house. They looked at the stars shining through the slit between the two barn doors. John wondered whether the princess could see those same stars that night and whether she had hope that he lived still and was on the road to rescue her. Morduc too looked at the brightest star and ran over in his mind all he knew about it and remembered many a time seeing it from the tops of trees, singing soft hymns in the moon-washed night of his home.

They began to talk quietly.

"John, we need to consider our road for tomorrow."

"I agree. There is the bridge . . ." He stopped speaking as he saw a round shape blacken the bottom of the opening Hubert had left. The huge barn doors rattled slightly as the shape squeezed through. John and Morduc sat up. Toward them, its nails clicking quietly on the barn floor, ambled the unmistakable shape of the gray dog who had welcomed them. He came up to where John sat on his hay pile and nuzzled his knee. Though John could not see the dog's face in the darkness, he imagined with pleasure its laughing, amused look.

"Well, dog-they-call-Anga, what are you doing here? Come to say good night?" said John as he scratched behind the dog's ears. The dog wagged its head up and down and then went over to Morduc. With a swift snap, he knocked off Morduc's hat, before sliding silently into the shadows against one of the inner walls about three feet behind them. Turning around in his place three or four times, he finally lay down and put his muzzle on his outstretched paws.

"I think he plans to stay the night with us, and that is welcome," said Morduc, "but I could do with less of his joking. Hey, gray dog, what do you mean by such tricks, eh?" he said affectionately back over his shoulder and received several soft thumps of Anga's tail in response. With that, Morduc and John resettled themselves and resumed their discussion.

"It's clear we can continue westward tomorrow on this road, but what do we do when we get to the branching?" said Morduc.

"I doubt the Master would drive all those people over the mountains, unless there is a low pass. My guess is that he took the southern route and that it goes around the foot of the mountains," said John. "How can we find out for sure, Morduc?"

"I suspect that signs of their passing will be as clear further on as they were here," said Morduc. He was quiet a moment. Then he said, "John, do you know what star it is that we see through the barn doors?"

"No," replied John.

"That star shines in my own land. It is a star that in your language could best be called something like 'Caracanta,' and it presides over romance and the search for love. It is a good omen that it shows itself to you tonight."

"And not to you?" said John, yawning. "Are there no elf girls for Morduc?"

"Surely, you jest," said Morduc sardonically, but was inwardly stirred with a longing such as he had never before experienced. John made no reply. *The smell of earth*, thought Morduc to himself. With several turnings, the two dropped off to sleep. The gray dog lay in the shadows with his large triangular head flat on his paws, his ears lifting and dropping silently, pointing this way and that, noiselessly in the dark.

After several hours, a small chill wind sprang up outside and, penetrating into the barn, lifted bits of chaff from its floor in swirling eddies. The sleepers stirred and burrowed deeper into the hay. Suddenly, the dog lifted its head.

From the other end of the barn, above where the stables were, came a faint rustling, hardly louder than the wind itself. The rustling came closer. In the deep darkness, a figure in white was creeping along the opposite inner wall of the barn on its hands and knees. The dog stood up and growled softly, sniffing to see who it was.

The figure stopped, shrinking back against the wall. A soft voice whispered, "Anga. Is that you?" The dog picked its way carefully around the sleepers and went across to the figure. It was Illanna. She stood up and crossed to where John was sleeping. She kneeled down next to him and put a hand lightly on his arm. He awoke with a start and reached for his sword.

"Sshh. It is Illanna."

"For Drefon's sake, Illanna, are you trying to get yourself and us killed?" said John.

"Sshh. Quiet," she whispered. She put her lips close to his ear and asked almost inaudibly. "Are you really going to the coast?"

"I don't know," answered John softly. "We are searching for the Master of Darkness. If his castle is on the coast, then we are going to the coast. Why do you ask?"

"I want to go with you."

"No, Illanna."

"Why? I wouldn't be any trouble."

"It would not be safe, to begin with. Your family would not understand either, especially Steingar. They might not even let you go."

"They wouldn't. Therefore, we must go now, before dawn. I am almost a prisoner as it is. If I remain here, I will die without fulfilling my life. Take me with you. Give me a chance to find L'Orka. I believe he loved me. I am not altogether sure that Steingar didn't compel him to leave and simply pretended that he left by himself. I dare not think he did worse. If true love means anything to you, take me along with you to the coast. I dare not travel alone, but with you and your friend, it would be possible."

They were talking so intently that neither noticed the dark shape of a man looming in the door slit. The man rested his hands on the sliding doors, tensed, and then thrust them open wide, rumbling along their grooved tracks. As he jumped through the opening, a sword flashed in his hand.

"Illanna, get away from him," the dark shape roared. "I will kill them both."

"No, Steingar, no! It is not what you think!" she shrieked and ran toward him. He threw her aside to the barn floor with such violence that in falling, her left wrist broke with a soft snap. She screamed and fainted, but Steingar stopped not for a moment and came plunging on down the barn floor toward John and Morduc.

"Arise and defend yourself, Red John!" Steingar yelled. "This is the last you will see of life and the last time you will dishonor a good woman."

"I have never dishonored woman, good or bad," said John springing up with his sword still in his hand, "Nor do I plan to let such a discourteous rascal as yourself choose my manner of death." John retreated, parrying Steingar's wild rush of blows until the rough stout planking of a wall against his back stopped him. "You make a serious mistake, Steingar. Don't compel me to kill the son of my host. Stop while you can."

"Death to all knights and sailors that travel the roads!" shouted Steingar as he lunged at John. Steingar's point stuck in a thick board of the dividing wall. In an instant, John slipped under the thrust and ran toward the wide open door. Steingar wrenched the sword out of the planking, whirled, and pursued John with a flurry of slashes, cuts, and thrusts that John was hard put to fend off.

"Listen to reason, Steingar. Listen," he said as he parried frantically. "I am not like L'Orka. I do not want what he wanted, if that is all you think he wanted. I'll be gone in the morning." As he moved backward over the uneven floor of the barn toward the door, his heel caught on a slightly upraised plank and he went down on his back. Immediately Steingar rushed forward to plunge his sword into the heart of the fallen knight.

Off from the side of the barn, a flying gray bundle of fur launched itself at Steingar and caught his sword hand in his teeth, knocking him off balance and causing him to drop the sword. He fell heavily and lay on the barn floor with the dog over him. John sprang up lightly.

"Kill me, Red John, and be done with it," snarled Steingar.

"I will not kill you, though you deserve it for attacking a guest."

"No less than you deserve death for seducing my sister when we accepted you under our roof."

"No, Steingar, no," said Illanna weakly from the floor where she had regained consciousness and was holding her broken wrist in pain. "That is not the case, though why it should concern you at all and why a brother should seem to be almost jealous of a sister, I cannot understand. I have nothing to do with this knight, but I did wish to go with him to find L'Orka on the coast. That I do admit, but it is not for you or anyone else to deny me. I will finally do as I will, and you shall not prevent me."

"You will leave this farm only over my dead body, Illanna," snarled Steingar.

Voices could be heard outside the barn, and Hubert and his other two sons came in carrying lanterns.

"What is this noise? Red John, what has happened?" cried Hubert. "Illanna, what are you doing here?"

"Anga has just saved John from being killed by Steingar," she replied, "and Steingar from being killed as well." She nodded her head to where Morduc could be seen with his drawn bow aimed at Steingar's throat.

"Steingar, is this true?"

"Had it not been for that damned dog, he would be dead now, this snake in human shape who came to steal away my sister."

Hubert looked at Steingar and then at Illanna.

"Well, Illanna, what *are* you doing here?"

After hesitating for a moment, she said, "I came to ask John to take me with him to find L'Orka, and I still wish to go, if John and Morduc will agree." She cradled her dangling left wrist. Though her air was defiant, pain furrowed her forehead and her fair skin was pale.

From the floor, Steingar muttered, "What woman will not lie to cover her sin?"

"Illanna may be foolish, Steingar, but she is not a liar," fumed Hubert. "This violence is disgraceful. To attack a guest this way runs counter to all I have ever taught you. The provocation did not exist. You have misjudged both your sister and Red John. Your perpetual rashness has betrayed you yet again."

"It may be so, Father, but it were best they leave, and take that traitorous dog with them too, who seems to love them better than he does us, who have fed him from the time he was a puppy."

"I pity your children to be," said Morduc from the shadows as he lowered his bow.

"Who are you, little green arrow man, to lecture me!" snapped Steingar. "Your shafts could not hurt so much as that dog's disloyalty."

"You have yet to learn, Steingar, that bread is only the half of love, and without the wine of justice, all food is dry fare. This dog has a better soul though in shape of beast than you in shape of man."

"If the dog stays," replied Steingar, "I swear I will kill him."

"Illanna," said John gently, "I am sorry we cannot take you with us, and particularly so now, with your injury. But I will undertake to look for L'Orka if—I mean—*when* I get to the coast, and I promise you that I will send word of what news I find, whether it be nothing or something."

"Illanna," said Hubert, putting his hand tenderly on his daughter's shoulder, "that would be best. I did not realize you held that man in your heart so strongly as to wish to risk everything on finding him. It is a hard thing for a father to think of his dear child out in the world alone, away from protection, and many a child has indeed been lost to the evils of the great world. Even to Red John's care and Morduc's I would have been loath to trust you. Moreover, they have their own search, which will bring them into dangers you need not face. If I could spare your brothers, I would not be unwilling to send them with you to search, but I cannot work the farm alone. I do promise you, I will try to think of something to satisfy your heart on this matter, yet what it will be, I do not yet know."

"And so it is, Father, that Steingar has kept me here by wounding me, and you give your approval to it under these words of concern. How strange your decision is, unless it is you yourself who wish to sacrifice my life for your own selfish comfort of mind, as Steingar wishes to do." She turned, and still cradling her wrist and grimacing in pain, she swept out of the barn, leaving the men standing there baffled.

The sky had begun to lighten and the birds long since to chirp sleepily in the trees. "Come," said Hubert, "we will put an end to this sad night. I will have Willa fix you breakfast and fill your bags, and then you can be on your way and leave us to our misery."

Hubert helped Steingar up, and the old man and his sons left the barn by the ramp and in the pale-blue morning first light entered the house. Morduc and John collected their gear and followed them out of the barn and down to the kitchen door.

CHAPTER 10

On the Road Again

Breakfast was not happy. Neither Illanna nor Steingar put in an appearance, and Willa herself was largely silent, though she fed them well and copiously with bacon, eggs, sausage, stacks of fried cakes, syrup, bread, cheese, fruit, and milk. Ingmar and Brockbear ate steadily and with appetite but silently. Morduc and John ate as quickly as they could in the embarrassed silence. Finally they were finished. Willa brought cheeses and bread and dried fruits and filled the sacks of each. John buckled on his greaves and cuisses, and Morduc helped him on with the rest. He slung his shield over one shoulder and his bag over the other.

"Willa," he said, "you have been a good hostess. I am sorry for the reopening of old wounds that my coming has made."

"Ach!" said Willa waving her hand and wiping a tear from her eye. "It is not you who bring troubles. It is evil men and evil women, not your youth and not even time itself. May ye fare well."

"You have been most generous with us," replied John, "and we will remember well of you in our journeys."

"And so I will of you, Red John. And you, Morduc, feed yourself up a bit, even on the road."

Morduc touched his cap with the tip of his bow but said nothing.

Then Hubert stepped to them and said, "Red John and Morduc, for my part, I welcomed you openly. I apologize for the assault on you by my son. Both he and you have had a narrow escape. I believe that your heart is pure and that you will fulfill your quest and that, in so doing, you will bring benefit to this house as well as to yourself, though in the moil of this past night and in the apparent poison of Steingar's heart, it is difficult for me to tell how that will come about. But I believe it will, and that you will live to do even him benefit and that he will thank you. As he is now, however, he cannot, and for that reason we give you as a gift our best watchdog, Anga, who has saved your life once. May he do so again. If you return this way, you may count on a welcome, at least from me, and I hope a better reception overall than you have had. May good luck lead you."

"Thank you, Willa and Hubert," said John. "I hold no blame for you. I will think of you often."

John and Morduc walked across the yard with Hubert and turned to look back at the huge stone house. From an upper window, her broken wrist in a white sling, Illanna waved to them with her good hand. John waved back and smiled and called out, "I will remember."

Hubert squatted down in the dust and took the dog Anga's face in his hands. "Th'art a good dog, Anga. I am sorry to see thee go. I raised thee m'sel. But you have always been a laughing dog and knew more than you could speak. You were a dog for adventures, not for farms, though you did your work well. Good-bye." The dog licked the old man's face.

Hubert shook hands with both John and Morduc. Then he unwound the stout chain that held the gate shut to the gatepost and swung open the purple bars. Just as the sun came up in the east, the three started down the road. John, in his red-steel armor, massive, strong, and eager, strode along with a step that seemed tireless. Morduc walked swiftly beside him in his seventy times seven shades of green. The gray dog trotted ahead of them, ever and again darting off to the side of the road to investigate what the weeds held and then frisking back in joyous excitement at being finally off onto the road of the world to discover the entertainments, the adventures, and the dangers it held.

CHAPTER 11

The Gorge

Morduc and John walked the dirt road west for several days, sleeping under trees or in fields. They encountered little traffic, only an occasional taciturn and suspicious farmer on his wagon smoking his pipe, who gave them a close, sharp look without stopping. None were going in their own westering direction. On the fifth day after leaving the house of Hubert the Gardener, the road began to slope downward. The vegetation beside the road became lush, dense, and wild. Tall mixed thickets of trees grew right down to the edge of the road. Vines drooping purple trumpet-shaped flowers snaked up the trunks. By midafternoon, they began to hear a rushing in the distance. At evening, they came to the rim of a wide, deep gorge, at the bottom of which a huge river tumbled along, white foamed and gnashing.

Where the road ended they saw two charred posts of a stout wooden bridge, standing like somber, silent sentinels at the edge of the gorge. The planking had been burnt. Fragments of blackened rope hung down the sides of the gorge. Morduc, John, and Anga looked across to the other side. Much too wide a space to jump. They looked down, down, down into the white water foaming over jagged rocks. Much too rough to cross. Anga pricked up his ears and trotted leftward in the downstream direction. Morduc listened, and John too put his hand behind his ear. Intertwined with the anarchic crashing and dashing of the water, they heard a faint thread of sound only slightly less chaotic. It was a kind of high, thin singing mixed with mad laughter. They walked carefully to their left, along the rim of the gorge and, after a short distance, found a path sloping downward beside it, twisting around boulders and large trees. As they descended into the gloom of the gorge, the laughter got louder and the snatches of wild song clearer. They could not catch its words nor could they follow its tuneless sequence of notes, rising and falling with no apparent rhythm or melody. Soon they saw in the distance, perched on one of the large rocks at the edge of the river, a rotund, white-bearded old man in a wide-brimmed yellow straw hat, fishing in the roaring river with a string on a pole. Gray hair streamed out from under his hat to merge with his flowing beard. He sang along with the roar of the river, punctuating his song with loud shouts and cries.

Morduc, John, and the dog stopped at this bizarre sight, and while they stood watching, the fisherman, with a wild whoop, jerked his line out of the river and landed a fat fish on the rock. With speed and dexterity, he removed the fish from the line, popped it down through the square hole in the lid of the wicker creel by his side, and, continuing his singing, baited his hook again and cast it back into the river. As they stood above and behind him, all of a sudden he twisted his head around and fixed them with two bright blue eyes looking out from under his hat's brim. Holding his rod in his left hand, he waved to them to come closer with his right. "Fish for dinner, lads?" he yelled over the rush of the river. "Or dinner for fish? Which is it to be?"

John and Morduc looked at each other in puzzlement, but the dog barked three times. "Very well, then!" yelled the fisherman. "Three guests for dinner. Ha, ha, my bold river. Yield up, yield up, yield up fresh fish for dinner, for these young but weary travelers." With that, he yanked back on his rod, and another fair-sized fish came flying through the air to land with a thud on the gray rock beside him.

"Wait, wait, wait for me, for me, for me!" he called out to them over the cacophony of the rushing river as he slipped this fish too off its hook and into his basket, rebaited the hook, and flung the line back into the water almost in one motion. John and Morduc sat down a ways back from the stream as the old man continued singing and laughing wildly as he plied his rod in the water. Anga stepped carefully up onto the rock and sat down by the old man. The dog watched the water intently as the old man fished and sang, and presently Anga tilted his muzzle upward and began to sing a joyful howling as well, as apparently random and inharmonious as the fisherman's song but forming nevertheless a high-pitched near counterpoint to it.

Morduc, with his usual blithe expression, sat back and relaxed on the bank of the river's cool glen. John, however, could not tear his eyes away from the river tumbling by him so closely. The torrent of water going past so fast made his head ache. Where did it all come from? Where was it all going? It seemed to come from nowhere, to be going nowhere, and to be doing nothing in between but pounding inanely and lethally as it passed. It could be his life, everyone's life. He looked up through the trees at the still-blue sky. From deep in the shadow of the gorge, he could see crossing the sky's vault a fan of the red-gold rays of the sun as it began to set. The sides of the gorge were dark rock. He felt swallowed by some giant, looking up hopelessly out past the giant's lips to light. He could see no stars yet. The river continued to roar in his ears.

He must have dropped off to sleep, for he felt himself awaken when he heard the mad, wild voice saying close to him, "Now here's a catch, a sleepy knight, a green reed, and a gray dog. Do you like finny fish filched from a fresh flow? Come on with ye, and we'll broil these tame trout trapped with fractal song."

John jumped up, ashamed that he had slept. How was a knight to succeed in his quest if he fell asleep when he most needed to be watchful? The old man led the way with his rod in one hand and his basket in the other. They went further along the path deeper down the gorge until they came to a bay in the high rock walls where there was a small shelving beach stretching from the water up to a hollow in the rock face. At the back of the bay, against the face of the rock, was a lean-to behind which John could see a cave mouth. In front, a blackened circle of stones stood on the sand. The old man put his basket down and leaned his fishing rod against the rock underneath the sloped roof of the lean-to. He got a fire going quickly in the black stone circle, cut the heads off the fish, and gutted them swiftly, tossing the offal to Anga, who ate them with contented slurping. Then he wrapped the fish flesh in wide wet leaves and set them down within the circle of stones to steam.

All the while, he sang to himself in his tuneless, random way. He laughed here and there in the course of it, either in exultation and delight or in a harsh, cynical bark at the invisible thoughts that flowed rushingly through his mind. Soon, all was ready, and in the deepening darkness, illuminated only by the embers of fire in the rock circle, the three ate their meal of cooked fish. John offered the old man some of the dried fruit he had in his pack.

"Wonderful," said the old man, inspecting the assortment and finally picking out some black raisins. Looking slyly at John, he said, "Thank'ee much. I hope you will always be so raisinable."

Anga moaned, and Morduc laughed. John merely stared at the strange old man. The white tops of the river rapids roiled and surged just a few yards away from them. High above, at the mouth of the gorge, a few faint stars had finally begun to appear in the dark sky. Where the upward soaring black rock walls ended and the night sky began, he could not tell.

After they had finished eating and had licked the last crisp flakes of fish from their fingers, Morduc spoke. "We thank you for this supper. My name is Morduc. My companion is John."

The old man settled back against the rock wall beside the cave and began to twist string from a pile of fibers by his side. "Yes, I know," he said.

"You know!" said John suddenly tense and alert. "How can you know?"

"And who is your dog?" replied the old man, wagging his beard, his eyes twinkling with mischievous delight, as he continued his spinning and twining.

With his customary grave and formal seriousness, John called Anga over to him from where he had been lying and formally introduced him to the old man. "Now then, if you please, who are you, and how do you know who we are?" asked John.

"Ask your dog," said the old man in a high-pitched giggle.

"I will ask him, if you wish," said John, "but how will he answer?"

"That, ha, ha, my young friend, would be well worth knowing, would it not?" crowed the old man.

"I must confess," said John, "that your manner of discussion, if you will not be offended, sir, upsets me some. I do not know what to make of it."

"And I don't know that I want you to. But here's a riddle for you. Do you like riddles, strong John . . . ?" John stood up abruptly and put his hand on his sword. "Noo, noo, noo—noo need for that," soothed the old man. "Sit down again and listen." John did.

"Is this river real, young man? Am I a fresh flesh fisher? Have I hooked you and can you swim free? But I really mean no harm, yet you have such a great deal yet to learn, *Red* John," he said, emphasizing that part of the name which Morduc had not mentioned. "Will you forgive me if I point that out to you?"

"That I have much to learn," said John, "I readily admit, since I do not know how you discovered that second word of my name, but I do pride myself on being ready to learn if you will teach me."

"Then how, oh Red John, and sometimes blue John, but never yellow John, how are you going to get across this river which doesn't exist any more than the bridge over it that was burned?"

"First, old sir," broke in Morduc, "I think we ought to know to whom we are indebted for supper. Won't you tell us who you are and why you live here?"

"You have a *most* remarkable, la, dee, da, dog there. Why don't you ask him?" replied the old man, whose nimble fingers had by now produced a stout length of cord from the fibers.

Though a bit irritated at the riddling replies, John and Morduc both turned their gaze on Anga, who sat in the firelight seeming to laugh silently at them out of his dark eyes.

"A *most* rare dog," said the old man behind them softly. "If a dog smells a mouse, what does he think it is? If he smells and sees a second mouse, does he sisterfy it with the first? Does he say to himself, 'Oh, wuf,' if that is the way dogs speak to themselves, 'Oh, wuf, wuf, here is another one of those things with the tiny-feet-long-taily smell? Where, wuf, have I met that before?' Does a dog do that? Does a house dog, watchdog, sheepdog, water dog think? Can canines count?"

John looked at Anga meditatively for a long moment and then said, "Do you know what one is, Anga?" The dog drew a line in the sand with his left paw. John stood up abruptly. "And two?" he continued. Anga drew another line beside the first.

"This is remarkable," said John excitedly, turning to the old man. "He understands what I say."

The old man tilted his head back and, in a singsongy, howly voice very much like Anga's, barked up into the dark night air, "A mooost remarkabable diggy daigy dogg, aroo."

"Well," said John, "how can he tell me your name?"

"Surely, a young man of your beard-red ruddiness of wit could figure that out. How will you ever defeat the M . . . of D . . . if you . . . ?" John started. "Oh yes, I know that too—and that Dastard of Markedness is really a very clever and persistent fellow—how will you en*light*en *him*, if you can't even figure out how to talk to your dog?"

"Well now, Anga," said John, giving the dog a hug and then settling himself down on the sand in front of him. "Let's sweep this sand slate clean and start again. Can you mark me a one for yes and shake your head for no?" Anga drew a stroke in the sand. "Good," said John. "Now, dear Anga, you who saved my life, is that mad old man's name the name of any animal?"

Anga shook his head.

"Is his name the name of a mineral, such as rock or copper or water?"

Anga shook his head in delight.

"Then," said John, "we must be dealing with some sort of vegetable or growing thing." Anga drew a single stroke in the sand. "Very good," said John, "but what green growing thing can it be?"

Behind them the old man sang out, "Illo ho, ho. Go to it. You are on the track. Sniff it out that ye be not snuffed."

"Then," said John, warming to this game he had not played since childhood, "we must discover what kind of vegetative entity it is with which we are dealing. Tell me, Anga, is this thing like a garden vegetable, low growing, green, and leafy, like a squash or beans or radishes?"

Anga shook his head.

"Well then. Is it long and thin and grassy like grain or bamboo?"

Again Anga shook his head. "Does it grow in the sea then, like kelp or algae?" Anga shook his head with such amused vigor that he tipped over backward and had to scramble around to sit up again and, in doing so, sent a small shower of sand into John's lap.

"You've forgotten land trees," put in Morduc from the darkness.

"So I have," said John. "Well then, Anga, is this thing we are looking for a kind of tree?" Anga reached out his paw and drew a stroke in the sand.

"Very well," said John, a tree it is. But there are so many—oak, elm, beech, birch, maple, apple, aspen . . . and on endlessly. Must I ask each one? I will be all night and never come to the end of the list."

"Don't be a *sap*-ling," said the old man. "*Spruce* up your thinking, and *yew* will see how to pro-*seed*. Divide and define. Define and divide."

"Very well, old man," said John smiling, "I will leave my former line of questioning and *branch* into something else. I see I am clearly *barking* up the wrong *tree.*"

"A hoo a roo roo," cried the old man into the darkness. "Go it, young fellow. You'll *root* it out yet."

"Now, Anga," continued John, "is this tree some sort of old *nut tree*?"

"What can the boy mean?" said the old man to Morduc.

The dog, however, shook his head. "Then is it a tree which produces only flowers?" asked John. Again the dog shook his head. "Perhaps then we must look for some kind of fruit tree. Is that correct?"

The dog drew a stroke in the sand.

"Aha!" crowed John, "Now we are getting somewhere. Is this a fruit with a pit?" Again the dog drew a stroke. "Is it a peach?" The dog shook its head. "Is it a plum?" asked John. The dog jumped up and landed in John's lap, tipping him over backward and licking his face.

"Hooray, Red John," said the old man. "You are doing well and have reason to appreciate your fine dog who sings as well as I do myself, if the truth be known."

"But," said John, giving the old man a quizzical look as he sat up with the dog in his arms, "can your name be simply Plum?"

"Not Plum alone," said the old man, "but almost there. What has just happened between you and I?"

"Why, I've met you."

"Right. Met Plum, Plum met, it's much the same. Here I am, Plummet the Fisherman at your service. Old enough and mad enough for anyone, but still no prune. I plumb the waters of this river and the waters of life with strings of song that I braid myself. I eat what I catch. My song is the sounding of the mad pearling waves of the river and any part is just like any other part, wild, whirling, and wondrous. So what do you say to that?"

John sat back, still not sure how to deal with the ancient silliness of this man who seemed to make as much nonsense as he could out of whatever sense he made. How could such a buffoon be of any help to them? Did he, perhaps, know a safe way across the river?

"Well, Sir Plummet the Fisherman," said Morduc, "We are finally glad to be able to thank you by name for the fish dinner. But to speak in your own vein, is there anything fishy about you? Do you know a sane way across this mad river?"

"Ah, Morduc, the green reed that will not break, however it is bent. The river is as mad as I am sad. I *knew* a way once and may know again, but really, that is not the main problem is it? For as I said, the river does not really exist, and crossing the nonexistent ought to be easy—or impossible. The real problem is the Mum of Dee—sssh! We must not say all of him, shan't we? What to do when you get *there*? Oh yes, I know that too. And that is how, perhaps the mad plummeting fisherman may be of some service to you."

Here he paused, becoming clearly serious for the first time. "I saw them pass over and burn the bridge behind them, a bridge I spent many days building and will rebuild again, but not in time for you to cross it. Yes, Plummet, the mad fisherman, is the engineer over the nonexistent, or *too* existent, who builds bridges out of frayed bark to keep wayfarers from plummeting into the abyss, but I warn you, the Master of Darkness, ah, at last we have said it out loud, he does exist, or at least as much as the river does, whose first cousin he is."

"I can hardly follow a thing you say," said John. "How can you help us? Will you take us across the river?"

"I will certainly try, my impetuous Red John, tomorrow morning if you wish. But again I ask, supposing you cross the river, what then? How do you bring light to the darkness? How unseat a sitting tyrant? What do you *know* of Der Herr Meisternacht?"

"We believe that he kidnapped the King of Time and his daughter," replied John, "and has taken them to, well, we don't actually *know* where. We think it must be somewhere by the sea on the coast because . . . because he *sounds* like the sea. I may very well have won a quest for the hand of the princess by answering a riddle, but before I truly understood my own answer, something strange happened. I have to rescue the princess to find out *if* I answered correctly and, *if* I answered correctly, why it was the correct answer. Then *if* I have won the quest, I must go off on it somewhere, and be successful somehow, and come back sometime and . . ."

Here Plummet held up his hand, "Stop, stop, stop, Red river John. You run on as fast out of your own gorge as this one does out of its. Do you really go ahead so blindly, without knowing where you are going and what you have to deal with?"

"We had no other choice at the time," replied John. "Of course, acting in ignorance is never best, but it was either go forward or die, and so far Providence has seen us through, and . . ."

"*Providence!*" shouted Plummet. "Ha, ha, thee's younger than me thought thee to be. *Providence!* What do you know of providence? What has this blessed providence provided you with other than threat and thrill and thrum?"

John was silent for a while. "You are right in one sense," John finally said musingly. "I have encountered nothing but trouble since I started my journey . . . except." He fell silent again.

Finally Plummet said encouragingly, "Except . . . ?"

"What I know," continued John, "is that along whatever road I travel, my love for the princess is absolute and my integrity as indissoluble as . . . well . . . as . . . my soul. Is not that all anyone needs to know?"

"Ah, what marvelous faith," said Plummet, "and faith is a kind of knowledge, I confess. But has your soul never—how shall I ask it?—been dissolved by wind or water, by tremor or terror, by death or . . . diamond?" Plummet shot out the last word.

John flinched as if stabbed. "And what more do *you* know about it, Drefon damn you? Anything at all?" shot back John, flushed and angry.

"A great deal," said Plummet calmly. "I have fished in and fled from the very flood in which you seek to swim. I know about the enemy you must face and I know the roads you must pass to find him." He paused and then continued gently, "I also know that fear of dissolution can lead to rudeness here and now. Do you suppose, dear boy, you might avoid it when you speak to me."

John's face turned almost as red in the faint firelight as his beard. "I do apologize, Plummet," said John, hanging his head. "You see the inner dark of my soul better than I do myself."

"Apology accepted," replied Plummet calmly. "But I am your friend and he is not, and what I just gave you now was a bit of an inoculation against the M of D himself."

"I don't quite follow . . .," said John.

"Never mind for now," said Plummet. "'The rash smash.' Just keep it in mind as you journey."

CHAPTER 12

A Bit of Dark History

Plummet rushed on. "You are completely right in supposing that the Master of Darkness lives on the coast of the sea. He lives there because he comes from the sea. His element is water and dissolution, and he thinks to sink Time and all belonging to it therein. More depends on your success than you are aware. The Princess of Time must be rescued, or all that has been won in this land and in all other lands will be lost."

Morduc drew closer. *Here is a journey worthy of a warrior elf,* he thought to himself. *What luck that I went for a stroll this morning!*

"Many years ago," continued Plummet, "before I sought out safety here, I lived on the shore of the sea myself. I was there when the Master of Darkness first established himself. The land on the far side of the mountains is narrow but fertile, and the folk there peaceful and industrious. Between farming and fishing, the families did well and prospered and over many years gathered gold and jewels. But living on a seacoast, they were subject from time to time to pirate raids. The pirates would slip into a creek at night and attack a village, routing out the people, sacking their homes, and killing any who resisted. The pirates were able to escape before effective pursuit could be organized. The people had grown soft in their peace and were not accustomed to this violent danger and risk. The fishermen were not willing to follow them onto the sea at night. Thus, by boldness, the pirates terrorized the entire coast. The townspeople and villagers met in council to try to provide some concerted defense, but any plan put forward by one would be criticized by another, and so nothing was done. Each one simply hoped that he and his family would not be touched, that the pirates would strike somewhere else, since the coast was a very long coast. In looking only to their own safety, the people permitted the water thieves freedom to pillage where they would and never meet any unified resistance. There was no leadership, and through envy, none was permitted to arise.

"About this time, there appeared off the coast a sleek black sloop with black sails. It anchored off one of the towns and put down a boat manned by trim sailors. They came ashore, saying they wanted to buy provisions. The well-spoken officer who ruddered the boat bought the best and paid in gold and announced that he would return twice a week for the same purpose. The farmers and the fishermen, of course, flocked to his twice-weekly visits, and since he conducted himself fairly and paid immediately, the people of the district came to see him as a worthwhile friend. This continued for several weeks. Then one night the pirates attacked that town, their boldest attempt so far. Just as the pirates were about to load their boats and make away with their haul, several boats from the black ship landed, attacked the pirates, killed several, and drove away the rest empty handed. In the morning, what the pirates had taken was returned to the citizens by the rescuers.

"You can imagine the effect such an action had. The citizens were immensely grateful and invited the captain to come ashore to a banquet to receive gifts for saving their homes, their lives, and their property.

"The Master of Darkness—for that is who it was, but he went by another name then, simply Captain Juncata—came to the banquet with several of his officers. He was tall, dark, bearded, and immensely strong, and exhibited a certain grave and reserved courtesy. His only peculiarity was that he kept his gloves on while he ate. Nevertheless, he conducted himself with propriety and accepted the thanks of the townspeople graciously. Surprisingly, he refused any additional gifts. While his ship remained off that town, there were no more pirate raids, and since he continued to purchase provisions from the townspeople, and since his sailors conducted themselves soberly, discreetly, and responsibly when they came ashore, the people had two reasons to be glad of his presence.

"The news, of course, spread along the coast in both directions. Somewhat further south along the coast was a wealthy port city which had been repeatedly assaulted by the pirates. It invited Captain Juncata to bring his ship into their vicinity to protect them, and they even went so far as to offer him land upon which to build a camp.

"He visited the place, said he liked it, and settled there. He built a stockade on a headland, and the proof of his efficacy was that the town was not attacked again by the pirates. They moved their operations much further north, and those villages along the coast which had been their usual targets were shielded as if by an invisible wall. The captain sailed up and down that section of the coast in his black ship, and the coastal inhabitants welcomed him everywhere as their protector and savior.

"This continued for more than a year. Men from the area sought to join his crew, and he did take a few into his service. These brought back reports of the captain's stern but just judgment in disputes among his sailors, and so it happened that in a boundary dispute between two farmers, which had come to a feud in which members of both families had been killed, the parties challenged each other to bring it to Captain Juncata to settle.

"Remarkably, he managed to settle it to the satisfaction of both parties, and so it gradually became a custom to refer matters of justice to him as well. Thus, in addition to protecting the towns and villages along the coast, he also became their magistrate, sailing to whichever one called him to render a judgment. He would make his decision and leave its execution in the hands of the village constabulary, which was a volunteer force drawn from the locals and supervised by the town councils. From time to time, his decisions would be blunted through inattention or favoritism or family connections in the constabulary, and he would have to be recalled to rehear a case he had already decided. He himself never complained about this, but the volunteer local police came to be perceived as inefficient and subject to local bias and influence. In spite of these inefficiencies, these informal arrangements went well until the pirate attacks resumed.

"Although Captain Juncata managed to beat off several, he was not altogether successful. He would arrive late, and one or two villagers would be killed. It was then that he went to one village after another and, amidst a show of grief and sorrow, said that if he were to protect them properly, he would need to station a unit of protectors in every village. This would mean larger forces, and for larger forces he would need some kind of monetary contribution from each village to help pay the Protectors, as he called them. If this were not done, he said, he could not guarantee their safety and he might even have to consider sailing away and leaving them once again to their own devices.

"The merchants, in particular, of course, were terrified at the thought of a return to the disorder and weakness that had preceded the coming of the captain. They had amassed wealth in his reign of peace and didn't want to see it lost to pirates again. The lesser folk objected most strongly to the thought of paying double taxes, first for their local police forces and now for a contingent of militia to protect them from outside attack. When, however, Juncata said he would hire the Protectors locally and have them perform the function of the local constabulary too, they jumped at the chance to keep their taxes low. So in the end, most supported his plan and he soon became a rather large employer of the neighborhood boys who might otherwise have been without job or wage or who relished the distinction of being part of his force. He dressed them smartly and fed them well and impressed them with the seriousness of their mission. Thus it came about that not only the external defense, but also the law, and the local police power all came together into his hands. It seemed ideal at the time. There was little extra cost, and the local disputes were removed from the family rivalries and jealousies that had plagued the villages all along. Some few voices were raised in objection, but in the end, he got what he wanted. What could the villages do? They were too scared and weak to do anything but put the government into his hands. They *could* have put aside their personal pride and petty differences and envies, they *could* have each one taken up a sword or staff and risked their precious flesh, they *could* have put up with the interminable turmoil of debate in the village councils, but they thought it was simpler and safer—and cheaper—to commit themselves to the care of the Captain, as he was now called.

"With the additional money and troops, he did what he said he would. He made the night safe. He became master over the dark time, and so earned his title. But what was once innocent eventually became malign. The voluntary contributions for the Protectors became involuntary. Over the years, the exactions became greater, and he extended his influence further and further up and down the coast. The more of the country he controlled, the more insistent his collections became and the richer he grew. With his extra revenue, he built a great two-towered stone castle that became the center of his operations. And he began buying jewels."

"Jewels?" said Morduc suddenly from the darkness. "What kind of jewels?"

"Any kind," rumbled Plummet. "But especially he favored green jewels."

"Why they?"

"I never asked him," chuckled Plummet.

"And the castle?" said John urgently. "Tell us about the castle."

"It sits on a granite island just opposite the headland on which he had originally been given land for his camp. It is not possible to dig under its walls or to scale them. Its catapults cover the entrance to the harbor so that attacking it by sea is impossible as well. From it, he supervises the defense of the coast, which depends on a series of smaller forts and stockades. The coast has been relatively secure since then, but the pirates have not disappeared entirely. In fact, there is even a rumor that one of the pirate chiefs, a pale, malicious killer called White Tom, has been seen in the castle.

"And why should the good captain exterminate the pirates, even assuming that he could? Without their threat, his own function disappears. Villages that are late in their payments receive a visit from pirate forces often enough, so that it is my suspicion he has bought them off and that they attack, when and where they do, only by his permission so that he can conduct his rescue when he wants. In this way, he keeps the population both in fear of the pirates and of himself at the same time.

"Once the citadel had been built, he began to try to make himself unchallengeable. Eventually he established a network of informers who spied on the people and reported any opposition to him before it could coalesce. If any individual started to propose doing away with the Captain's services, that person was visited by the Captain's forces almost before he had time to think his thoughts. That person found himself charged with some sort of treasonous crime, such as being in league with the pirates, and was taken to the castle. Sometimes such persons came back. Sometimes they did not.

"When I saw all this and indeed began to think I too should oppose him and had started to discuss with a few of my oldest and most trusted companions how it might be done, a feathered friend of long acquaintance lit on my shoulder one day and told me that the Dark Captain's troops were on the road to my village. I started walking westward toward the mountains, right at that moment, leaving everything behind—wife, children, house, friends, and craft. I crossed the mountains and continued walking eastward without stopping until I came to this gorge in which the river babbled on much as I do. Then I knew I had a place to hide which would sustain me and was fully congruent to my spirit as well. I have hidden in disguise in this gorge for a number of years now, keeping the road to the interior open, so to speak, hoping to someday participate in the Dark Captain's overthrow.

"So you see, my young friend, if you get to the coast at all—and there is considerable rough country between here and there before you do—you will not have an easy time of it. The Captain's spies are everywhere. Many of the people, even if not in his pay, will not hear a word against him, even though he has taken away their freedoms. They fear both him and the disorderly vacuum which would occur if anything happened to him.

"And now, by the looks of things, this Captain Juncata, the Dark Captain, your Master of Darkness, seems determined to extend his rule across the mountains and to regularize it by marrying the King of Time's daughter. From the coast to the mountains, he is supreme. Between the mountains and this river, his strength is growing. On the eastern side of the river, his influence can only be sensed, but his daring kidnap of the King of Time and his daughter shows what he can get away with even outside his own realm. So you see, young Master John, you have much to do if you are to meet him and survive, let alone triumph. Is your spirit up to such an undertaking, you and your half-elf friend and your smart dog? Are you really ready to take on so powerful an opponent?"

"Half-elf?" said Morduc from the darkness around the glowing fire. "He is a half-wit who says so."

"And do full elves summer in the snow?" replied Plummet.

"I do not follow you," said Morduc.

"I know. You precede me."

"I am ready," broke in John. "I will save the princess or die trying. I do not know how I will defeat him, but if he can be brought to combat, I will do all that strength can. I urge you, Plummet, take us across the river tonight. I am burning with indignation at this monstrous tyrant and his bold kidnap. I am on fire to rescue my beloved princess. Neither force nor fear must ever be allowed to rule in this world. Without free and understanding consent to marriage or to government, neither men nor women can hold up their heads. Their souls will drown in the swamp of tyranny. There is not a moment to be lost. We must leave now. Anga! Morduc!" John stood up, his eyes blazing with purpose. He shouldered his shield and his sack and strode off into the darkness.

"Wait, Red John," called the fisherman after him. "You no more know how to cross this river than you know how to defeat the Master of Darkness. I can show you one within the other, but the impatient mind will never succeed. You may trust in your strong arm, and I can see that it is an arm stronger than any other, but surely your father taught you that strength alone will not suffice to win. Have you had no schooling?"

"My father?" came John's pain-filled voice out of the darkness. He returned to the faint ring of firelight. Panting as if from an injury, he gritted his teeth and said, "No schooling. None. Not from my father. You know the right wounds to wring, old Plummet. What I know I learned from my uncle, my mother's brother, an old, wrecked wound of a man who used to rouse himself after dinner and drink to mumble wild stories of great wars and great battles during them. Then my uncle would put a wooden sword in my hand and show me cut and thrust before he collapsed snoring. From the other boys I learned to hold my own at quarterstaff and running and especially wrestling. I learned and practiced as I grew, until I could overcome any of the stout lads around me. It was always my superior strength that won. None of them had any skill in contest, nor desired any. It was as if I were fighting trees. I could knock them down or tear them up because their defense was nothing. But from my father, who must have known all the arts of war save how to save himself, nothing. He left me disinherited of both his love and his knowledge, leaving me only his own ungoverned raw muscle and the desire to use it."

"Loss like that is a great darkness," said Plummet quietly. "But not the darkest. Didn't your mother tell you of him?"

"What could be darker?" replied John angrily without waiting for an answer. "As for my mother, she was a bitter, depressed grimness who never mentioned him. When he did not return from . . . wherever and whenever . . . she never spoke of him again. Sometimes I even blamed her lack of faith in his return for his never returning. All he left her were his two children and an empty life."

"Two?" said Morduc, for Plummet's benefit.

"Yes, two."

"You have a brother, then?"

"No. A sister. Too young to speak of."

"You've mentioned her," said Morduc, lifting an eyebrow. "Your father's own child."

"Yes," said John.

"But you don't like her."

"I don't," said John.

"Pity. My own sister is almost my other self. A comfort."

"Ah, but not mine," said John. "She is a curse and a crime of an infant, no comfort or company at all." The stabbing of loneliness swept through John as he stood in the darkness by the gnashing and moiling river. He sat down again on the sand and gazed into the fire as if seeking to find there his lost father. He remembered a time long ago when he was so small that he could almost not remember it. He saw a huge man with a great red beard who had tossed him in the air, laughing, and then had held him close. He had put his face up into the giant's beard, his father's beard. He loved the smell. His father had held him and sung him long incomprehensible story songs in a strong, deep voice. And then, the beard and the man had simply disappeared. After a while his uncle had arrived, with his one arm left hanging wounded and almost useless off his bloated body. His uncle whom he had to pull out of bed in the morning to see the glory of the wild red and yellow poppies on the orchard floor, his uncle whom he had to pester to teach him how to read and write, his uncle who never spoke of war, or of great deeds, unless it was after dinner when he forgot and his eyes shone, shone for a while, and then he would weep and fall asleep. His uncle whom he knew loved him because he was with him, but to whom he could never truly talk about his plans, his ambitions, his visions. His uncle just nodded under the apple trees sitting on a bench, nodding, nodding with his cup of cider until his mother called them both in to supper.

John owed his uncle all the knowledge he had. He was grateful and respectful, yet there was so much missing, and more than that, there was also something else essential missing, some element in the teaching that would bring it all together and unify it, something that would give it meaning and significance. That something was in those songs his father had sung to him before he could understand them. That something was the meaning of the effort, and he had never learned it. His uncle could not give him that; his father had known but had disappeared before he could give it to him. The ache and pain within him was a burden heavier than a hundred suits of armor. It filled him with a cold weight pressing from the inside out, pressing, pressing, with a stone ache filling his entire being. He wiped his own beard with his red-steel-covered forearm. The steel glistened in the fire.

The mad fisherman watched him silently as did Morduc and Anga. The dog finally got up and wagged over to him, put his muzzle on his knee, and looked up into John's eyes. The dog whimpered in his throat and waved his great curly tail slowly back and forth. Slowly John reached out a hand and scratched behind the great dog's ears.

"Well, my pensive young friend," said Plummet finally, "I didn't mean to track stop you so stone sadly. I only meant to say that I can't take you across the river in the dark, but I do wish to help you. And perhaps I can just say to you what my father once said to me: 'He who lives for justice is never without a family.' Does that help at all?"

"It is a kind and noble thought, Plummet," replied John. "I thank you for it and for its intent. But nothing can fill the aching void of my father's absence—except my father, and that, I'm afraid, will never be. Yet I still wish to cross the river tonight."

"In light, my son, I think I can get you across the river without its pounding you to shredded fish food, but in darkness, never. I don't want you to lose yourself in this little rough rivulet of the Master's element before you have even had a single chance at fighting the main ocean. If you are successful in your quest and can release the princess from the Dark Captain, then I need no longer live swallowed by this gorge in exile. If you can destroy him, I can return to my beloved coast and see if any of my . . ." Here he paused and then went on, "Any of my friends have survived. I already know the Dark Captain burned my fishing smack and my little hut by the sea, and I suspect that my wife and children, whom I left there unprotected, were in it at the time."

John put his hand on the old man's shoulder. "I am sorry, Plummet. I didn't know. Your mad song conceals darkness of loss even greater than my own."

"You can see, Red John, that I owe Captain Juncata a great debt that I have so far been unable to pay."

"Seeing that I am fatherless and you are sonless," said John standing up, "perhaps I can be paymaster for you as well as for myself. Since the payment is long overdue, should I not make delivery to the Master as soon as possible and with interest and augment for the delay? Is there *no* way we can start tonight? Isn't the motto we are looking for something like 'Plunge in to win'?" said John, smiling grimly.

"Restrain your eagerness, John," said Morduc. "Let us wait until morning to find our way across this turbulent stream. We do not want to delay, but a delay that saves time and promotes our success is not truly a delay. I think the motto you are looking for is:
'The successful man
Has a plan;
The rash
Go smash.'"

John sat with his head down, wrestling inwardly, as the faint firelight reflected off his armor. Finally, he said reluctantly, "Very well, then. I will stay for the night. But as soon as it is light enough to see, Fisherman, we must be on our way."

"In other circumstances, John Red, I would say such haste is a refusal of hospitality, but so just a cause puts new excitement into my old bones and shaggy fat. If I had my life's work ahead of me, I suppose I would be as eager as you are too."

John looked over at the old man and said simply, "Perhaps, old man, you do."

Plummet stopped and looked sharply at John. "And just what do you mean by that?" he asked.

"I don't know, Plummet. It just came into my mind, like my answer to the riddle, and it made me feel good to think it, so I said it. Does it bother you?"

Plummet did not answer but said only, "Let us get some sleep. It's late, and we will be up early. Tomorrow I will tell you one or two more things I know about Master Dark that may help you, and I will take you across the river. If there is more you wish to know tonight, let it be asked."

"Now that you mention it, Plummet," said John, "there is the matter of the quest itself for the hand of the princess. It was never actually concluded that I had successfully answered the riddle. Yet the princess smiled, the RiddleMaster got upset, and the Master of Darkness, well, it's hard to describe *what* he did. I expected hard struggles and marvelous adventures on the quest, but I never thought I would have to be rescuing the princess in the first place simply in order to be able to then go on a quest to win her. I never thought I would be sitting on sand after a dinner of fish and water. That's hardly heroism at all, polishing the tail plates of one's armor by shifting on strand."

"Tell me this famous riddle," said Plummet. "Perhaps we can unplait it."

"I'll replay it," said John.

'Swiftest and most slow

Above and then below,

Beauty's best

In shadow's show.'"

"Hmmn," said Plummet. "Is that all?"

"All except the last line."

"And that is what?"

"It isn't that important. It only says to understand what the object is, discover it, and bring it back."

"Indulge me. It may be the fin by which we can catch this fish. How does it go?"

"It just says, 'Mind me, find me, bind me.'"

"Minding is not nothing, Red John. Perhaps it is the all."

"How can that be?" said John. "Does mere attention have such strength?"

"We will see. Sea we will," replied Plummet. "Were there any answers offered?"

"Yes. The wrong answers were 'the stars' and 'the sea.'"

"And what was your answer?"

"I didn't really give one. I was about to step up and speak, trusting to the moment for inspiration, the way a red . . . um . . . well, the way I had been advised to . . ."

"A red what?" interrupted Plummet.

John blushed. "A red squirrel."

"Indeed," replied Plummet. "I have such a talkative friend myself. Perhaps he has a brother."

"Or sister," put in Morduc sardonically from the darkness. John and Plummet ignored him.

"Well, then," said Plummet, "what happened?"

"All I could do was stammer, and then it was that the RiddleMaster became agitated, the Master of Darkness sliced the RiddleMaster's head off his shoulders, and I left my senses. I remember nothing after."

"What did you stammer?"

"Just 'I, I, I . . .'"

"Just 'eye, eye, eye', that with which we see?"

"No," said Red John. "'I, I, I,' as in, 'I, myself.'"

"Not 'aye, aye, aye,' as in, 'yes, yes, yes'?"

"When you put it that way," said John, "my answer dissolves into even more confusion. Which of the meanings of my answer do you think it was which disturbed the RiddleMaster?"

"In truth, Red John, I don't know. You certainly gave a three-in-one answer. Perhaps all three at the same time. I confess it baffles me," said Plummet.

"Well, what shall I say when I am asked the riddle again, as surely I will be?"

"Though I know this is a serious matter for you, Red John, my advice is not to worry about the riddle until you have rescued the princess. The why and which of your answer may occur to you as you journey, or as you fight, or when you see the princess again, or when you see her father. But most assuredly, Red John, if you can defeat Captain J. Dark, no mere riddle will defeat you. It is but a puff of air, a widdle of words, a bottle of breath, a mere some-none-thing, compared to the power and malevolence of the main counterforce. So put your foot on the road in the morning, and let the puzzle travel with you, but do not travel puzzled."

"That I shall not, good Plummet," said John, smiling and extending his hand to the old man who took it and gave it a single hard shake of agreement. "Let us take some rest," continued John, "and in the morning you can tell me what you know about the castle of the Master, you can name me your friends, and you can take us across the river."

CHAPTER 13

The Rains Reign

With that, the three companions and the old fisherman withdrew into the cave behind the lean-to where Plummet provided them with soft sleeping skins spread on spruce boughs.

Along toward that part of the dark morning, just before the birds have awakened and the air is at its most chill, a light rain began to fall. It came down gently for a few minutes and then began to fall more heavily. As the sky grew light, the rain fell more darkly, in solid sheets. The noise awakened the old man first, who shook the others.

"We must move, and move quickly," he said. "This much water will flood the river at any moment, and it would certainly not do to be trapped in the cave."

Morduc and John got up instantly, fastened their few possessions in their sacks, and were ready to go. Using one of the ropes he had made, the old man tied up all the skins in a bundle, hoisted it deftly on to his back, picked up his fishing pole and started off downstream. The river was roiling along louder than ever, and as it hit the rocks in its path, it jetted up in white geysers. As they trotted onward, inches from the racing edge of the water, the sky darkened further and let down such heavy flows of water that John could hardly see the fisherman ahead of him. Presently the path veered away from the channel and they came to rest under an overhang of rock. A curtain of water surrounded them. In their niche, they seemed to be under the waterfall of a river spilling into the one they were beside. The old man was puffing.

"Further on," he said, "is a pool. That is the only possible crossing place. You must immerse yourself to get through. The pool is deep, but because of its very depth and length, it is calm and there are no rocks, though the current is still strong. Now, even that crossing at the pool is risky. I would advise you to let me lead you up to another cave where you can dry out and then in two, perhaps three days, when the river has gone down, you can cross with no difficulty.

In the meantime, I can tell you all I know about the coast and the Castle of Darkness, and I can tell you how to find a friend or two. What do you say?"

"Show us the pool," said John without hesitation. "We will try to make it today. Every minute lost may mean the princess's life."

"Very well, then, though it is really quite foolhardy, especially in your armor. At least take that off for the swim."

John considered the advice for a moment. "And if I did, then how would I get it? You will not be able to cross until the river goes down. It would be just the delay I cannot brook."

"By this," said Plummet, unwinding the rope from the bundle of sleeping skins. "You can haul the armor across to you when you are on the other side."

John considered another moment as he stood in the pelting rain. "All right, Plummet. I'll do it. And you said you could tell me about the castle and some friends."

"There is hardly time for all I could say, but I will tell you the most important things." Almost shouting to make himself heard above the roar of the wind and the rain, the fisherman told John and Morduc and Anga that the Castle of Darkness could only be approached by a single road that was strongly defended by a gate. Beyond the gate was a drawbridge that spanned the rough ocean gap between the headland and the granite island. The castle's main gate was at the end of the drawbridge. The rock was partly cut away at its base on the seaward side so that lighters could come right under the castle and deliver their freight directly up into the castle by means of a winch within the main storeroom.

There was also thought to be an underwater exit and entrance from a saltwater well in the deep base of the rock. The existence of this entrance was not proven, but it had been postulated to account for the mysterious and invisible comings and goings of the Master himself. He would appear in a village, but his ship would not be near. Similarly, he would not be thought to be in the castle, but suddenly he would appear. How could it be otherwise than that he swam in and out like a dark shape-shifting squid, a were-fish if there ever were such a thing.

"And is there anyone you can tell me about who opposes him?" said John.

"There was one man and one woman who might still be alive. I have no idea where they would be or how they would have protected themselves. The woman you will know by her blue eyes that laugh and pierce at the same time. The man is mad about lost languages and spends his days and nights in study of them. Whether either can be found, I have no idea. These two you can trust. There may be others, but I do not know of them."

"Very well," said John, "I will remember. Take us to the pool."

They moved out from under the overhang, the fisherman leading. The rain was still coming down heavily, but not in the solid sheets of a few minutes before. The old man guided them along the slippery path to the side of a huge rock basin into which the river ran. Across it, on the other side, they could see a gently sloping sandy beach on which they would try to land. John took off his armor, wrapped it in his chain-mail battle sark, made of the same red-gold steel as the breastplate, cuisses, and greaves, and then bound them all together with his baldric. Finally he stuck the sword down through the center and slipped a noose knot around the bundle with one end of the rope the fisherman gave him. The other end of the coil he clamped between his teeth and let himself down into the deep cold pool and began swimming strongly toward the opposite shore. The rope floated and followed him across the pool like a brown eel.

Morduc took off his hat and rolled it up and put it in his pocket. Then he too plunged in, followed by the dog. All three were making good headway across the black swirling, churning pool, when suddenly they heard a distant roaring from further up the river. The old man called out to them as loud as he could, "The crest is coming."

From upstream out of the gorge came a huge wall of water crashing into the pool and causing the water already there to surge upward in a towering wave. John swam frantically, trying to reach the far side before he was washed away. He felt himself heaved upward from beneath and a moment later, a half-canyon-high wall of water poured down over him, pushing him down, down, down into the darkness. Just as he began to go under, he heard a faint voice calling, "The rope, the rope." He reached with his hand to grasp the rough, thick line, but just as he did, so it was torn from his teeth and he felt himself tumbling over and over deep under the water as he was carried away by the stream.

He looked up. Far above him he could barely see the bubbling mirror surface. He tried to push upward, to loft toward the air, but instead he sank. Far above him he saw the dog swimming strongly with Morduc hanging on to its tail. He called out, but only bubbles passed his teeth. He felt himself sinking, sinking, down, down, down into the water. He floated exhaustedly. Should he continue to fight? Perhaps it would be best to let the darkness take him. The surface was so far, far away. It would be such a terrible struggle to get there. Perhaps he should sleep a bit, just a short nap before going on. The princess would have to wait. Just a few minutes of sleep wouldn't matter. She could hold out for just a minute or two more . . . He felt his feet touch bottom and sink into the soft ooze there. He went down on his knees into the liquid cloud of muck. So soft, for sleep. The light began to dim in his eyes and a blackness, just such as he had felt in the King of Time's banqueting hall, closed over him.

CHAPTER 14

Morduc Meets Marianna

Anga and Morduc swam, struggling through the white-tipped water and finally dragged themselves exhaustedly out of the river on to the small sand beach they had seen from the other side. Amid the pouring rain, Anga shook himself furiously, sending a secondary shower on to the still-prone Morduc. The elf looked in both directions but did not see John. On his hands and knees he pulled himself further up the shingle, turned over, and sat there scanning the water for John. Anga pressed himself against the elf. After ten minutes of fruitless watching, Morduc got up. "Anga, we must see whether John has been washed ashore further down." Looking across the pool, Morduc saw Plummet standing on the other side with the rope coiled in his hands and the bundle of John's armor next to him. Morduc waved, and Plummet waved back. Above the wind and rain Morduc yelled, "I will look for John downriver."

The fisherman yelled back, "I will search this side." They began picking their way along the edges of the rough, roaring river. For close to an hour they worked their way down the rock-broken banks, but they neither saw John in the water nor on the shores. At last Morduc and the fisherman stopped opposite each other with the angry river between them. Cupping his hands to his mouth, Morduc called across, "What shall we do?"

"We must continue to look," called back the fisherman. "The riverbank is still passable for some ways yet. He may have washed up below." On they continued in the still-heavy rain, along the rocky, slippery banks. They continued to search for several hours, disappearing from each other's sight behind huge boulders and then again coming into view. The further they went, the broader the river became, until they could hardly hear each other across it. About midafternoon, as the rain began to lessen, Morduc came to the mouth of a tributary stream on his right, tumbling noisily out of steep rock walls. There he stopped, and the fisherman on the other side did so as well.

"I can go no further," called Morduc over the clashing foam.

The fisherman called back, "Go west."

Even though Morduc knew the fisherman was right, and even though he and John had agreed that the other would continue on to the coast if they got separated, Morduc was still unwilling to leave the river until he had found his friend or knew he was dead. Reluctantly, he called back to the fisherman, "Very well. I will go on. Tell John if—I mean—when, you find him." He waved his hand and turned his steps westward up the sidestream away from the river. Anga trotted after him.

They climbed up along the rocky bank of the tributary, picking their way over boulders and snarled driftwood, tracing its course westward. When it became a deep brook and turned south, they left it to continue west, climbing up on to a flat tableland forested with pines. The trees were spaced in regular lines, and the undergrowth had been carefully eliminated. The carpet of pine needles was uniform and smooth. Walking was effortless. The rain had almost ceased. Anga continued to stop briefly every so often to give his coat a vigorous shake. As the sun came out from behind the clouds, Morduc saw in the distance a large, white-columned house set on a rise. It had a portico in front of its center section and two wings made of white stone so pure that the entire building glistened in the sunlight. Most astonishing of all, however, was a blue dome, which sat atop the center section of the house.

"Habitation, Anga. Let us try what sort of hospitality we can receive. But we must remember that the influence of the Master of Darkness has penetrated to this side of the river, so we must be on our guard."

The dog wuffed assent.

They entered a long grassy aisle canopied with huge, rough-barked elms. As Morduc and Anga came up the avenue, one of the servants from the house saw them and stopped in astonishment.

He saw a short-legged gray dog, somewhat wet and bedraggled, and a short person who seemed a mere lad, likewise drooping wet and bedraggled, dressed in a suit of seven times seventy shades of green, with a bow and a quiver on his back, a soaked cloak over one shoulder, and a green leather bag slung over the other.

The servant ran down the avenue to meet them, blocking their way, and inquiring with a high, nasal superciliousness, "How, young sir, have you gotten past the gatekeeper? Go back, please. You can have no business here."

"We had hoped for a civil welcome," replied Morduc, "and a chance to dry ourselves off by your kitchen fire."

"A likely story. We want no young thieves here," said the servant, eyeing the bulging bag. "Be off with you at once." As he took a threatening step toward Morduc, Anga growled softly.

Before anything else could happen, the face and shoulders of a dark-haired girl appeared at a window under the portico. "Henry," she called. "That is no way to welcome wayfarers. Surely they have been out in the storm and need courtesy and shelter rather than being turned away to spend a night in the open. Welcome them in immediately. I will tell Father."

"But, missy, you know what your father said about people on the road."

"Henry. Please do as I ask. I will tell Father, and he shall decide." With that she withdrew her head from the window. Grumbling, Henry led Morduc and Anga a long walk around the side of the white, stately house to the back and to the door of the kitchen. Entering it, they found a long room ablaze with two fireplaces, one at each end, and a great bustle and hurry. A large woman with a white cap on her head was in the process of taking trays of crisp tarts out of the oven in the brick face of the nearer fireplace. The aroma of warm raspberry filled the room.

"Shoo, Henry. Out, out, out. Not yet, you knock noggin. I don't care how hungry you are. These are for dinner tonight." Morduc and Anga peeked around Henry. The woman looked up when Henry didn't answer. "I thought I told you Henry . . . What wee wandering waif have you picked up there?"

Morduc stepped forward and made a bow. "My name is Morduc, and I am traveling to see the world. I am not quite a waif, but if that implies you are disposed to give me fair treatment, I will be grateful and will not betray you in any way."

"Land, how the child speaks," said the woman, standing looking down at him with her huge arms akimbo. "Where did you pick up an educated parrot like this, Henry?"

"He just appeared in the drive, Martha. The little mistress says we are to take him in and she will settle it with the master. I don't like it, after what happened."

"Well, what the little mistress says, we do, and like it too, not because she's spoiled, but because she's right, whether a big lout like you, Henry, admit it or not, and now . . ." Here she stopped, noticing Anga for the first time, lying comfortably on the brick floor of the kitchen, wrinkling his black nose in anticipation of a substantial supper. "But that dog," Martha continued, "that dog must stay out. No dogs in my kitchen. It is an absolute rule."

"We will, of course, comply, even though, my good woman, he is a most well-behaved dog and would never steal anything from your tables or bins. He will wait outside for me, though I would rather not have him in the kennels. He should not have to fight for accommodation." Morduc bent down and whispered into Anga's ear, at which the dog went out the back door, turned right, and trotted away around the house.

"Land sakes," said Martha, laughing, "you'd think that dog understood your whisperings. But come sit over here by the fire. Your clothes are all wet. Henry, send for some dry things. He looks to be about the size"—she paused just barely, with a catch in her throat—"of the young master . . . three or four years ago. Some of his clothes must be left." Henry disappeared out the back of the kitchen.

"Sissy! Sassy! Come here and help," Martha called out loudly. Two kitchen girls appeared from a side room. "Help this boy into dry clothes," she ordered. They scampered forward and led him to a seat by the fireplace at the far end of the room. When, giggling, they took off his hat, they both stepped back and gasped at the green of his hair.

"Lor, young master, I never seed hair like that afore," said Sissy.

"Where come ye from?" said Sassy.

Before he could answer, Henry returned with a large towel and a complete set of clothing suitable for a young gentleman. Morduc took them into a small washroom behind the far fireplace, stripped off his wet green clothes, washed completely, dried himself, and then dressed carefully in the white knee-length stockings, black knee breeches, linen shirt, neck cloth, and medium-length brown velvet coat that had been brought to him. He slipped on the square-toed black shoes, which fit him well enough, and looked at himself in the small mirror on the washroom wall. He saw an elegant young gentleman with a dark-green, tanned face, who would have looked to be just on the innocent side of manhood, except for the mischievous wisdom and ancient gaiety that shone out of his green eyes. When he presented himself at the door of the washroom, Martha clasped her hands in astonishment.

"You look almost like the young master before he . . . . It is almost like having him here before my eyes again."

"You must have loved him a great deal," said Morduc gently.

Martha wiped the corner of her eye with her apron. "That indeed I did. We all did. And now, who knows where he is, or if he is at all."

"If the stranger is ready," intoned Henry with sarcastic pomposity, "the master is ready to receive him in the library."

Morduc hesitated. "What master is that?" he asked quietly.

"It is hardly for vagabonds like *you* to be asking the questions," snorted Henry. "You'll see soon enough."

"Oh hush, Henry," said Martha. "Before you go, little Mister Morduc, or whatever your name is, just try one of these raspberry tarts. The young master used to love them, and he would sneak, I mean, he would do me the favor of coming down here to sample them." As Henry made an exasperated noise in the background, Morduc took the proffered pastry and finished it quickly in two bites. It was delicious, with the flavor of the fresh berry warmed and intensified, yet still light and sweet in its delicate shell.

"Clearly, Martha, if you will permit me to call you that on such short acquaintance, you are surely the best cook in the land."

"Go along with you, Master Morduc," said Martha, laughing with pleasure. "You'll make me really cry in a minute. That's what the young master used to say. Still, I thank'ee much for saying it."

"Come along, now, *Mister* Morduc," said the lofty Henry. "The master wishes to speak with you." Henry led the way out of the kitchen and up a dark flight of stairs, then turned left along a narrow corridor, and then right, and then left again and right until they came out a small door in the wall into the large hall just inside the front door. The hall had a star-tessellated marble floor and a great sweeping stairway that went up to the second level of the house. Up yet another flight, Morduc saw a blue dome painted with gold stars looking down on the hall beneath.

"Come along. Don't gawk," said Henry. "The library is this way." He led Morduc leftward along a corridor which ran just inside a greenhouse wall of windows facing east. The setting sun already cast a domed black shadow on the large lawn which stretched beyond the portico to the trees of the park. At last they reached a large dark door, on which Henry knocked.

"Come in," said a deep voice. Henry opened the door and ushered Morduc into a large, rectangular room completely lined with bookshelves except for broad window bays on each of the outer walls into which maroon cushioned seats had been built. There was an iron track circling the shelves at the ceiling. From the track depended a ladder on wheels. Several dark leather wing chairs were dispersed about the room. Henry went out and shut the huge door behind him.

Behind a dark carved table with an inkwell and several quills on it sat a large, square man of about fifty. He had black hair shot through with gray. His jutting eyebrows projected over deep-set black eyes. His face was pale and gaunt, and the eyes looked as if they had not slept in many days. His large hawk-beak nose was slightly twisted, as if it had been broken at some point in the past and had healed without being straightened. When he saw Morduc, he started up from his chair. A look of joy and hope flashed briefly over his face before it abruptly fell again and resumed its gray haunted anxiety.

"Come here, young man," he said. "You do not look at all like the little green half-drowned rat that Henry said you were. For a moment I took you for . . . for someone else." He silently scrutinized Morduc for some time and finally spoke again. "My name is George Ravenstock, Lord Ballan. I am the master of this estate, and I welcome you. Who are you, where did you come from, and where are you journeying?"

Morduc debated whether or not to tell him the whole story. Although Lord Ballan seemed courteous, direct, and open, if a little gruff, Morduc decided to say as little as possible.

"My name is Morduc. Like many young men these days, I am far from home. I come from a considerable distance to the east. I am merely journeying to see the world. I tried to ford the river and was thoroughly wet and exhausted from the swim and the rain when I approached your house."

"Why did you not simply cross at the bridge?" asked Lord Ballan. "Why risk yourself in the flood?"

"Surely you must know the bridge is burnt," said Morduc simply.

Ballan looked at Morduc appraisingly. "You can confirm, then, that it was burnt?"

"I have seen the charred posts myself."

"And how did it come to be burnt?"

"It was burnt when I arrived at it," said Morduc carefully. "I saw no one doing it or leaving it."

"And so you came across the river. Higher up or lower down?"

"Lower down, this morning. The storm run nearly took us."

"Us?" said Lord Ballan sharply.

"My dog, Anga, and I," said Morduc imperturbably.

"It was indeed a dreadful storm," Lord Ballan replied. "You are lucky to have your life. This wayfaring is a dangerous business . . . especially . . . when you stray from the regular roads. Can you not tell me something of your family? Might I know them?"

Morduc understood that Ballan must know more if he were to trust him. He decided quickly to tell the truth about his origins as a way of concealing the quest in which he had joined John.

"I doubt, sir, very much, that you would know of them, unless you have journeyed in my part of the world. I am, as you might say, part elven, and my home is a great distance to the east. I have been wandering westward for a short time. My mother's name was Ayla, and my father's is Maqalan. He rules in a great forest where I was brought up. My mortal mother so loved my father that she forsook her own people to marry him and to live in the elven depths of the forest, though knowing he would outlive her. I have a choice, and that is why I am journeying, either to take up the life of a mortal, renouncing immortality forever, or to return to the deep forest where I can live forever and, where, if I am found worthy by the ElfMot, I may possibly succeed my father as king. This is why I journey about the human world to see what enlightenment it may hold."

"Then I am doubly glad to have you under my roof, young elven prince, for if you have seen much, and thought about it, your observations will be worth much, and you may perhaps even have news of some of my own friends. Living as I do, in the country here, I seldom see people from distant regions. It would give me pleasure if you would join my family and some few other guests for dinner tonight. And when you have rested somewhat from your obvious fatigue, we will send you on your travels with what I hope will be friendly memories of us."

A slight rustle from one of the huge leather chairs at the end of the library attracted Morduc's attention. He had thought that only he and the master had been in the room, but now he saw the ripple of a dress as well.

"Ah, yes, my daughter," said the master. "Marianna. Will you meet Morduc, who will be staying with us for a day or two." The figure from the chair got up and came forward. Morduc saw once again the girl who had spoken to Henry from the balcony. She was of about his own height, as slim and as light, with large dark eyes, long chestnut hair, and full red lips. She came forward confidently and held out her hand with neither bashfulness nor coyness.

"Good Master Morduc. I am pleased to meet you," she said.

Morduc extended his own hand, and as he looked directly at her, he saw in her eyes a vivacity and gaiety he had long sought but had heretofore never found. He looked so long and hard that he still held on to her hand.

"Why are you staring?" she said, neither offended nor puzzled, but saying it simply to tease him slightly, for she in her turn had seen in Morduc's green eyes a brilliance, a clarity, and above all an honesty which she too had not so far found in the world of men except in her father and brother. Though Morduc was dressed in her brother's mundane mortal clothes, his lean, tanned face and his green eyes transmitted a sense of invisible worlds seen and, because of having seen them, an unshakable reliability. Here, she felt, was someone whom she could trust as completely as she trusted herself.

"Staring?" he said. "Am I? Indeed, I am. Excuse me. I . . . I . . . I . . .," Morduc stammered. He paused, collected himself, and then finished his thought. "I seem to remember you from somewhere. But that, of course, is impossible."

"Yes, of course, that is impossible . . . but then again, we don't always know where we have been, do we?" said Marianna, smiling at him so frankly and so sweetly that his heart began to pound. She seemed to be talking of the Eolmalil. Could any mortal know?

"Perhaps, Marianna," said Lord Ravenstock, "you would be willing to show Morduc the library, garden, and house until dinnertime? And after dinner, Morduc, I may have something to show you, which will astonish you and delight you, if it does not frighten you."

"Thank you very much," said Morduc. "I would indeed appreciate being shown the house by Marianna, and I await your surprise with interest."

The master looked at Morduc carefully and intently from under his deep brows. "I have some other business to attend to at the moment, so I will leave you to your explorations." The master left by the large dark door through which Morduc had entered, and the two young people were alone.

"Where would you like to start?" asked Marianna.

"With you," he replied. He looked at her with a fascination, which he tried to conceal but could not. He believed he had never seen anyone so beautiful, yet, he thought, she was a mere mortal, destined to pass shortly out of elf time, as his mother had already done many eons ago, leaving his father lonely and bereft. How could he, Morduc, far from home—where there were innumerable resplendent, shining, perfect elf children—how could he possibly love this perishably short-lived mortal? Red John's passion came to his mind. Perhaps there was more than foolishness to it after all. As he continued to look at her, he realized that though she was small, she already had a fully formed figure, and he saw that she was physically strong as well, no doubt with a mind and spirit to match.

"There is not much to tell," she began, speaking in a low, musical voice. It was as if he had been hearing her voice for centuries already but still found it as fresh and as interesting as infinite novelty. "I have grown up here. My father teaches me every day—languages, literature, mathematics, poetry. My mother teaches me chemistry and medicine. I ride part of the day."

"Can you ride?" Morduc interrupted enthusiastically.

"Very well, indeed," she laughed. "I have been riding since I could walk. Perhaps I ride as well as you. Perhaps even better." Her tone contained no challenge but only the self-confidence of an equal. "At least," she went on, "I used to ride nearly as well as my brother when he was . . . home."

For the moment, Morduc let pass the mention of her brother. "And what else does your father have you study? Has he taught you to handle a sword as well?"

"And would it matter to you if he had? Would I seem too much of a boy to you and not a woman?"

Does she want to be a woman to me? thought Morduc. They sat down close together in the bay of one of the back windows of the library as it looked out on the gardens to the west. As the sun sank toward the jagged edge of the mountains its red rays washed the dark leather and darker wood of the room in a rich gold.

"Marianna, I can scarcely believe anything would ill become you."

"Then you are one of the rare few, aside from my father and brother, who so think. Most men believe a woman's place is necessarily only in the parlor and the nursery and not out in the world. Do you think a woman can be as good as a man at anything either can do?" she asked.

"In matters of the heart, mind, and spirit, there is no question. As for body, the raw strength of most women is simply not equal to that of most men, but given equality of size, as you and I nearly are, I grant you equality in physical performance and perhaps superiority as well. I think we might be equal as runners. Do you know how to handle a bow?"

"I can shoot any bow I can string," she said proudly, "and hit my aim."

"Then let us go hunting together," he said excitedly, "before I . . ."

"Before you . . . leave," she finished the sentence for him, turning away from him. Both realized at that moment that neither wanted Morduc to leave. He felt that he could stay with her forever; she felt that her life must be over if he left.

Morduc took her hand. She trembled but did not withdraw it. "Marianna, you are already very dear to me," he said. "Can you keep my secret?"

"If you truly know my heart," she said, her head down, "you must know that I would value any secret of yours as I do you and both more than my own life. Why must you leave?"

Knowing that he was perhaps endangering his mission by disclosing who he was to this girl whom he was sure he loved, but who might, through youth or inexperience or family loyalty, betray him, Morduc took a deep breath and said, "Do you know of the Master of Darkness?"

Marianna gave a shudder. "My father has spoken of him. He is a great power on the coast. His agents have visited here first with offers and then with threats. So far, my father has resisted, but he has been more watchful and worried than I have ever seen him." She paused, hesitated, and then tightening her hand on Morduc's, said, "In fact, he set me to discover if you were one of his agents. If you are, and you have deceived me, I will kill you first and then myself."

Morduc jumped up at the strong words, but she held his hand fast. They remained at arm's length for a moment, looking into each other's eyes. Then slowly she drew him to sit down opposite her again. In a low voice, he told her the entire story of his journey so far.

When he had finished, Marianna's eyes sparkled with excitement. "My father will be able to help you. I hope that your friend has not been drowned in the river. In any case, I see now why you must go. Clearly, the princess must be saved from that Would-Be-King Sir Dark, even if," she hesitated, "even if your friend is . . . unable to help you." She paused and then continued, "Yes, the power of this pseudoprince, this Master of Darkness must be broken forever. It is a noble, noble quest, and I wish you its true success. And perhaps afterward . . . ." She looked at Morduc with such admiration and love that the elf felt a giddiness he had never felt before, except perhaps in some distant, forgotten dream.

Seated in the window with the red sun shining on her face, Marianna seemed to Morduc the epitome of all femininity that he had ever hoped for. Her dark beauty, her long brown hair, the simultaneous slimness and fullness of her figure, the enthusiasm and liveliness of her spirit, and the steadfastness of her heart, drew him to her with irresistible force. She sat with her back against the wood, her hand still in his. Morduc slid toward her. She tilted her face upward. He leaned toward her, their lips almost touching, close enough so that they felt each other's warm breath on them.

The door opened and Henry entered, announcing in a loud, officious voice that dinner was served. The two young people separated and stood up. Marianna gave him a swift, teasing look, and said in a low voice, as she brushed past him, "Later." Morduc wanted to dance and burst into song but managed to maintain decorum as they followed the austere and gruff Henry out of the library and down the long, glassed-in, plant-filled corridor, across the high central hall with the blue-and-gold dome, to another large room just off the hall.

CHAPTER 15

Dinner at Eight

Through the open doors Morduc saw a long table set with pale-lemon-colored linen, blue plates, and sparkling crystal and silver under golden chandeliers that sent out beams of soft light to every corner of the room. Behind every chair was a server. Marianna's father was at the head; at the foot sat a small woman much resembling Marianna except for graying hair. She was addressed as Lady Ballan by the several other individuals whom Morduc had not yet met, who took their places at the table along with him. Morduc was motioned to a seat in the middle of the table while Marianna sat on her father's right.

Lord Ballan identified Morduc merely as a distant cousin. He had difficulty following the conversation with the others at the table because he looked only at Marianna, and she in return teased him with secret glances so swift he was not sure they had even been given. The talk started first with the weather, then turned to crops, then to poetry, philosophy, and finally on to politics. There were three other couples at the table who seemed to be residents of the district and who were clearly being sounded by Ravenstock as to how they stood in relation to the attempts by an unnamed force to extend its influence inland from the coast. Occasionally Morduc was asked to contribute information from his travels, but he carefully avoided seeming to have much knowledge of anything, and certainly not of matters related to the coast. Though he knew from Marianna that Lord Ballan was opposed to the Master of Darkness, it was not possible to tell which of the neighbors might be secret spies, or, horrible thought, even which of the servants might have been corrupted, if the Master's representatives had already visited the house. So Morduc kept his counsel and presented the appearance of an altogether dull young man.

Dinner consisted of a number of courses, each of which was exceptional, from the clear soup, through fish, salad, red meat, and on through the dessert of Martha's raspberry tarts. When dinner was over, the entire company, both men and women together, withdrew to the drawing room for coffee. Morduc noticed that Lady Ballan walked with difficulty, balancing herself with the help of two ivory-headed ebony canes. Marianna provided part of the entertainment, singing as she accompanied herself on a carved stringed box which she held on her lap and plucked with a white quill. Another guest played a piece on a seven-stringed violin, and a third sung a drum ballad of ancient times. Then most of the company turned to cards at leather-covered square tables or to a new game one of the visitors had brought with him, in which rather ugly gargoyles and dragons were moved in circles by dice on a segmented octangular board.

When the games began, Marianna brought Morduc over to where her mother sat, resting her folded hands on her canes. Her figure had remained nearly as slight as her daughter's, and even though she possessed all of her daughter's grace, humor, and lightness, a secret grief buried in her eyes made her altogether a grave, serious, and strangely enough, almost dangerous person. Marianna introduced Morduc with a pleasure and flutter in her voice bordering on indiscretion.

The mother, hearing the note in her daughter's voice, first looked at Marianna and then at Morduc with a deep and searching directness that nearly discomposed the elf. She shook his hand and said to him without a trace of humor or jollity, "Young man, let me compliment you on your tailor. Can you give me his name?" For a moment Morduc was dumbfounded by the direct indirection of the remark and wondered what he could say.

Finally he replied, "Lady Ballan, my tailor is a friend of my dearest friend's friend, and therefore your friend."

"Something of a riddling reply, young man, but then perhaps you are interested in riddles?" Morduc looked quickly at Marianna, but she shook her head. "Come sit by me, young man. We are not for the games, are we?" Even though they talked of apparently inconsequential matters, Morduc felt his measure was being fully taken. Her gravity and stern seriousness made him feel that in the mother too he had found an ally who could be relied upon absolutely, as much as the daughter, if she concluded that he was a friend, but otherwise a dangerous and effective enemy.

As the evening progressed, Morduc kept casting about in his mind for a way he could be alone with Marianna, but he could find none. Presently, however, Lord Ballan came over to Morduc and said, "Now is the time for the surprise I have promised you. Marianna, you may accompany us, if you wish."

CHAPTER 16

In the Blue Dome

Taking a candle in a glass chimney and giving another to Marianna, he led the way out of the drawing room where the others continued to engage in games or to read, into the hall and up the circling staircase. They went to the second floor and then up to the third until they were just under the blue dome and could go no higher. Morduc wondered what the surprise was. Then Lord Ballan pressed one of the stars painted on the blue dome and a small concealed, curved door in the wall opened and they went in. Morduc found himself at the bottom of a narrow iron staircase which spiraled up into the darkness above them. The three climbed around and upward on the cold, iron lattice steps until they came to a trap door in a slotted iron floor above them. This the master lifted open above him, and all three ascended through it. Morduc found himself in a domed room. Sitting in the middle of the room, he saw a large tube mounted in rings with a small bench at the bottom end, the whole suspended in an open iron cage. Lord Ballan concealed his candle in a baffled recess by the trap door while Marianna gave hers to Morduc. Then father and daughter went over to one side of the room and began together to crank a large wheel on the wall. With a low, rolling whisper, a crack began to open in the dome above them. It widened progressively to reveal the stars pinpointing the dark velvet of a cloudless sky. The moon had not yet risen. Only the clear white light of the stars shone down into the dome where the three small figures stood looking up.

"Cover the other candle now," said Lord Ballan. Marianna took it from Morduc and placed it within the recess, closed the baffle, and then came back to Morduc and took his hand in the semidarkness of the dome interior. Lord Ballan went over to the iron cage and climbed in. Sitting on the narrow bench seat, he began turning one or another of three handles mounted beneath the tube. The great tube began to swing until it was pointed out of the dome at a group of stars to the south.

"Come over here, Morduc," said Ravenstock. "Climb onto the bench, and look down into the eyepiece and tell me what you see?" Morduc did as he was directed. Instead of small points of light, as he had expected, he saw instead a great sweeping cloud of light with many thousands of brighter, larger lights within it. Shocked, he took his eye away from the tube and looked with his naked eye at the sky. All he saw in the direction that the tube pointed was a small, single point of light. Again he applied his eye to the tube. The great swirling arms of light were the small point. "I see a great ragged cloud of light where a small point should be," said Morduc.

"Is it not wonderful?" said Ravenstock. "The skies stretch out endlessly, and this instrument brings them closer. What seems to be a single small hard point of light becomes a great cloudy pinwheel of stars. There are billions of such clouds, and within each are billions of stars. The immensity of it overwhelms me, and if the multiplication of light were not enough, one may think as well of the extent of darkness around the stars. How small we are here compared to the magnitude of what we can see. At times I have spent the entire night up here scanning the skies for some answer to our troubles and insecurities here below. But I have found none so far, although sometimes I seem to be on the verge, not of seeing one, but of hearing one, as if a voice is about to speak to me out of the night, but speaking from a great distance among or beyond the stars. Yet with daylight comes the realization that only by my own unceasing vigilance and unrelenting work, work in the orchards and gardens and laboratories and on the battlefields and by perpetual alertness to the inroads of those who wish to control this land do I maintain even the limited freedom I have to undertake studies of this or of any sort, attacked as we are perpetually by those who wish to take our freedom, our land, and our thoughts together."

"And you have my love and gratitude for so doing, Father," said Marianna. "You know my opinion of these matters, that the stars give us reason for cheer in our troubles. In any case, while I live, your efforts cannot be in vain. I promise it."

"Thank you, Marianna. I will try to keep my spirits up." Then he turned to Morduc, saying, "Marianna is my most accomplished student, already a better astronomer than I. I hope you will not object to my leaving you in her care to show you whatever in the skies she wishes you to see. I am somewhat chilled by the night air and will return to the house."

"I have no objection, sir," said Morduc, his heart leaping with joy.

"We will rejoin you in a short while," said Marianna, as the tall, gaunt man crossed to the trap door, took one of the tapers out of the candle keep and, then by its light, slowly descended the iron spiral toward the doorway by which they had entered the dome. He opened it, went through, and then closed it behind him, leaving the two young people alone in the dome. Marianna took Morduc's hand and led him back to the cylinder of far seeing. "I will show you my favorite star," she said. Climbing onto the seat in the cage, she deftly twirled the handles, moving the great device soundlessly to point at another part of the sky. She bent over the small viewing tube a moment, and then instead of getting out of the cage, she moved over on the seat, making room for Morduc. He climbed up carefully and took his place on the short shelf which served as a seat in the cage and looked through the tube. He saw swimming in the glass a brilliant blue-white star, shimmering and iridescent, filling the entire eyepiece.

"Why," he exclaimed, "it is Caracanta, the star of love. We know this star in my home. And is this your favorite star?"

"Yes," she said, "and I searched the heavens a long time before I found it. It is the most beautiful star of any I have ever seen." Morduc turned toward Marianna in the semidarkness. He could feel her strong young thigh pressing against his. He put his arm around her and gently, slowly, put his lips on hers, and as he felt his kiss returned, sweetly, softly, yieldingly, as her full red lips opened to his and their tongues met within their kissed mouths, he knew he had found his true love.

Marianna laughed, her eyes shining. "Oh, that this kissing could go on forever."

"It does," replied Morduc. "This first kiss goes on forever. The interruptions are only apparent. This kiss of our lips is but the symbol of the kiss of our souls, which is eternal and unending. Your star and my star, always one, has joined us. We are truly one."

"Done," she said. In the silence of the stars broken only by the distant barking of a dog in the crofts below, they resumed their kiss, warmed by each other against the chill night air blowing down through the open dome. They were but two small figures, dark dots within a dark spot, on a dark orb, invisible in the immensity of the light-filled sky yet courageously equal to it all. Slim and small, both of them, but strong in spirit beyond the combined assaults of death, tyranny, torture, and the silent, dark, miasmic decay claimed of the universe itself. If any could combat it, they could, together the epitome of anentropy.

Eventually, they climbed down from the viewing cage. Marianna went off to the large wheel on the wall; Morduc followed, and together, they closed the dome. Then hand in hand, beneath the darkened dome, they found their way to the candle keep, extracted the remaining taper, and with their way lit only by the single candle for the two of them, went down through the trap door, quietly lowering it behind them. They crept carefully down the cold narrow, spiral iron stairs and just before they went into the main house, they blew out the candle and kissed again lovingly, passionately, deeply in the sheltering dark. Whispering so quietly that none but the one ear of each could hear, Morduc said, "One," and Marianna replied, "One." Then together they stepped out into the upper hall, their hearts full of joy and solemnity at the eternity of their commitment.

Chapter 17

Intruders in the House

They went downstairs and returned to the drawing room where Marianna's mother and father alone remained, the idle gamesters having either disappeared to their guest rooms or departed in their carriages for home.

"We are lodging you tonight in my son's room," said Lady Ballan to Morduc from her seat by the fire. "Is there anything else we can do for you before we all retire?"

"I would like to make sure that my dog is all right," said Morduc. "Would that bother you?"

"Not in the least," said Ravenstock. "Marianna will show you the way."

The two went off down through the house's dark passages. As they approached the kitchen, they heard low voices inside. Just as Morduc was about to push through the door and enter, Marianna laid a small hand silently on his arm to hold him back. They stood listening but could not make out the words, although they could distinguish three voices, one of them low and harsh.

Marianna pushed the swinging door open ever so slightly. They heard the harsh voice say, "Well, do what you can," and then, "Wait, someone is coming." There was a rustling, but before Marianna and Morduc could push open the door and descend the three steps into the kitchen, a black-hatted and cloaked figure had rushed out the back door while the owners of the other two voices had disappeared by other doors into the house. Though there was a lively fire in the near grate, no one else was in the room.

"Did you see who it was?" whispered Morduc.

"No," answered Marianna. "I must tell Father about this immediately." She slipped off the way she had come, and Morduc went to the back door and looked out. Even though there was now the beginnings of moonlight on the garden, he could see no movement there. He saw a light in the stables and heard distant low singing, but that was all. He whistled softly into the darkness, and presently Anga's compact gray barrel of a body separated itself from the shadows. He came up to Morduc, wagging his tail and looking up at him with his amused, intelligent, open-hearted eyes.

"Well," said Morduc, "did you find out anything?" The dog lifted his paw in assent. "Good," said Morduc. "Is there any danger?" The dog lifted his paw and shook his head at the same time. "What do you mean, yes and no?" asked Morduc. "Does the Master of Darkness have someone within the house?" The dog lifted his paw again. "Then," said Morduc, "we must be extremely careful." He squatted down and scratched behind Anga's ears while he thought. After a pause he asked, "Have you been fed?" The dog lifted his paw again.

"Good. Perhaps, it would be best if you slept on the floor of my room tonight." Just then, he heard a slight noise. He turned quickly to see Marianna slip back into the kitchen. "My father is most upset," she said. "He is not altogether sure that this intrusion is not connected with your presence here. He is even worried that you yourself may not be trustworthy. I have tried to reassure him that you are loyal to us, but he is in such anguish and perturbation of spirit that he wishes to see you immediately."

"Very well," replied Morduc. "I will go to him instantly. But first, this is Anga. He is an unusual dog. He can understand all that we say. I want you to take him to where I will sleep tonight and, if possible, to do so in a way that none but ourselves know he is there, both for my sake and for his. He is my ears in the night. I would sleep better knowing he is both safe and there. Can you do it?"

"Of course," said Marianna. "No one will see us. Go to my father. He is in the library. I will take you part way." They went back up through the house, moving slowly through the dark passages, the dog following behind. When they had come almost to the hall, Marianna stopped and whispered in Morduc's ear, "I must go a different way now. Straight on and you will find yourself in the hall." She squeezed his hand and was gone, with the dog following her.

Morduc continued on into the hall, which several servants were crossing to and fro with lights. As he was going down the corridor to the library, he saw Lady Ballan coming toward him, walking with her customary difficulty, but with a determined intensity of purpose. He gave her his hand, and as she leaned heavily on him, she spoke urgently. "Morduc, I have confidence in you, but we are under terrible threat if what you heard in the kitchen means what I am afraid it does. We had thought that at least the house was secure and the people all our own. I advise you to be completely candid with Lord Ballan. Only in that way can we help you and you help us. I urge you to make haste. I must see to another matter."

"Thank you for your confidence, madam. I will do so," he replied, and continued on down the hall as Lady Ballan moved resolutely away from him supporting herself against the wall with one hand and grasping both canes in the other. When he got to the library door, Morduc knocked firmly, and when the voice inside called out for him to enter, he did. Ravenstock was alone, pacing up and down before the fire with a worried look on his face.

"Morduc, I hope you are not out to bring disaster on this house," he said immediately. "For if you are, I want you to know that I shall oppose it with all the strength yet remaining at my command. If you intend to harm us, leave this very instant, for I will not harbor in my house spies and thieves, if such you be. What can you tell me about the mysterious visitor in the kitchen?"

"My lord, I know no more of that visitor than you yourself do, and I am equally worried about what it can mean. I will tell you truly of my mission, which may have some bearing on that visitor, but are you sure we are alone and cannot be overheard? That visitor left, but clearly it was not to himself he was speaking in the kitchen."

Ravenstock motioned Morduc to follow him. He led the way to one of the bookcases and reached over and behind the row of books on one of the shelves. Morduc heard the sound of a latch releasing. Ravenstock pushed, and a section of the bookcase swung inward, allowing them to enter a small room behind it. Morduc saw before him a large round iron vault door. Ravenstock twirled the dials on it, rotated a large wheel on the outside, and swung the massive door open. He motioned Morduc to enter. Morduc hesitated, but only for a second. He ducked his head, entered, and turned, half expecting the door to close on him. Lord Ballan, however, stooped low, followed him in, and then swung the door shut behind them.

The vault was lit by faint starlight sifting from a small, thick crystal port in the ceiling. "Now, Morduc, none can hear us, even if we both should scream aloud. What have you to say?"

Morduc told Ravenstock all that he had told Marianna, about finding Red John, about the riddle, about what Hubert the Gardener had seen on the road, and of their determination to reach the coast to locate and free the princess. He told of what they had learned from the fisherman about how the Master of Darkness had come to power, of the sudden rain that had resulted in John's disappearance in the river, and of his own obligation to go on to the coast. He did not, however, say anything about the compact between himself and Marianna.

The great gaunt head hung in thought for several minutes, and then Ravenstock said, "I am not sure whether the Master of Darkness knows of your journey's purpose. I suspect he does not and that our mysterious visitor is simply part of that dark lord's continuing effort to bring all the land on this side of the mountains under his control. In any case, we must prevent his learning anything more of you. When you are rested enough to travel, I will provide you with a pony or two, and provisions, and a map of a secret path over the mountains that will help you enter the plain of the coast undetected. It would be well if we could also construct some disguise for you to prevent the Master of Darkness from knowing, if he does know, of your association with Red John, which yet permits you to get close enough to the Master's castle to formulate a plan of attack. It is a momentous task you are undertaking. Drefon grant that it be successful. If you succeed, you save not only Red John's princess, but this entire region, from the paralysis and tyranny of that cold and perverse power. The aging you see in Lady Ballan and myself is not owing to time alone, but to our anxiety over the situation. My son set out a year ago to reconnoiter. He has not returned and has sent no message that has reached us. We do not know whether he is alive or dead or, worse, corrupted and converted by the Black Knight. That one has even had the effrontery to request Marianna's presence in his castle to attend his so-called sister, but really to serve as a hostage for my acquiescence. That is why we are so nervous about strangers."

"I can see it must be a fearful worry for you. I join in it," answered Morduc.

Ravenstock looked at him strangely for a second and then said, "I will think about the disguise and give you my suggestion in the morning. You should go to bed, but I think I shall prowl about myself a bit this night, patrolling the house at least."

They left the vault and returned to the library. Ravenstock pulled on a bell rope. In a minute or so, Henry appeared. "Show Morduc to his room, please, Henry." As Henry led the way down the glassed corridor, Morduc glanced out into the shadowed darkness. The moon had begun to rise. He saw nothing but moonlight on the white marble and gray grass, but the sense of peace and exaltation he had had in the dome had left him. Was all under the shadow of the Master of Darkness, even Lord Ballan's house? Was there no safe place among these mortals?

When he was finally lodged behind the locked door of the young master's room, Morduc looked around him. The room was notably different from those in the rest of the house. The walls were painted white, and it was furnished with exceptional spareness, almost like a monastic cell, except for several fine paintings of bright fields and trees hung on the walls and a small cabinet of old books which stood by the door.

Morduc murmured softly, "Anga?" Immediately from somewhere in the room there came the soft thump of a tail beating on carpet. Morduc knelt and looked under the bed and found Anga there, comfortably stretched out. Morduc undressed, put on the nightshirt which had been left for him on the carved walnut bed, and then got into that large curtained structure and lay back, looking up at the canopy above him. He was exhausted with grief and elation and worry all at the same time.

John had been lost in the flood, and he was left to carry on alone the fight to free the princess, yet in the meantime he had fallen in love with a girl whose heart and mind and spirit so fit his own that he could not fail to be happy with her forever, yet she was not a being of the forever realm. A mortal she was. So they would have to be happy for the rest of their lives. What was a life? So short a time. All that was left for them to do was to marry. Marriage! But when could that be arranged? Found her he had, but beyond finding her he had not, and, and, sleepiness surrounding him, and the quest—if it failed? He started awake as much as his overwhelming fatigue would permit him. *If* it failed, as like he and his true love would never, never, never—waves of dark pain and loss began to blow in from the stormy sea of his sleep. Drowned in death, drowned in mortality for a girl whom, after tomorrow, he might never see again, though with whom he was one, almost. He began to understand the courage of his mother, the grief of his father, the passion of his friend.

Perhaps he would just stay at Ravenstock House with Marianna. Perhaps the Master of Darkness would keep his distance. Perhaps . . . perhaps . . . John would send him a message: "Help no longer needed. All's well." If only all were well. No, he must fulfill his pledge to Red John, the friend of his heart. Yet to keep his promise, he must separate from Marianna, the joy of his being. So silly, slieepy, these mortals, to permit themselves to be bound in such sloopy, yawny paradouxes. Troubelees that are so soleepiuss . . .

He slept finally, soundly, undisturbed throughout the night, unawakened by the soft steps in the hall or by the rustlings in the grass behind and beyond the house. Once, Anga got up and went over to the west-facing window and stood there sniffing. But he eventually turned away, returning not under the bed but merely to its foot, his muzzle on his paws, his ears rotating silently this way and that, as he kept perpetual watch through the long and dark night.

CHAPTER 18

Second Awakening

John opened his eyes to palm-shaded sunlight and the brown face of a young woman. Her long black hair hung down on either side of her face and brushed his chest. Large, liquid black eyes looked down at him anxiously from under arching eyebrows. He tried to sit up, but a soft cool hand at the end of a long, slim, bare arm put itself on his forehead while the face smiled at him. She turned her head and spoke to someone in a language John did not understand. A small boy, hardly the size of a cat's shadow, slipped out of the hut. Presently, an old woman came in with a cup and gave it to the girl. She put her arm under his head, lifted it gently, and gave him a brief sip from the cup. It was a broth, rich, sweet, spicy all at the same time, like no soup he had ever tasted before. His body suddenly hungered and thirsted for the nourishment, and he took a large gulp. A bit of the warm liquid went down his windpipe and he coughed, sitting up abruptly.

The girl scolded him in her soft, liquid language. Leaning over him, she pushed both his shoulders gently back against the pallet. He felt the fullness and warmth of her body close above him.

The girl spoke to him again in her language and, tilting her head sideways, smiled at him showing two rows of perfect white teeth. Even without understanding it, John found her speech soft and beautiful, like the speech of orchids. She was wearing a large, red, four-petaled flower in her hair and a sarong. John looked around him. He was in a grass-roofed hut, raised on stilts and open on one side, with steps leading down into a large open space around which clustered other similar huts. He was lying on a pile of animal skins. The child who had been sent to fetch the old woman squatted on the steps watching him like a big-eared, bony brown cat.

John could remember nothing after the darkness in the pool. Where were Morduc and Anga? He tried to sit up abruptly but suddenly felt dizzy and sank down again.

"Nitono," she said to him. "Nitona, ne nulla na."

"Where am I?" said John weakly, lying back and trying to focus his eyes more precisely.

"Che changa! Che changa!" she cried delightedly, clapping her hands. Picking up the cup of broth from where she had set it, she slipped her smooth brown arm under his head again while he took a third sip of the hot, sweet broth. It went down easily.

"Alga, Lileia," said the girl. The old woman who had brought the broth fetched a brown folded animal-skin from a corner of the hut and put it behind the knight. He leaned back against it and drank again from the cup of soup. The girl kneeled down next to him, sat back on her heels, and watched him drink, following his every action with a mingled look of concern and worship in her eyes. He realized how hungry he was, but at the same time he realized he was a little nauseated by the soup. He handed the cup to her. She frowned.

"Poco ne milaraba oyne pi enar?" she said.

"I can't understand a thing you say," he replied, smiling wanly. "The soup is very good, but I suppose I haven't eaten for some time, and I feel a bit sick. I'll have some more in a little while." Saying all this was a great effort for him, and he slid down a bit on the pile of skins. He looked out through the open front of the hut and saw a bustling village. Tall, muscular, dark bronze-brown men were walking to and fro, clad in sarongs like the women, but only from the waist down. All the men had lank black hair bound in a blue fillet, but none had beards or hair on their bodies. Some carried bows and arrows, others ropes and hatchets, and still others had large bags on their shoulders. Extensive preparations of some sort were under way.

Through the throngs came a tall young man with a band of red feathers around his forehead. He came up on to the steps outside the entrance of the hut, looked in at John, and said, "Pala mirago, Cailloma." The girl stood up and went over to speak to the young man. As they were exchanging words, and she was gesturing at the warrior, John finally had a chance to see what a stunning woman his nurse was. She looked to be about eighteen, of medium height, with long arms and legs, long black hair hanging straight down past her waist, and a fine, full figure. She walked with a swaying motion that enchanted him.

The young warrior who had come up on to the hut's steps stood in front of her like a statue, listening to her impassively. Presently he turned, descended the steps, and went back across the packed earth square to a large, peaked structure of wood on the other side, likewise on stilts, with steps leading up to a wide door.

The girl came back into the hut with her swaying walk and kneeled down again beside John. She picked up the cup of broth and offered it to him once more. As he drank, she devoured him with her eyes. He took the cup from his lips and said tentatively, "Cailloma?"

"Cailloma," she said excitedly. "Liga Cailloma. Ai, ai, ai." She clapped her hands together delightedly. "Cailloma, Cailloma," she repeated, pointing to herself.

"LiLigora?" she asked, putting her finger on John's chest. "LiLigora?" she repeated.

"My name is John," he said. She frowned, puzzled.

"John," he repeated. "John."

With difficulty she tried to repeat the unfamiliar sound, "Dzshan. Dzshan." And then she began to laugh, tilting her head back and holding out both her arms. "Dzshan, Dzshan, Dzshan," she said over and over and over and got up and did a little swaying dance in the hut with her arms still outstretched. Then she came back and kneeled down beside him. She put her chin in her hands and her elbows on her knees and, looking at John, said, "Migol, Dzshan, migol," smiling a most radiant smile from between her full red lips.

By then, John had finished the cup of broth and felt somewhat strengthened. He sat up slowly and put his feet on the floor. He saw his tunic, his shirt, his leggings, and his boots, clean and dry, piled in the corner. He looked down and found himself clad only in a wrapper such as the men in the square had been wearing. He suspected who had undressed him and put him to bed. He stood up and pointed toward his clothes.

"I want to get dressed," he said. He went over to his clothes and brought them back to the bed and made motions of dressing. The old woman spoke to the younger, and after letting down a rolled reed curtain on the open side of the hut, they left him alone. Through the curtain, John heard Cailloma speak to the big-eared child on the steps. He ran swiftly across the square to the large wooden hut and spoke to one of the men standing outside the double doors.

John quickly shed the sarong in which he had been wrapped and put on his customary clothes. When he was finished, he felt somewhat better, but still only half of who he was without his mail shirt and his red-steel sword. Still, even without them, he looked formidable, massive, muscular, and immensely strong, with arms and wrists twice as thick as any other's and legs to match. With his pale skin, his red-gold hair, and the lengthening bush of red-gold beard spreading over his jaw and chin and shining in the sun, he looked like an uncanny and powerful visitor from another world amid the willowy, nearly naked, dark-bronze people of that village.

He pulled on the cord that had let down the reed curtain, and the curtain lifted. He stepped outside, onto the top step of the hut. All the people in the square turned to look at him. Spontaneously there arose a shout from the warriors around the square. In the doorway of the large wooden hut across the open space appeared simultaneously a great fat bull of a man with a tall red-feathered headdress. As he began to start down the steps, two warriors, one on each side, supported his thick arms and helped him to balance himself. He did not look where he was going. His attendants guided him. As he descended the steps, two other men followed behind him with a huge, squat chair. He walked several steps forward and stood waiting. The men ran up and placed the chair directly behind him. Slowly, his two attendants and the two chair bearers guided and lowered him, without his looking, down on to the large, armless carved chair. It creaked as he settled. Two guards, each holding a tall, vertical ceremonial axe, stood on either side of the seated man.

Now John saw a tall, thin old man come out of the building behind the seated man. His grayed-white hair stood straight up on his head. His white hair was streaked with the colors of the rainbow: red, yellow, green, blue, violet. He was dressed in a long, loose, rough, sleeveless white robe, belted with a rainbow-colored cord. Into the rainbow-braided belt was thrust a wooden flute. The child whom John had seen perched on the steps of his hut was beside the gaunt old man and helped him to descend the steps and come to stand just to the left behind the seated immensely fat man.

The people in the village square between John and the seated man opened a passageway. As they yelled and cheered and gesticulated, John began to walk between them toward the seated large man. The girl, Cailloma, followed John. The sun was hot, and John was glad to feel it on his face and arms and hands once again. He crossed the large space of the square, and when he was opposite the seated figure, he kneeled before him on one knee, at which the seated man gave a very deep grunt of satisfaction while the crowd in the square began yelling and cheering even louder. The seated man raised his huge ham of a hand, and instantly the entire square was silent.

"Pilla legolullan, sellu polastafan imellalu," said the man and motioned John to rise. At the same time, two men rushed forward with a low stool and placed it immediately to the right of the seated man and gestured for John to sit on it. He did so, and then the huge man spoke again to John. When he had finished, the thin old man in the white robe leaned forward ever so slightly and spoke to John in heavily accented words.

"Chief Guada welcome you. I am called Palla Nad."

Quite relieved to find someone with whom he could communicate in more than gestures, John replied, "Thank him for his welcome and hospitality. My name is John Houporos, known as Red John. Will you ask the chief if another man, smaller than I, dressed in green, and a dog, have been found after the great storm? They were my comrades."

The tall old man with the piercing gaze laughed aloud and said, "Good joke. Comrades! Ha! You no come with comrades. None like you found. You on riverbank after flood. You One."

Just at that moment, from the depths of the forest surrounding the large village, there arose a scream which was taken up by more and more voices in the forest until the entire village was surrounded by a wall of noise. The chief stood up from his chair. The warriors who had been watching the conversation began running off to the edges of the village, and the young man with the red band around his head with whom Cailloma had spoken earlier began calling out in a loud voice, giving orders to the other warriors.

Just as the screaming grew louder, missiles began to shower down on the square, a few rocks, but most were clay spheres which sent up a puff of dirty brown smoke when they hit the ground and gave off a powerful fecal stench. The chief, surrounded by a group of young warriors and preceded by the axe bearers, was lumbering across the square. Two of his men had run into the large peaked house behind them and now returned with a shield and two spears. The chief's attendants thrust the shield on to his left arm and put one of the spears into his left hand. The other they put into his right hand, with which he brandished it menacingly.

Slowly placing one giant leg before the other, the chief moved toward the fighting. Palla Nad grasped John by the elbow and said to him: "You One. We stay by Chief."

Along with the rest of the women, as well as the children, Cailloma retreated into the large, long wooden hut from which the chief had come. They closed the two thick wooden doors of the long house behind them. John heard a bar dropped into place within.

John stayed close beside Palla Nad. As they approached the edge of the village, they saw a line of men fighting not other men, but monkeys almost as large as men, with red eyes and bared yellow fangs. Some carried clubs, and all continued to make a horrible screaming din as they attacked the village. The beastly shapes would let fly a rock and then dash forward with a club to try to smash the head of the warrior who had been hit, and then retreat just as quickly. There seemed to be endless hordes of the monkey enemy, seething and swarming on every side, like the gigantic coils of a hairy snake slowly contracting itself tighter and tighter around the village.

Now and then a warrior fell to the rain of rocks and clay balls filled with the nauseating brown smoke. Palla Nad was thrusting in beside the chief, trying to reach the twisting, writhing bodies of the monkeys with a spear. Occasionally a villager's spear would slide home and a still-higher pitched scream would rise above the continual howling of the attackers. The fallen monkey would immediately be dragged to the rear of the monkey line while another, with red eyes fanatically gleaming and short yellow fangs showing, would take his place. The sector where Palla Nad had placed John slowly began to be forced back into the village. A pocket formed in the line of warriors bulging inward, filled completely with howling, screaming monkeys whirling their thorn-studded clubs about their heads.

John was standing just behind the chief when a warrior several paces from him went down, and the first monkey to break the line burst through, dropped on all fours, and turned his head this way and that, looking for a target. John grabbed the axe from the nearest bearer and leaped toward the monkey. With one whizzing stroke, he severed the monkey's head from its shoulders so that it rolled like a bloody, hairy ball across the packed dirt. He turned to face the others coming through the breach in the line. His axe flashing this way and that, John cut off head after head as the monkey horde tried to pour through the gap and enlarge it. Bit by bit, the young warriors around the chief redoubled their efforts and, with John's help, drove back the flood of howling monkeys that faced them.

One slipped past and was about to club John from behind, but old Nad speared him in the throat and he fell backward in the dust.

"I am in your debt," called John. "You have saved my life."

Even in the midst of battle, the old man could not keep himself from laughing. "Good joke. I write in story," he called back. John was very puzzled by this reply but had no time to either think further about it or seek clarification.

The threatening gap in the line was finally closed, but the fighting continued fiercely. John found himself fighting beside the young man with the red-feathered headband. The young man thrust swiftly with his spear, warding off club blows with his shield. Just as he was delivering a thrust to one of the monkeys in the front row, another dropped down on all fours, scrambled under his guard, and tripped him. As the young man went down on his back, two other monkeys rushed forward with clubs aimed at his head. Instantly John kicked one in the side of the head, breaking his skull in, and cut off the club hand of the other with a quick stroke of the axe. The young warrior scrambled back to his feet, giving John a grudging but quick look of gratitude. Side by side, the two continued to fight, preventing any new gap from opening. As John faced the howling waves of animals, he saw that one of the beasts several ranks behind the front line was larger than the others and wore a hide cap on his head decorated with teeth. John looked closer and saw that there were human teeth intermingled with those of other species on the cap. John called out to the young man with the red band and motioned with his head toward the large monkey and signaled with his eyebrows. The young man seemed puzzled, but John, without stopping his whirling cutting, pushed forward into the band of monkeys, making for the larger one. The young man with the red headband now saw what John was trying to do and gave a great yell, at which the remaining warriors fought even harder, pushing out following John into the seething mass of monkeys.

As they pushed the monkeys back, with John and the red-banded warrior in front, the large monkey became crazed with excitement, swinging his club wildly over his head and jumping up and down and gnashing his teeth. Every time John's axe swung, another little-eared monkey head flew off a body. Slowly the men pushed the line of monkeys back. Then with a great yell, John jumped over the backs of three lines of monkeys until, all alone, swimming in a writhing sea of monkeys, he came face-to-face with the larger one in the cap. He had a broad, flat black nose, with brilliant red patches underneath his eyes. He was whirling his club above his head, and just as he brought it close to John's head, John gave a tremendous cut with his axe and decapitated the beast with a single stroke.

The cries of attack suddenly changed into cries of fear and despair as the monkeys saw their leader killed. The nearest ones backed away from John as he continued to cut with his flashing bronze axe, turning this way and that. Even though a few club blows did fall on his back, they glanced off him and he was not seriously hurt. Just at that moment, with a cry of triumph the village men surged their line out to where John was. Back through the trees, the monkey soldiers were beginning to turn away from the battle and run, leaving their dead and wounded behind them.

The high keening which had begun when John had killed the large monkey spread through the forest around the clearing in both directions. On all sides, the monkeys began withdrawing, their voices growing fainter and fainter as they ran through the forest pursued by the human warriors. The pursuing village warriors returned, and they all stopped to breathe and to take account of their wounded. John suddenly saw that the chief was lying on the ground. Palla Nad was kneeling by his side.

"Chief say he not feel well," said Palla Nad. "He say tell red-hair man, he save us today." And then Palla Nad added on his own, "I think Chief be well." Eight of the chief's attendants ran up with a litter and, by rolling him, like a fallen statue, managed to get him on to it. Straining, they lifted it and carried him back to the large wooden hut at the far end of the village open space. The women of the tribe spilled out of the long house to take care of their wounded or dead.

The young man in the red headband came up to John where he was standing, exhausted, leaning on the handle of the axe he had borrowed and took him by both shoulders and held him at arm's length. Smiling broadly he said, "Dzshan? Dzshan? Dzshan gella pelanak. Planin geddafan."

John smiled back, and as he returned the nicked and bloody axe to him, said, "What is he saying?"

Old Nad stepped up, smiling too. "He say he be your brother forever. He very good man, Kurokum. Good fighter. War chief. You save him. He now your brother." John smiled again, clasping the man's arm in his, glad to have such an important and valiant friend in the village.

"Now time to bury dead. Now time to wash. Now time for victory feast. You kill monkey leader. Dzshan Red Fighter. They not come back again for many year. You Great Man-God with us, Red Dzshan. Great Man-God."

As they were standing there, still catching their breaths, Cailloma came running up the square with an anxious look on her face. When she got to John and saw a small scratch on his face, she spoke to him and put her hand on him to wipe away the blood.

"Tell her, Nad, that I am not hurt," said John laughingly, seeing her concern, but when he turned to speak to Nad, he saw on the face of Kurokum, the man who had just sworn himself his brother, a look of jealous shock and anger. The look was gone in a second, however, and Kurokum seemed the same warrior with whom John had fought shoulder to shoulder just a moment ago. Cailloma led John back to the hut where he had awakened, helped him up the steps, made him recline on the animal skins, and helped him drink some more of the broth. She showered so many solicitations and attentions on him that he began to feel uncomfortable. After a bit, he pointed toward the large wooden hut and said, "How is the chief? How is Guada?"

Immediately she got up, took him by the hand, and led him in that direction across the square. As he walked across, all the warriors continued to smile at him and give him greeting. As they came to the foot of the steps, two of the chief's guards, with their large hatchetlike weapons, stepped together and barred the way. She spoke to them angrily, at which they separated, and John and Cailloma entered the large building.

Inside the air was heavy with incense, and in spite of the several windows, the building was dark, cavernous, and gloomy. They advanced up a long room along the sides of which sat many old men cross-legged on mats conversing in low tones with one another. At the far end of the room, the chief was lying on a large raised bed, joking in a deep, rumbling, gurgling laugh with the people around him. Palla Nad, assisted by a man in a large feathered mask, was lowering a steaming pad of cloth over the chief's right eye. Seeing John and Cailloma approaching, Palla Nad spoke a low word in the chief's ear. With the cloth still over his eye, the chief broke off his conversation with those around him and spoke rapidly to Palla Nad.

"Chief say you number one guest at sacrifice feast tonight."

"I am honored," replied John. "I came to inquire after the chief's health. I hope he sustained no serious injury." Palla Nad translated to the chief, who smiled broadly, and in so far as he could from his reclining position, he nodded his head as he spoke in reply.

"Chief say only soft dark places. No cut. No break." As Palla Nad said this, the figure in the feathered mask lifted the cloth from off the chief's cheek and John saw that Guada had one of the largest black eyes he had ever seen. The chief smiled broadly and pointed to the bruise. "Tiga ral pleroma?" he said and laughed deeply.

CHAPTER 19

The Victory Feast

During the remainder of the afternoon, John rested in the hut in which he had awakened. Cailloma bustled about, singing snatches of song to herself. The boy who had been on the steps and who had then assisted Palla Nad sat at John's feet, fanning him. The entire village was busy preparing for the feast. A great long pit had been dug in front of the long house, and a fire had been started. John could hear the sounds of musicians trying out their instruments, the rattle of gourds filled with pebbles, tentative flute runs, the knocking of sticks on log drums, and a wail of three-stringed bowed instruments, sounding like large gnats whining in the dusk. Just as the setting sun touched the trees, a regular drumbeat began, and the square started to fill with people. A large oblong stone had been brought in on log rollers to a position in front of the chief's long house. Between the block of stone and the steps of the long house, a large square canopy of leaves had been erected on poles. Beneath this, John was led and this time was seated slightly ahead of the chief and Palla Nad. On one side of the village open space, by the big log drums, the other musicians had assembled; on the other, immense amounts of food had been laid out on large leaves. Joints of meat were already roasting over the fire pit. The rest of the open space was packed with people except for a circle just before the large stone. Suddenly the drumming stopped and there was silence. Into the circle suddenly burst seven dancers. Three had on monkey masks with fresh bloody monkey skins dangling down their backs, while three others were dressed as warriors. The seventh dancer had white paint on his body, wore a reddish brown wig, and carried a reddened wooden axe. Palla Nad leaned over and said to John, "They dance story of victory. You see self."

The drums began a new rapid beat accompanied by the rest of the musicians. The dancers began to dance. John did not understand the beginning where two other dancers brought in a large round tray with a yellow doll on it. They circled the square three times and then set it down in front of the stone block.

But after that, the dance was clearer. He watched in fascination as the dancers mimed the story of the recent attack and victory. He saw himself in the village asleep as the dancer playing him put both hands under his tilted head while the other three circled around him. He saw the monkeys sneaking stealthily through the forest until they sprang screaming upon the villagers. The dancer playing him jumped up, whirling his axe and, in a spinning, flashing dance, slew all the attacking monkeys.

John was ready to applaud, but the dance was not finished. Into the circle now came Cailloma. She was dressed in a purple-beaded sarong with a crescent crown of purple feathers reaching from ear to ear over her head. The music continued at a frenzied pace as she began to dance. She was illuminated only by torches and the coals in the pit before her. John was fascinated by the sinuous swaying of her body. Her arms and neck and feet were bare, and she had gold bracelets on her wrists and ankles which jangled as she swirled and stomped. She picked up a knife from the stone block and continued to spin around. Suddenly from the back of the crowd came four men dragging a struggling, still-live monkey. The beast was quickly stretched on the stone, Cailloma deftly slit its throat, and just as she did so, a great roar of triumph arose from the packed square. John started and nearly rose from his seat as he saw Cailloma put down the knife, dip her hands in the blood of the monkey, and smear it over her arms and chest and legs.

Then even more surprisingly to John, the figure who had been dancing John's role in the story of the fight reentered the circle. One by one, each of the three dancers playing warriors of the village mimed an attack against the figure representing John, and each time the white-faced dancer danced a victory over a warrior with whom he had previously fought side by side. As each of the warrior dancers was defeated, he left the circle until only the white-faced dancer and Cailloma were left.

Now they began a circling dance, first the dancer impersonating John pursuing Cailloma and then she him, back and forth, around and around, until finally John saw himself catch Cailloma, hold her tightly to himself around the waist as she leaned back, back, backward as the music increased in tempo and shrillness, until with a shout from the entire throng in the square, Cailloma sprang away from him and was dancing alone, whirling his axe in the air. The music immediately stopped, and both dancers sank exhausted to their knees before the stone wet with monkey blood. Palla Nad now stepped forward from under the canopy to the spot where both dancers were kneeling and lifted his voice in a short chant. After this, Cailloma and the other dancer stood up with an air of being well pleased with themselves, bowed to each other, and then separated. A low hum of excited chatter began among the people gathered in the square as they moved to seat themselves on the ground in long lines facing each other where the feast was set and began to fall to. Two of the villagers were carrying an enormous bowl from group to group and giving everyone a drink from it with a large ladle.

John did not especially feel like eating after the sacrifice he had witnessed, but all of his hosts had pleased and satisfied looks on their faces and spoke so cheerfully to him, that he felt he must keep up appearances. The big-eared boy, whose name Palla Nad said was Yanibo, brought him a broad leaf on which were several kinds of small cakes, some bits of roasted meat, and some roasted fruits. Palla Nad leaned over to him. "Chief very pleased with you. You eat little piece all. Each piece part of story of victory." John dutifully nibbled at a portion of each of the foods on his leaf under the approving eye of the chief and the benevolent smile of Palla Nad. By the time he had finished eating, the two villagers with the bowl had arrived at the canopy. Each person under the canopy, including John, dutifully took a drink from the ladle. It was a strong, fiery drink that raced like burning lizards down John's throat. When John and all the others were finally finished, Palla Nad spoke.

"Now, Red Dzshan, you, our people, one people. You eat monkey people. We eat monkey people. You, us, now same people."

John gagged slightly but kept his composure. "You mean I have just eaten some of the roasted flesh of that monkey Cailloma sacrificed?" John said faintly to Palla Nad.

"Yes, yes," Palla Nad answered with a broad grin. "We beat 'em, we eat 'em. Good, eh?"

"I'm not sure," said John as he suddenly broke out in a cold sweat. "Perhaps monkey meat doesn't really agree with me."

"What else you want?" said Palla Nad, belching contentedly. "Yanibo get for you," he said, signaling for the child to approach him.

"No. Nothing just now. Thank you," said John and waved the boy away, who went back to squatting on his heels at the edge of the canopy, happy to be John's servant. The feast went on animatedly around John. The villagers were eating, talking, and shouting to one another with a gaiety which John began to feel somehow was in excess of the victory over the monkeys. The celebration had an undefined anticipatory quality to it, which suddenly made John suspicious.

He turned to Palla Nad and said, "I wonder if you could explain the beginning and end of the dance to me. I'm not sure I understood it all." On hearing this, Palla Nad went off into another of his spasms of laughter and chattered excitedly to the man in the feathered mask and to the chief, who shook with a low, deep, mountainous laughter and looked at John in rumbling knowing amusement.

Still laughing, Palla Nad turned back to John. "We know all story. We know you make fun. We know you test us. You know where you come from. You know where you go. All we know is our religion say one day Gold God come on silver river to save us from enemies. He fight for us. He beat strongest enemies. He marry princess. They have many children. They sail away in silver boat and live forever with stars. Gold God very funny. Not understand dance! Ha! That part not in story how Gold God make good jokes. Ha, ha. I add to story. Children hear many year after now."

"And you think," said John, "that I am the Gold God?"

"Sure, sure," said Palla Nad. "I see it all in dream. We find you at edge of river very deep asleep, all tired out from long journey from the stars. Princess Cailloma know as soon as she see you. She say you Expected One. She say you defeat all other warriors to win her. She say she be chief's daughter told of in old legend. You Cailloma have many warrior sons and tribe never be defeated in war again. All sons Cailloma Dzshan fight like Dzshan. Then you take Cailloma to live by silver river in sky. Stay young forever. Watch over village forever. This true from beginning in old story. Now it come to pass. Have more monkey, Red Dzshan."

John felt even sicker than before. He had no intention of remaining to fulfill the myth of the tribe, in spite of Cailloma's beauty, sensuality, and willingness, offerings which he found difficult to ignore in spite of his devotion to the princess. But what could he do? He could not afford to offend his hosts, and furthermore, he needed provisions and a guide to continue his journey. He surmised that the myth required him to fight his brother warriors, in reality or symbolically, he didn't know which, in order to win Cailloma and then marry her. But how was he to get away before that happened?

He could hardly sneak out in the night. He might run into the monkey people, and they would surely kill him if they found him. And if they didn't, the people of Cailloma's village would track him and bring him back, saying something like 'Old story not tell how Gold God like play hide, seek. We add to story.'

The feast was breaking up, the torches were being extinguished, and the men and women and children were going to their huts. The clouds seemed to have come down close to the jungle, making the night close and humid. The chief stood up, turned, and, with the help of his attendants, heavily reascended the steps of the long house. Cailloma, Yanibo, and Palla Nad escorted John back to the hut he had awakened in just that morning. He ascended the steps, entered, and let down the rolled curtain behind him. Outside of the hut, Cailloma, Palla Nad, and Yanibo sang a soft song to him. He lay down alone on the pile of skins to try to think of a way out of his difficulties. The village was gradually becoming quiet. He smelled a faint, rank odor, but couldn't quite identify it. He turned on his side to try to get comfortable, but he could not find a position that would allow him to rest. Back and forth, over and over he turned in the humid heat of the night, like a sausage being roasted on a spit, restless and twisting in the heat of his troubled thoughts.

Suddenly he heard a slight movement at the curtain. A figure slipped into the hut. Instantly, John was fully awake and sprang to a crouch, ready to fight, weaponless though he was.

"Cailloma," the figure said softly. "Cailloma, belada. Cailloma." The figure slid over to him. He saw by the faint light that it was Cailloma. He relaxed and sat down again on the pile of skins. She kneeled beside him and pushed him gently down until he was lying on his back, and then silently she straddled him. He could feel the full, strong, young body straining against his. She lowered her head and kissed him passionately, full on the mouth. John smelled on her breath the heavy, musky odor of the drink he had drunk after supper. She waited a moment, but when John did not respond, she laughed a delighted whispered laugh in his ear, got off his bed, and as quickly as she had slipped into the hut, left, leaving the faint aroma of monkey blood on the air. John, his pulses racing wildly, stood up, and through the slatted curtain followed with his eye her fleeting shadow as it silently flew across the square and disappeared within the chief's hut. Then he lay down again on his bed, breathing rapidly, wondering what the morning would bring. He still felt Cailloma's kiss on his lips, rich, soft, and deep. He still smelled the smell of monkey blood. Then it came to him. The pile of skins he was lying on were monkey skins. He moved off the pile and slept the rest of the night on the plank floor with his arm for a pillow. He looked through the slats in the reed curtain up into the night sky, remembering the talk he and Morduc had had in Hubert the Gardener's barn. Though he could not see the stars in the clouded night, he knew they were still there, silently watching, guiding, shining.

Chapter 20

Not the One

The next day dawned cool and fair, with a brilliant blue sky showing above the tall green jungle trees. John awoke feeling surprisingly rested after the anxieties of the night. He sprang up from the floor, refreshed in mind but hungry. As soon as he pulled up the rattan curtain, the old woman appeared from the hut next to his and, seeing him, ducked inside her hut again and returned immediately with a leaf on which were spread several ripe fruits. John thanked her smilingly and, standing there looking at the sun, vigorous and ready, ate them all. The young warriors were assembling from the various parts of the village dressed in their best finery. He guessed that in several hours, whatever the charade was in which he was supposed to participate would end with his marriage to Cailloma.

The warriors came to the chief's building in their finest feathers, bringing with them spears and shields and bows and arrows and fighting staves. Everyone who assembled at the chief's *tantum*, his long house, was in excellent spirits, and when John, having finished his breakfast, strode across the square, the sun shining in his hair, lighting up the gold among the red brown and setting his rapidly growing beard alight too, a spontaneous cheering arose from all the warriors in the village. The chief descended from his house slowly and massively, followed by his throne bearers carrying his carved chair. As on the day before, they set it before the steps, and the chief, guided by his attendants, slowly sat down. One of the attendants stepped forward and began to make a long speech. Palla Nad, grinning like a proud father, motioned to John to stand next to him, just behind and to the left of the chief. Having done so, John watched each of the tribe's warriors present himself to the chief and each put a bead of a different design in a small jar that one of Palla Nad's assistant priests was holding.

"They make choice. Number one bead, number one fight."

The priest swirled the jar around faster and faster until one of the beads leapt out of its mouth, and a huge roar went up from the crowd. The warrior to whom it belonged stepped forward and claimed it. The priest swirled the jar again and another came out. He did this seven times. Among those chosen was Kurokum. As he stepped into line, John caught his eye and signaled to him with his eyebrows, just as he had done in the fight the day before. Kurokum looked at him in puzzlement, then quickly looked away.

Toward noon, the contests began. The first contest was spear throwing. The man whose lot had flown out first stepped up to a line at one end of the open space and let fly his spear toward a large post which had been sunk in the ground at the other end. His spear hit the post and stuck in it for a moment and then fell out. John stepped up to the line, was given a spear, and made a mighty heave. His spear thumped solidly into the post and remained quivering there. The crowd cheered wildly.

In the next contest, with bow and arrow, the warrior shot at a bird that was thrown into the air. He brought it down with a single shot. John stepped up to the line and spoke to Palla Nad, saying he wanted two birds thrown into the air at the same time. When this became known, a murmur of expectation ran around the crowd. Both birds were thrown into the air at once and flew away in opposite directions. John shot first at the one on his left as it flapped above the square. Spinning to face in the opposite direction even before the first arrow had hit, he shot again at the swiftly diminishing shape of the second bird as it ascended high above the trees. When the second feathered body hit the ground soon after the first, the crowd went wild with cheering and shouting.

Cailloma sat by her father, her head held high, conscious of her destiny as the bride of a god and the mother of a race of invincible warriors. She was dressed in a brilliant red sarong, with ropes of blue beads around her neck and had never looked more vibrant and alluring. As with the spear throwing and archery contests, the next two events, stone throwing and running, were also won by John. Every time John won a contest, Cailloma would bow to him in grave admiration. The fifth event saw the beginning of the true fighting, the staff fighting, the wrestling-boxing, and the sword and knife fighting. A huge young man named Puolo, two heads taller than John, stepped up with a staff. They took their places in a circle marked out in the dirt in white chalk. Puolo stepped in fast, delivering a shower of blows with both ends of his staff, grinning broadly, knowing he was fighting the god for glory, thinking that even though he knew he would be beaten, still he might fare well enough against John to win great renown for himself and his children in the future. John parried quickly and skillfully, so fast that the ends of his staff were a blur. As he was walking backward around the circle, he leapt suddenly to the side, giving Puolo such a sound crack in the ribs that the larger man gasped at the pain and the crowd roared its approval. Faster and faster John moved the staff, whirling around

Puolo, until suddenly, with a deft upward movement, he lifted the larger man's staff out of his hands and sent it sailing over his head behind him.

A cry went up from all the watching men and women and children. "Yelado verada. Yelado verada!" they shouted.

As Puolo and John approached the chief, Palla Nad said, "They are saying 'He wins again. He wins again.' This is a very great day for us. We will never be beaten by our enemies again."

In wrestling, which had always been John's special delight and skill, the opponent hardly had a chance and was on his back in the dust in less than thirty seconds. Then came the last of the sports, close-in knife fighting. John and Kurokum finally came face to face, but Kurokum alone of the contestants stepped up unsmiling and grim. Palla Nad opened a long black case lined in red velvet. Inside were two ceremonial blades, each eight inches long, wavy, gleaming bronze set in a horn handle. Kurokum selected one. John took the other. They took their positions opposite one another, crouched, intent, watching the other and circling cautiously. Though everyone knew there would be no killing here, the god might nevertheless draw blood from Kurokum, and so the warrior fought cautiously, for a wound of any sort was always a danger, and besides, who knew what a god would do? Furthermore, if the god was to have Cailloma, whom he, as war chief, had hoped to marry himself, the god should be made to win her honestly.

Slowly they circled. Kurokum leapt and slashed, but John jumped lightly out of the way, at the same time returning a thrust, but not before Kurokum could parry it expertly. They continued to circle, feinting, thrusting, parrying, and recovering. John maneuvered carefully and, seeing an opening as Kurokum thrust forward, pinioned Kurokum's knife hand under his own arm. Locked together for a brief instant, John whispered in the other man's ear, harshly and insistently,

"Kurokum yelado, Kurokum yelado."

No one but Kurokum heard, and when they broke, and John stepped back, the warrior looked at him with dawning half understanding. As they circled again looking for an opening, John imperceptibly shifted and slightly opened his guard, looking at the other man intently and lifting his eyebrows. Kurokum saw but did not yet completely know what to make of it. As Kurokum leapt forward, John deliberately slipped beneath the thrust and appeared to lose his footing. Instantly, John was on his back and Kurokum's knife was at his throat. The warrior looked down at the man prone beneath him and held out his hand for John's knife. John gave it to him.

The crowd, after a shocked drawing of breath, stood in absolute silence. Kurokum looked into John's eyes and then, throwing his head back and his arms wide, one of the wavy blades in each hand, yelled to the sky,

"Na Kisabo. Na Kisabo."

After another interval of shocked silence, a wailing began to rise from the direction of the chief's throne. Cailloma was standing rigid, her head thrown back, screaming. When she had finished, she turned her head downward toward John on his back on the ground. In a tone of absolute grief, she screamed again, repeating Kurokum's words, "Na Kisabo, na Kisabo," and ran weeping to the far end of the village and out of sight into a hut. At that, the entire crowd took up the words,

"Na Kisabo. Na Kisabo."

Kurokum, now holding both blades in his left hand, held out his right to John. John reached up and took it, and Kurokum pulled him upright. As they walked over to the chief, Kurokum put his hand on John's neck, and when they got to where the chief was sitting, pushed him down on his knees in front of the throne. The chief slowly lifted his great bulk from the carved dark-wooden chair and said viciously to Kurokum the one word, "Nakoda."

And then, with an air of resignation, he added, "Kurokum yelada Cailloma." He raised his thick arm and then let it fall by his side. His two chair attendants quickly lifted the throne and scurried with it up the steps into the long house. The chief turned and, aided by his two walking attendants, slowly climbed the stairs without a further word.

Palla Nad, with an incredibly sad look on his face, came up to the two. "Na Kisabo. Na Kisabo," he said, shaking his head. "He not the one. He not the one." He came over to John, put his hand on his shoulder as he knelt in the dust, and tenderly touched the hair of his head.

"Yala Kisabolota. You not one, Red John. You no god. You fight good good, many many. But no god." He began to weep, shaking his head sadly from side to side, looking as if he had aged twenty years in two minutes. He turned and slowly began to mount the steps of the chief's residence. Kurokum spoke to him sharply. Without stopping, he nodded his head up and down, and still weeping spoke with his back to John.

"Yes, I go join ancestors. I die too." John jumped a little at that and tried to stand up, but Kurokum kept a firm grasp on his neck keeping him on his knees. Palla Nad went on, "My life finished. I die for my mistake. I told chief you true one. One old story tell come. No matter. You gone. My life gone too. You become three days like son. Now we both . . ."

Before he could finish, Kurokum spoke to him again, and Palla Nad stopped on the steps, straightened suddenly, and then turned and came back down briskly.

"If you do that, Kurokum, I go too. Red John, Kurokum say he give you boat, food, instead of kill you like Chief order. But you need guide. I know river. I dead anyway. I go with you. If we stay, we die. If we go, get caught, we die. Must hurry."

John looked at Kurokum, who moved his eyebrows up and down and then half smiled, thinly and quirkily at him. He spoke again to Palla Nad, who translated. "He say he know you are true one, but Cailloma not true one. He keep your memory until you come again. You marry his daughter daughter daughter. Make tribe strong forever. Make no sense to me. But he say."

Palla Nad turned and spoke softly and quickly to Yanibo, who had remained standing by them. Then he turned back to John and said, "Now we go with Kurokum."

CHAPTER 21

A Hair-Raising Escape

The villagers watching this scene from the doors of their huts next saw Kurokum tie a thong first about John's neck and then about Palla Nad's and then lead them both, bent over, hands tied behind them, off into the bush. As they passed each hut, the village inhabitants made a guttural, vomiting noise in their throats. Kurokum made a good show of it, brandishing both daggers in his right hand and holding the prisoners' rope in his left, dragging them along. Meanwhile, Yanibo slipped off among the village huts unnoticed.

They walked quite a long way from the village until they were well screened. Palla Nad said to John, "Now we stop. Kneel down." John did as he was told, but when Kurokum seized his hair and bent his head back and brought one of the knives close, he suddenly wondered whether this was not all a trick to make his execution easy, and he began to struggle and thrash.

Palla Nad hissed at him. "No, John. All good. Still, still." John looked at the old man and saw such a look of love and concern on his old, wrinkled, tattooed face that he stopped doubting. He waited patiently as Kurokum came closer to his face with the knife. Then he moved it past his eyes and quickly cut off as much of his great bush of red-gold hair as he could. He held it up grinning, and then deftly slit the neck cord as well as the one binding John's hands.

John jumped up and began rubbing his wrists while Kurokum went over to Palla Nad and gathered as much of the tall, frizzy, rainbow-streaked gray hair on his head as he possibly could and sliced that off too.

Kurokum held up a knife and a handful of hair in each hand and grinned broadly.

"Now we go river. Fast, fast, no noise, no noise." Palla Nad quickly led the way through the jungle in a wide circle away from the village. John followed Palla Nad silently. Presently they saw the silver shimmering of the river through the trees, and crept ahead cautiously as they approached the bank. They waited hidden in a tangle of roots at the water's edge for what seemed hours as the afternoon wore on and night descended. At one point, they heard a huge shout go up from the village.

"Kurokum say John dead. Kurokum say Palla Nad dead. Now he marry Cailloma. He be chief. Why my dream not tell truth, John? Why you not god? Why you not be chief?"

John said nothing, knowing that the two questions did not have one answer as Palla Nad assumed. Presently, just before the moon rose, there came sliding noiselessly down the river a log canoe which seemed to be adrift and unoccupied. It came closer and closer to the bank, rocking slightly on the water. Palla Nad made a sound like a frog in his throat and chest. A small round head with big ears popped up just above the gunwale, put a hand over the edge, and began paddling the log canoe toward shore.

As it bumped the shore, Palla Nad grabbed it and held it. John pulled himself into it and lay down on several bags in the bottom. Palla Nad continued to hold it while he conducted a heated discussion in whispers with the boy. Finally, Palla Nad got in and whispered to John, "Yanibo say he come with us. He say if he go back village, he tell what happened. They come after us. He say I must throw him in river for water dragons if we not let him come. Throw him in, Dzshan. I not let him make you dead."

John could barely see the child's shape in the darkness. Finally John said to Palla Nad, "Let him come. If he must, he must." At which, even without understanding what John had said, but guessing what it meant, the boy broke into a broad white smile, pushed off from the bank, and began paddling with both hands, sliding the canoe swiftly out into the center of the river.

Palla Nad put a hand on John's shoulder and said into his ear, "You good god, Dzshan. Too hard for me to kill own grandson.

CHAPTER 22

The Snake from the Sky

When Morduc awoke the next morning, the day was already full light. He sat up with a start in the carved walnut bed. Anga got up from the foot of the bed, yawned capaciously, stretched his front legs and then his back, and then came around to the side of the bed with his tail wagging—eager, alert, and, as always, amused.

"It's late, Anga," said Morduc as he jumped out of bed and went to the window. The estate's gardens, orchards, and fields stretched out to the west before him under the morning sun. Beneath him, within the shadow of the house, he saw Martha taking a basket full of raspberries and yellow and green squash from a boy who had just come in from the gardens. Another maid was on her way into the house from the chicken roosts, likewise with a basket in which Morduc saw piled white and brown eggs.

"I have slept much later than usual, Anga," said Morduc as he tossed off his nightshirt and began to dress quickly in the clothes he had been given the day before. Just as he had finished, a light knock came at the door. "Who is it?" called Morduc.

A soft voice answered in low tones, "Marianna."

He opened the door to find her looking even lovelier than she had the day before. She was wearing a powder-blue silk dress that fitted her slim figure exquisitely. She had tied back her long chestnut hair with a matching blue ribbon. Morduc's heart skipped a beat.

"Are you all right?" she asked, seeing him tremble and sway a bit. "Did anything happen last night?"

"Yes. No," he said. "Nothing happened. I'm fine. Was there any trouble last night?"

"Not so far as Father could tell. You looked very strange there for a moment."

"Oh, nothing. Just your beauty. Nothing serious," he said, smiling gravely.

"Probably just hunger," she said teasingly but pleased he had noticed.

"Hunger and thirst, both," he replied.

"Would you like some breakfast then, or something else?" she asked teasingly, linking her arm in his as they went down the long hallway.

"For the moment, breakfast will do."

"It had better, for we know not how long the drought and famine may last," said Marianna, pausing and smiling at him with shining eyes, "but we both hope for a bountiful harvest."

Morduc swayed again.

As they came to the large stair, she dropped her voice, saying, "I'll take Anga down the back way. You go on into the dining room, and I'll be there in a moment." Giving him a quick kiss on his lips, she disappeared into an almost invisible door in the wall. Morduc continued on down the hall, descended the curved stairway, and entered the dining room. Lord Ballan was standing with his back to the door, his hands clasped behind him, looking out the eastern windows.

"Good morning, sir," said Morduc quietly. Ballan turned tiredly, showing a worried face. "Good morning, Morduc. I trust you slept well, and without interruption."

"Yes, I did, and I feel much refreshed. Marianna said . . ." but before he could finish, Ballan stopped him with an abrupt motion of his hand and a brief scowling look. "Let us not discuss that here," he said in a low but intense voice.

"Very well," said Morduc. Lady Ballan entered the room from the hall, supporting herself on her two ivory-headed ebony canes. Almost at the same time, Marianna appeared through another one of those almost-invisible doors in the wall, startling her mother and drawing a look askance at her. They sat down to fresh red raspberries in cream followed by eggs and ham and toast. For thirst, there was milk. The morning light streamed into the dining room and almost banished the weight on Morduc's heart. Yet over their conversation about the weather, about the skies they had looked at last night, and about flowers and herbs with Lady Ballan, and about painting, books, and music with Ravenstock, hung the dark, inescapable knowledge for Morduc that he must leave his beloved Marianna and this lovely house, at a time when, in some unclear way, the Master of Darkness, either on account of him, or for other reasons, was threatening Lord Ballan and his family. In order to save them, he must do what he wished least to do: he must part from them, to face the uncertainty of the certain risks which lay ahead.

Breakfast over, Lord Ballan motioned Morduc to follow him and led the way to the library, and then again into the vault behind the moving bookcase.

"You look tired, sir," said Morduc once they were inside the metal cylinder and the great iron door shut.

"I am indeed, but I am also convinced that without having myself kept watch last night, the forces of the Master would have achieved some advantage.

The house was secure, but I think he will try again this evening to gain a further foothold here. In any case, I shall sleep today and watch again tonight. Now, tell me, how long do you think it will be before you are ready to travel?"

"I would judge one, or at most, two more nights of sleep such as I had last night will restore me completely."

"Very well, then. Let us say that you will leave, not tomorrow, but the day after. As I said yesterday, I will provide you with a map of a route I know across the mountains, and although there is a rather large forest and a marsh between us and the foothills, you should not have any difficulty traversing both. I will provide you with a mount and another pack pony and supplies. Until then, I suggest that you discuss your plans with no one and rest as much as you can. Unless something suspicious happens, we will not confer again until the morning of your departure. Unfortunately, as of yet I have not been able to think of a suitable disguise or role for you to play which would enable you to get close to the Master of Darkness. However, I will continue to give thought to the possibilities. You are not quite large enough to recommend yourself to him as a member of his guards"—and here a distant look of pain passed over his face—"nor small enough," he continued, "to pass as a real child. Thus, we must look for something else, yet I have so little intelligence of his present activities that I do not know what needs he has that you might pretend to serve. Perhaps you yourself have some suggestions."

"At present, sir," replied Morduc, "I have none. But I too will continue to turn the problem over in my mind, and perhaps before tomorrow something will come to me."

"Very well, then. If you do think of something, speak to me this evening, at a time when we can come to the vault, or early tomorrow." With the conversation concluded, the two left the vault and returned to the library, where Morduc found Marianna waiting for him with a covered tin pail in her hands.

"May I show Morduc the grounds, Father?" asked Marianna.

"Yes, you may, but do not go too far afield," he said glancing at the pail. "You are aware of the reason." Marianna shuddered slightly as if a chill wind had blown at her back. Taking Morduc's hand, she led him through the long plant-lined passage from the library into the high entrance hall and out through the great main door on to the eastward-facing lawn across which Morduc had come the previous day.

Laughing, they ran around the corner of the house, glad to be together and, for the moment, almost carefree, two lithe figures running down the alleyways of the flower gardens to the west. Presently, they came to a small rotunda set on seven slim white pillars at the far end of the garden. Within it was a stone bench. They entered and sat down and looked back at the large, symmetrically elegant stone house at the other end of the garden.

They sat there for several minutes, hand in hand, saying nothing. Finally Marianna murmured, "When will you have to leave?" Morduc hesitated before answering. He looked around him. They seemed to be alone, yet he remembered what Lord Ballan had said about not discussing his plans outside the vault. He drew closer to her on the stone seat.

"Your father thinks it is dangerous to speak openly of any of these matters. He talks to me only in the vault in the library. Do we dare to speak here?"

"It seems safe enough," she said, "though I know my father's caution is never misplaced." Off in the distance, one of the gardeners moved among the flowers with a hoe. They looked around themselves. The rotunda sat on a small circular lawn, with a ring of flowers around it. The entire scene seemed completely innocent and peaceful. Several small birds flitted silently from branch to branch in the trees above. Putting his head close to that of Marianna, Morduc said in a low voice, "I plan to leave the day after tomorrow."

"So soon," she gasped. "There is so little time."

"But I will return for you," said Morduc. "I don't know *when* you can expect me, but you *can* expect me."

"Yes, I know that," she replied. "I have no doubt of your faith. But not being able to fix a time for your return makes your departure seem so . . . final." She cast her eyes down. "I know we are pledged forever . . ." Here she faltered a bit but then continued, "If there is any small fragment of forever as future for us."

"Yes, forever," said Morduc thoughtfully. "And the future will be soon and last long."

"It is my wish and my hope," said Marianna. "Until it comes, will you wear this for me?" she said, slipping off from her middle finger a gold signet ring with the recessed figure of a swan on it.

"Usually, among mortals," laughed Morduc, "I understand the man gives the woman a ring. I have nothing that I can give you in return, but I'll wear this ring for you if I can get it on. He tried it on each of his fingers, but the only one on which it would fit was his left little finger. He held it up for her to see. "How does it look?"

"Better than on me."

"And what does the swan stand for? Surely it's not just a cygnet ring?"

"You should receive *pun*ishment for a joke like that," she laughed as she jumped up and grabbed his hand and started to run. "Come, I'll show you." He allowed himself to be pulled out of the rotunda by the slim figure in blue. She led him out beyond the garden into the fields to a large silver lake in the midst of a high meadow. When they reached the edge, Marianna sat down, put the tin pail on the grass, and then drew Morduc down beside her. She whistled shrilly three times and was silent.

"Well?" said Morduc after a short time.

"Wait," she said. "Look across the lake."

Morduc looked and detected some movement, as if a patch of white caps were moving toward them across the blue water. As the white ruffles came toward the shore he saw they were a group of fifteen large white swans with an equal number of sooty-brown-feathered hatchlings following. As they approached the bank, Marianna opened the hinged half lid of the pail, reached in, and brought out a handful of corn kernels. She began throwing the kernels out into the water for the swans. A few they caught in the air, but for the rest they had to go end up and search with their beaks on the shallow bottom of the lake.

"This is my game of swans," she said.

"What sort of game is it?" asked Morduc.

"No, silly. 'Game' just means group. They are mine. I raised them myself. They are beautiful, strong, faithful, and fiercely courageous. They are my ideal, and that is why the crest on my ring is a swan. I seek to live their virtues every day. And the ring is to remind you why you should return to me, your own swan."

"I need no such reminder, but I am grateful for it nevertheless."

As they sat watching, the families of swans swam right up to the bank and climbed out on their short, strong black legs and came up to Marianna for more grain.

"This is William," said Marianna, "and here is Jane, and their chicks." They all came up to her, bobbing their necks and rubbing their bills on her cheek as she gave each one a few grains from the pail. One even stuck his head inside the pail and then could not get it out so that when he lifted his head, he looked like a swan with a knight's helmet on. "Greedy Gustav, into trouble again," she scolded as she removed the bucket carefully from the swan's head. Soon the noble birds were all around them, smothering them in white, stretching and fanning their wings in a whispered thunder. When the pail was empty, Marianna held out her hands and said laughingly to them, "No more. No more." The birds, knowing that signaled the end of her gifts, took again to the water and swam off from shore a small distance.

"Come," said Marianna, "I want to show you my private cove."

Again she took Morduc by one hand and the now-empty pail in the other and pulled him, running and laughing along the edge of the pond. The swans followed them, swimming silently in the still, clear water, their white rippled images reflected on the blue surface, gliding along with the silence of serene thought. Finally they reached a small dam. The birds turned back while Marianna led Morduc past the spillway and down along the course of the stream through thick grass. Presently they came to a hollow in the bank grown up with grass and wildflowers. Into this, Marianna led Morduc and pulled him down on to the hot, blossom-filled summer grass. From where they sat, they could see the brook purling on in front of them; across the brook was a cool grove of maple and birch. Above them, the sun shone straight down, concentrating all its heat in their small cup of earth. Grasshoppers jumped across them. Marianna lay back in the sweet-smelling wildflowers, and Morduc leaned over her and kissed her. The two lay there together in each other's arms.

"This is my secret place," said Marianna. "I played here as a child. I showed it to you because I want everything that is mine to be yours. Everything."

"I wish I could take you to my home country right now and share my own secret place with you. It is the interior of a giant tree. Several shoots from a single root had grown up and out, and as the trees grew, they thickened and touched and joined to form a hollow that lifted higher and higher from the ground. In it, two children could sit. We might both still be able to sit in there now. I never took anyone there, but I used to climb up and sway in the wind imagining myself a bird flying among the branches."

"Let's go there . . . when you return," she said and then fell thoughtfully silent. They both lay back on the grass and wildflowers, their hands touching, looking up at the bright blue sky through a leafy ring. A squat black crow, calling raucously, flapped across the patch of sky they could see from inside the hollow.

"Yes," said Morduc, "when I return."

"I think," said Marianna hesitantly, "I think I ought to go with you when you go."

"What!" said Morduc, sitting up abruptly. "That's absurd. I have no idea what kind of dangers I'll be in, and I have no intention of exposing you to them."

She then sat up too. "Well, I don't see that that matters. Two of us would be better than one. I can ride as well as any boy and shoot too. It's true that I don't know how to handle a sword, but I can wrestle and fight, and I can beat anyone my weight about half the time, and more if he isn't careful."

"Is that *so*," said Morduc, laughing, as he threw himself upon her. Even though Morduc thought he would have an easy time pinning her, she was strong and quick. She twisted in his grasp and had slipped behind him, searching for a hold almost before he knew what had happened. Laughing and rolling in the grass, Morduc finally had her on her back.

"You wouldn't have won," she said, "if I hadn't had this dress on. Now let me up."

"And I, for my part," said Morduc, "won't be inclined hereafter to underestimate your ability. You did, indeed, almost have me, and that is truly rare, as rare my dear girl, as you yourself are." He looked down into her large, dark eyes which looked up into his own with complete openness and confidence. Then she was looking past him quizzically.

"What is it?" Morduc asked.

"A strange long bird, diving."

"You are the strange bird," he said bringing his face closer to hers.

Suddenly, her eyes darkened; she opened her mouth to say something and instead screamed. Morduc jumped up and saw that a long black snake with a red pit under each eye had sunk its fangs into Marianna's ankle. He snatched up the grain pail and began to beat the snake on its head. The snake coiled and raised itself poised to strike again, this time at Morduc. Just as it launched itself, Morduc leapt to the side, and as the snake fell stretched out at full length on the ground from its strike, he crushed its head with the bottom rim of the pail.

Quickly he loosed the blue ribbon from Marianna's hair and bound it around her leg above the wound, inserting a stick to twist it tightly. Tossing the limp snake into the empty tin pail, he closed its hinged half cover and put the handle over his arm. Then he lifted Marianna and started toward the house at a run. Back up the path beside the brook, past the lake, back across the fields, into the garden he ran. As he carried her, she said nothing, but he felt her growing limp and a cold sweat had come out on her limbs.

"Are you there?" he said tensely as he ran on.

"It burns, it burns," she said. "I feel sleepy and cold."

Martha was outside the kitchen door. "What is it? What is it?" she cried as she saw Morduc speeding toward the house through the garden with Marianna's limp body in his arms.

"Snake bite," said Morduc.

"Take her up to her room," said Martha. "I'll call Lady Ballan." Dropping the pail by the back door, Morduc carried Marianna in through the kitchen door and up the narrow passageway stairs to the main hall, and then up the stairs to the second floor.

"Open her door," he called to one of the maids who was in the hall and had turned, startled, to see him running with Marianna in his arms, wisps of grass still clinging to her dress. The maid flung open the door to Marianna's room and Morduc placed her carefully on the bed. The wound had begun to swell with an angry red color while the rest of the foot had turned pale and blue. Before he could wonder what to do next, he heard Lady Ballan's sticks in the hall. She came through the door, followed by Martha, who was carrying a large black box.

Without turning as she bent over Marianna on the bed she abruptly asked Morduc, "What kind of snake was it?"

"It was completely black with two red pits under the eyes."

"It is not from this area" she replied. "Where is it?"

"I left it in the covered grain bucket by the back door."

"Martha. Run and bring me the snake. If I can tell exactly what sort it is, I won't have to guess which antidote to use." Martha left at a run, and Lady Ballan began to work over Marianna. Opening the large box, she first lit a small spirit lamp. She spread a rubber-backed protective cloth under Marianna's leg, and then taking a pair of small scissors from the box, she quickly cut away the stocking from around the wound. Then she took a small knife and, after passing the blade through the flame several times, made two small cross-shaped cuts in the skin where the fangs had gone in. Blood and pus drained out and down her ankle. She sprinkled an orange powder in the cuts, and after she had done that, she wrapped a new band around the girl's leg above the spot where Morduc had tied and tightened the blue ribbon. Then she untwisted the ribbon and took it off. Martha returned wringing her hands.

"Madam, the snake is gone. The bucket is still there, but there's nothing in it but some black blood and slime."

"Are you sure, Martha?" said Morduc, in amazement.

"Right, sure, indeed. You don't think I'd want it, do you?"

Lady Ballan looked piercingly at Martha for a moment and then said, "Very well, Martha. You are not to blame." Then turning to Morduc she said, "Now, tell me again, exactly what this snake looked like."

"It was about three feet long and completely black except for those two red pits, one under each eye, that looked as if they were on fire."

"Very well," she said. "I will do what I can for Marianna. I want you to go directly to Lord Ballan and tell him what has happened." She bent over the figure on the bed and lifted Marianna's eyelid gently. She felt her pulse and her forehead. Finally, she turned to her box and, selecting a vial from its inner recesses, unstoppered it and took from it a large purple lozenge. This she slipped under Marianna's tongue.

Reluctantly Morduc turned to leave the room. Marianna lay limply on the bed, her head to one side, her eyes closed, her breathing shallow and rapid.

"I will be back after I have spoken to Lord Ballan. Will she be all right?"

Lady Ballan turned on him abruptly. "Are you still here? I do not know whether she will be all right. If she survives this weakness, and then the wound heals cleanly, she should recover. Much will depend on how much poison she took into her blood. You acted very quickly, Morduc, and you may have saved her life. You have done well. But now, you must go immediately to see my husband. We must assess the degree of danger instantly."

Morduc left the room and went to seek Lord Ballan. He found him in the library. As soon as he saw Morduc, he said in alarm, "What has happened? Where is Marianna? Why is she not with you?"

"Marianna has been bitten by a snake," said Morduc.

Lord Ballan jumped up from his desk. "I must call Lady Ballan. Where is Marianna? Hurry. Take me to her. I was afraid something terrible would happen."

"She is in her bedroom, and Lady Ballan is attending to her now. She sent me to find you to inform you of the circumstances."

"Good," said Lord Ballan, sinking again into his chair. "If anything can be done for Marianna, Lady Ballan will know what to do. My knowledge would be superfluous. Where did this attack take place?"

Morduc related to him their expedition to feed the swans, where the attack had taken place, and the strange appearance and then disappearance of the dead snake.

Lord Ballan shook his head, "So close, so close. On this side of the stream, you say? Things are worse than I thought."

"How do you mean, sir?" asked Morduc.

"Let us go into the vault," said Lord Ballan. Once inside he said, "Morduc, that attack was not, I believe, an accident. That particular snake is indigenous only to the lands across the ocean, to Argusturia. We have never had that sort around here. Are you sure you saw no person?"

"We saw no one. Or at least I saw no one. Marianna said something about a diving bird just before she was bitten. Can it be that the snake came hurtling down through the air and struck at Marianna as it landed? After she was struck, I didn't stop to look for anyone but brought her to the house as quickly as I could."

"Morduc, it is clearly more important than ever that you start for the coast tomorrow."

"But with Marianna wounded, how can I leave without knowing how she is?"

"I understand your sentiments, Morduc, but if Marianna—assuming she survives—is to be saved, if I and Lady Ballan, this house, and this entire district west of the mountains and north of the jungle is to be saved, the Master of Darkness must be stopped. At the moment I know of no one else." And here a dark look of anxiety swept over Lord Ballan's face even as the sea is darkened by a puff of air moving across its surface. "No one else is willing to try or likely to succeed." He paused and then continued slowly, "If I were able to send a message to my son, perhaps he . . . but in any case I have had no word of or from him for many months, and if he is still alive, his identity may be known to the Master of Darkness. You have the advantage of possibly going unrecognized. And just this morning, you have proven your resourcefulness. Moreover, I have thought of a disguise for you that will possibly enable you to enter the Master of Darkness's castle."

Morduc mused for a long moment before replying, "I am reluctant to go, but if you think it best, I will do so."

"It is not merely best—it is essential. Now, do you know anything about magic?"

Morduc smiled to himself. What elven man, woman, or child did not? But he suspected Lord Ballan meant merely the material imitations of magic which prevailed in the human world, the tricks, the sleight of hand, the deceptions of the street performers. Morduc, having occasionally seen such deft old entertainers, had sometimes wondered whether their sly demonstrations of misdirection did not sometimes overlap elfin magic, so marvelous they were. But even of the lesser magic he knew something, since prestidigitation was part of the education of all elf children, learned as preparatory enactment, before they were allowed access to the full knowledge of the secret powers whose flashing forth the ignorant call magic.

"Yes," said Morduc, "I do understand a bit of it."

"Good," said Lord Ballan. "Then it might work. I think you should appear on the other side of the mountains in the character of an old astrologer-conjurer. You might claim some such fictitious origin as to be a twenty-first child of a twenty-first child of Dalfan and Merquitana. I suspect the Master of Darkness, as an impostor, will welcome all such to his realm, and if you perform in public, either he will hear of you and send for you himself, or you will be required to apply to him for a license. If you give the appearance of corruptibility, he may think he can use you. In any case, you will be able to get a look at the castle's layout and defenses. But you will have to determine what to do when you get there, for I certainly have no ideas about how he may be defeated or routed. Does my suggestion seem sensible?"

"Yes, Lord Ballan. I think so. I believe I can carry off the role of what you call an impostor fairly well if you can provide me with the usual paraphernalia such wizardlings use."

"That I can. I have, in fact, a substantial collection of ancient conjuring apparatus that came to me from a distant relative. I believe he wished me to take up its study, but I was never able to see the point of such childish diversions and turned myself to the study of science and the stars instead. I wish I had other resources to offer you, but I have nothing else."

"Let me see the equipment as soon as possible. Even 'childish diversions,' as you call them, may require some familiarization. Nevertheless, I believe you have provided me with a useful mask, and I accept it gratefully."

They emerged from the vault to find Henry waiting in the library.

"Yes, Henry," said Lord Ballan.

"Lady Ballan wishes to see you in the mistress's bedroom as soon as you are free."

"Thank you, Henry. I will go immediately. Henry, I need you to bring some things here to our guest."

Morduc remained in the library. He went to the window seat where he had first become aware of his love for Marianna. Sitting, he let his eyes roam vacantly out over the deserted gardens. He caught the faint glint of the lake in the far distance. The sun was dipping toward the mountains, its rays beginning to slant into the room, washing its dark wood in red light. A pattern of rhomboid-shaped shadows spread over the dark-figured carpet. The room seemed utterly safe, stable, and secure, with its ancient panels, heavy furniture, and its rows of leather-backed books, yet all their accumulated knowledge and wisdom seemed unavailing against the impress of the poisoning snake and the disruptions of the Master of Darkness.

What wisdom in words could compensate him for the loss of his beloved Marianna? What knowledge could break the grip of that grief or of the Master of Darkness on their land and life? None!

A flying shadow veered fleetingly across the mingled patterns on the floor but was gone before Morduc could turn his head to see what beast had made it. The sun sank, a red disk in a sky of purple-tinged haze. Presently Lord Ballan returned, looking worried and grave, but not defeated. He was followed by Henry and another servant carrying between them a long black box with handles at either end, which they set down on Lord Ballan's desk. Two other servants followed with another similar box between them.

"How is Marianna?" asked Morduc.

"She has sunk into a deep sleep," said Lord Ballan. "She is breathing strongly and is neither cold nor feverish. Lady Ballan is watching over her and expects her to awaken recovered in mind, if not in strength. We may hope for the best." Lord Ballan pointed to the two large boxes. "You may take anything you think you may need from there." Morduc went over to the nearer of the boxes, unlatched the two large blackened brass clasps, and raised the cover. Beneath a dark velvet cloth, whose color shifted between midnight blue and black-night red, sat a collection of the standard equipment of conjurors—cups and balls, ropes, large silver rings, decks of large cards with curious figures and designs on them, knives, juggling gear, spangled picture frames, dice, coins, tubes, bottles, large and small silk squares, feather flowers, hats, caps, bowls, decorated boxes and screens, fans, and bags. There was even a white wooden egg, a plaid bag, and an ebony wand with ivory ends.

In spite of himself and his worry about Marianna, Morduc could not help taking pleasure in this profusion of what where to him familiar toys of his childhood, whose functions he knew well as disguise for the mightier magic of his people. He picked up one of the coins and rolled it expertly over the knuckles of his hand and into his palm. But when he turned the hand over and opened his fingers, it was gone.

"I see," said Lord Ballan, somewhat surprised, "that you are adept at this kind of manipulation."

"If it is manipulation," said Morduc wryly. "As for the children of Dalfan and Merquitana," said Morduc smiling, "I played as a child with one of their forty-first generation."

"Ha! Very good, Morduc," said Ravenstock. "Most convincing. You are catching on to the manner quickly."

"With respect, Lord Ballan. I really did know the forty-first son. In any case, there will be quite enough equipment here for this old impostor's needs."

"Very well, then," said Lord Ballan. "I will leave you here to familiarize yourself with these deceptions until dinnertime."

Morduc went over the entire contents of the boxes carefully, these boxes which were to be his arsenal. By the time he had finished, the sun had dropped behind the distant, mute jaggedness of the dark western mountains. Henry announced dinner. Morduc and Lord Ballan ate alone with little talk.

Following dinner, Ravenstock rejoined Lady Ballan at his daughter's bedside while Morduc slipped down through the passages of the house to the back door of the kitchen. He whistled for Anga and soon saw the gray body appear from behind one of the outbuildings and trot in a diffident, amused, and leisurely fashion over to him. Morduc spoke softly to Anga in the deepening darkness for several minutes. He then turned back into the house with Anga following him. They returned to the main hall through the passages of the house, and then climbed the stairs to the second floor. Morduc knocked softly at Marianna's door, and after a short wait, he and Anga were admitted by Lady Ballan.

"Any change?" he asked.

"None so far," she replied. "She has always been a strong girl, and if anyone can surmount the assault of the poison, she can. Her recovery should be complete." Morduc went softly to the side of the bed in which Marianna lay. Although he had been prepared to see her looking ill, he was shocked by her pallor. Her eyebrows and eyelashes and her dark hair contrasted with her pale skin even more starkly than before. Gone from her lips was their previous redness. They were slightly parted and gray. She lay back against the pillows, scarcely seeming to breathe. As Morduc leaned over and kissed her lightly, air from her nostrils brushed his cheek with a faint odor of decay.

He turned to Lady Ballan with an alarmed question in his face.

"She is casting out the poison," she whispered. "All will be well." Anga put his muzzle on the covers at the foot of the bed and whimpered once. Marianna stirred and smiled faintly. Partially reassured, Morduc and Anga quietly left the room and retired to their own. Morduc dropped off to sleep quickly but was racked by difficult dreams which tossed and turned him. Anga raised his head to growl softly at the shape of a giant dust-brown moth, as large as an oak leaf, which again and again bumped and thumped against the window before it flew off. In spite of these disturbances, Morduc nevertheless slept the night through without waking.

Chapter 23

On the Great River

Red John, Palla Nad, and Yanibo paddled swiftly and silently downriver through the night. When morning came, they were enveloped in a ghostly fog. Palla Nad pointed toward the right-hand western shore. Yanibo pointed to the left. John agreed with Yanibo, and they paddled as silently as possible toward the east shore until the canoe bumped the roots of a large overhanging tree looming out of the mist. John let the canoe drift slowly down the bank until it came opposite the mouth of a small creek. He and Yanibo turned the canoe into it and then paddled until they found a thick, overhanging willow tree. They tied the canoe to the trunk of the willow and lay down under the tree concealed by the drooping yellow-leafed branches. They slept all day under the golden dome of the tree, safe from being seen, even after the mist lifted. At dusk, they descended the creek and pushed out onto the river again. After three days of paddling only at night, they concluded that they were not being pursued by anyone from their village and began to travel down the broad, flat expanse of the river during the day.

Though Yanibo, the boy, was young, and to look at seemed not particularly strong, he was able to take his turn at the paddles along with John and Palla Nad, and so their progress downriver was steady. Moreover, he was unusually cheerful and smiling and adept at making jokes, at which Palla Nad would laugh until he almost fell out of the canoe. One time Palla Nad laughed so hard, his precious priestly bamboo flute fell overboard, and Yanibo had to dive in and retrieve it. As he was hoisting himself back into the canoe, he felt something brush his heel. It bumped the bottom of the canoe, rocking it, and would have succeeded in overturning it except for John's quick action of leaning toward Yanibo rather than away while steadying the craft with his paddle. They waited in silence watching every ripple fore and aft, port and starboard, but whatever great bulk it was that had passed beneath their fragile craft did not return. After several days of exceptionally quiet watchfulness as they traveled, they relaxed again and their good humor returned. Yanibo resumed his joking. Palla Nad would try to translate the jokes for John, but John was seldom able to see their humor.

When they camped, Palla Nad and John together began to teach Yanibo how to speak John's language. After the language lessons, Palla Nad would sometimes play his flute softly for them, and Yanibo would sing the songs of his people. All in all, though they were constantly cautious, their time on the river was more of a holiday than a tribulation. It made the three of them fast friends, and by the time they were within five days of the port city of Imbal, Yanibo's progress in the outer-world tongue was such that he could make himself understood to John about simple matters and actions. He even began to try to make jokes in his new language, some of which John could almost begin to see the point of. One concerned an elephant with a frog up its trunk being like something else, but John was never quite able to grasp the analogy.

They were grateful that their journey had been, except for the mysterious bump on the keel by some river beast, largely uneventful. They did once have to outrun a canoe of hostile warriors, and after that they took care to pass by villages on the opposite side of the river, now wide enough so that they were either not seen or not challenged. They survived a storm that nearly swamped the canoe, and they escaped from an alligator by stuffing its jaws with one of the food bags and poking it in the eye. After that loss of a quarter of their supplies, they fished and gathered wild fruits and berries from the shore to eke out the remainder of their stores. The closer they came to the coast, however, the thinner became the vegetation and the less they found to eat. Thus, they were considerably leaner and hungrier by the time they neared Imbal than they were when they had left the village.

As they came closer to the city, they increased their caution. When they began to see other canoes on the river, they once again took to hiding during the daytime and drifting carefully and slowly down river at night. They hoped to slip into the city undetected, but since a half-scalped knight and a similarly tonsured bush priest would surely cause the most question, the two somewhat unwillingly acceded to Yanibo's suggestion that he go ashore alone to find food and safe lodging. They began to be aware of the smell of saltwater and to feel the tides, and finally one night they came upon a small oceangoing ship moored in the estuary. Slipping past it, they eventually found a dilapidated low wharf, ran in under it, and tied up to wait for morning.

At sunup, while Yanibo climbed up onto the wharf and started for town, John and Palla Nad remained in the bottom of the canoe in the deep shadows beneath the wharf. Yanibo did not return until nightfall, but when he did, he had on frayed trousers belted with a piece of rope, a shirt somewhat too large for him, and a straw hat. He looked just like one of the local street urchins. He brought with him a single loaf of stale bread. While they ate it in the darkness under the wharf, Yanibo talked in a rapid whisper to Palla Nad. Finally, Palla Nad leaned over to John and said in his ear, "He find man from village to hide us." In the middle of the night they took up their nearly empty food bags, and Yanibo led them stealthily from beneath the wharf into the town.

Behind them, in the darkness beneath the wharf, the bottom of the canoe they had just abandoned was bumped again. A black wrinkled snout with spider legs for chin whiskers rose onto the canoe's gunwale. It had an arrow stump in its right eye pit. The SpiderSnake flicked its forked tongue all over the canoe,,especially the stern from which had John steered. After waiting more than an hour with its snout on the gunwale, while its long black bulk floated out behind the canoe, the SpiderSnake slowly dragged its length into the rocking canoe until it filled the craft like a heap of slimy, tarry hawser. It had a second arrow stump in its belly, surrounded by a white festering swollen ring. Finally, it lay motionless and went to sleep, exhausted by its until-now fruitless and arduous pursuit.

Meanwhile Yanibo led John and Palla Nad through the narrow twisting streets of the town to a small, dark stable. Yanibo knocked quietly three times.

"Kirando," whispered Yanibo into the darkness. There was a rustling within. The door opened a crack, and they slipped inside. When the door had closed, a shadowy figure opened the dark slide of a small lantern and held it up. They saw that there were many kinds of animals housed in the stable: camels, mules, an elephant, horses and ponies, and even, in two cages at the far end of the shed, a lion and a tiger. The holder of the light was a muscular young man with a blue headband and a long, wide scar on the right side of his face. When the young man saw Palla Nad, he gave the lantern to Yanibo and embraced the old man with a broad smile. Yanibo brought him over to John.

"This Kirando. This Red John," said Yanibo. The two young men looked at each other carefully. Kirando ran his eyes all the way down John and up again. Suddenly he moved quickly to the side and around behind John, and almost got a choke hold on him, but John, with the instantaneous response of his long boyhood practice, immediately countered, reversed the hold and began in turn to bend Kirando forward to the ground. Kirando put up his free hand in the universal gesture of submission. John released him, and Kirando smiled broadly, a smile that could not be made completely unmenacing because of the great gash scar on his cheek, and said to Yanibo, "Yes. He do." He held out his hand to John, saying, "Strong red-hair man very fast. We can use." And then laughingly he said, "You, Palla Nad, both have funny haircut. Who barber?" Over in the corner, Yanibo nearly fell over laughing noiselessly.

"Where is here?" said John, ignoring the joke and still on his guard as he took Kirando's offered hand and shook it firmly but cautiously.

"The Chauri Circus," he said. "I get you on maybe as tiger wrestler or strong man, or if you know tricks, as a wrestle-any-who-come. We need new acts. Circus go downhill."

Yanibo stood behind Kirando with a broad grin, nodding his head emphatically up and down to John, yes, yes, and yes. John deliberated. What would it be best to do? They had no food, yet how would being bogged down in a fleabag circus bring him closer to the castle of the Master of Darkness? Who knew what pressures the princess was being subjected to? He must hurry to her side, but what risks did haste hold?

Palla Nad said, "I think this be good plan."

"Very well," said John, reflecting that he himself had no other or better. "I'll try."

"Good," said Kirando with his broad but seemingly wicked smile. "Now all we have to do is get Mr. Boss Chauri to have same idea we do. First we change clothes so you look like wandering act. Then this afternoon we get Mr. Chauri to notice you. Yanibo figure out a way. Stay out of sight in stable now. I get clothes. Then go quickly. Others come soon." He fished out a large loaf of bread from beneath a hay pile and gave it to Yanibo, taking the lantern back from him. He closed the slide on the lantern until only a narrow bar of light lit his way to the stable door. Then he closed the slide completely and slipped out. While they waited in the dark among the animals, they breakfasted hurriedly on the bread and the few dried red berries left in the food bags. Soon Kirando returned with two dirty old cloaks and some ragged shirts and pants for John and Palla Nad. He also carried a bowl of water, some soap, and a razor. When he held up the razor in the light of the lantern, John stepped back.

"Red man shave head," said Kirando.

John hesitated. "I think I would rather keep what head hair I have left," he said.

"Last strong man in circus have no hair. Chauri maybe hire you for strong man if you remind him," Kirando explained. "Lose hair, keep life. Keep hair, lose head. Can get new hair. Cannot get new head. *Mimtaka*, freckle skin?"

For some reason Yanibo thought that remark was incredibly funny and once again rolled on the dirt floor of the stable, laughing silently.

"Mimtaka?" said John, confused.

"Uncle Nad, explain Red-Hair," said Kirando, turning in disgust to the older man.

Palla Nad put his hand on John's shoulder and said, "Mimtaka means, 'Do you understand?' Mimtaka now, John?"

Ruefully, John replied, "I understand now. Mimtako."

Kirando grunted with satisfaction. John sat down on a bale of hay, and by the light of the lantern, Kirando shaved off what was left of his red hair. When Kirando had finished and held up the lantern, Yanibo chortled in the corner.

"Sun rise already inside animal house," said the boy. "Shiny, shiny. I go blind to look. Freckles on top, spots on sun." He laughed so hard at his own joke, he fell over on to the ground for a third time.

They dressed themselves rapidly in the old clothes Kirando had brought, put on the tattered cloaks, and slung the three remaining empty food bags over their shoulders. Kirando opened the door carefully and looked about outside. The deep black of night was slowly transmuting to the dark blue-gray of dawn. They moved quietly away from Kirando and the stable door with Yanibo leading, the tall, gaunt figure of Palla Nad in the middle, and the massive hooded figure of John bringing up the rear.

They came to a ring of wagons, one of which, in the shape of a boat on wheels, was painted white with red and gold trimming. It had a ticket window at the square stern end, and in the faint predawn light, they could just make out the words painted on its side: *Chauri Sea-Land Circus*. As they went past the wagon, they heard loud snoring from within. Once beyond the wagons, they moved quickly through the dark streets toward the edge of town.

CHAPTER 24

Chauri Strikes a Bargain

By the time shapes could be clearly distinguished, they were well into a stretch of tall, marshy grass that nearly hid them as Yanibo led them carefully from hummock to hummock across the damp, squishy ground. Finally they came to a small white dune. Climbing it carefully and slowly and crawling as they reached the top, they peered over the edge between the spear-grass blades on its top. The immense, dark, blue-green sea, flecked with white, lay spread out before them. As they watched, several of the foaming whitecaps suddenly flew up into the morning sky and became gulls. When the gulls reached a certain height, their belly feathers turned rose red as they caught the rays of the sun from beyond the horizon. The beach was deserted. From the top of the small dune, the three watched the bright disk of the sun suddenly lift clear of the dark sea on their left to flash scalloped gold over its entire expanse.

"The sea!" exclaimed John, standing up and raising outstretched arms almost involuntarily. He pulled back his hood and turned up his head, letting the light and the breeze fill his face and beard. *Wherever Morduc may be,* John thought, *at least I have reached a coast which can be followed to the lair of the Master of Darkness.* Out of frustration and distraction had at last come progress. *But,* he asked himself, looking first to the east and then to the west, *in which direction on this coast must I go to find that dragon's den?* He had no answer.

They went down the seaward face of the dune. At its base, they found a sheltered hollow surrounded by tall grass. They threw down their bags, tore off their clothes, and ran naked, all three, across the beach and into the waves. Diving and plunging into the morning-cold water, shouting, laughing, and splashing, they washed from their bodies the grime of their month's journey, scouring their ankles and elbows with sand.

Far out to sea, a single black gull flying high above the water caught the joyful commotion in his eye and turned purposefully toward the west, but in a brief flurry, which went unnoticed by the three naked men in the shallows, a cloud of white gulls surrounded it forced it down to the surface of the sea and then tore at it again and again with their hooked beaks until it was but a bloody, twisted lump of black feathers.

Oblivious to the drama in the skies, the three travelers finished their sea bath, and then, clean of body and refreshed in spirit, returned to the beach. After they had dried off in the hollow and put on their clothes again, they ate the remainder of the bread from the large loaf that Kirando had brought them that morning. When they turned the three food bags upside down, nothing came out but a light sprinkling of berry stems.

"Well," said John, "if we don't get work tonight, we'll surely go hungry. How do you plan to manage it, Yanibo?"

For answer, Yanibo jumped up and, dashing through the long dune grass to the tide line, quickly came back with six small smooth stones. Striking a nonchalant pose and smiling broadly, he began to juggle first two, then three, then four, then five and finally six oval shapes. Reducing the number of stones he had in the air to four, he suddenly dropped to his knees, sat back on his heels, still juggling, and then jumped to his feet again. Dropping one more stone and continuing to juggle three, he slowly leaned over backward, juggling all the time. Now he dropped one more stone until he was juggling only two with one hand. He continued to bend backward until his head touched the sand, and then ever so carefully, with his legs bent and balancing himself with his free hand, he lifted first one leg and then the other off the ground until he was juggling while standing on his head. Then with utmost care, Yanibo straightened his arm. He was now juggling in a one-handed handstand. John and Palla Nad clapped and shouted, "Bravo!" Yanibo caught the stones and quickly flipped his feet over his head and sprang upright, facing them again.

"Brilliant," said John, "but what do I do? I can't learn to do that in an hour."

Quickly Yanibo ran to John and said, laughing loudly, "I do that on face place."

John looked puzzled and ran his hand over his eyes, nose, and beard. "I think," said Palla Nad, "he means he will stand on your head."

"Well then," said John standing up, "let's give it a try." John locked his hands together to make a step. Yanibo put a foot into the stirrup of interlaced fingers and sprang easily up on to John's shoulders, where he steadied himself by putting one hand on John's head. He turned to face forward with one foot on each of John's broad shoulders and stood upright as John wobbled a bit under him. He was not heavy enough to be much of a load for John, but balancing him was not immediately easy.

By flexing his knees, Yanibo found he could ride easily and remain stable wherever John walked. Then he began juggling. He found he could handle three quite easily. They made an imposing picture, the slim, brown, agile boy juggling atop the massive shoulders of the bald, red-bearded man. "Holla!" he shouted and tossed the three stones down to Palla Nad.

John braced himself, stiffened his neck, and turned his face slightly upward. Yanibo placed one hand on John's forehead and, holding on to one of John's upraised hands, slowly rotated himself upside down. When he felt himself fully balanced, he let go of John's hand and slowly bent and crooked his knees.

"*Now!*" he shouted to Palla Nad, who deftly tossed him one stone and then another. Yanibo started juggling the two in his one free hand. John struggled to keep steady. Sweat broke out on his brow. All of a sudden, with an "Aieee!" Yanibo's hand slipped and he fell, only to be caught by John before he hit the ground.

"You juggle me, Red Strong," said Yanibo, laughing. "Not bad for begin. You gotta learn no sweat. We do again."

"How can I not sweat?" said John.

"We get good. You no worry then."

"Maybe," John said doubtfully. Suddenly, he reached down, scooped up a handful of the white beach sand, and drizzled it over his own smooth scalp. As it ran off, some caught in his eyebrows and red beard. "How would this work?" he asked gravely.

He looked so silly with a little cone of white sand on the top of his head and whitened eyebrows and beard that Yanibo fell down laughing once again. "Old man sandy head very funny," said the boy when he could speak again. "We try again that way."

John held out his hands, and Yanibo sprang up to John's shoulders again with the agility of a monkey. Facing forward, there he rode, juggling furiously. Finally, he tried the one-handed stand on John's head again. This time he did not attempt to juggle and did not slip. Palla Nad drew forth the flute from his belt and began a swift, shrill tune. Atop John, Yanibo yelled, "Aieee!" in pleasure and delight. When the music stopped, Yanibo somersaulted directly to the ground and landed lightly on his feet, doing a little jig.

Knowing now what they were going to do, the three lay down in the hollow of the dune out of the wind and slept several hours with the empty food bags over their faces. When the sun was two-thirds up the sky, they awoke and set out along the beach toward the town. Eventually they saw a road running parallel to and a bit inland of the beach and climbed up on to it. As they walked along, a closed carriage drawn by a troika of frothing black horses came rushing behind them. The three scrambled down the bank into the ditch as it swept past them with a rattling clatter of wheels. Black curtains were drawn over its windows, and the coach itself was black. The coachman and his companion upon the box, as well as the two footmen riding behind, were dressed in a black livery and took no notice of the three shabby travelers in the ditch.

John said nothing to Yanibo and Palla Nad. The crest on the coach door was a black briar rose pierced by a jet-jewel-hilted black sword. Some minion of the Master of Darkness rode therein, John judged, and each contact, though a risk, was also an opportunity.

The three travelers climbed back onto the road and continued their journey into town. Almost two miles further along, they came upon a peasant seated by the side of the road whose cart had tipped over and whose unyoked bullock stood placidly in the ditch, munching what strands of grass it could reach. The small, wiry, red-faced peasant lamented and cursed, and his black eyes alternately snapped and wept at the bags of grain strewn about the road and ditch.

"What happened, Granfer?" said John.

"Carriage run me off the road," replied the old man disgustedly.

"Need a hand to get going again?" asked John politely.

"Ha," barked the farmer. "Ye look ta be a strong 'un, but even thee canna lift yon bullock out sa deep a ditch thyself."

"Maybe not, but let me at the least try."

"If ye can do it, I'll be much obliged ta ye, young man. Maybe I'll only miss half the market day. Flarin' great lords riding hell-bent on country roads. It sickens."

Together, John and the peasant first righted the cart and reloaded the bags on to it. Meanwhile Yanibo had tempted the bullock at the bottom of the ditch closer to the bank near the cart by dangling some especially juicy flowers before his nose. John slid down into the ditch. The peasant and Yanibo grasped the ring in the beast's nose, and Palla Nad made ready to sound a note on his flute. John put one massive shoulder behind the beast's haunch, and just as Palla Nad shrilled forth a piercing shriek on his flute, John heaved upward while the peasant and Yanibo pulled on the bullock's nose ring. The surprised bullock scrambled up the steep side of the ditch and suddenly found itself on the road again. While John crawled out of the ditch, the peasant hitched up the beast and made ready to travel again in the direction of the town.

"Goin' ter town, then?" asked the peasant.

"That we are," said John.

"Weel, then. Ya kin ride if ye wish, but it's no fast trip," said the man. "Name's Gat. These bags 'r filled wi' rice."

The three climbed into the back of the wagon and leaned back contentedly on the rice-filled sacks as the wagon moved slowly toward the town. "Tell me, Gat, who ran you off the road? Do you have people like that around here?" said John.

"Drefon's fool if I know," replied Gat. "Some great gambock in a hurryin' black carriage. But nat frum 'round hereabouts. The great folk 'round here be a leetle better mannered'n that, tho nin sum be that good mannered ta 'gin wi. Naw, sum great nasty traveler that be. Wicked lookin' vehicle too, don ta think?"

"Sounds like it," said John noncommittally.

They reached the city gates of Imbal about one o'clock and entered through them without anyone giving them a second glance. The cart crept through the streets, giving John, Yanibo, and Palla Nad a chance to see everything they passed. The streets were filled with bustling people. Many ships were anchored in the harbor, and their sailors filled the dock area, opposite which were a number of large warehouses intermixed with many small taverns and hostelries. Further back was the commercial district of the town with large shops and ship chandlers' stores. Constables in leather jerkins carrying long, pointed batons patrolled the streets in pairs. Eventually the cart came into the market area, where stalls were still filled with people and goods, bread, fruit, vegetables, herbs, and utensils. Off to the side stood the butcher shops.

"This be far as I'm goin'," said the peasant.

"Thanks for the ride," said John as they got down.

"And thank'ee fer liftin' yon flaysome ox out ta ditch. I wish't I could pay ye, but I haven't a coin to spare till I make the market. Find me after market if thee's still hungry. I doan kin tell what yer up ta, but yer a good lad, and I wish 'ee well. My blessin' on ya. If'n ye need bed ever, come work wi' me. I got five daughters. Any one a 'em ye kin have."

John smiled at the old man. "No sons, gaffer?"

"Nay, nary a one, but yer such as I wish't I'd got."

"I'm spoke for already, good Gat. But your blessing means more to me than any coin."

"Knowed ye was a good boy. I hope ta see ye ag'in." Gat drove on, and the three travelers stood inconspicuously out of the way in the milling crowd. As they stood there, they heard a bass drum thumping somewhere behind them and a trumpet playing a fanfare over and over again. They waited for the sounds to draw nearer. Finally into the marketplace came three people dressed in red-and-white satin quartered suits. The one in front was the trumpet player, the one in the middle carried a small white dog under his arm, and the third, leaning back, was banging a bass drum strapped to his chest, on which was painted a picture of a ship on wheels and the words "Chauri Circus."

When they reached the center of the marketplace, they stopped, and a ring formed around them. The man with the dog set it on the ground and made a circling motion in the air with his hand. The dog lifted itself up on to its hind legs and began to spin around in a circle. Then the man clapped his hands and formed a hoop with his arms, through which the dog jumped back and forth. Then the man bent over, and the dog leaped up on his back and barked twice. As the crowd gave scattered applause, the man picked the dog off his shoulders and said in a loud voice:

"Come to the Chauri Circus this afternoon. Wonders and marvels from the far corners of the world. Two o'clock at the old bear ring. Come to the Chauri Circus. A penny each. Box seats a silver shillin'. Whole box fer gold."

When he had finished, the man with the drum began banging out a beat, the trumpet sneered out its metallic blare, and the three began marching out of the square. John, Yanibo, and Palla Nad followed at a distance. The dog, drum, and trumpet stopped three more times in the street to give their performance before they finally turned their steps directly toward the center of the town. They eventually led John and Yanibo and Palla Nad to a large octagonal building. From inside, one could hear animal sounds and an occasional shout. Presently people began to arrive at the building, pay their penny at a little wicket in the wall, and enter a narrow door next to it.

At this point, Yanibo led John and Palla Nad to a spot somewhat off to the side of the wicket, placed his hat on the ground in front of him, and began juggling the stones he had picked up on the beach. Palla Nad played a merry tune on his flute. Yanibo began to do a little jig at the same time as he juggled. One or two of the adults going to the circus turned aside to watch. Children who wished to miss nothing dragged their parents in Yanibo's direction. Yanibo danced and juggled so engagingly that presently a small crowd had gathered and very few were purchasing tickets to the circus itself. Some of the spectators had even thrown a small coin or two into the hat.

Suddenly there appeared in the narrow doorway of the arena a short, fat man in white riding breeches, black boots, a red swallowtail coat, and a black top hat. He also had an immense black handlebar mustache waxed so that it stood straight out to each side of his jowls and then curled up.

"Show starts in fifteen minutes!" he bellowed toward the crowd. "Don't stand there waiting. Hurry, hurry, hurry. Show starts in fifteen minutes."

Yanibo turned, John held out his hands, and just as they had done on the beach that morning, Yanibo almost instantly appeared on the top of John's shoulders, juggling furiously as the flute in the background dropped into a more exciting tune. The people in the crowd tilted back their heads and let out an "Ahhh!" and clapped their hands. Then Yanibo dropped all but two of the stones. Carefully placing his hand on John's up-tilted brow and head, he slowly lifted his feet off his shoulders. When he was standing on one hand, with his feet in the air, Yanibo began juggling the two smooth stones with his free hand.

The crowd applauded wildly, calling out, "Bravo! Hooray! More! More!" Additional coins began to tinkle into the straw hat. From the doorway of the octagon, the fat man in the tailcoat strode forward, crying, "What is this? What is this?"

Slowly, with his arms out for balance, John turned in a circle, letting the crowd around them view Yanibo from all sides. The fat man thrust his way through the circle of people until he stood facing the three.

"*You!* Vagabonds!" he said loudly. "What are you trying to do? Get away from here. You can't perform here. I'll report you to the police."

A voice from the back of the crowd called out, "Hey, Chauri,"—for the furious bustling rotundity was Chauri himself, the sole owner, traveling manager, and presiding ringmaster of the Chauri Circus—"You got better inside?"

Chauri spun around, trying to identify the mocker. "Sure we got better inside. We got the best in the whole world. These mangy pip-squeaks got nothing to show. Get your tickets now. Show's over out here."

Yanibo had indeed stopped his juggling and had jumped down from John's shoulders, and Palla Nad had stopped the strange exciting music he had been drawing from his flute. Yanibo scooped up the money from the hat, put it back on his head, and said to Chauri with an engaging smile, "We go. No trouble. All cheery?"

Chauri seemed somewhat mollified by Yanibo's easy submission and looked at the trio keenly. "You know circus work?" he asked.

"I know good," said Yanibo. "They learn fast," he said, nodding his head toward John and Palla Nad.

"I hire *you*," said Chauri pointing his finger at Yanibo.

"You hire *us*," said Yanibo with his broad white smile. "Bald ox man very strong. Old man very funny. Not work without them."

Chauri looked at Yanibo and grunted sullenly. "These take all your pay from you. Work for me yourself and take it all. Silly boy. You work for Chauri and be big star."

"Chauri," said Yanibo. "What would they do without me? Big one not smart. Old one not strong. I feed both. They take care of me. I feed you too. Feed you good. You like feed good?" said Yanibo, nudging the portly belly of the circus proprietor with his elbow and grinning mischievously.

Chauri laughed at the boy's effrontery. "Oly Woly, little smart boy. Follow me. See show from inside. We talk after." Yanibo grinned at John and Palla Nad. Chauri turned and bustled off around the building. John, Palla Nad, and Yanibo followed Chauri around the side of the octagon past the crowds of townspeople who were now streaming toward the entrance wicket. Chauri disappeared into a huge double door at the back of the building that led to a dark tunnel running underneath the seats and out again into the bright afternoon light of the arena. Some of the performers were waiting outside the double doors, tossing juggling clubs into the air or stretching, while others lingered in the shadow of the tunnel. Off to the side they recognized the stable where they had spent the night. Its doors were wide open now and the animals were lined up, all cleaned and caparisoned in preparation for the show's opening parade. Kirando stood impassively at the head of the line, holding the halter of a large chestnut horse on which a pretty young girl in a pink sequined costume was sitting. The girl smiled at Yanibo. Kirando, however, looked straight past them, giving no sign of ever having seen them before in his life.

Chauri led Yanibo, John, and Palla Nad through the tunnel, out in front of the seats and then up three steps into the bandstand to the right of the tunnel. He pointed to an empty space on the very last tier and said, "Sit there, and don't move." The excited buzz of the audience mingled in the arena with the band's testing of its instruments.

Chauri went back down to the ring and waited nervously in front of the bandstand. The arena had a packed-dirt floor surrounded by five-foot-high walls. Above the walls were seats surrounding the circle. To the right of the bandstand, another tunnel ran under the seats into the arena. Suspended above the ring, and glinting in the bright afternoon sun which shone down through the open roof, was a delicate tracery of poles, lines, webs, and nets. Directly opposite the band were a series of boxes in which the wealthier people of the town were seated. The central box, which had a rust-colored plush canopy over it, was still empty. The people in the seats were getting restless and calling for the performance to start.

Presently there was a great bustle as a small group moved down the aisle toward the canopied center box, preceded and followed by several servants in mustard-colored livery. When they were seated, John could see that a large man in a yellow velvet suit wearing an immense, rust-colored, saucer-shaped hat was seated at the center of the box's second row. As he gestured, several large amber rings on his fingers flashed in the sun. To his left sat a woman of similar bulk and comparable age, dressed in a long red silk gown that emphasized rather than concealed the immense doughnut rings of fat encircling her. She also had on a ridiculously high orange turban with a big purple jewel at its center. A waving red feather was stuck behind the jewel. In front of them, lolling noisily over the arena rail were three fat children, likewise dressed in tasteless, garish clothes. Two of the liveried servants sat at each end of the row of children, both to contain them and to go on errands to fetch them the ices and sweetmeats they were constantly ordering from the vendors walking through the stands. Most striking among the group, however, was a very tall, very thin, unnaturally white-faced man who hovered behind the fat man's right ear. He was dressed completely in black, even to a close-fitting cloth cap over his head, whose tie strings dangled down each side of his face. His eyes were so dark and deeply set in hollows underdrawn by dark bags that he seemed a clothed skeleton with only his skull face and two bony hands showing. When they were all finally settled in their seats, the large fat man in the middle made a signal with his hand to Chauri, who was standing in front of the band, watching him.

Chauri bowed as low as his round belly would permit and, stepping to the center of the ring, shouted in a loud voice, "Lord Mayor of Imbal, distinguished guest, and ladeeez and gentlemen and children of Imbal, it is time to begin the show. I give you the Chauri Sea-Land Circus." He then put to his lips a shiny silver-colored whistle he wore on a cord around his neck and blew three loud, quick, shrill blasts. The band behind him, consisting of several horns and woodwinds of various types and a set of drums, immediately struck up a wheezing but fast-paced and mostly on-pitch march.

Into the arena trotted a line of performers and animals from each tunnel, spreading left and right and following the sides of the ring. The two lines met in front of the box of honor, bowed, even the elephants, and returned across the ring toward the band and then out the passages through which they had entered. As the performance progressed, with a trained dog act, with three spotted horses trotting in tandem around the ring, with members of the troupe jumping onto their backs as they moved, and with interludes from the clowns, the most notable thing John saw was the fat man in the center box leaning back toward the tall skeletal man in black seated in the row behind and talking to him behind his hand almost continually.

Suddenly Yanibo slipped out of the bandstand and down the left-hand tunnel. Two acts later, in came Yanibo riding a huge gray draft horse and carrying a tambourine in one hand. He had stripped off his shirt and trousers and was wearing only the jaguar-skin winding about his middle that he had worn when he had escaped. The girl in the pink sequined ruffly skirt paraded the horse around the ring at the end of a check rein and then clucked him into a trot. Yanibo stood up on the horse's back, balanced himself for a moment, and then carefully bent over backward into his one-handed stand on top of the rhythmically rocking horse's hindquarters and began tapping out a rhythm with one of his heels on the tambourine. The fat children in the front row all stood up and cheered and the lord mayor even stopped his conversation with the skull-faced man behind him. Suddenly the entire arena exploded in cheers and whistles and clapping. John saw the man in black lean over and for the first time speak to the lord mayor, who nodded his head vigorously and then likewise struggled to his feet and applauded.

The girl brought the horse to a stop in front of the mayor's box. Yanibo lightly vaulted from his handstand down to the earth of the arena floor, bowed quickly, and then the two turned and rapidly went out the right-hand exit with the horse.

Several other acts, including aerialists, followed, but finally the band struck up the music for the finale, and as the reddening afternoon light slanted ever more acutely into the arena, covering the westernmost seats with shadow and shining directly into the faces of the band, the performance came to an end, and the people began to depart.

The fat man and his party in the box of honor remained. Chauri danced toward them on his tiny toes in black boots like a large bouncing ball. He exuded a mixture of oily gaiety and bobbing servility. He doffed his top hat and made a flourishing bow with it. The lord mayor had by now moved to the front rail of the box among his dumpling children. They shrunk back out of the way in silence when the tall man in black joined their father there. The lord mayor leaned awkwardly over the edge of the box and extended his fat hand to Chauri, who reached up, shook it, and bowed all at the same time. The mayor began to speak to Chauri and at one point tilted his head toward the man in black, who similarly leaned over the rail and extended a long, thin, bony hand and shook Chauri's hand gravely but held on to it tightly as they began to talk. Chauri bobbed up and down, this way and that, like a balloon on the end of a stick. With his other hand, still holding his hat, he tried to brush away the strings of the sepulchral man's cap which dragged repeatedly across his face. The tall man in black could not be seen moving his lips while he talked, nor could John, Yanibo, and Palla Nad hear anything of the conversation from where they now stood at the left tunnel entrance. Finally, still held by the thin man's bony grip, Chauri broke into such a spasm of bowing and sweeping of his hat that he looked like a desperate red-and-white blowfish caught by its flipper. The man in black finally released Chauri's hand and turned to go. The rest of the people in the box rose. Chauri continued to stand below on the dirt floor of the ring, bowing as they left, massaging his hand and apparently still trying to wipe imaginary cobwebs away from his face.

John slipped out of the arena through the left tunnel and walked rapidly around the curved side of the building in time to see the mayor and his party emerge from the main entrance. Two lines of constables held open a path through the crowd to a large black carriage into which the mayor, his family, and his guest climbed. The crest on the door was a black rose pierced by a black-diamond-hilted sword.

When John returned to the performers' entrance, he saw Chauri talking excitedly to Yanibo and Palla Nad in the mouth of the tunnel. Inside, in the ring, a few roustabouts were coiling ropes and stowing tackle. The circus owner was wiping his profusely sweating head with an immense purple handkerchief. He was arguing angrily with Yanibo.

"I can't do it now," Chauri was saying. "You come yourself. Do horse thing with Marjorie like today. That sell whole circus. No risk new act now with red-beard ox. I got to keep acts I got. No risks now."

Yanibo continued to smile and speak cheerfully and cajolingly. "Yes, yes, yes, Mr. Chauri. You take all of us with you. Three for price of one. You no pay till we make money for you. Just feed. Strong man, Yanibo do many works."

Chauri looked again at John, estimating the work he thought he could get out of those massive shoulders and thighs. "All right," he finally said. "I take you all, but no trouble. We try him out on way. This my real big chance. But any trouble from big one, from old one, out they go. Bump on road. Splash in water. *No trouble! You understand?*" he yelled. "Very important. Very, very, important.

This my big chance. But if I make mistake, maybe I ruined, maybe I even . . ."
He shuddered. "You do good for me, I make fortune and you make fortune
too. Enough we no have to work again. But if we make mistake, no can work
ever again." Here he thrust his big, round, bulging-eyed, oily face into John's
and lifted his eyebrows in a significant gesture John did not quite understand.

"Where go?" John asked directly and innocently but with as stupid an
expression on his face as he could muster.

"Trouble already!" Chauri yelled throwing up his hands and turning away.
Clenching both his fists, he yelled at the top of his voice, "*Bolta!* I need you." A
small-eyed, scraggly-faced man with a brown cigarette dangling from the corner
of his lips separated himself from the roustabouts on the far side of the ring
and slouched over to Chauri.

"Bolta. This man new roustabout. You, red ox man, this Bolta. He boss
roustabout. You do whatever he tell you. You understand 'boss'? Boss! Boss!"
he repeated, shouting. "*Understand?*"

"Ya!" replied John, smiling. "Boss. Bolta my boss. You Bolta boss. Ya!"

He looked at John closely. "Good. Maybe you not so dumb after all," said
Chauri. "Bolta, get rigging down. Pack all, pack all. We no stay here longer. I
go tell performers." He put on his black top hat and started toward the right
exit tunnel beyond the bandstand. Halfway there, he turned toward the three
standing with Bolta in front of the left-hand tunnel.

"You! Yanibo. *No trouble!* Understand?"

Yanibo waved back cheerily, showed his white teeth, and called back,
"Right, boss. No trouble." John too smiled and waved his massive hairy arm as
Chauri continued toward the tunnel and disappeared under the stands. When
John let his hand fall, it came down gently on Yanibo's shoulder. The boy turned
around, his strong teeth showing in a broad smile. "I do it, Red John," he said.
"Chauri got to go play for big man on ocean coast. Yellow fuzz man make him.
Kick him out Imbal circus house. Bone man pay him. Chauri not like too much,
but they give much gold and he too scared not to go. We sail in three days. I
do it John. You like?"

John felt his heart jump within him. Were they really going to perform
before the Master of Darkness himself? Would they be able to enter his region
and even his city undetected? And if—*when!*—he came into the presence of
the Master, this time, thought John, grinding his teeth, the outcome would be
different.

"Yanibo," said John intensely, "we must be ready."

All of a sudden John felt a rough hand on his shoulder. He turned his head
to see long, dirty, bruised fingernails on an equally filthy hand. He braced and
flinched ever so slightly. He smelled a sickening sweet smell in the air. The hand
dug its nails into John's flesh.

A raspy voice said to him, "Ox. Hey, Leatherhead. Yeah. You. Red Ox. Are you an ox or a bull? You got red hair everywhere? Ha, ha, ha. Get to work over there. Pick up those ring sections and take 'em to the wagon."

John turned slowly and then said carefully.

"Ya?"

"It's me, Bolta, your boss. Remember, stupid? Your boss. You gotta do what I say." Bolta coughed up a mouthful of phlegm and, not turning his head aside from John's face until the very last second, spat in the dust.

"Hey, Bolta. He good worker," said Yanibo, smiling his charming smile.

"Insect," said Bolta. "Pretty insect. Boss's favorite. This ox has to do what I say. He don't follow *your* orders no more. Get it?"

"Ya, Bolta," said John. "You boss. I carry. Work good. Good ox. Ha, ha. Good joke. Best ox."

John started moving toward the ring sections, chortling. Bolta looked suspiciously at all three of them but could not penetrate their disguises. Concluding nothing, he took a drag on his brown cigarette, inhaled deeply, held it, and then let it out slowly into the late afternoon light. Yanibo kept smiling. Trying to appear senile, Palla Nad started to chew his lip. Finally, Bolta looked away and followed John toward where the rest of the crew was lounging.

"Now hear this," Bolta called in a surprisingly loud voice for his small frame. "Tear down, tear down, tear down. Pack up, pack up, pack up. We sail in three days. Three days, sailing." The roustabouts bending over the equipment stood up and looked at each other in amazement. "Get moving, you apes. Look. We got a new ox to help us. Chauri's Dumb Ox. Give him a good welcome, boys." The boys said nothing but laughed easily.

John continued to chortle to himself, but when he bent over and picked up by himself a ring section which usually took four of them to move, they stopped laughing and thereafter kept a friendly but respectful distance.

Yanibo seized Palla Nad's hands and danced him around in a ring, stomping joyously in the dust. The old man followed as best he could in the diminishing light, his white head bobbing and his old skinny legs tripping from time to time in the dust.

In the blackness of night under the low wharf, the wounded and exhausted Lady Topalak awoke in the bottom of the canoe. She flicked her forked red tongue in and out, tasting the air for the scent she wanted. She snuffled all the parts of the canoe again, but finding nothing new, lifted her snout toward the wooden ladder on the side of the wharf. Slowly she flowed up the ladder and onto the rotting wharf. Like a thick black ribbon, she undulated landward following the scent of the steps of her quarry. From time to time, the arrow stump in her side caught painfully on a rock or on the corner of a building as she moved around it. A small hairless dog trotted down the street. It started barking at a shadow sliding up the street. Suddenly the Lady Topalak launched herself toward the dog, seizing it in her jaws and breaking its back. She repositioned the dead dog and swallowed it head first. When it was deep within her, the snake went on undulating through the nighttime streets. Eventually she came to a stable. When the animals within started a racket, the silent stalker moved away from the building. Eventually she came to a wagon shaped like a ship. She explored it from every side but found no opening. Finally with great effort, she got her head up over the side and flowed onto the deck of the ship-shaped wagon. Again she found no way within. Carefully, she disposed herself beneath the gunwales of the pseudoship, like a huge piece of tarry rope, ugly but seemingly an integral part of the vehicle. There she lay, blind, wounded, and deadly with vengeful pain.

CHAPTER 25

The Forest and the Cup

Morduc set off on his journey from Lord Ballan's with a heavy heart. He had visited Marianna early that morning, but she had scarcely been able to speak. As he bent over her, she had put her hand on his neck, drawn his ear to her lips, and whispered, "À bientôt." Then her hand fell back strengthlessly on to her pillow. He had kissed her cold forehead and left the room to begin his journey. *So unnecessary*, he thought as he checked the ponies' pack saddles. *There is anxiety enough in peaceful life*, he thought. *Why must men augment it by evil?*

Now riding with Anga toward the forest and the dim mountains that rose beyond it, he wondered whether he would ever see his beloved Marianna again, ever feel her tender touch, her kiss, or see the light of her eye. He rode in an old brown homespun outfit covered by a patched gray cloak. On the small red pony that Lord Ballan had given him and leading a second pack pony freighted with two long burlap-wrapped boxes, he looked and felt like a poor country lad on his way to a distant croft rather than the deposer of tyrants Lord Ballan expected him to be. Did the joys of love necessarily entail the burdens of war? Was there no easy, obscure life to be lived among mortals? Must war always be the prelude to love? And the afterlude. And apparently the interlude and everlude too, as it was for Lord Ballan? Morduc wondered why his father had not told him this about life among the mortals. His father had merely said that he would find a unique jewel among mortals. Was the jewel Marianna's love? Was war and the threat of death what made it valuable? He too now had a riddle to solve. It had forced itself upon him, he who had come forth from the blissful world beyond the mountains looking for adventure. And now, his life had become serious. He had found love, but inside that rose, would he find the worm of war and death?

While Morduc mused, Anga trotted in front of the ponies, sniffing the path directly ahead and to either side, pleased once again to be on the road. They ambled on all morning across the fields and then up the meadows that stretched westward from BallansHold. At noon, they stopped for rest and a brief bite. Morduc looked back at the lake and the serene fields leading to his beloved's house. He could barely see the blue dome of the observatory on the roof. The house itself was now but a speck of white in an expanse of green field and forest. Marianna's swans were indistinguishable from the white caps on the surface of the blue water. Morduc lay back on the grass of the mountain meadow and looked up. Far above him in the hot noon sky floated a silent solitary crow. The world seemed at perfect peace, yet through those serene fields, a concealed malevolence of immense strength and bitter determination had already snaked its way into the life of Marianna and her parents and was likely to attempt to do so again. Here he was, going to seek out that evil at its head and try to cut it off, when it had not even been his fight. It was neither truly safe to leave his love nor safe not to. Did mortals face these dilemmas all the time? Anga barked once, calling him to resume their trek.

"Indeed," said Morduc to the dog, "I should show more spirit. Although we have a powerful opponent with many strong pieces on the board, the game is not finished, perhaps not even really begun, since I and John are only just newly in it. He does not suspect our attack. Even a pawn can defeat a king." By midafternoon they had reached the edge of the forest. The trees rose up like dark columns in a giant maze, their high, round, dense crowns cutting off all direct light to the forest floor. The ponies shivered as a chill breeze blew out at them from among the trunks. Morduc patted their necks and spoke reassuringly to them as they slowly entered the shade beneath the dark trees. As before, Anga trotted on ahead, snuffling the ground, leading the way on the zigzag path through the gloom.

Although there was very little underbrush, the trees grew so thickly together that, once among them, Morduc could see no more than fifteen feet in any direction. The wall of tall trunks opened before and closed behind them like shifting curtains as Morduc and the ponies followed Anga along the faint path. Occasionally off to one side or the other, there seemed to be movement, but no shape of beast or other being showed itself.

Just as night was falling, they came around the foot of a huge tree and saw a clearing ahead of them next to a sizeable pool in the forest. In the clearing, a small stone hut was built at the base of a cliff which extended toward the pool. At the top of the cliff, above the pool, a small clear spring bubbled out of an outcropping and down the cliff's brown rock face into the pool. They went forward a few feet and stopped, waiting to be noticed. No one came out of the hut. There was no sound from inside and no sign of life without. Morduc dismounted and walked slowly toward the door, saying neither loudly nor softly, "Hallo? Anyone there?" The dog went ahead and peered into the open door of the hut. He turned and came back wagging his tail.

"Well, Anga," said Morduc, "I take it there is no one home." The dog drew a stroke in the dirt. "Then let's have a look." Tethering the ponies to a tree trunk, Morduc went to the door of the hut, swung it slowly back, and looked in. After his eyes had become accustomed to the gloom, he saw a cold hearth opposite the door. He entered and inspected the hut's single room further. It contained nothing else—no tables, chairs, cupboards, beds, books, tubs, larders, basins, churns or chests, just the fireplace, a stone mantel and a chimney rising up through the roof. A fire had been laid, but it was covered with spiderweb. On the mantelpiece sat two large conical cups, mouth down, one white, one black.

"Looks like no one lives here," said Morduc to the air. "I guess she won't object to our staying the night." Morduc went back outside and took the saddlebags and saddles and boxes off the ponies and then led the small shaggy beasts to the pool to drink. After they had drunk their fill, Morduc tied them by long ropes near the pool where soft moss and grass grew. Anga barked once and slipped away to hunt supper for himself. Meanwhile Morduc returned to the bags and saddles and boxes, dragged them inside the hut, and then he too began to consider what he would have for supper. He looked longingly at the fire ready to be lit. Hot food. The warmth and light of fire against the night. Desiderata. It was a courteous and gentle gesture of his host or hostess. Any traveler would welcome it on a cold and dark night. But tonight was not cold, nor was the darkness deep. The absence of trees above the pool admitted starlight into the forest. Best to leave the fire for a traveler in greater need. Black bread and water for supper tonight. He picked up the white cup from the mantelpiece and went to the waterfall beside the hut. As the ponies chomped on the lush grass nearby, Morduc dipped the cone-shaped cup in the pool until it was full, and then brought it with both hands to his lips, and . . . dribbled water down his cloak, his leggings, and onto his shoes. He looked into the cup. It had no bottom. He turned it over and held it up to his eye like a short telescope. All he saw was the trees on the other side of the pool. He examined the cup, turning it around in his hands. Small black letters in a fluid brush script ran around the body of the cup against its pure white background. With his thumb, Morduc felt the slightly raised black letters that lived under a transparent glaze. He could not read either the script or the language. Why would anyone make a cup without a bottom? He returned to the hut and picked up the black conical cup. It too had a hole in its bottom, though the radius of the cone was narrower than that of the white cup.

"Now what kind of a potter would make cups like that?" said Morduc to himself. "Neither will hold water. They're both useless. It's a stupidity beyond thought." He replaced the two cups on the mantel, mouths down, and looked and looked and looked at them, puzzling over their presence, the sole bizarre furniture of this isolated, uninhabited hut. The white cup with the flowing, brush script stood out in the growing dusk. The black cup receded into invisibility in the gloom. As Morduc stared at the two shapes, the white cup seemed slowly to rise into the air, as if lifted by an invisible hand, and was rotated mouth upward. It floated slowly toward the black cup, and gently settled down on the black cup's upturned peak. There it sat, a white cup seemingly suspended in dark air but sitting on a black base, invisible in the dusk. Morduc took a step forward and then blinked. The white cup was back in its place on the mantel, mouth down beside the black cup. Slowly and carefully, Morduc reached for them and, as in his vision, placed the bottom of the white cone over the peak of the black one. The combined cup looked like a chalice or a large egg cup with a white top and a black foot. When he lifted the white cup this time, he did so by the black base. Within the white cup, the cone of the black base penetrated up into the bowl nearly to the rim.

"Fancy that," said Morduc and went off again to the pool. He filled the white cup up to the height of the black cone's tip. Now the white cup held water. Morduc brought the cup to his lips and drank deeply.

The cup imparted an effervescent minty quality to the water, or perhaps it was the water itself. Morduc scooped up some water from the pool in his hand and tasted it. No, it was the cup which gave to the water its exciting tingle on the tongue. He looked at the double cone cup in wonder. "Even in Elfland, there is nothing like this. Separately, the two halves are useless—together, a marvel." He filled the cup again and drank deeply a second time. He returned to the hut and put the two truncated cones away in one of his saddlebags by the side of the fireplace. "Such strange and curious things," he said to himself. "I will take them with me to show Marianna." By the time he had arranged the bags and saddles into a bed for himself in front of the hearth, Anga had returned, licking his lips and cleaning his muzzle contentedly.

With his saddle for a pillow and the dog beside him, Morduc lay down on his back in front of the fireplace with his face toward the open door of the hut. By now the sun had completely set and only the faint starlight filtered down through the opening among the trees above the pool, just barely defining the door as a slightly lighter blackness against the blackness of the inner cabin walls.

CHAPTER 26

Night Beast

As he began to fall asleep, Morduc became conscious of something happening within him. He felt a darkness creep out from the corners of his body and invade his mind. It was a delicious, smooth, smoky liquid seeping into his brain from deep within his body. He opened himself to it, letting it extend its flavored rivulets into his consciousness. As it came more and more boldly forward, extending itself even into his ears and eyes and tongue, he tasted it and found it had the same mintyness he had found within the cup. *What new delicious dream drink is this*, he thought to himself.

Anga stiffened by his side. Morduc heard a faint rustling outside the hut. The blackness in front of the door thickened as if some great bulk had interposed itself between the door and the faint star shine under the trees.

Over the taste of the invigorating dark mint, Morduc smelled a foul odor, like fat and hair that had been rotting together in the bottom of a pit. A large shape blocked the doorway. Its head rested on the roof of the hut while one of its arms reached within the hut toward the fireplace. Anga stood and growled with his fangs bared. The arm was replaced by the nose of the monster completely filling the door, sniffing, expanding, and contracting its black nostrils. Then the muzzle was withdrawn and replaced with a single bulging eye, rotating this way and that, trying to see what it smelled. The head retreated and the arm reentered, groping again toward the fireplace. Just as the hand was about to reach Morduc, Anga darted forward and sank his teeth into the large, shaggy, shapeless arm. The arm shook off the dog as if he were a mouse, scraping him off on the hut doorframe. A howling of rage began. Simultaneously Morduc felt himself dropping over the cliff of consciousness, falling down through endless space into the dark abyss of nightmare.

Spiraling down dizzily into complete darkness yet remaining at the same time motionless on his back on the floor of the hut, Morduc saw suddenly, like a silent exploding star, a noiseless, blinding flash of light behind the shape. Even through his closed eyelids, Morduc saw silhouetted a huge head with upturned horns. It turned toward the flash, lifting its arm to shield its face as another stunning blast of light went off. The shape cowered before the exploding blue-white flash. Two more flashes of immense power followed from other directions.

The shape began to scream in fright as it ran away from the hut door into the woods, crashing through branches and leaves. The flashes, as if from several large swooping stars, pursued the shape through the woods. It stumbled, crashed, and fell, but the flying stars dived upon it and harried it back up again. The black shape fled through the forest. The flashes became dimmer and dimmer, the crashing fainter and fainter. Anga crept toward Morduc, curling up painfully next to Morduc's waist. Both relaxed, and with the warm presence of the dog by his side, Morduc eventually gave himself up to a haunted sleep.

CHAPTER 27

Daybreak in the Forest

Long after the faint gray light of dawn had become the strong light of morning, Morduc was still sleeping deeply in the hut. The dog painfully stood up from his nestled bed by Morduc's side and walked limping down to the spring. After admiring himself in the pool, turning his head first one way and then the other, he dipped his black muzzle into the water and lapped noisily. The ponies were where they had been, patiently cropping grass and blowing small misty clouds of breath into the cold morning air. Anga walked slowly back to the hut, still favoring his left front foot and stood in the doorway, looking at Morduc. The dog barked, and Morduc stirred. His head ached and his eyes still had points of light burned into them. When he opened them, he saw triple golden auras around everything he looked at.

He tried to sit up, but felt so groggy and dizzy, he couldn't. After resting another minute, he tried to stand but could not. He was safe, he acknowledged, but he felt as if the shapeless, foul-smelling, horned beast in that dreadful not-dream still possessed him, still lived somewhere within him but had merely withdrawn into a secret cave. Morduc lay back against the saddle and tried to eat some of the tough, dark bread that Lord Ballan had given him. As he chewed a small piece, he thought of the cup from which he had drunk. With immense effort he turned back the flap of his saddlebag. The two bottomless, conical cups were still there, a black and a white. Taking a piece of paper from his pack, Morduc tore it in half, held it taut across the curved outer surface of the white cup, and then, with an old piece of green crayon he took from his pocket, he carefully made a rubbing of the script. Carefully, he unrolled the paper from around the cup and then rerolled it into a small scroll with the image of the lettering on the inside and tucked it into a corner of his saddlebag. After a short nap, and as the food took effect, Morduc began to see more clearly and to feel better. After another quarter of an hour's open-eyed rest, he struggled again to stand, this time succeeded, and wove his way dizzily to the spring, drinking from his hand. After another rest, he collected the ponies, loaded them, and made ready to start off again on the path. Though still somewhat dazed, he was determined to get away from the hut while he still had light. Another night in its shadow was something he wished not to spend. Before he left, he replaced the two cups on the mantel and then took the crayon with which he had made the rubbing and wrote as well as he could on the remaining half sheet of paper, "This cup causes death dreams in those who drink from it. Beware." Rolling up the message like a small scroll, he placed it in the narrow opening of the black cone cup where it sat inverted on the hearth mantel. "Not for that monster, certainly, but maybe someone, sometime, passing this same lonely way again will drink forewarned."

With immense effort, Morduc pulled himself up onto the lead pony and, clucking to it, started again westward along the woodland path.

He labored to stay in the saddle all through the afternoon, but finally he felt he could no longer stay erect. They had come to a small clearing on a rise where a circle of pale-yellow grass received full light. Morduc looked up, as if from the bottom of a deep well, to see the bright blue of the late afternoon sky overhead and, around the rim, the tops of the tallest trees sun-touched with green gold.

"We'll stop here for the night," said Morduc to Anga. Slipping off the pony clumsily, Morduc slumped in the grass while the still-loaded pony cropped the small island of prairie at the foot of the trees. Morduc lay resting on the grass, his mind still giddy with the black mint that he had drunk from the mysterious cup. His mind had gradually been clearing all through the day, enabling him to reflect on his experience and on the bursting flashes of light which had saved him from he knew not what. Yet he remained weak and unable to make his body do his will.

After resting a while, he dragged himself over to the loaded ponies and released them from their saddles and boxes. After tethering them and aligning his gear beneath a tree at the edge of the circle, he sat down exhausted on the burlap-covered boxes. Anga disappeared as he had the evening before to hunt dinner for himself. Too weak to eat, Morduc lay down on the boxes, looking up beyond the circle of three tops as the light slowly left the sky, changing it from bright blue to dark blue and then slowly to black. As he watched, the first stars came out, and eventually he saw above him Caracanta, the star of love. "Perhaps too," he said to himself, "Marianna can see this star tonight, and it will strengthen her as it does me."

In a while, Anga trotted up, looking amused as always and a degree more satisfied. The dog made a thorough tour of the clearing, sniffing every stone and log on the perimeter. He ended by scratching his side against the rough bark of the tree under which Morduc had placed the boxes. He jumped up on the box next to Morduc and dropped down contentedly next to him. Morduc drew his cloak over them both. With Anga by his side, Morduc went to sleep. The stars—strong, steady, serene, and pure—moved slowly through the night across the clearing's window.

Chapter 28

King Ranagnathus

When morning came, Morduc awoke much refreshed. He sat up quickly and found himself clear headed. Feeling considerably stronger than he had the morning before, he quickly loaded the ponies and set out on the path leading from the clearing. Ahead of him the path began to descend ever so gently from the rise on which they had camped. He knew the mountains would begin some days westward, but he could not tell from Lord Ballan's map how many more. He rode on within the forest for half a day. By noon the vegetation began to change.

The hard, dry floor under the tall trees became moist enough to produce low-growing lilies. The number of insects increased, and Morduc became conscious of a gentle, ever-downward-sloping grade. Toward the middle of the afternoon, he stopped at a point in the path at the top of a fairly steep decline. At the bottom, extending as far as he could see, was a broad, flat marsh. A causeway path ran across it, but only a few inches above the water. Numerous ponds interrupted the huge expanse of tussocky grass in front of him.

If he must go down, he thought, before he could go up, he would. He got off his pony and carefully led both animals down the bank and on to the narrow dirt track. He began to hear a faint peeping. It was weak and persistent, though not alarming. Progressing along the causeway across the marsh, Morduc and the ponies moved in a bell of silence, the peeping noise receding before them and closing in again behind them.

As the sun slipped behind the distant mountains, shadows settled over the marsh. Morduc continued to lead the ponies along, watching their footing carefully. The further they went along the path, the taller the vegetation grew up on both sides of them. Huge fronds of fern towered above them. Rooted in the dark water along the edges of the path stood tall stalks with bulbous red shapes at the top of them, like lightless, velvet-covered lanterns. Eventually the sound increased until Morduc, Anga, and the ponies were enveloped in a thick blanket of choric, cacophonous peeping. It was so dense, it seemed to sound inside Morduc's head.

They paced forward for some time in the declining light until, abruptly, the path simply disappeared ahead of them. It slanted down, vanishing under the dark, dank water of the marsh. Morduc and Anga and the ponies stood at the edge of the water, surrounded by the thunderous high-pitched peeping, wondering what to do next. Suddenly Morduc felt a soft plop on his shoulder, like a large raindrop, and then another on his head, and suddenly all around him, the water was erupting, with small squat frogs leaping up on to him.

They landed on the ponies too, which stomped, snorted, and shivered but stood their ground. Anga jumped this way and that, snapping at the small animals catapulting themselves up out of the water at him. He caught none, and several managed to land on his back and ride there. Morduc started to brush off the numerous little vermin which were beginning to accumulate two and three deep on his shoulders and arms, when from across the water he heard an immense booming and splashing. Rushing toward him with the speed of a small ship skimming the surface was the largest and greenest bullfrog Morduc had ever seen. Like two rushing lighthouses, its great green eyes sped nearer and nearer. Presently it came to rest several feet from shore, a huge beast, towering above Morduc, the dog, and the ponies the way a great sailing ship towers over its dock, its passengers, and its crew.

The frog swelled its neck and boomed like a giant bass viol being played by an angry god. "My children call me," he roared forth. "Who may ye be that intrude upon my marsh?" Looking not much bigger to the gigantic frog than an insect, Morduc answered, throwing back his cloak in a bold gesture.

"My name is Morduc, and I am a wandering magician, off to seek my fortune."

"Oh *ho*! Magician, are we?" said the frog in his thick rosin gut voice. "Do we really presume to magic and do we presume to say so to *us*? Indeed! Why, you meager thing, with just one quick flick of my sticky tongue, I could lick you up and put you away." And as he said it, there was an invisible moist swishing in the dark air above Morduc's head as the frog flicked out and retrieved his long red tongue in a monitory demonstration. The ponies shied backward, and Anga barked once in defiance.

"Great King," said Morduc, doing his best to keep his voice steady, "We mean and have done no harm to you or even to the least of your children, and surely it is best for power to show justice. Moreover, in return for passage across this marsh, I would willingly show you such marvels as are at my command. May I inquire, O Great Green One, to whom I am speaking?"

"Ah, little green one, you speak much for so small a gnat. But you also speak truly, and for that truthfulness, as well as for the pleasingly green tint of your skin, I am inclined to test your claim, though there have been some recent attempted invasions of this marsh which would better advise me to dispose of you promptly and go without your marvels. If I had not just recently snacked on a dozen giant dragonflies, perhaps I might be more tempted than I presently am to make tasty morsels of you and your three companions."

"Thank you, Great Green Monarch. Even the supremely powerful may find restraint benefits them in the end."

"Harrumph," replied the giant frog. "You are a cheeky wasp. Nevertheless, if you get clear of here, you may say that you were the guest of King Ranagnathus and was well-treated by him, but if not, my reputation for hospitality won't suffer much from your report, will it?" The frog let out a bellowing chortle in which he was immediately joined by the high-pitched laughing cacophony of the peepers. Even though the ponies snorted and shifted uneasily from foot to foot and Anga continued to look about alertly, Morduc remained standing stolidly at the edge of the water.

When the huge frog had laughed sufficiently at his own joke and the ripples in the water from the shaking of his sides had nearly subsided, Morduc drew his emerald sword and, holding it aloft, spoke three words softly to himself. Immediately the green blade began to glow brighter and brighter. Suddenly Morduc flashed it down toward the surface of the water and a great green spark leapt from the tip of the blade to it. All the peepers in the water twittered deliciously at the mild shock. The great frog moved backward a bit in the water.

"Aha," said the frog good-naturedly. "The little green wasp has a sting as well. My, my."

"I accept your hospitality, great Rana," said Morduc, "and swear by my father's sword neither to betray my guesthood nor to speak ill of you in the time to come, as you do right by me."

"Nobly said, little green one," replied the giant frog. "But will your actions agree with your words? For many beings these days, a word is but a paper mask, to be used and then discarded when convenient. Even as I welcome and accept you into my kingdom, I warn you again, beware of injuring me or any of my children, however diminutive and seemingly unimportant they are, for I am a jealous father and hold eternal warfare with those who would diminish my breed. This is my stronghold, and though you are my guest, I urge you to treat me with circumspection and care. If you do, you will be welcomed and sped. If not, you will become food for the fishes and for the flies, who in turn become food for me and mine. Now climb on my back. I will ferry you to my palace for the night. There we will feast and enjoy merriments, your magic marvels among them. In the morning, I will land you on the opposite side of this marsh provisioned to your need."

With that, the giant frog approached the path and extended a large foreflipper. Leading the ponies, Morduc splashed through the shallow water, up on to the back of the webbed hand, and then up the arm and shoulder on to the broad green back of the king frog. The ponies hung back when the mottled skin yielded to their hooves, but Morduc led them firmly and gently onward across the broad back until they were just behind the gigantic head. Anga followed, being careful not to slip on the wet skin.

"That dog's toenails tickle," boomed the huge frog, chuckling. "Hang on," he called as he turned in the water and pushed off from the path's end with a mighty thrust of his long, bulging, gleaming green thighs.

Keeping his head and neck above water, the beast swam slowly and effortlessly through the dark waters carrying Morduc, the ponies, and the dog atop him. The last light caught the tops of the trees on the high land behind them. Ahead, Morduc could see only water and darkness.

The great frog swam steadily for half an hour before Morduc saw lights in the distance. As they drew closer, he made out a large compound of reed-walled and rush-roofed buildings on an island. Large numbers of frogs somewhat smaller than King Rana were entering and exiting from the main gate. There was a small beach, and as soon as they reached it, Rana stopped and let his passengers descend his steep shoulder and arm on to the sand. Once they were off, he lumbered out of the water and led them forward toward the high reed hall. They passed through several reed-walled corridors and finally arrived at a large room lit by torches. At the far end, on a round dais sat another frog, nearly as large as Rana but considerably lighter, almost white green, on whose back swarmed hundreds of small frogs of a similar hue. As the two exchanged croaks, which Morduc did not understand, he and the ponies and the dog waited patiently on the green stones with which the hall was paved.

Presently, Rana turned and said, "May I present my wife and queen, Phyllosodon." Morduc bowed deeply; the queen returned a nod which quivered her several chins. "Perhaps," said Rana, "you would like to see to your mounts first. I will have some of my servants supply you with what is needed. When you have taken care of the ponies, return here, and we will contrive an appropriate feast for you, and you may entertain us and the princes and princesses of our line with your magic. Though we live on a path that is, or at least once was well traveled, it is nevertheless quite some time now since my queen and I and our brood have witnessed jugglery of that sort."

"I would, indeed, be most grateful for the ponies' sakes to find them food and rest," replied Morduc. He led the two loaded shaggy ponies though the door to which Rana had pointed and down a long reed-walled corridor. At the end was a comfortable room, dry and warm, with a small window. There Morduc took off the saddles and the bags and the boxes, rubbed the ponies down, and saw that the frog servants had put grass and water within their reach. Then he considered his attire. After reflection, he decided to replace the country homespun in which he had been traveling with his own suit of seven times seventy shades of green. Having redressed himself, he selected several tricks from his boxes of magical paraphernalia, put them in a red velvet bag, and, with Anga at his heels, returned through the passage to the main hall.

As he entered, a low appreciative murmur at his green attire ran around the room. Rana and Phyllosodon remained on the dais, massive and dominant, while the servants bustled to and fro, bringing dishes heaped with various kinds of fish and insects to a number of low tables that had been set close to the walls around the perimeter of the room. Clustered around the tables were the young princes and princesses of the realm, eagerly awaiting the entertainment.

Rana called Morduc and the dog to him. "You seem almost one of the family in those colors. Sit here by me." He indicated a smaller table by the side of the dais. More and more frogs of various sizes, shapes, and even colors began crowding for places at the tables around the walls, twittering and talking as the servants filled up the tables with tray upon tray of delicacies and succulents.

Presently a quavery, watery gong sounded, and a hush fell over the assembly. Rana lifted a cup between his webbed fingers and chanted a prayer in a language Morduc did not understand. Then everyone fell to, but in as strange a way as Morduc had ever seen. As each dish passed, the eater would extend his tongue faster than the eye could follow, and a morsel on the plate would be snared and gone. *Almost as good as my magic*, thought Morduc to himself. When the trays came round to Morduc, and he took up some of whatever looked edible with his fingers rather than with his tongue, the frog princes and princesses around the hall stared and pointed in astonishment, humming and brumming excitedly together. Anga ate from a dish one of the servants had set on the floor for him.

After all had eaten in good measure, Rana slapped with one of his webbed hands on the dais. An old frog harpist came forward into the center of the hall, squatted on the stones, and sang in the strange tongue of the prayers, accompanying himself on the harp. Following this, Queen Phyllosodon leaned her smiling Silurian head toward King Rana and spoke something to him. Rana turned to Morduc and said, "What else now, oh Morduc, can you do with those tiny flippers with which you picked up food? What else can you do to entertain your hostess and her children here tonight? Children must be entertained, you know. If you please them, you please her. If you please her, you please me. If you please me, you will have my help and friendship forever. Such is the chain of fate in this hall."

Morduc picked up his bag and proceeded to the open space in front of the dais. He reached into it and produced a large silver tube. He put his arm through the tube, wiggled his hand at the end of it, and then withdrew his arm to show the tube empty. Standing it on end on the floor, he waved his hands over it and slowly, up from the tube, began to grow a slim green plant. It continued to grow, and as it grew, blossoms of blue, red, yellow, and white appeared. These, Morduc plucked off one by one, and as he did so, each became a silk handkerchief the color of the blossom. Morduc draped these over his left arm until it was completely hidden by a cascade of colored silk squares. Suddenly, he put his other hand on top of them, waved the bundle quickly up and down, and then, moving his hands apart, displayed between his outstretched arms a single, large, rainbow-colored scarf of silk. A gasp of pleasure arose from the courtiers, the queen, and the many younger frogs, who filled the room with the sound of flapping, slapping applause. Stepping forward, Morduc proffered the multicolored scarf to the queen who, smiling with pleasure, caught it up on one large fingernail of her webbed hand and drew it gently around her neck, being careful neither to smother nor dislodge any of the froglets riding on her back and peering over her shoulders to see the performance.

Next from his bag Morduc took a handful of shining hoops. At first he merely juggled three of the metal circles in the air. Next he spun them ringingly on to the floor so that they first sprang away from him and then returned under their own power. All of a sudden, two of the rings linked, and then a third, and then all of the rings began to link and unlink rapidly in Morduc's hands forming shining ladders, spheres, and rosettes, folding and unfolding in glimmering designs. Finally, just as they all seemed inextricably intertwined, the rings suddenly shook loose one by one and fell into a neat stack on Morduc's arm. Again a noisy, flat, slapping-wet applause filled the room.

As his final trick, Morduc produced a stack of three large cups. Pulling the small table on which he had eaten out into the center of the room, he placed the three cups in a row in front of him and looked up at King Rana.

"Now," said Morduc, "I need your assistance, King Rana, and the help of several of your smallest children." All of the tiny frogs on the queen's back began to make excited peeping noises and crowded down over her shoulders, eager to volunteer. At this, the king looked long and hard at Morduc but finally spoke a word or two to his queen. For once, she seemed not to be smiling and leaned her head toward Rana and spoke in protest and expostulation. King Rana overruled her with a gesture, and three of the excited peepers on her back jumped down on to the floor and hopped over to Morduc. He picked one up and put it on the table before him and stroked its back until it was motionless.

"Be cautious how you proceed, oh guest," said King Rana. "Neither terrify nor harm even the least of these who are precious to me."

"Do not fear," said Morduc, "but I do ask you to let me finish what I start before you conclude I have done wrong." So saying, he quickly popped one of the cups over the small motionless frog, at which Queen Phyllosodon gave a gasp. Moving the three cups over the table slowly in intersecting paths, he brought them to rest again in a line in front of him.

"Now, King Rana," said Morduc, "Where is your child?"

"It is," replied the king, glowering somewhat at Morduc, "clearly under the end cup after you moved them." Morduc immediately lifted the cup, to show there was nothing under it at all. At this, the queen began a noise of anguished wailing. Morduc swiftly lifted to the table another small frog which he again deposited under the center cup. Shifting the positions of the cups again, he again asked where the frog fry might be. Again the king was wrong; the cup he pointed to was empty. Morduc placed the third peeper under the center cup and again it disappeared. By this time, the queen was rocking from side to side, and the king himself was looking progressively unhappier.

"Well, Morduc," said Rana, "on your life, resolve, resolve, resolve this mystery immediately." Morduc swiftly stacked up the three cups, tapped the one on top and then lifted the bottom one, showing the three little frogs, riding one on top of the other, blinking confusedly, beneath the bottom cup. They immediately jumped off one another and hopped excitedly back toward the queen, peeping in tiny, happy, chirpy voices. The queen gave a squeal of relief as she gathered them up and saw that they were unharmed. Rana too relaxed, sinking back on his haunches on the dais.

"You are most bold and reckless, little green one, to sport with my children in that fashion. You have saved yourself this time, but I urge you not to attempt such feats again."

"Indeed, King Rana," said Morduc, "it was perhaps a little more than others would have attempted in such a house as yours, but I assure you that I hold all of your children as tenderly as I do those three and will preserve them as you would yourself. Let it not be said that Fellows of the Green, such as yourself and I are, should not trust one another completely. You will find neither disloyalty nor danger in me."

"I am almost convinced," said Rana. "The Fellowship of the Green is a bond I myself recognize, but there are many outside the marsh who love us not. We have lost many, many children to predators of the air and the land and some even within the water, especially recently, though I believe the lake and marsh itself are for the moment free of such. You must understand our caution. Nevertheless, you have fulfilled your portion of the agreement. We thank you for the entertainment, and after your night's rest, I will see you to the other side of the lake myself where you may resume your journey, none the worse for us."

"All beings are of the green, if they but knew it, great king."

"Not quite all, little Morduc. Your sentimentality will be sore tested before your journey is over. Green is of the heart and spirit, not the skin, and some be foul, crusted, and dried of heart, though smooth and fair and even green of skin. Water and light meet in green to make leaf and limb. But water wants all, without limit, and burning light too, would have all. Thus the war between them and within us."

"Is there no rest from this war?"

"Ha, ha, little green leaf. *You* are the rest. Do you feel like you rest?"

Morduc considered the agitation within him. "No, wise king. I do not feel at rest."

"Ha, ha. *No rest*, then. Only marsh mash. How do you like this little 'frogment' of wisdom?" King Rana laughed so hard at his own joke that the reed walls shook. Suddenly he stopped and looked at Morduc piercingly. "Verily, small green slip. Do these matters interest you? You should stay with us. Our OWO might consent to teach you."

"OWO?" said Morduc. "What is an OWO?"

"You do not have an OWO in your tribe? Indeed you do have *much* to learn, leafling. I urge you, delay your journey. Remain a while with us."

"Kind king," Morduc replied, "would that I could. I am eager to learn more 'frogments' of your wisdom, as you call them. Yet I am even more eager to proceed on my journey. Perhaps another day I shall return this way."

"Not likely," said King Rana, "if you are really only a wandering magician, as you claim, with no pressing appointment or destiny. Take the chance while you have it."

"Have we not all a pressing appointment, even those, such as yourself, who travel not?" asked Morduc.

"You speak OWO, Morduc. Be it as you wish."

Morduc bowed, collected his equipment, and retired with Anga down the passage leading from the main hall to the room in which the ponies were stabled. There Morduc lay down on sweet-smelling rushes with Anga next to him, and covered by his cloak, he sank into sleep, well satisfied with the evening's work, and feeling safe and secure on the island in the middle of the lake.

CHAPTER 29

The Attack of the Air Thorns

As Morduc slept, he began to have bad dreams again. He heard, far off, thunder and screams, thrashings in water, and the rush of dark wings. He stirred but did not awake. Anga, however, did and lifted his head. The sounds came closer. Through the passageways could be heard the movement of many bodies. Anga poked his nose into Morduc's side. The elf awoke and heard in reality the distant noises of his dream. Quickly he leapt up, threw off his cloak, and, snatching his bow and quiver, started out into the passage, only to be pushed back by a rushing troop of helmeted frogs carrying halberds. He followed them down the passageway and into the great hall. There were other troops coming from the other doorways and running out to the main gate. Morduc and Anga went with them. When they reached the gate, they saw in the dim light of flaring torches a battle being fought all along the edge of the water. Morduc could not see who the adversary was. Suddenly, he was knocked down by a large swooping shape which picked up Anga in its claws and flew off.

Immediately drawing a green arrow from his quiver and fitting it to the string of his bow, he shot in the dim light just above where he could see the dog struggling in the air. The arrow went home, and a black-winged body faltered in flight, releasing the dog. Anga fell back to the water and landed far out in the lake with a loud splash. The dark shape wheeled in Morduc's direction as he waded into the lake, struggling through the water toward Anga. All around him frog warriors were fighting other assailants of the air. The dark shape descended screaming toward Morduc. It came closer and closer and then dropped dead in the water just ahead of him. Morduc finally saw the enemy.

It was a giant bat, with long yellow fangs, small red eyes, long black ears, and an immense span of thin skin wing. The dead bat was foaming at the mouth and bleeding stickily into the surrounding water. Morduc pushed the floating corpse away with the end of his bow and waded out into the dark lake where he could hear Anga whimpering. As he finally went beyond his depth and began swimming, Morduc heard another screeching bat swooping down to attack him. He turned in the water, drew his sword, and waited. At the last moment, Morduc threw himself aside and held up the sword so that the bat ripped his entire belly open on the emerald point as he skimmed low over the water.

Others came diving down, their fanged mouths open. Morduc slashed again and again. Of one, he cut off a foot. From another, he ripped a wing like a bloody black sail. Struggling to defend himself, to keep afloat, and to find Anga, Morduc slowly went further and further out into the dark water. Finally Morduc saw Anga swimming feebly toward him, every now and then turning his head to snap at the dark swooping bats.

The air seemed filled with them. All around him Morduc saw the bats diving toward the water, snatching frogs from its surface, and then flying off with them, the white underbellies of the frogs showing against the dark sky in the torch light, their legs writhing in dangling agony as the bats' talons dug into their soft sides.

Morduc at last reached Anga, and together, they turned back toward the land, swimming as best they could in the moil of water and blood. As they struggled into the shallow water, they could see King Rana fighting furiously on the beach as several bats attacked him simultaneously. On to the ground now bat after bat was dropping in attack. The shore was covered with huge, flattened mouselike faces. One of them began to advance toward Morduc, balancing unsteadily with its wings dragging. For a moment, Morduc felt he was going to be sick from the bat's furry stench of filthy caves. As it came closer and closer baring its fangs and hissing, Anga barked and charged the beast, limping though he was. Morduc recovered his resolution, remembering there still lived those he loved and who loved him, and striking out with his emerald sword, he severed the head of the bat just as the beast was upon him.

Whirling as he felt a fetid breath on his back and heard more scraping of wings on the sand, he struck another straight through the throat. Slowly retreating along the edge of the water in front of the great gate of the hall, Anga and Morduc fought their way to the side of King Rana, who was stabbing into the air with a long-handled trident. Bat after bat fell, pierced by the swift thrust of his triple-pronged weapon.

Finally standing beside Rana, Morduc continued to wield his emerald sword while the king bellowed and the wounded bats fell screaming. All over the island and far out into the lake, the frogs and the bats kept up their furious battle. From a dark, cloudy sky thunder rolled down on the battle.

Suddenly from out of the sky dropped a great gray bat larger than any of the others, right down on to the king's back and sunk its talons into his skin. As the frog king twisted and turned, trying to throw it off, the bat sought for a place to sink in its fangs. Each of the gray bat's wings ended in a sharp white thorn of bone with which it tried repeatedly to pierce the skin of Rana. Morduc retreated several steps to get out from under the thrashing figures and waited his chance. As Rana rolled toward him, the bat's body, clenched on top of the frog, came almost level with the sand.

Morduc grabbed the top of a pinion and swung himself up on to the back of the beast and scrambled up toward its head. Reaching around with his bright green sword, Morduc plunged the blade into the throbbing sinewy gray neck of the king's assailant and twisted it back and forth. The wrinkled ugly face of the bat looked around at him in surprise and rage and, with faltering strength, tried to bite him. Morduc loosed his hold and slipped down off the furry body and down the side of King Rana to fall flat on his back on the sand. Above him, the two great shapes thrashed in deadly battle. As the bat's grip weakened, Rana twisted savagely and dislodged the creature from him and thrust his trident through its heart.

As Morduc lay watching Rana plunge his weapon into the shuddering monster, a dazzling streak of lightning seared down the sky, illuminating for a moment the entire island and lake. Morduc saw the lake boiling with the defense of the frogs. All around him the bodies of dead and half-dead bats lay. An enormous peal of thunder followed immediately upon the lightning stroke, and Morduc felt rain begin to fall. Large drops hit him on the face and fell on the surface of the lake with a hiss. The rain pelted down harder and harder until it seemed as if the entire sky had opened and sheets of water were pouring out. Most of the bats still in the air veered up and away, though some were beaten down by the falling sheets of storm and were killed by the frogs where they fell.

Soaked, Morduc lay watching the dark shapes struggling up through the rainy air, leaving the lake and the island behind. A great bellowing cheer rose from the lake, a cheer of triumph from the frogs. From the sky, as if from the other side of the storm, there came in response an angry cacophony of hostile screechings dying away into faintness in the dark clouds above them.

Morduc sat up and turned to find Anga. He was lying bloody and gasping on the beach, wet through to the skin, his feet awash in the lake. Morduc scooped the dog up in his arms and started for the main gate. Behind him the booming of the frogs continued, as more and more pulled themselves from the water and sent their deep, defiant song of victory up into the night. Morduc rushed into the hall and down the passageway to the stable room. The ponies were still there, nervous from the storm and the battle noise but reassured by the sight and smell of Morduc.

Morduc laid Anga down on the rushes and, taking a cloth from the bags, began to dry him off and to examine him. The four places where the bat's talons had gripped him had bled and were now clotted and did not look serious. One of the hind legs, however, was strangely twisted. Morduc touched it gingerly. Anga whined in pain and drew it away.

Going to his pack and drawing forth from it the box of medicines that Lady Ballan had given him for his trip, he took out one vial after another, pulled out the cork-encased stone stopper of each, and sniffed carefully. Finally he found the one he wanted. He poured a small bit of the substance on to a corner of the cloth and, speaking softly to the dog, held it to his nose. The dog at first twitched when he smelled it, but then as the fumes began to take effect, he relaxed and went off into a deep sleep.

Carefully, Morduc felt for the bones beneath the unbroken skin and discovered that only one had been snapped, and in only one place. Gently, he manipulated the two ends back together until they slipped into place under the tension of the tendons. Even in his deep sleep, Anga whimpered at the pain. Binding together several of the rushes from the floor with strips of red bandaging he found in Lady Ballan's medical box, he made a splint and carefully fitted it to the leg, tying it on firmly but lightly with more of the red bandaging. Then he took off his own wet clothes and dried himself off. He found dry ones in his pack, put them on, restored the medicine box to its place, and finally sat down by Anga to wait until the dog woke up.

As he waited, he heard noises throughout the palace and outside it. The low drone of a chanted singing came from the distance. Eventually the dog gave a snuffle and a start, opened his eyes, and lifted his head. As he tried to get up, Morduc moved to him and held his head.

"Don't move just yet," said Morduc. "You've been doctored, but you won't find it easy to get around." The dog lay back and slapped his tail feebly on the rushes. "I'll get you something to eat and drink." Morduc walked back down the passage to the main hall. King Rana was on the dais, looking tired but relieved. The queen was nowhere to be seen. Servants were washing out the hall.

"Morduc, my friend," said the king solemnly. "We have won a great victory this night, though at considerable sad cost. The Queen has tended to the injured of her children and is now leading a lament for the lost. You fought well for us. I do not doubt that I owe you my life. That big gray bat almost had me. What resources I have are at your disposal. I am a fierce and implacable enemy, but an over- and ever-flowing fount of benefaction when a true friend has awakened my gratitude."

"I am glad I was of help," replied Morduc. "At the moment I only ask some food and water for my dog, who was wounded in the fight." Rana spoke to two of the servants crouching by him, and they immediately went out.

"Later," said Rana, "when the wounds of all have been washed, and the bodies of the warriors who fell in the fight given proper funeral, and the dead bats burned on the beaches, we will have a proper victory feast. Then you may claim your boon, whatever it may be. It was a grievous confrontation, and you did not shrink from risking all to help us when you might have hung back. You had no obligation other than not to hinder us. Yet you entered the battle and made the crucial difference. We do not forget such devotion and courage."

Morduc bowed in acknowledgment. "Your kindness as a host, King Rana, permitted no less on my part. I shall be happy to attend this victory celebration and feast." Then he turned and went back to watch by Anga.

When he reached the stable-guest room, dishes of food and water had already been placed near Anga and he was standing, holding his splinted left hind leg off the ground, lapping thirstily at the water. He stopped when Morduc entered, looked up, and tried to come forward, hopping awkwardly on three legs, nodding and wagging his tail.

"Easy does it," said Morduc, and the dog nodded his head up and down, yes. "And now, in what's left of this night, perhaps, we can get a little sleep. I think the sky is beginning to lighten already, and I hear some birds being fretful." They lay down, and both dropped off into a deep sleep. The ponies stood drowsing, shaking their heads from time to time as they nibbled the hay and alfalfa put before them.

The dog and the elf slept long, and when they did finally wake, it was near noon. The day was clear and bright. The sun shone on the lightly rippling blue surface of the lake, and a brilliant blue sky was filled with huge white balloons of clouds, marching in slow, stately ranks eastward across the sky. For a moment, the horrors of the night seemed only a dream, until through a small window, far off on the beach Morduc caught sight of pinpoints of yellow fires burning, giving off a faint dark smoke which drifted along with the clouds back to the east.

"We must consider, Anga," said Morduc as he stood looking out the window at the serene and only slightly stained scene. "We must consider what to do now. You are in no condition to travel, but I should get to the coast as soon as I can. Every day lost leaves the Master that much more unchallenged. I do not wish to leave you here, but neither do I wish to delay as long as it would take for the bone to knit. What is to be done?"

Even in his pain, the dog's look of slightly bored but loving amusement had not left his face, and from where he lay on his side, looking over at Morduc almost quizzically, he gave a chirp of a bark, not loud enough to be heard outside the room but strange enough to startle both Morduc and the two ponies. The reclining dog arched his back into the shape of a bow, stretching all of his legs unconcernedly, as if he had just awakened from a safe snooze on a warm hearth rug. The torn strips of red cotton cloth that bound the splint to the leg looked more like the beginnings of a party costume than bandages. Anga put his head back down on the rushes, and if a dog could whistle, Anga looked as if he were whistling quietly to himself.

Morduc was a little angry. The dog didn't seem to care. *Why is he so unconcerned?* thought Morduc to himself. *What can give him such perfect peace when we have this terrible difficulty to resolve?* Morduc turned again to the window. Where was Red John? He must find him. He must proceed to the coast. This was the most important journey of his life. It was what he had been born for. How could he delay? Yet how could he abandon Anga? It was this business of mixing with mortals that created such dilemmas, such difficult choices between comrades. Could the dog, perhaps, come later, by himself over the mountains? Dogs had been known to do such things. It would make the decision so much easier.

Suddenly he felt a faintness around his heart. A kind of darkness passed swiftly before his eyes. What was he thinking of? He saw himself as a small, shameful, squirming worm. He saw now why the dog was so relaxed. The dog had known all along what was right, what was due to a comrade, what he himself would have done had Morduc been sick or injured.

"The dilemma is really no dilemma at all, is it, Anga?" said Morduc softly. "The Master of Darkness, Captain Juncata, whoever he is and whatever he is, will simply have to await our pleasure." The dog rustled his tail on the rushes.

Immensely lightened in spirit, now that the decision had been made, Morduc took up the green garments on the rushes that had been so wet last night and found them dry. He shucked off his spare clothes quickly and reattired himself in his proper apparel. "And perhaps, Anga, we can gain some intelligence of the road ahead while we wait for you to heal. And I too perhaps would be at my best strength with a chance to rest and to exercise." Sprucely clothed, and with his spring restored to his step, Morduc strode back down the passage, purposeful and alert. Only a few servants were in the main hall, and Morduc continued through it, out into the open forecourt and then through the gate and toward the shore. At various points along the beach, the pyres of the enemy dead were burning with a dun mist that rose up into the noon air. King Rana was on the shore, surveying what had been the battlefield, the shallows of the lake. His servants were busy pulling enemy carcasses from both the shallows and the deep water, dragging them up on to the beach and then tossing them on to one or the other of the fiercely burning piles. A dark fetor occasionally blew over them when the breeze changed direction. As Morduc came up to him, Rana turned his massive green bulk and rumbled, "Aha. The sleeper has awakened. Here you are at last."

"Yes," said Morduc. "And I have come ahead of time to ask my favor, and perhaps also to offer what help I can again."

"I will be most delightedly happy in both," said Rana, closing and opening a great eye as he cocked his head downward toward Morduc. "Name what wealth or position you wish, and if it is within my gift, it is yours."

"If it is acceptable," continued Morduc, "I would like to prolong my stay with you until my traveling companions are all entirely well and fit enough to journey over the mountains."

Rana looked at him, surprised. "Is that all? No shining mud from the mountain streams which feed this marsh? No sparkling stones we keep at the bottom of this lake? Those things for which so many others of your shape have assaulted us? Is this all you ask, that which I most desired myself, your company and conversation?"

"Yes, that is all," said Morduc. "Just rest and sustainment until we are ready to cross the mountains."

"And" said the Frog King, "are you sure you will ever be truly ready to do that? There is bad business beyond the mountains. We have been feeling it even here, for many years now. But of that, more later. Nothing would give me greater pleasure than to have you stay with us forever, if you thought such a water-bound life would suit your fancy. We will have some fine talks, and I will teach you some of the frog language and games. The only way to learn the language is to play the games. We are a highly metaphorical people, and all our names are taken from the games. It might amuse you."

"I would like that," said Morduc, "and since it is not against the rules of hospitality for a guest to be useful as well, I would welcome any assignment you could wish to give me or any method by which I might show my continued gratitude for your entertainment here."

At this, King Rana swiveled his huge body a bit on the shore, snared a purple dragonfly from right above Morduc's head, gulped contentedly, and then bowed toward Morduc as much as his bulk permitted, saying, "Your companionship and conversation alone are the greatest service you can do me. We are now comrades in arms, and I need not say again that I owe you my life. But if you wish, perhaps there are ways you could help us to defend ourselves better against the attacks of these"—and here Rana said a word in Froggan which Morduc took to be a curse—"these . . . hawking bats.

"From the birds by day," he continued, "and from the black falcons of the mountains, and from the long-legged, body-gulping cranes, we know well enough how to defend ourselves, though we eternally weep for all our children since we know some must die. But about the bats, who are the hawks of the night, we know little what to do. If you could assist my counselors and me to devise a strategy to help there, not only would you have my redoubled gratitude, but you would have that of the entire nation of frogs as well. We are a peaceable people of the water and are accustomed to live, to love, and to grieve the inevitable death, but not to fight. It has been forced upon us."

"It is the lot of the peaceful, sometimes, to fight," said Morduc. "But you speak of the bats as a new viciousness, one to which you are not accustomed. Is this true?"

"Indeed," said Rana in his throat. "They have only attacked twice before, and last night was the first time in force. Before that, they only raided the edges of the lake. This was the first time that they have dared to attack the island precinct."

"Where do they come from?" asked Morduc.

"We think from somewhere either within or beyond the mountains, but we do not know for sure. We have cousins through all the world, and we hear much by way of the toads, the salamanders, and the newts. Even the snakes will sometimes condescend to speak to us in the ancient language of the water folk—that is, when they are not hunting us. There has been a disturbance amongst all the animals recently, and from somewhere west of here. Out of this, we think have come these fishers by night, but specifically from whence, we know not."

"Perhaps," said Morduc, "I know something of this myself." A short silence followed, while Rana regarded him intently, looked away, and then looked back.

"Indeed," grumped the king. "Then I would like to know of it, and I would also like you as well to speak to our OWO, who has theories of his own that I do not well understand, yet who has always given me the best of advice."

Morduc considered whether he would ask again what an "OWO" was, but in the end said only, "I am willing to do that, whenever it shall suit your pleasure."

CHAPTER 30

The OWO

The far shores of the lake seemed calm and untroubled. The soft sound of the water slapping the sand and the faint hum of the clouds of purple dragonflies surrounded them as they stood side by side, looking over the water. The clouds continued to float serenely overhead, and high up in the sky, dodging between the clouds, so far above them that it was almost less than a dark speck in the sky, a solitary carbon mote of a crow wheeled and circled for a time, and then drifted silently off toward the north.

The funeral for the dead Froggan warriors was held in the afternoon. Their bodies were carried on reed floats to the head of the lake, where they were buried ceremoniously. When all had returned to the island, a solemn banquet was held to honor the fallen and to celebrate the victory. The queen reappeared with her multitudinous royal brood still riding on her back, peering eagerly over her shoulders. Toward the end of the banquet, King Rana called Morduc to the center of the hall and, after reciting his deeds, addressed him formally as his comrade in arms and presented him with a necklace of large green gems. Finally he proclaimed Morduc an eternal friend of the frogs and all amphibians and ordered it so recorded in their annals. He said nothing, however, about how long Morduc would be staying with them, what he would be doing while he was there, or where he was going.

The next morning, a messenger came to Morduc in his rush-walled room, saying that King Rana would be pleased to see him as soon as possible. When he arrived in the great hall, the king said simply, "Follow me," and started down a passageway behind the royal dais. They proceeded in silence between the rush walls for several minutes, but as the passage began to descend, Rana said, "We are going to see our OWO." Down, down they went, deep into the earth. The walls of the passage changed from rush to earth, from earth to rock. Glowing fungus patches on the walls gave enough light for them to see their way. Finally they came to a small grotto in which was a pool fed by a constant trickle of water down the grotto walls. In the middle of the pool was a rock, and on the rock, there was a mound of green slime. The space was lit by the same faint-green fungal glow that had illuminated the corridor.

Although Morduc could see no one there, King Rana began speaking in the frog tongue. When he had finished, there was a silence. Rana spoke again. From somewhere there came the muffled sound of a reply, and then with a start, Morduc realized the slime mound on the rock was moving. It slid off the rock, splashed feebly through the water, and then crawled up on the rock shelf in front of them. Morduc saw that the creature was indeed a frog, and a very old one at that, but one that seemed to have a different jaw and face than the other frogs did.

It looked almost like a lizard, with a green horny crest rising on each side of its eyes and sweeping back across its head and down his neck. The creature wove his head back and forth as he spoke in the strange combination of clicks, hisses, boomings, and croakings that made up Froggan phonetics. Occasionally, a slim red tongue, forked like a snake's, would slide forth from the OWO's mouth and then back in. In spite of himself, Morduc shuddered slightly, remembering the attack on Marianna.

"This is our OWO, our Old Wise One," said King Rana. "He will teach you the frog tongue, and when he thinks you can understand it well enough, we will talk again with him about the threat to the marsh. It is the severest one in my memory, although probably not in his. He will ask you what he wants to know and will perhaps be able to help you with what you want to know. I urge you to apply yourself. You can be of great help, both to us and to yourself."

"Thank you," said Morduc, excited at the prospect of learning Froggan. "I will follow where my teacher leads me."

"A good answer," said King Rana as he turned and went back up the passageway leaving Morduc and the OWO alone. Morduc stood before the ancient form, not knowing where to begin. The OWO squatted on the rock shore. He patted the stone with one of his paws. Morduc sat down on the wet stone and waited. The Old Wise One produced from among the folds of his skin a small rough pebble of gold and put it on the flat rock between Morduc and himself. He covered it with one of his webbed green hands and then said something to Morduc. Morduc tried to repeat it, and the old one waved his crested head up and down. Then he uncovered the pebble and made a slightly different sound. This too Morduc tried to reproduce. As the lesson continued, Morduc found himself becoming better and better at making the two sounds. Then the OWO gave him the gold pebble. Morduc covered it with his hand and made one sound, uncovered it and made the other sound. The old one was delighted, hissing and flicking his long red tongue in and out.

They went on to other simple motions and sounds. Although Morduc could not say that he really understood what was going on, he found he could imitate the actions of the OWO and make the sounds that went with them. He was eager to continue, but the OWO suddenly slumped on the rock slope, waved toward the tunnel, and turning slowly around, paddled back to his rock in the center of the dark pool. Morduc understood that the lesson was over for the day and reascended the passage. When he came back into the hall, he noticed over at the side, two of the small royal brood squatting on the floor playing the same game he had played with the OWO. He found he understood the sounds, or at least recognized them and associated them with the action. Much pleased with himself, he went through the court, out the front gate, and down to the shore. Along the beach he saw the two ponies trotting along together with several piles of young frogs on their backs, bouncing up and down, screeching and peeping in excited delight. Anga hobbled along behind as fast as his three-legged gait would permit, the red of the bandage flashing like a distant light wherever he went among the greens of the marsh.

Each day thereafter, Morduc descended the long passage into the grotto. Each day, the Old Wise One reviewed all the sounds that Morduc had learned since the beginning of the lessons, and then went on to new ones. The OWO knew many games, and gradually, Morduc began to see why one sound was appropriate to one action and not to another. His ability to use and make the sounds grew more and more precise, until he found he could almost do so without thinking. He learned salutations and good-byes, yeses and nos, goings and comings, appearances and illusions, living and dying even, and the sounds of all the things he could see.

One day, the OWO put two of the sounds together in a new way that Morduc had never heard before, and he was puzzled all over again. "'Eye'?" said Morduc, "combined with 'life'?" What is "eye-life"? The old one said the new combined sound again and again, until, finally, in a flash, Morduc saw that the meaning of the two things put together was utterly different from each one used separately. "Aha," he said, "'eye-life' must be to see with the life of the mind and to see with the mind is to understand. I see it, my OWO, I 'eye-life' it."

The OWO became excited. He slapped his flippers on the rock, his crest rose, and a blue-white glow filled the grotto.

The OWO uttered another combination. "Dark air thorn! Dark air thorn? What is dark air thorn?" Suddenly in a rush, there returned to Morduc the memory of the bats descending in the dark with their sharp claws on both wing and foot and their smell of rotting blood. "Ah, the bats, the bats," said Morduc out loud in his own language. The OWO rocked back and forth in delight as his crest rose again, and the light in the grotto grew stronger.

After he had seen the basic principle of the frog language, Morduc's progress was swifter than ever. He learned combination after combination in Froggan. The OWO began putting the puzzles to him more and more quickly in excited croakings, and every time he did well, the grotto would fill with the blue-white light that had appeared when he had first understood how Froggan transmitted its more abstract meanings. When the lesson was over, the light always disappeared. Morduc puzzled over the matter, but for the time being decided not to ask Rana. In due time, the OWO himself would explain if he wanted Morduc to know.

Eventually Morduc began to understand what he heard not as mere sounds associated with objects or actions which he then translated into his own tongue, but as images and ideas which sprang into his mind along with the sound, and when he wished to speak, he was no longer conscious of remembering sounds for meanings; when the image of what he wanted to say came into his mind, he now merely uttered the combination of croaks and bellows that went with it.

Finally a day came when King Rana accompanied Morduc back down the passage and all three of them crouched on the dark wet stone shore in the pale-green light to the soothing sound of water trickling continuously down the walls.

"Now," said King Rana in the frog tongue, beginning to laugh even before he had uttered the words, "We all three can *pool* our knowledge." The OWO and Morduc laughed along with him, slapping and splashing on the wet rock. When King Rana's chortles died away, he began to speak seriously. "On what bush grow the air thorns, the dark, blood-eating air thorns? And how can that bush be cut, for surely it produces no blossoms, only never-waking sleep for us. Tell me again and tell Morduc what you know."

The OWO wove his crested head back and forth and began to speak in what sounded to Morduc like a somewhat older version of the frog language. "Many sky-lights ago, I began to hear things from the newts who walk within the deep-earth waters. I lie here all nights listening to songs of the earths, smelling the waters and talking with all the beings of water birth who come to me with their stories. Many lights ago, I smell thick red-in-water, I smell blood in the outwaters of the earth. The newts say they hear from the toads that over the mountains much red-in-water runs into the ground, much blood mixed with the sky waters goes into the ground.

"The red-in-water comes from beasts who will not run for black rose. One Black-Rose Man-Beast seeks to compel all tribes of beasts. Black-Rose Man kills any beast who not runs as he say. Why he compel, the newts not say.

"Shame to our tribe. The belly walkers stop speaking to the toads and frogs. No longer give ancient greeting. Keep to themselves first on other side of mountain, now this side of mountain. The snakes no longer talk brother with amphibians, though we are their ancestors. They no longer talk of people of the water birth, but speak of power they serve. Say they plant all world to black rose. No longer marsh, no longer sand world. All must be black rose place. Unwaking-sleep-garden. Even some of the birds, shame, our descendants too, have begun to turn, though not all.

"Black Briar Rose tries to go east beyond mountains. It claims rule of all land on sea-wash-side of mountains, but toads tell me this not fully so. The snakes move unopposed through sea-wash land, but only through passivity of animals and men there. Hearts of men have not yet been won, but their thought lines are tangled. They worry about day, not about aeon. They live in dream. They say, 'I will wake up later'. Black Briar give them sniffing powder. They forget troubles. They feel god power. They be briar slaves. They worry much but resist not. They worry much but become not wise.

"Until attack of bats, Black Briar not come here. They seek control of lake on night you arrive, Morduc, on night you save King Rana. Some of King Rana's ear-talkers believe we should seek alliance with briar force rather than oppose it rather than risk destruction. They forget, there always destruction, not always freedom. If no hope of resistance, as many think, you can see how they feel alliance only good step. My heart is knowing resistance is possible, necessary. Can succeed but difficult. At the moment we are at disadvantage because we do not know this power or how it operates or where bats come from. Rumors of deep earth-mouth in the mountains, half-night flying from here, but I learn no more than that. I send questions to the newts and others that breathe the water."

"My Old Wise One," said Morduc, "the story I live says the same as your story. The force which attacks you I know as Master of Darkness. He has kidnapped the daughter of the King of Time and holds her, I believe, in his castle on the coast, where I am going to try to free her. His sign is the black briar rose. My own true love was attacked by one of his snake agents, on the other side of the forest. My journey watched by crows. If you can tell me how to safely and secretly cross the mountains, I may be able to reach some of those on the coast opposed to the Master of Darkness, though what I can do, once I get there, to lure him into a fatal error, I cannot tell. What is most important, however, is that I arrive secretly. As for the bats, I may have solution to marsh defense."

"So much to say, student!" said the OWO. "Very good, oh green young shoot, oh Morduc. I can help you through the mountains, and give other advice for when you get there. If you can stop the black briar master, you give us much future defense. Yet if you can baffle bats now, we can live till you succeed in great task."

"Hold a perpetual festival over all the island and the lake. Flutter decorations to jangle their ear sight," said Morduc.

For a moment, the only sound in the grotto was the trickling water. Suddenly the OWO hissed, his crest rose, and the blue-white light appeared.

"Our OWO approves," said King Rana, "but I myself do not yet give it eye life."

"Ears!" said the OWO jubilantly. "Of course. Gaudy to blind their ears. The frog friend speaks well. Now I must rest."

As King Rana and Morduc went back up the long tunnel, Morduc outlined his plan to King Rana and explained the reasoning behind it. By the time Morduc was ready to leave several days later, the island and the lake had been covered by a network of stakes sunk into the marshy ground and the bottom of the lake. Between the tops of the network of stakes were stretched strings. Hung from the strings were various lengths of cloth of multitudinous colors, strips of wood, metal circles, spirals and stars, and lamps of various shapes and sizes. Turned, twisted, and jangled by the wind, the objects formed an ever-moving canopy over the entire island and much of the lake, yet one which was still open to the sun.

CHAPTER 31

The Water Road

Anga was almost recovered. He could easily put his weight on the leg which had been broken, and although he still limped slightly, he was strong, sleek, rested, and fit.

Morduc too was in excellent health, even if he did pace for long hours back and forth on the shore with his head down, pondering and thinking. Now was his last day on the island. No one had been told. Only King Rana and the Old Wise One knew. He had yet to have his final interview with the OWO in the greenly lit grotto, but otherwise, all was in readiness. His bags were packed with enough food for the journey both for himself and Anga and the ponies and his boxes reswaddled in burlap and made watertight against emergencies. The OWO would give him his route, but how he would help him defeat the Master of Darkness was as yet unclear. They had agreed it would be best for him to leave after nightfall to escape the prying eyes of the day. The OWO had said he would tell him the way. He thought of his beloved Marianna left far behind at her father's house. He longed to hear her laugh, to see her teasing, loving look, to feel her touch.

Finally it was time to see the OWO. Morduc walked through the forest of flutterings that had been suspended above the island. He did not know whether the idea would actually work, since there had been no subsequent attack, but all had agreed it was an ingenious tactical effort. He entered the gate and went through the hall. King Rana was on his dais, surrounded by various of his functionaries to whom he was talking about the administration of the lake and marsh. He merely nodded as Morduc passed him and entered the passage that led to the Old Wise One's grotto.

Down, down, down he went, wondering what the venerable amphibian would say to him. As he came closer, he heard violent splashing below him. He began to run down the dim, damp passage. On the rock, he saw the OWO struggling with a dark, horn-covered shape. A great black bony head, with a huge jutting jaw, held the OWO by the back of the neck and was lifting him and crashing him down on the rock again and again. The creature did not have legs but supported itself on bony fins, half in the water and half out.

Morduc drew his sword and, giving a battle yell, sprang into the water and made for the rock. Meanwhile the OWO was twisting and turning, trying to free himself from the black bony beak. The green light of Morduc's sword filled the grotto, startling the creature momentarily so that it stopped crashing the old one on the rock. As Morduc reached the wet rock and climbed out of the water on to it, the creature dropped the old one with a muted, wet hissing sniff of frustration and turned ponderously toward Morduc.

Morduc saw two gleaming red eyes under horny projections and two air holes in the front of the hard bony beak. Morduc lifted his sword and struck with all his strength directly on the coal-black snout. The sword glanced off, making no impression at all. The huffing and snuffling beast, ungainly on its bony fins, continued to lurch toward Morduc, trailing a huge coiling tail behind it. As the beast hoisted itself along, Morduc could hear the clacking and scraping of its armor plates on the wet rock. Morduc backed away slowly. He could hear the rasping labored breath of the OWO on the far side of the rock where the beast had thrown him. The creature humped forward, and the hooked beak opened as if to snatch Morduc and bite him in half the way a bird might bite a worm drawn up from the wet earth.

Morduc sprang to the side and then up on to the back of the beast. Working the point of his sword down between the plates of the neck, he cut and dug and thrust. The great bony beast writhed in agony and let out a piercing scream that echoed in the cavern and seemed to pierce right up through the rock. He twisted and coiled, trying to shake Morduc off. He lashed his pointed tail across his back trying to brush off this little green stinging fly, but Morduc hung on to the sword, now sunk deep within the beast's neck. Morduc worked the emerald sword ever deeper between the plates, searching for the fatal node. The creature increased its contortions and just as it resorted to flinging itself on its back to crush its attacker, Morduc felt the sword separate the final strands of a fibered toughness and slip free. Morduc flipped off backward into the water as the creature went completely limp.

Morduc swam back to the rock and clambered up to see what he could do for the OWO. The green sword blade was covered with the same tarry black blood that was oozing out of the beast on the rock. The OWO was still alive when Morduc reached him but was gasping hoarsely. "Water Road. Take Water Road. Safest now. Bone Faces dead," and then he sank back. Morduc lifted the old one's head and cradled it in his arms. As he did so, the crest on the OWO's head rose up and forward and the blue-white light shown out from beneath it, brilliantly, filling the entire grotto with light. The OWO was speaking again. "Take StarStone." The OWO turned in his arms toward him, and Morduc saw that the light came from the back of the OWO's head beneath his crest. Resting in a pouch in the soft green skin beneath the crest was a huge, brilliant, transparent blue stone. Shifting and trembling within the blue clarity was a white multipointed star like a creature of light swimming effortlessly in a clear blue sea. Morduc gasped. He had never seen anything so beautiful, either in mortal or elfin realms. The life of the elves resembled it, but diffused and intangible rather than concentrated and perceptible as was this. Such things existed even for elves only in stories of their lost kingdom beyond the horizon of time.

Morduc heard noises in the tunnel coming toward the grotto. "I must not take it from King Rana and the Frog Kingdom," said Morduc.

"Not Froggan," hissed the OWO. "For you, my best pupil, loved. My last gift. *Take it!*" Morduc reached under the raised crest behind the OWO's head, lifted the jewel out of its pouch, and slipped it into his pocket. The crest fell back limp, covering the stone's now-empty socket, as the OWO slumped in Morduc's arms.

Rana and a troop of guards appeared on the bank. Rana immediately splashed the short distance to the rock. "Is he still alive?" he asked Morduc.

"Just barely," replied Morduc. The king went to the OWO and spoke to him but received no reply.

"He is gone," said Rana simply. "The best counselor and friend a king could have." The frog guards dragged the bone-face fish out of the water onto the sloping stone and then entered the pool, churning it to foam as they searched it for other enemies. They found nothing and returned to King Rana on the rock. He dispatched one for more help. Then, turning to Morduc, he said, "When we are alone, we will discuss what has happened here. The OWO had said to me that there might be an attack in some other way than through the air, but I had no idea he meant on himself. For now though, enough."

Presently other guards arrived, lifted the OWO, and carried him up the passage. Others attached ropes to the bone face fish and began dragging the scaly carcass laboriously up the stone incline, scraping as it moved. Morduc and Rana followed. When they had attained the surface, Rana ordered preparations for the funeral of the OWO to begin and directed that the remains of what he called the HalfFish be burned at the place where the pyre of the bats had been. Rana also ordered a general alert to be sounded.

The frogs in the hall looked frightened as the shapes were carried by. All over the island the sound of the alarm bellow was carried from one distended throat to another. Rana gave directions to his chief of guards to search the entire island and lake for any signs of intrusion and then report to him. When these directions had been given, Rana indicated to Morduc a small rush door on the other side of the main hall. They entered it, and Rana closed the door behind them.

Within the room was a large silver-green sphere that reflected their faces and bodies in the curving mirror of its surface. "Let us enter the bubble before we talk."

Morduc looked. "I see no door, King Rana. You will have to instruct me."

"Just step through its wall. It will accept you." Morduc stepped up to the green-silver surface and reached out to put his hand on it. The hand slipped right through, disappearing within so he could not see the end of his arm, his wrist, or fingers. He lifted a knee and a foot and put them inside as well and leaned forward. With a soft pop, he was through. He stood in an arched sphere filled with a soft green light and a tuneless music that Morduc was sure he had heard before but could not place when or where. He looked out through the walls and could see King Rana clearly, yet knew he could not be seen. Suddenly, Rana's huge head came through the filmy, seamless silver wall and then the rest of him.

"We will not be disturbed or heard here," said Rana. "Now tell me, Morduc, what happened." Morduc did not reply, still lost in the miracle of the music-filled green-silver surface of liquid light. "Morduc," said Rana gently. "Time is short. The attack on the OWO is significant. This place in which we talk was one of his gifts to me." Morduc turned his attention to King Rana and told him the little he knew, how he had simply come upon the fight, how he had splashed to the rock, and how he had killed the HalfFish. Of the jewel, however, he said nothing.

"You did well, Morduc. The OWO told me about these HalfFish many years ago when I was young, but I thought they were creatures of the sea."

"Creatures? Are there more than one of such monsters?" asked Morduc in alarm.

Rana paused, looking at Morduc calculatingly. Then he said almost off handedly, "No. I don't think so. Not any longer. I have never seen one before, nor do I think the OWO had either. I did not think they, or rather it, could even reach us. Did the OWO manage to say anything to you before he died? I know he had much to tell, and you will be the worse for not hearing it, but if he managed to say even one thing to you, it might be your salvation."

"The only thing he said was something about taking the Water Road," replied Morduc.

King Rana looked astonished. "The Water Road? Did he really say *you* should take the Water Road?"

"I am quite sure that is what he said, but I don't understand how there can be a water road over the mountains."

"It isn't over. It's under," replied Rana. "Perhaps the OWO has come to think of you as truly one of us. The Water Road will be the way through the mountains you will like least, though for frog or OWO, it would be the easiest. You have a choice. I can easily put you at the continuation of the Land Road.

If you could fly, you could take the Air Road, but, of course, you cannot, and besides, would be most easily seen that way. But the Water Road instead of the Land Road! Most puzzling. Did he say anything else?"

"Only something about the bone faces being dead," answered Morduc.

"Ah!" said Rana. "That means the OWO believed you had killed the last of the HalfFish. Now I see why he thinks the Water Road is safe for you. Nevertheless, it is still up to you to decide. And you must do so soon if you wish to keep to your original plan of leaving tonight. That the OWO himself was attacked means the adverse powers grow bolder every day. The Water Road leads from beneath the OWO's rock into the mountain. I don't know where the exit is, but perhaps the OWO did. In a sense, he may have attracted the HalfFish to himself in order to save you and to make the Water Road safe."

Morduc's heart ached within him at the thought that his teacher had sacrificed his life for him. Could it really be so? Could such love exist? Rana continued, "The Land Road rises from the marsh on the other side of the lake. It goes over the mountains in various ways by several passes, but I am told that it is an exposed road. What do you think you will do?"

"I'm not sure yet," said Morduc. "But I will know this evening."

"I think further," said Rana, "that even though he was your friend and teacher, you should leave during the funeral of the OWO. There will be no one in the hall, if you decide to go by the Water Road, and if you wish to go by the Land Road I can detach a few of my trusted guards to take you on a rush boat to the opposite side of the lake."

"Very well," said Morduc reluctantly. He had come to have deep love for the OWO, whose jokes and wit and puns had amused him greatly during their long sessions of frog language learning. And now, considering the immense gift of the star stone and the further possibility that the OWO had given his life for him, Morduc was even less willing to leave without paying his last respects, but clearly Rana was right in saying that if he left during the funeral the fewest number would be aware of his departure. "I will think of which road to take and inform you as soon as possible."

Exiting the silver-green bubble, he left the rush-walled room, crossed the great hall, and went along the passage that led to his own room, where the two ponies were stabled. Anga was not there. Morduc went outside looking for him and finally found him on the shore, running back and forth, completely healed, snapping at the dragonflies which occasionally swooped down on him. Some of the other frogs watched him, greatly amused at his ineffectuality, and enjoyed themselves by snapping a snack out to the air with ease to show him how it should be done. Although he no longer wore the splint, some of the frogs had tied the red bandages around his neck to make a cloth collar.

When Morduc came up, Anga stopped playing. They walked out on a sand spit that was surrounded by flat-leafed lilies. Speaking softly, Morduc told Anga of the choice that lay before them. Which road did he think they should take? Were the ponies up to it? Morduc smoothed a spot in the sand. "Anga. Draw me one stroke for the Water Road and two strokes for the Land Road." The dog hesitated, sat back on his haunches, turned his head to the sky, then to the water, and then to Morduc. Finally he lifted his paw and slowly drew a single stroke in the sand.

"Then water it is," said Morduc quietly, and with a quick motion, he brushed over the sand until it was smooth again.

Afternoon was approaching. Morduc knew that he should prepare, but he was reluctant to leave the island to face the dangers in the water beneath the earth. He had faith in the OWO's advice, but the thought of traveling a blind road through the earth in water made him shudder, even if he knew why it was safer. What if they were to meet another HalfFish, and in its own element? At least in the open air, you can see where you are going half of the time, and even at night, there are the stars to guide you. He thought back to the night in the forest when stars had saved him.

Could stars penetrate the earth? But that was the point of going under mountain, to keep eyesight that flies from seeing him. Yet going under the mountains to go across them seemed to increase the risk. Could the agony of death have distorted the OWO's judgment? Could he have said the opposite of what he meant? Anga had thought it would be best, and it had appeared to be the Old Wise One's advice. He was committed to it, but he faced it with trepidation. He forced himself to return to the palace. He found King Rana outside the gate and signaled to him with his eyebrows that he had something to say. They returned to the silver-green sphere of the soft singing music and slipped within. "We have decided to go the Water Road, but we don't know exactly what it is. You said that it starts in the OWO's grotto?"

"Indeed, it does," said Rana. "I will tell you what I know. Beneath the rock in the center is a tunnel through which water from the grotto flows. Water fills it for twenty feet, but then it emerges, so the OWO has told me, into an open stream bed in the rock. If you are to go that route, you, your dog, and the ponies will have to swim under water for seven yards in order to reach a spot where you air breathers can live again. You must then walk along the stream bed until you find a ledge on which you can climb out. The one element in your favor is that the current will be with you. The HalfFish would have had to swim against the current for many miles, and then straight upward through the WaterGate to enter the grotto. That is how he must have reached the OWO. I gather from what little the OWO told me that after you pass down through the WaterGate, you are to follow the stream through the mountain."

"Very well," said Morduc. "How will I know when to leave?"

"The funeral will take place on the shore before we place the OWO in the rush boat to go to the burial ground. When you hear the drums and the singing, then you should go. The hall will be empty."

"Good," said Morduc. "I will say good-bye to you now. I do not know whether I will ever see you again, any more than I know whether I will ever see my dear Marianna, but if all goes well, perhaps you and your queen will be able to attend our wedding."

"Not only attend, my dear Morduc, but sing as well," said Rana, puffing himself up with pleased enthusiasm.

Morduc continued, "I appreciate your hospitality greatly. I fear that I have been responsible for these cruel attacks on your subjects. Your graciousness in never mentioning this possibility affects me deeply."

"Do not worry yourself," said Rana. "Even if it were so, it is the attack of evil on goodness. *That* we must all bear and are bound to oppose. Your love of Marianna—is that her name?—and your defense of us has been in no way deficient, and in these situations we must think only of love and courage and the future. I wish you every success and luck on your journey. If anyone deserves it, you do."

"You are most kind, King Rana. The assaults of Darkness make one feel small and singular and lonely. One wonders whether one can merely survive, let alone triumph."

"Where evil is concerned," rumbled King Rana reflectively, "perhaps the only survival is triumph. Yet even if there is no survival, some say there may still be triumph. But that is difficult Drefon's doctrine. Farewell, good Morduc. May you and the good and the green triumph. I will remain here a moment longer and listen to the music."

Morduc stepped out through the seamless green-silver surface of the bubble, left the room that contained it, and walked across the hall and down to the stable room. Anga was there with the two ponies.

"Have you told them?" asked Morduc nodding toward the ponies. Anga drew his one stroke for yes on the floor. "Good," said Morduc, and went over to the two beasts. They shifted nervously as Morduc began to load them carefully, making sure all of the bundles were watertight. Outside, the sun had already gone behind the elevated horizon of the mountains, putting all the lake in shadow. The sky was still light and reflected in the water of the lake making its surface a mottled mirror.

As he tightened the saddles, Morduc spoke softly and soothingly to the two ponies. Anga sat on the floor, occasionally scratching his ear with a hind foot or running his tongue over his muzzle. With the raffish red cloth collar around his neck, he looked completely satisfied with the situation—relaxed, confident, amused, and ready for anything. Morduc looked musingly at Anga's collar. He went over to the dog and untied the red cloth from around his neck. Putting his hand in his pocket, he brought out an object, tied it in a knot in the cloth, and then retied the cloth around the dog's neck. For the first time in their life together, Morduc saw the dog's relaxed amused expression vanish from his face and become somber and serious.

"Yes, good Anga. This greatest of all treasures I entrust to you to carry through the WaterGate."

As the sky darkened, a slight breeze sprang up, fluttering and rattling the lanterns, scarves, tin, and thin-wood shapes that hung over the island. Morduc heard a solemn drumbeat begin far away on the shore. Soon a deep, booming chorus joined it. As silently as possible, Morduc led the two ponies and Anga out of the room that had been their home for six weeks, back through the passage to the great hall, and then to the passage behind the dais. Down they went, quietly on the rushes until they reached the rock portion of the tunnel where the echo of the ponies' hooves began to sound cloppingly on the walls. Down, down, down they went, the faint fungal light on the walls weaker now than Morduc had remembered it, until they stood once again on the beach of the grotto of the Old Wise One with its incessant murmuring trickle of water and its now-empty rock in the center.

Morduc looked around him for any sign of life but saw none. Stepping into the water, he led them all behind the rock where they saw a partially water-filled hollow beneath the stone. Gingerly Morduc felt his way forward, leading the ponies. Anga, already swimming, brushed past them and ahead into the black hole in the rock. Suddenly he dropped under the water and disappeared from sight. Morduc took a deep breath and plunged beneath the surface of the water holding on to the halter ropes and pulling the ponies behind him. It was pitch dark, and he felt his head bumping on rock above him. Suddenly he lost his footing and fell down, down, down amid swirling water. He felt the halter ropes loosen as the ponies behind him fell too. He continued swimming vigorously, swimming blindly along with the current, pulling the ponies behind him. In the utter darkness as he swam, he wished for just a candle's glimmer in the water-filled, rock-bound tunnel. Suddenly there flashed ahead of him a brief burst of light which illuminated the silhouette of Anga swimming strongly below him. Encouraged, Morduc swam on. Finally, just as he thought his lungs would burst, he and the ponies splashed into calm water with air above it. He gave a great gasp, sank beneath the water again, but bobbed immediately to the surface. He continued swimming and pulling strongly on the ponies to bring them through the water. He felt rock under his feet and stood up. The ponies too stumbled to their feet and stood in the shallow water, blowing and gulping air. Somewhere up ahead, he could hear Anga sneezing and snuffling. All of a sudden he felt a shower of drops hit him.

"Anga, is that you?" he said cautiously into the darkness. A single small bark and a brief whine answered him. Slowly and carefully, but still in complete darkness, he led the ponies onward in the ankle-deep water. The air was warm, and there was surprisingly little echo from the splashing of the ponies in the stream. They had come through the WaterGate safely but were only at the beginning of the Water Road.

"Well," said Morduc to Anga and the two ponies, "let's see if we can tell where we are." Taking his sword out of its scabbard, he held it up. The faint green glow showed him that they were in an underground rock canyon not much higher than twice his height. The tunnel extended straight before them into the darkness. Anga was already a short distance ahead, nose in the air, looking back expectantly, waiting for them to follow. Follow they did, slowly and carefully on the damp, slippery rock with the water pushing them gently forward. They went on and on through the darkness.

Presently, the rock walls sank closer to the level of the stream. Cautiously, Morduc peered over the edge. By the light of his sword, Morduc still saw only the walls of a tunnel, but with a ledge on one side. On they went until the rock rill channel was only a few inches deep. Wearily and wetly, they finally climbed out on dry rock and stood there exhausted. By the light of his sword, Morduc got a bit of food for them all. After they were rested and refreshed, Morduc led the way onward beside the stream. At one point, the walls widened out into a pool full of fat, eyeless white fish, with long, trailing white whiskers on each side of their muzzles.

CHAPTER 32

Through the Mountains

They continued on their way hour after hour with no change in the tunnel or the ledge. They rested periodically, standing right there on the ledge with the stream running rushing by at their feet. Morduc was tiring. He estimated that they had been walking most of the night, but they still had found no outlet. He began to wonder how long they would have to go before they reached light again. Suddenly ahead of him, in the soft green glow of the sword, Anga had come to a stock-still stop with his head and tail down. He growled ever so softly. Morduc stopped too. He felt a faint wind on his face. Cautiously he moved forward. The sound of their steps began to change. Morduc could no longer see rock around him in the reflected green glow of his sword. They were in a vast cavern.

Up above them, Morduc saw hundreds of faint points of light, like hazy stars clustered together in irregular patches in a black sky. Since the river flowed straight across the cavern, Morduc led the ponies onward along its edge. As they continued, he felt the ground begin to rise ahead of them, even as the riverbed began to sink once again into the rock. That was a welcome signal. Perhaps the path would lead back up to the open air soon. As they continued across the great open rock room, one of the lights began slowly to descend. Swiftly and silently it came down and very gently settled on the neck of the second pony, which suddenly reared and neighed loudly, trying to shake it off.

Morduc turned and with his sword quickly lifted the saucer-sized creature off the neck of the pony. It looked like a huge headless spider, a pale, white glowing puffy circle from which extended a tangled multitude of filamentary legs like the tendrils of a luminous, air-swimming jellyfish. It flexed and explored with its legs the flat of Morduc's sword, from time to time dropping its central mouth to the glowing green sheen, trying to pierce it. Wherever the mouth of the medusan touched the sword, it lifted it quickly as if it had found the gem blade's surface unpleasant to taste. As Morduc swung the sword aside to deposit the soft white shape on the ground, it lifted itself up and off the green glowing blade, swinging on its invisible thread and began climbing slowly back up toward the ceiling. As he watched it ascend, Morduc saw that other of the lights had slowly begun to descend.

"Quickly," said Morduc quietly to Anga. Tugging hard at the two ponies' halters, Morduc began to move as quickly as he could up the incline they were on to get out from under the many pulsating patches of luminescence on the ceiling. When they came to rough-cut steps in the rock, Morduc bounded up them as fast as he could, still pulling at the ponies behind him. They struggled up the notched slope as rapidly as they were able, slipping occasionally but recovering and going on quickly.

After ten minutes of frantic scrambling, they reached a level space before a small arch in the rock. Morduc pushed the ponies through it and turned to look behind him. The whole path across the cavern was covered with the white nodes softly undulating and palpating the rock, trying to find what had passed. A few were following the trail in the direction of the steps, but most had begun to climb their invisible lines back toward the roof. Morduc ducked through the arch and found the ponies and Anga waiting for him.

"Close," he said. "Very close indeed." He pushed on through the narrow arched corridor which continued to slant upward at an easy rate. They could hardly hear the stream. After several hours of steady climbing up the sloped tunnel, Morduc saw ahead a faint shaft of light falling sideways on the path. Cautiously he approached and found a jagged window in the corridor which opened into a high chimney within the rocks. He stuck his head through it, looked up, and saw the faint blue of the morning sky far above him, still dotted with one or two bright stars. How uplifting they were, how different from the spurious star light of the cave polyps.

"It's morning," he said, "and we are on the westward side of the mountain, Anga. We have been traveling all night, but we must push on still. We can't rest so close to those caverns." Taking the rein of the lead pony, he continued through the corridor. A little further along, they came to another break in the interior corridor wall, and this too admitted a little light from above. Morduc saw that the ceiling was cracked next to the window. They continued along the corridor by the light of the cracks or by the light of Morduc's sword until they saw up ahead of them a clear, open patch. When they got there, the light indeed was coming fully into the tunnel, but the roof over the path ahead had completely fallen in, blocking the path, though leaving a large, rough-walled open-rock cylinder leading up to the sky. It was wonderful to be able to look up and see the dawn light, but utterly baffling to see such a huge pile of rock in front of them. Water had collected in a small pool just outside the tunnel mouth; otherwise, the rock chimney was barren.

"We'll rest here for a while," said Morduc, "and consider what to do next." Morduc slipped the packs off the ponies, got out some grain for them, and let them munch within the shelter of the tunnel. He let them drink from the pool in the open air, but then brought them back inside the tunnel. Then Morduc and Anga ate, sitting just within the tunnel's mouth. Morduc rested with his back to the passage wall and his legs out in front of him. The light came straight down the cracked chimney in the rock, making jagged black shadows under the large rock chunks which blocked their way. Morduc chewed his dark bread thoughtfully. Suddenly he felt immensely weary.

"Anga, can you keep watch while I take a nap?"

The dog stroked yes. Morduc curled up at the entrance of the tunnel and immediately fell asleep on the rock floor of the tunnel.

When he awoke several hours later, the sun had already passed its zenith. The light coming down the chimney reflected off the back wall. Morduc climbed the pile of shards in front of him and looked down on the other side. The mouth of the tunnel on that side was completely blocked. He looked up the vertical sides of the chimney. What would he see, he wondered, if he climbed up to the top? He gauged the distance and looked for foot and handholds. He chose the western side, and looping a coil of rope over his shoulder and chest, he stepped from the pile of fallen rock to the wall, and slowly began to climb. Inching his way carefully up the nearly vertical rock, he slowly gained the top and disappeared over the rim. Anga sat just within the tunnel mouth, looking up, whining a bit, and watching. After about ten minutes, Morduc's head appeared again. Two lines of rope streamed down, and Morduc descended rapidly, pushing off from the inner wall, sliding down the rope, and then pushing off again to swing easily down in a few seconds the height which it taken him so long to climb.

"Anga, I can just see the ocean," he said excitedly, as he yanked on one end of the rope and it too swiftly slid down hissingly into a pile at his feet. "It is still very far off, but I can see it! We are closer to our goal than I expected."

For once, Anga too, usually detached, amused, and imperturbable, was excited and jumped back and forth. "But," continued Morduc, "the big problem is how to get out of here. There is no way down from the top of the chimney for the four of us, except falling, even if I could haul you and the ponies up. I can see a faint path descending the hills a mile or two further on. It runs from the scarp into the trees below. I suspect the continuation of this tunnel eventually runs into it. But we can't get past the rock pile into the tunnel."

Morduc made a thorough examination of the entire area again, but he found nothing that he had overlooked. A huge heap of rubble prevented their entering the tunnel that presumably lay beyond. "Well, Anga," said Morduc, "there seems to be nothing left but to get to work."

Moving stone by stone and handful of rock chip by handful, Morduc began the tedious task of clearing a path through the mound before him. All the rest of that day he worked, until he dropped into an exhausted sleep as the sky darkened above him. He slept soundly but awoke with a start in the middle of the night as some rock flakes tumbled off the pile with a granular hiss. He looked up to see the same stars he had looked at with Marianna when they first discovered their love. He could not see Caracanta, the star of love, but the soft, deep blackness of the sky and the pure points of light comforted him nevertheless, and he returned to sleep comfortably and easily.

Anga both slept and watched back down the tunnel a bit, but from that direction as well they were left in peace. When morning came, Morduc resumed work on the rock pile. Slowly he began to reduce its height, and by nightfall of the second day, he had exposed a small gap between the rocks and the tunnel roof beyond the mound just large enough to fit his hand through, a hand thoroughly scratched and roughened by the work it had been doing.

Sitting just inside the lip of the tunnel at nightfall, and eating his dinner, and drinking sparingly from the small trickle of water that flowed into the shallow rock basin nearby, he again watched the stars come out. On the third morning, he wrapped strips of cloth around his hands and continued to enlarge the opening. By noon it was just large enough to admit a single kneeling pony without packs. After a short rest and a meal, Morduc led the first pony out of the tunnel, across the small basin and to the foot of the large rock pile. Carefully, carefully, they mounted the shifting rocks. At every step, its hooves slipped on the gravel flakes. But slowly, slowly, the pony mounted higher and higher on the pile until it reached the top. Then Morduc slipped through the hole and, trying to keep his footing on the steep slide down into the dark tunnel on the other side, pulled the halter rope. The pony hesitated and then came forward, slipping and sliding down into the tunnel on its knees.

"Good girl," said Morduc, looping the halter rope over a rock and scrambling back up the rock-flake slope for the other one. The second pony managed to squeeze through with no less difficulty than the first. Now Morduc went back, and in four more trips brought all the bags, boxes, packs, and saddles, dragged each up the rock pile, and pushed it down into the tunnel through the hole. Finally he went back for Anga. The dog went up the pile easily and easily slid down the other side into the dark tunnel where the two ponies were waiting patiently amid their loads. Finally Morduc himself slid once again down the pile. By this time he was hot, dusty, and tired. Nevertheless, he loaded the two ponies, tied them together, one after the other, and, taking the halter rope of the first, pushed on cautiously down the tunnel.

Back at the chimney, in the still heat of the afternoon, a glossy black crow lit high on the east rim. As he perched there, cocking his eyes about, some rock flakes on the pile far below shifted, sliding down into the small trickle of water. The crow looked carefully, searching the bottom of the chimney for any further movement for several long minutes. Finally, seeing nothing, he took wing again and flew off.

Morduc continued down the dark tunnel. This section too was broken by clefts in the roof where water had come through, but the small party encountered no other total collapse to stop them, and just as the sun began to grow huge, red, and round in the west, as if it would displace a world's weight of water, they came to the end of the tunnel, hidden behind a screen of cedars. The path continued on to a ledge that zigzagged down the side of the mountain. Morduc stopped briefly on one of the switch backs and looked up at the huge rock peak towering high, bare and gaunt above them, through which they had come. The further down the mountain side they went, the thicker became the trees, and by nightfall they were in a dense woods.

Pushing off the path some distance, Morduc found a small grassy dip in which to camp for the night. One of the streams that came off the face of the mountain tumbled through the forest nearby. The ponies, Anga, and he all drank deeply and settled in for the night.

The next morning, they got up, ate quickly, and packed. They began to move forward but more cautiously than ever, now that they were in the open again and would be coming eventually to paths undoubtedly watched by minions of the Master of Darkness. They moved carefully and quietly down the trail during the whole morning. Around noon, they reached a point in the path where it fed into a larger trail coming from the north. Morduc looked to his right, north up the larger trail and then left to his south but saw and heard nothing in either direction. Carefully and quietly he led the two ponies onto the wider trail, and they continued their descent.

They encountered no one as they moved through the scattered light on the floor of the forest. Twice during the afternoon, however, Morduc thought he heard something behind him on the trail, but when he stopped to listen, he heard nothing more than the scramble of squirrels, the nattering of insects, and the calls of small birds. They went on through the cool aromatic air of the forest with increasing care and caution. Toward evening, they again pulled off the trail. Morduc relieved the ponies of their burdens and let them graze. He fed Anga and himself and lay back on the packs, looking up through the tall trees at the darkness deepening the blue of the sky.

Clouds were coming in from the west. He had not seen the ocean since he had climbed to the top of the chimney, but every now and then he caught a faint whiff of salt tang and fishy decay carried far inland by the breeze. The sky continued to darken and fill with clouds as the breeze became a strong wind. He could only see an occasional star in the rifts between the scudding clouds. There was no moon yet. Lying on the forest floor, looking up into the high rustling leaves of the treetops, he felt that the wind was not just moving leaves, but blowing lives here and there. He was but a green leaf himself, blown about the beautiful earth. Would he be a dry leaf eventually? Between golden unfolding and brown desiccation, what? Budding and flowering in a day's light with whatever excellence and beauty he could summon? With Marianna, it would be enough, but this Master of Darkness did not want that. He wanted to swallow all light, to gather all buds to himself, to kill, to rot, to discard.

Morduc tried to think of a plan. How should he approach the city? How could he keep himself safe until he decided what to do? How would he find Plummet's friends, if they were still alive? He especially wished he had John's help now. Together they could certainly have formulated a strategy. Without his friend's energy and Marianna's counsel, he felt unequal to the task he had accepted.

Suddenly, he thought he heard the flubbering blow of a horse in the distance. Silently he crept to Anga and whispered in his ear, and then Morduc slid off through the bushes back along the trail. Anga stayed put. A few faint taps of rain began to fall on the leaves. Morduc continued creeping through the trees slowly and carefully, moving parallel to the trail. After he had backtracked for a little more than an hour, he suddenly saw a slight movement ahead of him through the bushes. As he crept closer, he saw two horses tethered and munching contentedly on the lush forest grass around them. One of the horses lifted its head and blew air out of its nostrils noisily. He could see no one with them. The two horses just seemed to be there.

Morduc drew back silently the way he had come and began to circle the horses carefully. As he did so he caught sight of two figures huddled together under a dark-brown blanket at the foot of a tree. The rain was now beginning to come down heavily. He stopped and watched, but they did not move. As quietly as he could, he went back the way he had come.

Obviously, these figures had been behind him on the trail. He was certain they had not followed him through the mountain. Where had they picked up his track then? Perhaps they were not following him but were merely going in the same direction. He slithered back through the damp leaves toward Anga and the ponies, pondering his difficulty. He did not relish the prospect of taking on two enemies at once, nor did he know what quality of fighters they might be. Perhaps the Master of Darkness had his spies at the frontier, alert to track whoever entered his territory. If only John had been there, the Red Knight's strength and speed would have been decisive in a situation like this.

By the time he got back to Anga, he was cold and wet. He huddled under his thick cloak. The figures probably had stopped for the night if the tethered horses meant anything. They were not likely to come up upon him in the dark, though that was not an impossibility. Would it be best to stay put and simply wait for them to pass in the morning or should he get moving again now in the dark and storm and so perhaps outdistance them? Since no one had passed him on the trail, it was unlikely that they had sent a message on ahead. Perhaps these two were merely meant to drive him into the arms of others. On the other hand, they had not seemed to wish to be known, as they would have if they had been mere beaters, intending to flush the game for the true hunters.

He decided eventually it would be best if he were to move on that very night. Quietly, wearily, he loaded up the ponies again, and in the rain and darkness, split now and again by flashes of lightning striking down on the looming mountain behind him, he slowly returned to the trail. The four moved forward carefully on the soggy ground for several hours until they came to one of the many streams that cut the forest on their way to the sea. The path slanted down steeply to the ford through two high banks. Morduc suddenly saw the possibility of setting a trap there. First he took the ponies across the stream, down the trail a ways and off into the trees, where he tied them. Morduc and Anga went back up the trail, reforded the stream on foot, and climbed up the back of the right hand rise until they found themselves looking down fifteen feet or so from the lip of the bank on to the path below. They looked around for a thick bush to protect them from the rain, crawled under it together, and waited for the dawn.

In spite of the storm, Morduc fell asleep, and it was full light when Anga lifted his muzzle from his forepaws, turned to Morduc, and licked his face. The elf sat up with a start and asked the dog whether two other travelers had passed yet. The dog drew two strokes, "No," with his paw. Morduc explained to Anga what he wanted him to do, and the great gray triangular face seemed especially amused at the thought of the joke they were going to play. He trotted silently away through the underbrush in the direction of the ford. To Morduc, it was not a joke, however, and he wondered whether his plan would work. He lay flat on his stomach at the edge of the little earth cliff. Beneath him ran the path and to his right was the ford. The water purled along softly. Butterflies and bees searched through the wood and along the stream edge for nectar-filled blossoms.

Presently, from up the trail, Morduc heard the soft, cautious footsteps of two horses. They stopped for a considerable length of time and then came on again very, very slowly. As they came in view of the ford, they stopped again, and Morduc could see the two figures on the horses, cloaked both in dull brown robes with hoods over their faces. They had packs on their saddles as if they had ridden a considerable way. They hardly seemed as threatening as Morduc imagined servants of the Master of Darkness would be. One carried a quiver of arrows at the horn of his saddle and wore a strung bow over his back. The other carried a large quarterstaff under his arm, like a lance.

What was more distressing to Morduc, however, was their attempts at silence. They did not seem to wish to be heard or seen by anyone. They started moving again in single file, the one with the bow riding behind and the larger one with the quarter staff in front, approaching the ford cautiously. Just as the second rider came directly beneath him, Morduc whistled shrilly and jumped directly down on the second rider. At Morduc's whistle, Anga had charged out of the bushes at the side of the trail, barking and snarling and nipping at the hocks of the first horse, driving it in panic, splashing across the ford and down the trail. The rider struggled in vain to rein it in, but the dog drove the horse ahead of him, thus separating the two travelers.

Morduc had knocked the second traveler off his horse and now the two of them rolled over and over on the ground struggling for advantage. The brown-robed figure was quick and difficult to control. It tossed back the skirt of its robe and quickly pulled a short knife. Morduc was astraddle the figure, struggling for control of its knife-thrusting arm, when suddenly the brown hood fell back and Morduc looked into the face of—Marianna.

CHAPTER 33

Middock the Magician

"Marianna," he screamed. "It's Morduc."

Marianna stopped attempting to plunge the knife into him and looked in amazement. "Morduc?" Another pause. "I could have killed you!"

"Indeed!" said Morduc laughingly as he rolled off her on to his back in the middle of the trail. "Are you so bitter I won the wrestle the last time we played this game?"

"Ah, but this was no game, and I might indeed have killed you. I have been in continual practice since I recovered." And then smiling mischievously, she added, "Besides, I let you win last time."

"Did you?" said Morduc, delighted. "But why aren't you at home?"

"And why aren't you on the coast? Where have you been?"

"I'll tell you all about it later. Who's with you?"

"A young woman named Illanna. She says she knows you."

"Good grief," said Morduc, jumping up. "Anga will terrify her. But no, I forget, he will know her." And sure enough, as they both turned their heads toward the ford, Anga came bounding and frisking back, and close behind him came Illanna with the horse now under control, riding swiftly back to save her traveling companion. She rode up and sprang to the ground, brandishing the staff which she had held on to even as her horse had bolted.

She was about to brain Morduc when Marianna cried out, "Wait, Illanna. Wait. It's Morduc."

Morduc sat plump down on the trail, laughing joyously. "Don't worry, Illanna. Your traveling companion can take care of herself. She almost took care of me."

Marianna casually resheathed her knife and offered a hand up to Morduc, who accepted it. "Well, now that we are here," he said, as he and Marianna brushed themselves off, "let's get off the trail a bit and have a talk. We need to devise some sort of effective plan." Morduc led the way across the stream and down the trail. Soon he turned off to the left and burrowed into the woods where his own ponies were tied.

They all sat down and looked at each other. Illanna sat scratching Anga behind his ears, and Morduc, his heart full of joy, looked into Marianna's young and beautiful face. With her hood back, her dark brown hair fell about her face, her large dark eyes sparkled, and her full red lips shone like living rubies.

"How did you get here?" he asked.

"Oh, I just ran away," she replied archly. Morduc doubted that. There would be more to the story.

"Are you all right?" he asked.

"Yes. At least, I think so. I recovered fairly steadily after you left. Only just occasionally I feel a passing chill at the bone still, when the memory of the snake passes through my mind. But aside from that, I am as strong and quick as ever, as you learned, and I am so glad to see you again that I can hardly sit still." Taking Morduc's face in her two small hands, she gave him a strong, hard kiss full on the lips.

Illanna sat watching the lovers, thinking wistfully of her own lost love. Anga remained contentedly stretched out, his tongue lolling, as Illanna continued to scratch behind his ears.

"It really is too dangerous for you to be here," said Morduc.

"Pooh," said Marianna. "Are you of all people going to talk to me like an overprotective father or brother? Would you rather not have me here to see—and touch?"

"I would rather have you safe."

"And where is that, these days? Better to be here and take the risk of battle with you than languish in some silly surface safety back home. What have I to live for if I lose you anyway? But perhaps Morduc is saying indirectly that I would be a hindrance to him in this battle?"

"Morduc is never indirect with his beloved," said the elf. "I apologize for what might have seemed doubts."

"Well then," said Marianna. Better to be here and with you than back home. I would have come with you anyway if the snake had not bitten me. What I am amazed at is that you are no further along than I am. I only left nine days ago. What happened to delay you?"

Morduc was again amazed and admiring of the spirit of the girl. In the warm sun, which was making the rain from the previous night steam off the damp ground, Morduc told her briefly of his stay with King Rana and of his journey through the mountain.

She in her turn told him how when she had regained her strength she had broached the subject of following him to her father. She had said she was going with or without his permission and had spoken only so he would not think she had been abducted. With Lord Ballan's knowledge then, though not his agreement, she had slipped away one night and gone north to hit the road over the flint fields and the pass of Durbaneen. On the way, she had met Illanna and learned of their common goal.

"And you too," said Morduc, turning to Illanna. "Are you another one of these runaway women?"

"It's not as funny as you think, Morduc," said Illanna. "Steingar became impossible, and I am not altogether sure that he may not have followed me out of some misguided notion that he must protect me. He really intends to decide how I live my life. So yes, I did run away, but it wasn't a real life, a life of my own choosing which is one's only true life, that I was living back there on the farm. I am here, and I will help if I can, and in the process I hope to find L'Orka. We have made it this far with no more difficulty than smart, tough, country-raised girls can handle, but I am, nevertheless, very glad to see you, Morduc. I think two such women as Marianna and I are a match for much, but nevertheless, I am glad to see you, as an ally and man at arms."

"Well, Illanna, as surely as I am man, I am ally. I thank you for your gladness. We may be able to go on all together." Here Marianna gave him a sharp look of inquiry. "To determine that, however, I need to know what problems you have had? What kind of opposition have you met with in your efforts to enter this district?"

"None really," said Marianna. "We encountered rough weather on the mountains and a kind of foolish, boasting land pirate whom we made short work of. There were dark nights and interested animals, but no other attacks. Why do you ask so urgently?"

"We need to know if the Master of Darkness is tracking us. What animals showed interest?"

"Forest pigs, large cats, a bear or two."

"Was that all?"

"Yes."

"Bats?" asked Morduc tentatively.

"No. What a horrible thought," said Illanna.

"Birds?"

"Birds! Of course, there were always birds, but none showed any interest in us, and what could they do anyway? We are a match for any birds even if we are not for bears."

"But," interjected Marianna, "there were the crows."

Morduc shivered.

"Tell me, Illanna."

"Well, now that you mention it," answered Illanna thoughtfully, "and curiously so, we were dogged always by those black birds. Is it significant?"

"All or some of these beasts might have been the agents of the Master of Darkness. If they were, they may know of our mission."

"Morduc," said Marianna, "none were like the snake that bit me, though we seemed to see the same crow day after day. All the beasts we met were fell and terrible in their way but seemed mere nature, disinterestedly interested, you might say, deadly but without malice. I think we have been ignored by the powers of the Master. I doubt very much he knows we are here. We came past the border guards very carefully, and they did not seem any too careful of their job, to tell you the truth. Though I am sure that the Master is always a force not to be underest—" She broke off and listened intently. The ferns in the woods nodded silently in the soft breeze sliding off the morning mountain. The others too looked into the woods and listened.

"There it is again," said Marianna softly.

"What?" said Morduc.

"A sort of a song, on the trail behind us. Not like human song. More like the noise of nature itself, without intense, focused human harmonies, but not orderless either. Tuneless, but repeating, in a self-similar way, yet peaceful for all that. It has been behind us off and on in our journey here, but we never saw or could imagine its singer."

"Could it be Steingar?" Morduc asked.

Illanna shivered. "Unlikely. He has no music of any kind in his soul," she said quietly, "even tuneless music."

"Stay here," Morduc whispered. "I'll try to see who or what it is." He crept silently off through the bushes in the direction of the trail, knowing full well that to an experienced eye, the place where they had left the trail would be completely evident. He crept silently onward toward the sound which rose and fell on the breeze. As he approached the trail, the faint sound suddenly stopped, and Morduc froze. Through the grass and bushes, he saw a large shadow on the trail. He heard a voice softly calling,

"Morduc! Morduc? Show yourself." Morduc chilled to his bones and shrank as close to the soil as he could get. No one should have known of his presence there. Had the Master of Darkness sent one of his talking mastiffs? Had he tracked him down now?

"I know you're out there somewhere, you green blending elf," said the voice, which began again to hum a tuneless sequence of variations that Morduc had heard before, going up and down in an apparent randomness that nevertheless had a kind of emergent order to it. Morduc heard a flapping over his head, and just as he looked up, a crow perched on a branch above his head. The bird cawed raucously.

"Have you found him, then, my airy friend," said the voice breaking off its humming. "Come out, come out, wherever you are. Though you are green, this fruit is not, but rather ripe ready to assault the pits of Darkness, to plumb them without pity but without plummeting into them. Now, Morduc, appear, I do conjure you. We have so little time and so much to do."

At last recognizing the voice of Plummet the Fisherman, Morduc stood up and came forward through the bushes in joyful wonderment that his acquaintance from the gorge would be there. "Plummet! Are you really here?"

"Shhhhh. Not so loud," said the fisherman. "Spies really are everywhere, but perhaps fewer out here than closer in. Their elements are water and darkness. They but seek control of light and air. Still . . . Let's get off the road and quickly, good friend. Then we can see where we are."

Morduc led the large old man, with his broad-brimmed yellow straw hat and his long white beard back through the trees and underbrush to the small clearing where Anga, Marianna, and Illanna were waiting for him. When they got there, the old man threw down a large bundle which gave a muffled clank as it fell and then took off his hat and wiped his head with a large purple handkerchief. The crow, silent for once, flew to his shoulder and perched there.

"Oh, ho," he said, looking at the women, "The green reed has caught himself some fish, and slippery fish they look to be too." The girls looked at each other and shifted uneasily, not knowing what to make of the strange old man.

"It's all right. He is a friend," said Morduc. And then turning to Plummet, he said, "Do you have any news of Red John? You seem to have his armor with you."

"No, Morduc. I have no news of John. I went up and down the river for seven days and found no trace of him, and that leads me to think he may still be alive, and if, I repeat, *if* he is still alive, then, he may be making for the coast, and if, I say only *if*, he is making for the coast, he may want his armor, so I brought it along."

"How did you get here, then?" said Morduc.

"Just followed the pretty girls," said Plummet. Marianna and Illanna started and exchanged looks.

"So it was you," said Marianna, "behind us all the time?"

"And even before *us*, behind you," he said, turning to Illanna.

"How so?" she asked.

"When you walked on water," he replied.

"I never did," she said.

"Then you never crossed the deep river?" he inquired, "and so you are not really here then?"

"I came over a rough bridge. When I took the road from home, I came to a burned bridge over a wide, deep gorge. At that bridge there was a purple arrow pointing north. I followed the river for many days until it narrowed, and I did find a bridge to cross over on, several logs lashed together with vines. I felt it move under my feet, but I did get across, and it was soon after that I met Marianna on the road."

"Call me Bridgeman then, the architect of walking on air or water as the case may be. By the same route I came before you, by my crow friend's caw,

wing, and claw I saw you, let you pass, and then when you became double lass, I
followed fast. Say hi, say ho, say ha de li do." He started humming his mysterious
tune again.

"Yes, indeed," said Marianna. "Here we are, and hi, and ho, and ha and all
that. What now?"

"Why," said Plummet, "On to the big city. Lights, bustle, crowds, conspiracy,
action, success. Surely such things are before us? And if not, come late, come
soon, dear death will come, drear at night, noble at noon."

The crow cawed quietly on his shoulder in a way that sounded slightly like
sardonic laughter.

"Your zest for death is remarkable, old man" replied Illanna. "Speak for
yourself in that matter, not for me."

"You do not want to die for your children before they are born. Is that it?"
the old man said gently. Illanna looked away and made no reply. He went on.
"Though I jest, I do not do so frivolously. Adventure and exertion and crisis
surely lie before us. And perhaps success. In the port of Kerballa, there we will
curb Mr. Dark's portable darkness. Oh, just a bit of rough sport in the twilight.
Since the fight *may* not be avoided, what a fine opportunity."

"If we survive," said Marianna.

"When we win!" said Plummet emphatically. "Methinks the vineyard may
just be ripe for harvest by now. But I grant you, it will be tricky, wresting
the vineyard from Dr. Dark's hands without wrecking it or"—holding up his
hands—"losing these pickers and stealers in the process. Such keepers of dark
do not like to have their vineyards taken from them, but you see, we must try,
for *their* wine is made of the blood of grapes." He leaned close to Morduc and
whispered, "It goes to their heads. Did you ever see a grape fight back?"

There was an awkward silence.

"Well? Have you?" Plummet asked.

"You baffle me, old man. I can't fathom your meaning."

"Vinegar, Morduc. Vinegar. We'll dress his salad yet. *Good!*"

The two women looked at each other a third time. Was this old man crazy?
Why did Morduc listen to him at all?

Illanna spoke up. "*You* seem eager, and *you* seem to have a plan, old man,
but we have had so much trouble getting this far that we haven't really thought
about what to do when we get there. But now, I presume, it is the time to do so.
What do you suggest, Plummet?"

"To enter the city, I propose that we split up once again. You, Morduc, I
would like to see disguised in some fashion. Meanwhile, I shall try to make
contact with my old friends, if they are still alive, if their blood has not become
wine for the tyrant."

"Very well," said Morduc. "I had planned to present myself in the character
of a magician."

"Excellent, excellent, Morduc. That will attract just enough attention, but not too much. Try to make it a sort of shabby magician, a wanderer with a bag of tricks, but not too clever, and a little venal in addition, quite unscrupulous in a timid and small-change sort of way. The Master will understand that. Can you manage it?"

"I can, indeed," said Morduc, warming to the role as it took shape in his mind. "Perhaps I shall call myself Mordukane the Magnificent. What do you think?"

"Pleasantly pompous," said Plummet. "Perhaps a bit more than I had in mind. It sounds like something one might see in a theater. We want something that might be painted on a tawdry canvas for a circus side show. Try for something scruffier."

"What about Slandar the Slippery?" said Marianna archly.

"Am I to be married to a tease?" said Morduc.

"If you please," rejoined Marianna. "But you wouldn't really want to strip me of my tease, would you?"

Morduc was about to answer in the method but then merely smiled and gave her a look that said love and delight together. "I'll work on the name," he said to Plummet.

"What about us?" said Illanna.

"That would be thought on," said Plummet. They sat there for several minutes in the sunlight-flecked green wood, talking over possible poses for Marianna and Illanna, but none suited the purpose of keeping them together. Finally Morduc suggested somewhat tentatively, "Perhaps this magician could be supposed to have two pretty assistants to, ah, shall we say, do his bidding. How does that strike you?"

"Two?" said Marianna in mock horror.

"I think you have it," said Plummet jumping up. "That does make you a somewhat more successful and impressive magician than I had wanted you to be, but there would be a significant additional advantage *if* you can make yourself into a rather old dotard of a magician and present the two pretty assistants as, shall we say, your 'daughters.' Can you do that?"

Marianna laughed, waggling her hand under her chin. "Oh, Father. What a gray beard you have!"

"Be careful there, daughter. If you don't have proper respect, I'll take you over my knee."

"Oh, la, *Papá*. What *would* people say? Me on your knee. That is not nice, Papá."

"More respect, young woman, or I'll sell you to the first pirate I meet."

"Oh, but, Papá, you have always sold me heretofore without respect of any kind."

"Wonderful. Wonderful," said Plummet. "You understand my idea, perfectly, of what I want the Master of Darkness to think of this traveling magician. If he thinks the magic is disguise for sleaze, the Master may not look beneath for the squeeze. That will be your disguise. He will suspect the worst and possibly miss the best, which will be the worse for him."

"Oh, Papá. And we your daughters too. What a shameful disgrace," chortled Marianna.

"Enough joking now, you two," said Plummet. "When the deed is done and all safe, there will be time enough to jest in joy. Is the plan agreed to?"

"I am worried," said Illanna.

"About what?" said Morduc.

"Two things. I am worried first that I will be so clumsy and ignorant in the magic performances that I will spoil the disguise."

"Don't worry about that," said Morduc. "I will teach you all you need to know. That really is no obstacle at all. Anything else?"

"Just one other trifling matter."

"Yes?" said Morduc.

"What if you are required to really sell us, oh my magical father? Despite what Steingar thinks, I would kill the man first."

"It is not a possibility," said Morduc. "I would die myself before I would let that happen."

"Good."

"Illanna," said Plummet carefully. "Would you feel that way even if it admitted you to the presence of the Master of Darkness himself?"

After a moment she spoke. "I see what you mean, perhaps, about the additional value of the disguise." And she said no more.

Thus it was settled that Morduc would travel toward the port city of Kerballa in the disguise of an itinerant magician with Marianna and Illanna as his assistants and that Plummet would go separately.

"I had best be off," said Plummet. "You remain here for a while, get your disguises together, and train your assistants." Here Marianna threw an acorn at Morduc. "Then come on by the best road you can find. Once in the city, come at least once a day to the fountain in the center, and I will find you myself or send someone with a message. For the moment, that is all we need to plan, I think. Do you agree?"

None had anything more to add. "Well then, with a ho and a hee and a hi, it's off to our games we go." Plummet shouldered his bundle again, picked up his staff from where it had lain, and started off through the copse back toward the path. The crow flapped its wings and sailed up through the trees. The fisherman started his tuneless tone sequence again. Morduc, Marianna, and Illanna remained behind in the green shade, listening to the song fade away into the distance. They sat silently for some minutes, resting in the peace of the woods, listening to the breeze in the tree tops and to the occasional quick scratching scamperings of squirrels on the bark. Finally Morduc said, "Well, we had best get busy with our preparations."

The two girls looked at each other slyly before answering almost in unison, "Yes, Father."

CHAPTER 34

Docked at Last

John, Palla Nad, and Yanibo stood on the deck beneath the sails of the slow, fat freighter as it approached the port city of Kerballa. It had taken them nearly a month to sail from Imbal, out the gates of Caracassoa, and up the coast to Kerballa. The Chauri Circus had been called by General Juncata to perform first for the public and then possibly for the general himself in private entertainments within the castle fortress. As they slid through the mouth of the Bay of Kerballa, they saw off to the north two black towers rising high into the sky above the battlements of the massive castle which rose above the town. From their position, the castle rock seemed to be attached to the tip of the peninsula, but John remembered that Plummet had said it was an island, connected to the mainland by a single bridge from the shore. They could just barely see a swarm of small ships clustered around the seaward base of the rock from which bales and boxes were swung up into the bowels of the castle in huge cargo nets. No ship could ascend the river to the town's docks without first passing the castle.

"So that is our objective," said John quietly to Yanibo.

"Yes, Red John. Big Rock. We crack. Ha, ha." The boy smiled broadly and began a dance on the deck of the ship. Chauri came bustling toward them in his black boots, white jodhpurs, red frock coat, yellow vest, and high silk hat. "Raaaadeeee to unload!" he bawled to no one in particular. "Get raaadeeee to unload." Other members of the circus troupe began to appear on deck, as did the sailors who took their docking stations. The ship continued to sail north across the bay until they sighted the mouth of the river, up which they must sail to reach Kerballa's docks. Then the ship turned east by north and slowly with the tide and a light breeze approached the estuary of the river Sokotra. The river ran along the south side of the town, and the closer they came to its mouth, the closer came the great castle on their left, which seemed to increase in height as they approached. Now they could see the high bridge which launched itself from the shore side of the city and attached itself to the huge front gate of the castle. The two tall towers loomed above the main bulk of the building like gaunt black claws or the spines of a damaged pitchfork. Anchored north and seaward of the castle's base, a large black sailing galley rose and fell at anchor as the wash of the sea waves flowed under it, breaking in white foam on the base of the rock.

Their broad-beamed freighter slowly made its way into the river mouth proper. Before they had come to any of the docks, they saw shoot out from a stone house on a jetty by the shore a smart cutter manned by four oars and a tiller man. In the bow of the cutter sat two tall, thin men dressed in black uniforms. The boat circled behind the freighter in order to align itself parallel to the ship and be going in the same direction. The tiller man hailed her through a megaphone. The port oarsmen caught hold of a ladder thrown over the starboard side of the freighter and held the cutter steady while the two men in black climbed somberly aboard. They stepped on deck with an air of decisive authority, asking no permission to come aboard. The captain of the freighter came down from the steering deck, and as he went past John, he said under his breath, "Juncata's port police," and passed on to the starboard bow to greet them. Chauri, bowing and scraping in his usual oily fashion, was dancing from one foot to the other off to the side amidships. The two men in black glanced at the rotund circus owner as they would have at a swollen insect, a brightly-colored fly gorged on offal and dung.

The captain handed a paper to the taller and thinner of the two port police, who looked at it carefully and then nodded curtly. The two in black stepped past the captain and began to stroll down the deck to where John, Palla Nad, and Yanibo were standing. Yanibo said something to Palla Nad, who quickly drew his flute out of his twisted rainbow-rope belt and began playing it. Yanibo flipped up on his hands and began walking up and down the deck on them. The two officers walked past, giving Yanibo and Palla Nad bored looks, but when they came to John, who had remained standing, holding on to the shrouds with one massive hand, they stopped and looked at him carefully. His bald head, carefully shaved each day by Yanibo with a razor bought from an Imbal barber, was now as brown and tanned as leather, complementing his by-now broad and long red-brown beard. Even in the rough leather vest and crude leggings which Yanibo had crafted for John's disguise, his massive shoulders, arms, and legs drew attention. One of the two policemen was about to say something when a shining string of saliva slowly dribbled out of John's mouth and down his beard. His head wobbled a bit and a soft, strange, empty laugh bubbled up out of his throat.

Yanibo did three backflips, landing on his feet in front of the policemen. Smiling broadly, he gave them a wink and tapped his head with his finger and said, "Big Man got baby head."

The thinner of the two policemen looked down coldly and unsmilingly at the small boy's upturned grinning face. "Just be sure he stays out of trouble," said one.

"No trouble," said Yanibo. "He do what I say." And then leaning confidentially toward the policemen, he cupped his hand around his mouth and said to them, "Look like bull. Fixed like ox. Think like ox too. Gotchee?"

The heavier-set, thicker-faced officer laughed a crude laugh, and said, "Gotchee, you little forest monkey. Just see that he doesn't do any damage when he gets drunk."

"No drinkee. No damage. He do what I say."

"See that he does for your own sake," said the thin one. They passed on down the deck, followed by the captain and Chauri, and descended the main companionway, where their progress through the hold could be heard by the noises of the animals below. Finally they returned to the deck after their inspection by way of the fo'c's'le ladder and checked even the bowsprit. By now Chauri was sweating with such nervousness that he had taken off both his hat and his coat and was mopping his head with his large purple handkerchief.

Finally the thin policeman who held the paper took a small carved stone stamp and a covered ink dish from his pocket. His companion held the dish while he inked the stamp and pressed it firmly on the captain's paper. He put the stamp and ink dish back in his pocket and returned the paper to the captain, saying, "Everything seems to be in order. Permission to dock granted. Proceed to number 13."

Then the officer in charge called sharply over the rail, "L'Orka!" John started at the name and moved as quickly as he could to the rail without attracting attention to himself.

A voice from below floated up, "Standing by, sir." The voice belonged to the tiller man, a dark-skinned, broad-shouldered sailor with a wide smile.

"Ready to receive us!" the police officer said.

"Aye, aye, sir," returned the voice, and the two officers disappeared over the rail, descended the dangling ladder, and stepped deftly into the cutter, which had stayed alongside the ship as it continued to move slowly up river on the tide. The cutter veered off to starboard and, cutting back downriver across the merchantman's wake, returned swiftly to the stone custom house and jetty, now well behind the freighter.

Well, thought John, *there can't be two such. It is a hopeful sign. At least Steingar didn't do him in, but can he really be working for the Master? When this is over, I shall send news to Illanna.*

The captain finally brought the ship to berth at a long low wharf with a drab, elongated cargo shed on it. The freighter was secured to the pilings both fore and aft, the broad cargo door in the side that led to the lower deck was let down onto the wharf to serve as a ramp and, out from the belly of the ship, awkward and reluctant, came the menagerie of the circus, the elephants and camels, the horses and ponies, the apes, the lions, and the tigers in their wheeled cages, blinking and snarling at the unaccustomed light. Chauri had even brought the ship-shaped wagon which served as the business office of the circus and in which he lived while the circus traveled by land.

Chauri was running up and down the wharf, trying to see to everything at the same time. John worked along with the other roustabouts, helping wherever his extra strength could be of use. Within a couple of hours, the entire substance of the circus was either on the open loading space of the wharf or under the shed.

Just as the disembarkation had been completed, a black coach stopped at the wharf's foot. Out of it stepped the skull-faced figure whom they had seen in the mayor's box in Imbal. He was followed by a tallish, dandified young man dressed in a suit of plum-colored velvet who held a scented handkerchief beneath his nose. He had on a soft hat of the same material as his suit, with a white ostrich plume floating above it. He carried a long, silver-headed ebony staff and stroked his little black silky mustache and goatee with a small gold comb mounted on top of a gold lorgnette. The skull-faced man and the dandy picked their way down the wharf through the wagons and animals and rigging until they reached Chauri. On seeing them, Chauri went into another paroxysm of bows, but this time with such great intensity and depth that John thought Chauri would surely tip over on the dock and fall on his head.

"You have finally arrived," said the skull-faced man sourly to the circus owner.

"You are so grim, Maksohn," said the other. "Give them a welcome, why don't you?"

"My superior welcomes you to Kerballa," said the man in black dourly. "Lord D'Orcade here is the Master's Master of the Revels. He is the one who will decide your fate."

"Such disharmonious discourtesy, Maksohn. That is no way to welcome visitors. Moreover, you overemphasize my importance. It is the general himself who makes all the final decisions. I am but his servant and agent. You always put things so coldly and bluntly, Maksohn. The joy of life resides in delicacy, but you are not accustomed to either I suspect, are you, Maksohn?"

"No," said Maksohn, hardly moving his thin lips. "It is not a delicate world."

"Indeed," said D'Orcade, looking at him through his lorgnette. Returning his attention to Chauri, he said, "Let me give a proper welcome to you, Mr. Cheeri. I am Marivaux D'Orcade, Master of the Revels for His Most Supreme Excellency, General Wansisterax Lanaltoolamie Juncata. I am completely at your service. We are all delighted and excited you were able to favor us with this engagement. Now about your accommodations . . ."

"Chauri, your most delicate honored sir," interrupted the circus owner.

"Excuse me?"

"Chauri, sir. Not Cheeri. My name is Chauri, Meestaire Lord Sir D'Orcade, by your most excellent pardon and leave, high mister, the name is Bombadorison Chauri. You may call me Bombi if you wish, sir lord."

"Yes," replied D'Orcade pausing, as he brought the lorgnette up again and inspected the fat circus owner through it. "Chauri, to be sure." He brought his lace handkerchief to his nostrils briefly, inhaled its perfume, and then went on. "The general has provided you a rent-free place to house and show your circus. It is the old arena building in the center of the city. It should prove ample in size. Mr. Maksohn here will remain with you and guide you there. But you understand, *you* will be responsible for your own support through public performances. The general is not unmindful of the sacrifices you have made in traveling here from Imbal, but he feels any further subsidy would diminish your, how shall I say it, your ambition to please. You and all your troupe should try to do your very, very best because I myself personally will be inspecting the performances."

"Yes, Mistor Lord. I understand that," broke in Chauri.

"But," said D'Orcade, tapping Chauri on the chest with his lorgnette, "after attending several of these performances, I *may* feel that one or two of the acts are of sufficient merit to recommend to the general. He *may* then order them to appear in a command performance within the castle before himself and his bride-to-be and her father and certain other selected noble guests."

In spite of himself, John started at hearing these words and could not help leaning forward with eager interest. Yanibo carefully put a hand out to restrain him and to remind him to retain his mask of idiocy. But Yanibo's gesture attracted the eye of D'Orcade, who began walking slowly toward John as he continued talking. "If these acts are satisfactory, you and they may receive some additional bonus. The general is a generous man to those who serve him well. Nevertheless, you must understand that there is no guarantee of this preferment and that your main responsibility is to provide the general populace with entertainments, as I am sure Herr Maksohn made clear to you in Imbal. If you do well, the general may condescend to become your official sponsor. If you fall short of expectation, well . . . that remains to be seen."

"Yes, my lord," sweated Chauri.

"Finally," said D'Orcade as he stopped and turned and spoke sharply to Chauri. "You do understand as well, Mr. Cherry, do you not, that the general holds you and you alone fully responsible for the good behavior of your troupe while you stay with us. If any one of them gets into trouble of any sort, if any of your wild animals should get free, or anything of that sort, the general will be displeased, and," leaning toward Chauri, he said in a low voice in which menace and his own fear were mixed, "we all know what happens to people with whom the general is displeased."

"We do? Yes. Yes. I mean, no, no, I don't know. I don't even want to know. But yes, yes. You have no worries at all. All my people are complete professionals." And here he glanced nervously at Yanibo, Palla Nad, and John as D'Orcade moved ever closer to them. "Absolutely complete professionals. Been with me for years. No trouble from any of them at all. We do our job and keep to ourselves and don't complain."

"Good, good, I am so very glad to hear it," said D'Orcade, who by this time had reached John. As he turned away from Chauri, his eye suddenly lit on Yanibo standing off to the side, with his young brown face and white-toothed smile. "What have we here, Chauri? Introduce me to this beautiful boy."

"Ah, Lord D'Orcade. That boy is a nobody, a troublema . . ." He stopped in midword as he realized what he had almost said. "He is a nobody, no troublemaker, of course, but just a jungle juggler we picked up rec . . ., ah, ah, I mean, sometime ago. I brought him up like he was my own son, but really, sir, a nobody, no one worth Your Lordship's notice. A mere savage still."

"Indeed," said D'Orcade as he inspected Yanibo through his lorgnette. "I must come to know you circus people better. I am not so aloof as I may seem. Call the boy."

"Yanibo," Chauri said roughly. "Get over here." Yanibo sprang forward, did two flips, and landed smiling in front of D'Orcade. "Stop that!" yelled Chauri. "Behave in a civilized manner. This very great man, Lord D'Orcade, the Master of the Revels himself of General Juncata, the one who has the complete decide whether to hire us or fire us"—Chauri gave these words heavy emphasis—"has shown great condescend to want you speak to. Now speak nice."

"Yes, boss," said Yanibo, saluting and smiling.

"Now, young man," said D'Orcade, placing his hand on the bare shoulder of Yanibo and looking him in the eyes, "What do you do?"

"Me juggle. Best acrobat. Juggle in circus."

"Most excellent, excellent," said D'Orcade, turning the boy around in a circle. "Perhaps you would accept an invitation to come to one of my private parties sometime to entertain and to meet a few of my friends? What do you say?"

"Mr. Chauri. Him boss. He gotta say. You ask boss. If good by boss, good by me."

"Charming, charming," replied D'Orcade, pleased at the boy's complaisance as he turned to the much-relieved circus owner. "Well, Mr. Chewi, or shall I call you Bumbi, now we are better acquainted? What do you say? Do you think you could arrange this charming child's appearance sometime?"

"Most surely, most gracious lord," said Chauri.

"Me juggle. Me make good show. Me make everybody laugh," said Yanibo.

"Fine, fine. And what was it that Mr. Churi called you just a moment ago?"

"Me Yanibo. You call Yano for short. What you say? You got coin now for Yano, your friend?" Yanibo held out his hand.

"What bad behavior," said Chauri, huffing and puffing. "Don't you recognize the great honor that is being paid to you? You shouldn't be begging like a mindless monkey. Don't I pay you enough?"

John suppressed a laugh at Chauri's foolish presumption. Chauri raised his hand to strike Yanibo, but D'Orcade stopped him.

"Oh, no, no, no, Bumby. Never strike a child." Then, smiling, he reached in his pocket and took out a gold coin and put it in Yanibo's outstretched palm and closed Yanibo's fingers over it. "Take this, my boy, for yourself, and there is more where that came from. He is a fine boy, Chauri, a fine boy. Be careful of him. I do not want anything to happen to him. Do you understand?"

Chauri had taken hold of Yanibo's shoulder and was holding him so firmly that the boy began to feel pain but still continued to smile. Chauri, bowing and scraping, replied, "Yes, of course, Meestaire. I understand very well."

D'Orcade stepped back and regarded Chauri closely through his lorgnette. "*No harm!*" he said emphatically. "Do you understand?"

In silent answer, Chauri lifted his hand from off Yanibo's shoulder and held it palm upward, as if to say, "See, I wasn't hurting him," and smiled guiltily at D'Orcade.

Meanwhile Yanibo skipped away from Chauri and, in full view of D'Orcade, tested the coin with his teeth. "Good money, Mr. Play Boss," he called out. "Yano play for you." And then turning to Chauri, he put the coin in the surprised circus owner's hand and said before skipping away, "Here Papa. You keep for me."

"Delightful, delightful indeed," said D'Orcade, turning away and strolling back up the wharf, talking over his shoulder to Chauri. Chauri turned quickly to Yanibo and hissed under his breath, "What are you up to, you young scamp?" but feeling the money in his hand, he looked at it again, bit it himself, and, finding it sound, pocketed it and hurried after D'Orcade.

"Now, Charri," said the Master of the Revels, suddenly all business, "the general expects you to perform regularly. The people need diversions. You must be ready to perform by the last day of this week. That will give you three days. I expect to see a superior job. I expect you to perform up to your recommendations. The general is counting on you. If you fail, that means I fail. I do not like to fail the general. In fact, I have never failed to secure what he wants. I always get what the general wants, even though it has not always been pleasant for, shall I say, my contractors? I become very, very angry when people displease me. Spare yourself that painful experience, Mr. Cheirry. Do I make myself clear?"

"Yes, Master Sir Lord D'Orcade," said Chauri as he bustled after the perfumed lord up the wharf.

"Beastly smell, this," said D'Orcade, waving his handkerchief in front of his nose as he passed by the elephants. The Master of the Revels picked his way through the confusion outside the dock shed and went on to where the carriage was waiting. Maksohn opened and held the door for him as he climbed in and then closed it after him. D'Orcade let down the window by its leather strap and, leaning out, spoke a last word to Chauri. "See that you don't fail me," he said, fixing the little fat man with a steely gaze through his lorgnette.

"I will not," replied the sweating circus master, bowing again, an action which brought his nose just level with the crest on the door, a black rose transfixed by a black-jewel-hilted sword. The carriage jolted forward, drawn along the dock road by two large black horses. The driver was in black as well as the two footmen on the back. Chauri shivered as he watched the coach leave. He pulled out his huge purple handkerchief to wipe the sweat of worry and exertion from his head. He then turned back into the shed and began talking to himself, "Why did I come? Oh, why did I come? Because I had no choice is why. Now what are we into? When I catch that little monkey, I'll . . ." But as he put his hand reflexively in his waistcoat pocket and felt again the large piece of gold, he stopped his tirade of threat, smiled and said, "Ahhhh." He turned and saw Maksohn, who had come back down the pier to guide the procession. Chauri smiled limply and said no more.

All the boxes and bales and cages and equipment were finally loaded and the wagons set off in something close to their usual order upon entering a town. With the loud and brassy circus band marching ahead of them, they began their progress along the dock road and then turned right, mounting a steep street into the town to find their quarters. The procession struck northward from the docks, straight across the westward-jutting peninsula upon which Kerballa had been built. Up the steep streets from the wharf side they went until they crested the large plateau that formed the center of the peninsula.

Riding on one of the elephants, John was able to see the Master of Darkness's castle and citadel to his left looming above the town. The drawbridge to the castle was protected by a gate on the land side at its entrance, and extending both right and left away from the gate, there was a large walled military encampment with flags and pennons flying.

Away east, to landward, stretched the remainder of the old town. The procession turned eastward when it came to the main avenue at the center of the peninsula. As John rode along, he could see the old city ahead of him, and beyond it the old city wall. Outside that was a newer section of the town, itself enclosed to the east by still another wall. Here no doubt lived the people who had been attracted to Kerballa since the coming of the general. Off on the northern side of the peninsula, by the sea, but still inside the old wall, was a forested area within which John caught glimpses of large white marble villas.

Looking south to his right across the river, John saw extensive farms stretching away from the river bank side. A continual traffic of small boats plied the river between these farms and the city's dock area which they had just left. A bridge would not be out of place there, thought John. He turned and looked westward behind him from his moving perch on the elephant. Over the entire peninsula brooded the high, tall shape of Juncata's castle. It seemed to peer down into every alley and street of the city, into every window, and even into every cellar. From the castle and its guardian military camp ran five jagged roads reaching down the peninsula into the land like the five tendons and fingers of a gnarled hand. The builders of the old city had been careful to misalign the main gate and the roads so that any invader could not sweep from the wall to the tip of the peninsula with a single rush. He would first have to turn right or left within the city wall and then inward again and jog again and again before he could make his way toward the pinnacle. The streets running north and south from one side of the peninsula to the other were likewise jogged. Outside the old wall, however, the five streets ran straight through the suburbs like the ribs of a fan to the new outer wall.

In the middle of the old city, the jagged center road straightened out and broadened for several blocks. To its north was a large park. At the southern edge of the park, a fountain marked the site of the original well around which the city had been constructed. On the other side of the main thoroughfare was the large town square where the daily market was held. To the south of the market square and back a bit from it was the old gracious building which had been the original seat of government. Since Juncata's assumption of full powers, however, that building had stood largely empty. It was used occasionally only as a guesthouse for visiting dignitaries and others whom the general wished to flatter. In the middle of the market square stood a large column, erected by General Juncata when he had defeated the pirates many years before. On top of the column was a statue of the general himself, one gloved hand extending in protection over the city and the other on the hilt of his sword. As the sun progressed each day from east to west, the shadow of this column fell all the way from the castle end of the city to the outer wall, like an accusing finger.

Around the edge of the plaza were the market stalls for the city. In the smaller buildings facing the plaza and behind the stalls were located the butcher shops and the other stores which vended the necessaries of life to the citizens. Ten blocks east of the market square, but twenty through the twisting streets, was the old stone-walled, timber-roofed horse-training arena in which the circus was to perform. The procession made slow progress through the streets, with the band at its head followed by Chauri's own personal wagon, the ship on wheels, on whose seat rode Chauri and Maksohn, calling instructions to the drum major. The elephants and horses were interspersed among the wagons carrying the performers, who waved gaily to the people in the streets. At the end came the carts carrying the heavy equipment.

When they reached the arena, they turned back south down a side street to reach the huge entrance doors for the animals. Inside, beneath the arena's seats, they found ample and comfortable holding space for the animals, with room to park the wagons as well. When Chauri looked into the arena, he discovered it was much bigger than the old Imbal bear garden. They would have room to expand their performance to three rings, although Chauri immediately realized that to do so would shorten the show unless he could find some new performers, or unless the people they had could double up even more than they already did and appear in different acts. On the other hand, the seating capacity was immense; they would be able to handle all the crowds that might come in from the suburbs and even from the country. Perhaps, thought Chauri to himself, this would not be so bad after all. He might make enough money to quit this terrible business. But to do so, he would have to put on the show of his life. Yes, yes, just possibly, he might be able to do it.

Chauri was everywhere at once, shouting and yelling, telling the various drivers where to pull their wagons into the space beneath the arena seats which would serve as both barn and living quarters. Finally the entire line of carts was stowed, even Chauri's boat on wheels, but work had to begin immediately on rigging for the first performance in three days. Trapezes and nets had to be erected and the large performance cage for the lions and tigers set up. People had to rehearse in the new setting and get the kinks out of their joints after a month at sea.

CHAPTER 35

The Old Man and His Daughters

Several hours before, at about the time that Chauri had been having his first conversation with Lord D'Orcade on the wharf, there had appeared at the main gate of the New Wall beyond the suburbs a most amusing sight. An old wizened man in a tall conical hat, with stars, moons, and suns affixed to it, accompanied by a large gray dog and two young girls, whom he called his daughters, had applied for admission to the city to "tell fortunes and do magic on street corners and in theaters."

"Hey, Grandfer, what are you anyway?" said one of the guards holding on to the halter of the old magician's pony and ogling the girls sitting on the horses behind him.

"I'm the most quizzical wizard you every saw, snapper whipper," said the old magician. And indeed he seemed strange indeed, with a long, scraggly white beard, bushy white eyebrows, a pallid green tint to his skin under the high spangled hat, and a short, rather tattered once-golden cape with a high collar which still glistened in the sun in a few spots. "If you've got a girl, soldier, give her this from me," said the magician, leaning toward the soldier and pulling a somewhat tattered feather flower out of his ear.

"Easy, old man, don't play tricks on me," said the soldier. "I'm too old for your silly children's stuff. Go join the circus that's coming to town."

"You silly fool," wheezed the old magician in his high, cracked voice. "You think I'm some cheap trickster?" He withdrew the extended hand which had held the flower, unaccepted by the soldier, crumpled it up in his fist, and then opening his palm, showed in its place a small gold coin. "See what you could have had?" said the old man, looking down fixedly into the large potato-shaped face of the guard. The other guards guffawed at the confusion of their companion until the old magician did in fact slip the gold piece into the jerkin pocket of the man holding his horse. "If your sweetie doesn't like flowers, soldier, take her out for a drink instead. Now I've shown you my wares, perhaps when you are off duty, you'll come to my performance and give me back some of that gold you've won by treating an old man and his daughters honorably. Wouldn't you like to see my pretty assistants get stuck full of knives?"

The soldier made a coarse joke and winked at the taller of the girls and then said, "Old man, anyone who comes into or goes out of the city must register and be searched, so get ye down off your pony and come in and put your name in the book." The old magician leapt off his pony with surprising agility and followed the sentry into the guard house, leaving the two women seated on their horses at the gate.

"Say, girlie," said another of the guards to the smaller and darker of the women who was sitting on the second horse, "That old man can't be much fun. Why don't you slip out some night and meet a real man?" The woman did not answer but just sat quietly, looking straight ahead. The guard sauntered over and, putting out a hand, lightly and carelessly stroked the mane of the horse. Then he slid his hand down the horse's neck, across its shoulder and toward the legging-wrapped thigh of the rider. Just as it touched her, the guard heard a deep growl behind him. Looking over his shoulder, he saw a large gray dog with a tattered red cloth for a collar, snarling up at him.

"Just joking, lady, just joking," he said carelessly and lifted both his hands shoulder high.

The taller girl in front had turned in her saddle and said good-naturedly, "No problem, soldier, but you and the sailors are all alike, always after the same thing. Come down here and talk to me."

"Aye, aye," said the guard, "If it's sailors you like, you'll find plenty down at the port, and I've got many a friend among 'em, but they can't hold a candle to us when it comes to showing a girl a good time." The soldier drifted ahead to stand by the tall girl's horse, leaving the dog back by the other horse. The tall girl leaned down slightly from her saddle and said quietly, "Wrong time. Wrong place. Daddy isn't always around. Look for us and bring some of your sailor friends with you."

"And what about the dog?" said the soldier, tilting his head toward the ground.

"Oh, he's no problem. But he's very expensive to feed," she said and gave the guard a wink.

The soldier stared at her for a second or two and then looked back carefully at the dog, which now seemed to have an amused look on its face. The guard's face slowly lit up in understanding, and he turned back to the tall girl with a lewd smile on his coarse lips.

"Righto, girlie. I gotcha now, but it don't look like yer sister there gets it."

"She ain't in the game—yet," said the tall girl, looking significantly at the guard.

The soldier looked back at the slim, aloof figure on the horse and whistled softly to himself as the old magician came out of the guardhouse with a paper in his hand followed by a customs officer dressed in black.

"Any weapons, jewels, bottled spirits, or special medicines to declare?" said the customs officer. The magician showed a small knife, a bow, and a quiver of arrows which the customs officer duly noted on the form.

"What's in the boxes?"

"Magic paraphernalia," replied the magician.

"Let's have a look." The magician opened the two long boxes on the second pack pony. A stale dust arose from them. The customs man pawed through the rings, cups, and feather flowers and saw nothing that captured his interest. He looked over the girls carefully but saw nothing suspicious there either. Neither wore jewelry of any kind. Satisfied they were no more than what they said they were, the customs man stamped the paper and handed it back to the magician, who, despite his age, climbed nimbly back into his saddle again and led his small procession through the gate and into the town. As they rode through the streets, Morduc, for, of course, Morduc it was, took note of the many pairs of policemen dressed in black boots and uniforms and sharply peaked caps. They seemed to be strolling idly about wherever one looked, apparently unoccupied but always watching. There was no direction one could look without seeing either near or far off in the distance the two black strokes of Juncata's policemen marking the landscape side by side. As Morduc rode on, they eyed him as he passed, and he in turn bowed low from his saddle and called out, "Come see the magician in the plaza, by the fountain." They gave no reply or even an indication that they had heard or comprehended what he had said but just returned silent, cold, suspicious looks.

The dog, the pack pony, and the three riders went on until they came to the gate in the wall of the old city, where the paper Morduc was carrying was rescrutinized carefully and he himself questioned again. The paper was stamped a second time in a different-colored ink and returned to him. As they continued on down the main thoroughfare toward the square of the old city, the girls were nearly overwhelmed by the bustle and noise, the crowding and shouting. They turned every which way to see the carts and the pack animals and the people rushing everywhere. Here too, as in the outer city, the general's special police were much in evidence. At one point, one pair even stopped the travelers and demanded to see their gate passes. As they were inspecting the pass, Morduc snatched off the peaked cap of one of them and, before he could protest, pulled a live dove from it to the surprised irritation of its owner and the amused attention and applause of the small crowd which had immediately gathered around the two officers and the three strange-looking travelers and their dog.

The officer took back his hat and fitted it carefully on his head, saying sullenly, "You ought to be more careful, old man, what liberties you take with the general's Special Police. You could easily get killed playing tricks like that."

"I apologize, sir," said Morduc in an old, cracked voice. "Publicity, you know. But no true insult offered. If we should be so fortunate as to be able to perform indoors, just present this card at the door for free admission for yourself and your girl. Entertainers must live, you know."

The policeman took the card and read it: "Middock the Masterological Magician and His Dancing Daughters—Performers Extraordinaire." Then he turned to Morduc and said, "Well, Master Middock, that was an extraordinarily dangerous act you just performed. For some reason, the general is big on performers and entertainers just now, or you'd be in my dank dungeon. If I had my way with you charlatans"—here he flexed his hand—"but that is not for me to say, at present. Move on now, and make no trouble." He handed the gate pass back to Morduc, who folded it up and tucked it under his cloak, and then, clucking to the ponies, proceeded down the street. When they had passed out of sight in the crowd, the special policeman cast his eyes down again at the card in his hand and then stuck it thoughtfully in his tunic breast pocket.

Morduc, Illanna, and Marianna, with Anga and the two pack ponies behind them, continued on into the town. At one point Morduc stopped to ask directions. Several blocks before they reached the main plaza, he turned south down a side street that led in the direction of the waterfront. Just after they had turned, a circus procession passed behind them, with band blaring and a long train of carts and animals following. Morduc and Marianna and Illanna continued some distance down the side street and then turned to the right into a narrow alley.

At the end of the alley hung a small gold sign with a green dragon on it over a low inn yard gate. Morduc stopped at the gate and looked about. No one came out to meet him. He got off his pony and led it and the pack pony under the gate into the yard. A small open door led off the yard to the left. To the right were closed stable doors. Illanna and Marianna dismounted and held all four of the animals while Morduc entered the open door. He found himself in a low, dark room, with a fireplace at the far end in which a fire with a pot over it burned feebly. Behind a counter opposite the door was a small round dumpling of a woman with a huge white cap on her head.

"What can I do you fer, darlin'?" said the woman without looking up.

"Lodgings for three people, myself and my two daughters, as well as stabling for four mounts, and for you the honor of housing the greatest street magician in the land." At this she looked up sharply, and Morduc saw a pair of small black-currant eyes in a round, doughy face that seemed to take him in instantly and weigh him out not all that favorably.

"And a dog," she said sharply, looking down past Morduc at Anga, who had followed him into the inn room.

"And a dog," replied Morduc calmly.

"Ye be not the only street magicians about these days," she answered cryptically but noncommittally. "We can put you up, and when you're run out of town, we can see you gone. Two rooms, though," she said, looking past Morduc out the door at the girls standing in the sunlight. "We're a decent house here. Payment for a week in advance. Dog free. Fourth pony extra."

"Done," said Morduc, when she had told him the amount. "I'll just *fish* around here in my bag for the right coins," he continued, emphasizing the one word in the sentence. The short woman's eyes contracted to even smaller black points than they had been before. She took the money in her outstretched hand and regarded Morduc carefully and suspiciously.

"How did you say you came to choose my inn to stay at?" she asked.

"I didn't say," replied Morduc. "But it is close to the square where I intend to start performing."

"Indeed. I'll get the boy to show you your rooms. *Harry*!" she bawled into the air, and while they waited for an answer, she asked casually. "Do you want to order anything special for your dinner?"

"No. Whatever you have will be fine. Though if they're in season, some fruit for dessert might be nice. Some plums, for instance."

"Indeed," she replied, "dried rotten prunes is more like."

"You'd be surprised what fresh plums we saw in the country," said Morduc offhandedly.

A youth appeared. "Look alive, Harry. Help this magician and his assistants to unload, and then stable his horses." The boy, whose brown hair looked like an inverted bowl on his head, stared stupidly at Morduc. "Come, Harry," said the short innkeeper, sharply, "hast thee never seen an old trickster like this?"

Harry looked at Morduc, focusing his eyes. "Never, Mother Gump, unless it be old Pl . . ." But before he could finish, the innkeeper snapped sharply at him, "Hush, Harry." Harry looked as if he had remembered something very serious, but in a moment or two his face brightened again, and he said to Morduc, "Pray, good magician, show me a trick."

"What, right here?" said Morduc, laughing.

"Ay, master, if it please you."

"Harry, you big lout. Off with you and help this geezer, or I might say guiser. None of your nonsense today," said the innkeeper.

"Please, Mother Gump. Let him show me a trick. Just a small one."

"Have you a coin, Harry?"

"Yea, sir, but it be nawbut a small nothing of a coin."

"So much the better, Harry. Let me have it."

"What be ye to do wi' it, master?" inquired Harry doubtfully as he rooted in his pants pocket.

"Do you want to see a trick or not, Harry?" said Morduc.

"That I do, zir."

"Then give it me now."

"Here it be, zir, wi' the face of the general's mother on it." Morduc took the coin and looked at it carefully. He rolled in swiftly over the backs of his knuckles and then let it disappear inside his right hand. He held out both fists to Harry.

"Now, my boy, tell me where is the coin?"

"It is in that 'un zir," laughed Harry, "'cause I saw it go in," as he pointed to Morduc's right hand.

"That may be so," said Morduc as he held up the closed fist and drops of water began to fall from it onto the brick floor of the inn barroom. "See, Harry, the general's mother is weeping."

"Why do she do that?" said Harry.

"Why do mothers generally weep?" asked Morduc.

"I don't know," said Harry. "My mother's died. I weep for her sometimes."

"Shall we ask the general's mother why she weeps?"

"Yea, zir, but a coin face canna talk. Ye be joking me. I want to see a trick."

"I'll open my hand to just check on the general's mother." He did so, and there was nothing there but a wet palm.

"It canna be," said Harry, taking Morduc's hand in his own and turning it over and then back. "What ha ye done wi' my coin," said Harry, becoming quite agitated. "I was goin' to buy candy wi' it. Gi' it back to me. It's no good trick to steal from the poor people."

The short landlady snorted.

"Look over here, Harry," said Morduc opening his other hand to show a different coin, more valuable than the first. "Here is a coin you can have in place of the other."

Overjoyed, the boy took the coin and looked it all over. Concluding it was sound he said, "Thankee, sir, thankee. That was a rousing good trick, sir. Now I'll help you with your things, zir. Have you got more wonderful tricks?"

"That I have, Harry," said Morduc, "but I warn you not to go poking into any of my bags or boxes, or I'll turn you into a cheese." And with this, he glared at the boy until he quivered and looked down.

"No, sir, no, zir, and I won't let none other touch 'em neither."

"See that you don't," said Morduc in a magisterial voice, "and there'll be more coins for you."

The boy went out and began unloading the ponies and the horses. The girls came in and Mother Gump showed them to a room while Morduc watchfully oversaw the unloading. Harry and another servant took the bags and boxes up to Morduc's room, and then Harry himself took the ponies and horses to the stable across the small cobblestone-paved inn yard. Anga lay down out of the way by the door, watchful and quiet. Presently, Morduc came down again with Marianna and Illanna, but without his high conical cap or his tawdry gold short cape on. He was in his old cloak and brown homespun. He looked like an old farmer, hardly worth a second glance. They went out rapidly and up the alley, followed by Anga. After searching in the streets for a short while, Morduc found what he wanted, a tailor shop, and went in. There he ordered two suits of shimmering material to be made for the two girls and three gray cloaks and then came out again. Off they went, walking the streets, learning the geography of the town. They went up to the square and walked all around it, scouting out the place of their intended performance. Toward evening, they returned to the Green Dragon Inn, had a simple meal, and went to bed.

On the next morning, Morduc was up early, went to the tailor shop, picked up and paid for the now-finished suits and cloaks, and returned to the Green Dragon. The two girls carefully put on their tight-fitting golden garments, each of which included a tight-fighting hood with a built in mask. They looked like two creatures of the air, brilliant, sinuous, and mysterious. Throwing their gray cloaks over their costumes and carrying their equipment, they and Morduc and Anga once again set out for the plaza.

When they arrived, the fountain was playing in the air and the broad space with the column in its center was filled with people milling about the stalls of the vendors. Morduc found a space at the foot of the column. The girls threw off their cloaks and spread them on the ground, and then to the sound of a small drum played by Marianna and a tin whistle played by Illanna, they began to dance in a circle around the cloaks, on which Morduc stood motionless in his short cape and his high conical hat with the stars, moons, and symbols on it.

The sharp beat of the drum, the squeal of the whistle, and the shapely beauty of the girls immediately attracted a crowd, and as soon, as a fair number had assembled, Morduc drew out his wand and a cup. He showed the cup empty, waved his wand over its mouth, and then drew forth a dove, which flew up and away to perch on General Juncata's head on the top of the column. Morduc continued to perform small miracles, such as producing a mountain of silks from his empty hands and making a ball float in the air at the edge of a scarf, to the oohs and ahs of the crowd. By the end of the performance, a rather large crowd had assembled, and thus the attention of the omnipresent special police had been attracted. Several pairs stood around on the outside of the crowd. When the performance was over, Morduc placed a bowl on the ground and invited coins to be put in it. The crowd responded generously. He then packed up and moved away while the police urged the group to disperse now that the show was over. He continued this procedure the next day. On the third day, just as Morduc was to begin, an ornate carriage with a black rose crest on the door drew up in the broad street opposite the column, and from it descended an ornately dressed figure with a long curled wig carrying an ebony silver-headed walking stick. He was accompanied by two young men, also elegantly dressed, one of them carrying a small, carved ivory folding stool. This trio, with lace collars and cuffs adorning velvet suits, dawdled toward the crowd around the column.

"Make way for Lord Marivaux D'Orcade, the Master of the Revels of his most High Excellency and Protector of the Realm, the Lord Chief General Justinian X. Juncata!" shouted one of the black liveried footmen from the carriage. The always-present police parted the crowd less gently with their quirts to allow the three young men to come to the front.

D'Orcade took a small card from his waistcoat pocket and, after looking at it, asked, "Do I have the privilege of addressing Middock the Magician?"

Morduc bowed and replied in the creaky, wizened voice of his disguise, "You do indeed, sir. May I ask where you got that little card?"

"It does not matter to you. Suffice it to say that we have connections everywhere. Your name has been recommended to me. Do you object?"

"Not in the least, your honor."

"Well, then, Master Magician, show us what you can do. Your daughters are pretty things. You yourself, if I may say so, do not look terribly prepossessing. Play on."

Morduc bowed deeply, stepped forward, and out of thin air and with a flourish of his cape presented D'Orcade with a bowl of water with fish swimming in it. Quite startled, D'Orcade lifted his lorgnette from where it hung on a silk cord around his neck, looked at the beautiful creatures swimming within the globe and exclaimed, "Most remarkable. Most remarkable. Is it an illusion?" Morduc dropped the glass bowl at his feet where it shattered, splashing water on the stones and leaving two multicolored carp gasping for breath. One of the special police at the outskirts of the crowd barked a harsh, cruel laugh. In spite of himself, Marivaux D'Orcade was impressed, and that business of leaving the fish gasping and dying on the stones was just the sort of taste in entertainment he knew his Master favored.

Morduc performed several other tricks, making a white rabbit appear first under one large bowl on the ground and then under another. He made a canary in a cage disappear, cage and all. He produced a small fountain of rainbow-colored water from a handful of silks. Then, stepping up to Marianna, he appeared to put her into a trance, placed her on the ground, and covered her with a large gold cloth. Slowly the recumbent figure began to move upward, first just a bit off the ground, then higher and higher until she was at Lord D'Orcade's eye level. Then, all of a sudden, with a loud yell, Morduc yanked the cloth away, and there was nothing at all in the air. She had vanished completely. The crowd gasped and then broke into applause and loud roars of approval. The Master of the Revels was thoroughly shaken. From his seat on the ivory stool, he moved his stick through an arc in front of him where the girl had been floating but encountered nothing.

"Oh my dear," he finally said. "It is impossible. Quite absolutely impossible."

"Nothing, my lord, is absolutely impossible," said Morduc innocently, "where vanishings are involved."

Marivaux D'Orcade, twenty-seven years old, actor, dancer, musician, poet, painter, designer, and newly rich Master of the Revels of the Master of Darkness, thought about that for a moment but contented himself with replying in equal innocence, "Indeed, can you make her reappear? Can you restore her?"

"Indeed I can," responded Morduc.

"Well then, do it. Do it immediately, old man."

Morduc paused, and then said slowly, "I shall wait to do that at another time, with Your Grace's permission."

Marivaux paused. "And what if I refuse my permission, weak old wizard? What if I command you to do it now on pain of torture?"

"Where my will consents, I can perform that and many other marvels for you unendingly, but where request becomes command, you are but commanding water, light, and air, Your Excellency. Can you do that?"

"This makes little sense, Magician," said D'Orcade, becoming slightly irritated. "No one can command water, or light, or air. But where people are concerned, we do not deal in consent in this city. We deal in command and in prompt performance. Do I make myself clear?"

"Perfectly, Your Worship," said Morduc without moving.

One of D'Orcade's companions leaned over and whispered in his ear, "He is not right in the head, Mari. Be careful."

"Something like, perhaps, Tommy," said D'Orcade softly to him. Then turning back to Morduc, he said, "For the moment we will suspend our command. A most excellent illusion, nevertheless, Magician. Most excellent. Are you able to perform these wonders in any location?"

Morduc laughed his wizened laugh. "If I can do them here, surely I can do them anywhere. What nonsense you do talk."

"Well then, Master Magician Middock. You know who I am. You will be hearing from me soon. I think I will be able to give you employment. Where can you be found?"

Morduc bowed low. "Your humble servant, Lord D'Orcade. Send but to the Green Dragon Inn, and I and my daughters are yours to command."

"I am glad to hear it." He stood up, and turned toward the coach. A footman opened the door. His two companions followed him with the stool as he pushed his way back through the crowd. The three entered the coach, the door was shut upon them, and the carriage wheeled about and clattered off rapidly westward in the direction of the citadel.

The magician and his one remaining assistant began packing up his equipment on the pony. When they were nearly ready to go and no one was paying attention to them anymore, out from under a pile of rags appeared Marianna with a cloak around her. She put on a hat that covered her sleek golden head, and the three of them, along with the pony and Anga, moved quietly out of the square.

By afternoon the whole city was talking of the remarkable performance that had taken place that morning before Lord D'Orcade in the square. The Master of the Revels himself had immediately hurried down the broad avenue in his carriage to deliver the news of his find to the castle. The carriage rattled along over the brick paving, with the three figures inside it. As it approached the castle, the very air seemed to darken. They came to the third wall on the peninsula, the wall enclosing the military garrison which occupied the land at the very tip of the city. Rows and rows of neat soldiers' huts filled the walled-in area, and through it ran the broad central way leading to a pair of gates at the back of the camp. Today they stood open and disclosed a great bridge with not only a lane for carriages, but a walkway as well, spanning the narrow, deep, sea-filled chasm between the headland and the great rock upon which the castle was built.

The sentries recognized the carriage and, seeing the well-known face of the Revels Master at the window, waved it through. The wheels rattled thunderously on the planking as the carriage passed between the huge suspension chains extending from two massive towers flanking the castle's maw. The bridge ended at a huge iron portcullis which barred their way. The sentries, with their halberds and helmets and short swords, looked into the carriage and then gave a signal to the soldiers behind the giant iron grating. With an immense grinding noise, the great grid rose, and when it was high enough, the carriage sprang forward under the touch of the lash on the backs of the two horses. Once inside, the grating fell behind them with a ponderous clang, and the carriage came to a stop in a large open yard in which a small squad of soldiers was drilling under the stern eye of a sergeant. Other soldiers stood guarding the many doorways out of the open space.

D'Orcade and his two companions descended from the carriage and went toward a great flight of steps that led to the main portion of the castle, continuing to talk all the while about the performance they had just seen. Soldiers stood on every third step, and as they passed between the lines of armed men, D'Orcade began to feel once again the dread and apprehension he always experienced when he approached his employer, even though he had long since become familiar with the procedures of the fortress. In spite of the oppressive atmosphere, the other two dandies nevertheless continued to chatter gaily as they approached the two huge main doors. They were locked closed, with only a small one-person wicket in the left-hand leaf operating, and even that had a grate in place over it.

D'Orcade tapped on the grate with his stick. The sound echoed cavernously within. Presently there appeared behind the grate the pale face of an especially severe young man dressed in an especially dark version of the uniform of the special police. Though his face was youthful and unlined, his thin hair was totally white. The pallor of the face and the white hair against the background of black made his head seem to float in the stygian recesses of the hall.

"Business?" the pale face snapped.

"Come, come, Sprok. You know I have to see the general about the festivities. You shouldn't, my dear, have to ask me again and again."

"Business, specific!" Sprok bit out coldly, ignoring the endearment.

"Just because you are the general's chamberlain, there is no need for you to lord it over me," said D'Orcade petulantly. "We went to school together. Don't you remember? You should loosen up a bit and come to one of my parties sometime."

The pale man in the black uniform said nothing nor did he move to open the grate either. Finally D'Orcade said, "Oh, I've found a new magician to entertain the general and his guests, and I wish to know when to order the performance, if you must know."

"Wait here," said Sprok. The severe young man disappeared. D'Orcade peered inside but could see nothing. It was as if the man had simply been swallowed up by the dark air.

"These beastly delays," said D'Orcade. "I don't know why the general permits this upstart to wield so much power. It is really so very, very outrageous." Yet he realized, even as he said it, that he himself was in a similar position. Presently, Sprok returned, swung open the iron grate, and pointed at D'Orcade. "You, in. Others, wait."

"This is nonsense, Sprok," Marivaux protested and started forward. "My friends come with me. Ricky, Tommy, attend."

"No," said Sprok, smiling icily, and drew a short dagger with lightning speed. "I'd love an excuse to cut you both to . . ." Ricky and Tommy stumbled backward down the steps with as much composure as they could muster.

"Oh, very well," said D'Orcade to them. "Wait in the carriage." Sprok stepped out of the way permitting the Revels Master to step from daylight past the small iron grating into the cold cavernous darkness of the castle. Sprok clanged the grating shut and then the thick wooden wicket door. It took a minute for D'Orcade's eyes to adjust to the gloom. When he could see, he proceeded along the hall, which was just barely lit by an occasional feeble torch in a sconce. He felt a chill go over him and through him and touch his bones, and yet it was not a mere surface chill of the air. It was as if needles of ice were being inserted into the marrow of his bones, needles that produced a screaming pain as they went in and left a lasting deathly ache as they melted.

He wondered why he had ever taken this job, but he knew why—because he liked the power and because it permitted him to live in his villa on the north shore in splendor and riot. But he knew he was not really cut out for the work. Now Sprok, there was a born villain. Something was wrong with that boy, dreadfully wrong. But what?

D'Orcade continued to walk down the dark corridor toward an arch through which he saw a dull red light. Once past the arch, he was in a rather large hall, at the end of which stood a raised stone platform with an ebony chair on it. In the chair, scarcely distinguishable from the black wood itself, except for the faint red light playing on his strange, rough skin, sat a tall, bearded figure with piercing black eyes. The thick face struggled to give an appearance of openness and composure and courtesy but failed consistently to conceal the smoldering anger, the churning rage, the envy, and the hate that roared silently and perpetually up within his skull like a black fire.

"Your Most Gracious Lordship," began D'Orcade obsequiously as he swept off his large purple plumed hat and bowed. The figure in the chair said nothing but merely nodded stiffly to him. "It is a great honor to inform you that by extreme effort, I have once again managed to discover a diversion for Your Excellency that will please and delight you, as I think you have never . . ." The figure made an impatient waving gesture with his gloved right hand and clenched his other gloved fist at the same time in a way that disconcerted the flamboyant courtier.

"Do you think," said a deep voice seeming to roll out of the figure's chest without coming through his mouth, "that I care for pleasure and delight? You have not yet, D'Orcade, understood the purpose of these diversions, confusing your own degraded, sensual, and frivolous nature with mine. The purpose of life is not to seek pleasure, but to advance the cause. I make allowances for the weaknesses of the masses of the people until they can all be brought to see how they must work ceaselessly to bring about the new order, but that I should continually have to make such allowances for one of my own trusted lieutenants is utterly disgusting."

D'Orcade saw the inner dark flame in his eyes, that focused, intense, fanatic black gleam, which was more frightening than any scowl of anger could be.

"That I continue to keep you in office is a tribute only to your successes so far. I suspect that you only serve yourself, but I hope that someday you will, in fact, be truly converted. Now, D'Orcade, begin again, and try to speak correctly. We must have correct words."

Marivaux took a deep breath and began again. "Your Excellency, ah, in the interests of promoting the advancement of the New Order . . ."

"Better, D'Orcade, better," said the black-steel voice.

"I have discovered yet another . . . demonstration of the benevolent paternal regard of the general for the welfare and interests of the people, and . . ."

"Good, D'Orcade, good. And true too. Go on."

"And in particular, a demonstration that might appeal not only to the great bulk of the people but also to a certain person who has so far remained unconvinced of your generous . . ." His voice trailed off. D'Orcade was stopped neither by any motion nor by any sound the general had made, but rather by a sudden freezing of his face which gave it the bony, mindless predatory sheen of an ancient deep-water fish. The general's previous faint, half smile turned down at the corners of his mouth and his visionary, mad, absolute eyes glistened like smoked gold foil around expressionless, depthless pupils as his inward mind experienced the cold anger of unsatisfied illegitimate passion.

Seeing he had gone too far, D'Orcade left his previous sentence unfinished and began another. "He is a most remarkable old conjurer in the way of levitations and vanishes, productions and disappearances, and he has two very pretty assistants too, I may say, whom he chooses to style his daughters. Shall I engage him for the city and for the castle?"

Juncata sat for a moment or two, regaining control of himself, his mind rising slowly from the solitary black depths up to renewed awareness of D'Orcade, and finally said, "Pretty assistants?"

"Yes, indeed, Your Grace. The image of these two innocent young girls serving so willingly beside their old father, all the generations, you see."

"Indeed. Yes, though for their innocence, I imagine it to be less than you suggest. Engage him for tomorrow night. Are there others as well?"

"A new circus has come to town, but they only give their first performance this afternoon. I will attend and report to you."

"Very well, D'Orcade. You have not failed me yet, though, as you say, a 'certain party' remains unable to see the light of my vision. I need to have tangible results soon. So far, your entertainments are the only social functions she will condescend to . . ." His voice trailed off and then resumed again. "She will yet live to thank me—and to love me—as the people do." Here D'Orcade gulped silently in his throat. The general was clenching his black-gloved left hand. "She will yet! She will see that she must submit to . . ." The General stopped himself, and then continued less intensely, "Ah. But, D'Orcade, I am speaking too much. I am losing my patience, and 'He who loses patience loses all,' eh, D'Orcade? Who said that? You have pretensions to an education in the books of this land. I have read them too. Do you not recognize it?"

"Your Grace will have to identify the source," said D'Orcade, bowing low, "for I do not recognize it."

"Indeed! Never mind! Here," said Juncata, holding out to the Revels Master a small purse that dropped with satisfying weight into his hand. "You may go now."

"Thank you, Master. I shall not disappoint you," said D'Orcade. He bowed low as he backed away from the ebony throne, yet was thinking to himself all the while as he retreated, *If I could get away safely with my money to some place where your steel finger did not reach, I would do it and be well satisfied to be out of this constant insecurity. A pox on your money and proverbs and your steel-spined claws.*

Not until he had reached the arch at the far end of the hall did he stand straight and turn around. Though still not free in his mind, he nevertheless walked down the long entry passage with a much lighter step than that with which he had ascended it. Coming finally to the narrow swinging iron grating set into the rightward leaf of the much-larger massive double doors, he bid the unpleasant Sprok good day and rejoined his two companions, who had been playing dice on the carriage floor and were arguing when he came up. D'Orcade jumped into the vehicle and thumped the interior roof of the carriage twice with his ebony cane.

The horses sprang forward under the coachman's lash and drew the rattling carriage down the courtyard, where it waited briefly and impatiently for the portcullis to be raised, and then rumbled out across the bridge. As the carriage thundered over the planks, D'Orcade looked down more than a hundred feet at the sea which washed the granite base of the castle. From that height, the water could scarcely be heard as it moved in ever-new, ever-same combinations on the rocks below, sliding and shifting silently in an eternally serene motion, breaking on the immobile motion of the rocks which bounded it.

D'Orcade sat morosely beside his two companions, who chattered mindlessly on about their dice game, altogether unaware of the radical insecurity of all of their lives. They rattled on through the camp and toward the city. As they neared the center of the town, where the great market square occupied one side of the widened avenue and the cool, tree-filled plaza the other, D'Orcade rapped twice sharply on the under roof of the coach, which brought the carriage to an abrupt standstill. "Drive to the Green Dragon Inn," called D'Orcade out the window to the coachman.

"Never heard of it, Your Excellency," said the driver.

"Well, learn of it, and go there," replied D'Orcade in exasperation. The driver resumed moving down the main avenue, stopping from time to time to inquire about the location of the inn. Finally he got clear directions and turned down one of the cross streets that led in the direction of the docks. Deep in the oldest part of the town, the coachman stopped at the entrance to an alleyway.

"Well," called D'Orcade to the driver. "Why have you stopped?"

"We are here," replied the driver.

"I see no Green Dragon Inn."

"It is at the far end of this alley, sir. Too narrow for the coach." D'Orcade looked out the window down to the end of the alley and, with a gesture of both impatience and disgust, called out, "Footman. Go to the inn, and tell the magician I would speak with him." The footman jumped down from the carriage, ran down the alley, and disappeared under the inn sign.

A minute passed. Then another. The footman finally reappeared, with a somewhat simple-minded-looking young man in tow and brought him back to the carriage and stood him on the cobblestone pavement in front of D'Orcade.

"Well? What is your name, boy?

"'Arry, zir."

"Why haven't you brought the magician?"

"He is not in, sir."

"Well, fool, where is he?"

"He's gone out, zir."

"You idiot. *where* has he gone out?

"To the circus, zir," said Harry smiling. "And I be going there now myself."

"Then climb aboard, Harry, because we are going there too," whooped D'Orcade. The footman jumped back on the carriage, and Harry swung on behind too. The coachman wheeled about, nearly knocking down a large fat man wearing a broad straw hat who was crossing the street to enter the alley. Off went the carriage clattering up the street toward the main avenue and, once there, turned to the right, and then to the left, and then right and left again until they arrived in front of the arena. A huge banner across the stone front proclaimed *Chauri Circus Today*. Two drummers were standing outside the main entrance, beating with controlled abandon. People were streaming into the main entrance of the arena, and interspersed throughout the crowd were the police, in pairs, simply strolling, looking, remembering.

Despite D'Orcade's distaste for mingling with the crowd, he and his two companions, with the footmen and Harry following, entered the arena and laid claim to the general's box. They entered it, sat down, and D'Orcade scanned the crowd. Eventually he located the old magician and his two assistants in the front row at the eastward end of the arena. He dispatched a footman with a slip of paper. Morduc read it, wrote a short reply, and sent it back. When D'Orcade received it, he looked up, Morduc rose and bowed, while Harry waved wildly from his position front center in General Juncata's box. Then everyone settled back contentedly to watch the performance.

CHAPTER 36

Within the Dark Towers

The Master of Darkness watched the bowing velvet-suited shape of his Master of the Revels recede down the hall until D'Orcade turned and disappeared under the arch into the passageway. "Overdressed insect," he hissed to himself. Frustration at the weakness of the instruments through which he was forced to work gripped him. Slowly he pounded the right arm of his ebony chair with his gloved hand as he considered his next step. Though much had been accomplished, magnitudes remained; moreover, the time he had been given for the delivery across the sea was now almost two-thirds gone. He had brought the entire coast under his control, from the southernmost Rocks of Caracassoa all the way north to IcePort, yet the realms beyond the mountains were still resistant. And then there was the king and his daughter. Though he held them captive, they would not agree to join him, and only if they joined him would he be able to swiftly gain control of the inner lands without a careful, clandestine, and protracted campaign such as he had conducted on the coast, but for which he no longer had time.

When he had threatened the princess with the torture of her father if she continued to refuse to marry him, she had merely said, "And so you would treat me if we were married. Do you take me for a fool?" Nor had she succumbed to the spells he had tried to put on her. She had pierced easily all illusion he had at his command. As for threat to herself, she seemed indifferent. "You will not get me to love you by mistreating me," she had said simply. "Try pleasing me, instead." Mere stalling and deviousness, of course, but perhaps worth a try.

"And what would please the princess?" he had asked.

"To be taken out to shows and entertainments in the city," she had replied. Another ploy, of course, to get free of the citadel, to permit the people to see her in hopes they would rise and rescue her and her father. He barked out a short contemptuous laugh. Little chance of *that*, he thought to himself, at least not the way the souls of the populace were now, dependent on him for everything from public order to even their entertainments. And the puzzle was that for such a serious girl, the princess had the same tastes as theirs: a low devotion to color, music, image. Such frivolities were not suitable for a future queen. Well, there would be time enough to alter that when once he had her in his . . .

But really, he could not risk taking the princess out into the town, no matter how docile the population seemed. He would humor her here in the citadel. He would pretend to please her by bringing entertainers in. It truly galled him to be reduced to practicing courtship rather than command, but through her lay the only route to quick victory, and his allotted time to collect his lord's "necessaries," as the Great Snake called them, was running out. Perhaps he had spent too much time on the coastal campaign, but the region was totally *his*, without dispute or contest from anyone. He had collected in his ship a few of the sorts of gems he had been sent to find. If he could command the inner lands in the name of the princess and her father, he could, no doubt, discover the rest quickly. But by pursuing the route of legitimacy, he had to have patience, and moreover, he had to put up with his sister's mockery and contempt as well. "You, a lover? Absurd," she had said. But he would try. Perhaps the princess was innocent enough to be taken in by the show of courtesy. Surprisingly, that mincing fool, D'Orcade, had been fairly successful in scouting out diversions and in mounting masques to please her. She had clapped her hands and smiled at the stupid jugglers, the country dancers and singers, and the mythic tableaux that D'Orcade had arranged. She had behaved most regally, in fact, bringing credit to him among the fat burghers that competed disgustingly for the "honor" of being invited to one of the castle's command performances. And he made them pay gold into his coffers for the privilege of falling asleep at the puerile entertainments. So cows pay for their keep by being milked. Yet the red-gold-haired princess, in her perversity, still persisted in asking to be taken into the city, claiming that there were shows there that could not be brought to the castle. He had assured her that he was able to command the appearance of any performer or troupe anywhere on the coast, and well beyond. She had challenged him to provide her with regular entertainments. "Even a princess can only work at her loom weaving the fabric of a wedding dress for so many hours a day," she had said.

"Ha!" he snorted to himself in the empty hall again, in the dim red light. Did she think him stupid? Wedding dress indeed. His shroud, perhaps. Of course, she was merely a pawn in the game, a pawn which could, if necessary, be sacrificed, but the time for that had not yet come, and sometimes, just sometimes, the pawn became a queen, and the true queen then fights on the side of her king. If he could only get her on his side. What strength! What beauty! What intelligence! She would, if anyone could, figure out where the hidden green crystals were. He was convinced the father did not know. Impressive-looking figure but totally ineffectual. And the princess too did not seem to know where the caches were, yet if they were anywhere beyond the mountains in the fertile lands before the desert started, she, Aleth Trealthweow, would be able to discover them if she set her mind and heart and beauteous charm to the task. She was smart, smart, smart. Why would she not join him? While he waited for luck or craft to work, he would pretend to please her by bringing entertainments into the castle. Perhaps he would visit her now, to tell her of the performance scheduled for the following night and to try her mood once again.

He lifted himself from his black chair using the strength of his arms, limped heavily down the three steps of the dais, and moved painfully toward the corridor on the right leading to the south tower.

"Slug," he called as he came to a locked door with a small barred window and a sliding food slot in it. There was a liquid rustling behind the door, and a pair of frightened bulging eyes poked up over the bottom edge of the window. "I am going up, Slug," said the Master. The eyes disappeared and a bolt shot back behind the door. It swung slowly open. A short, shapeless figure groveled at the edge of the door as the Master entered.

"How is she today, Slug?" asked the Master. Slippery syllables, but unintelligible, issued from the mouth of the gatekeeper. "Never mind, Slug. I will see for myself." The fat puffing boy twisted his face up toward the Master and nodded with a mixture of fawning and fear. *So it is with such animals,* thought the Master as he went toward the stairs. *They respect only power, never goodness. It is their curse and my opportunity.*

The Master began climbing the spiral stone steps. Slowly, limpingly, up and up he went in the dim light admitted by infrequent narrow loopholes in the tower, until he came to a broad landing in front of a massive door which, like the other below, also had a sliding tray in it. A large beam resting in two wrought-iron staples barred the door shut. He heard within a high, pure song like clear water endlessly falling through sun-washed open air. He rapped sharply on the door. The singing stopped.

A soft mocking voice called out, "Enter—if you can." The Master slid the beam sideways into a deep receptacle in the wall and pulled the handle of the thick door toward him. The door did not move.

"Princess," called out the Master with annoyance, in a voice like the cruel sounds of stones clacking on one another underneath the sea. "Unlock the door. Slug is not with me.

"I am not accustomed to being commanded, whoever you are," said the soft, lilting, mocking voice. "Rather it is I who prefer to give the orders."

The Master ground his teeth. "Open the door, Princess. Now. I am alone, and I have a message for you."

"You may write the message down and slide it through to me. Or not, as you wish. I care for messages only if I am free to speak with the messenger myself. I shall not unlock the door."

Swearing under his breath, the Master fished a key on a cord out from underneath his high-necked tunic, inserted it in the keyhole of the door, turned it, and a latch snapped open. He pulled on the handle again, and the door ground open.

He was in a high, spacious, light-filled room whose windows looked out over the sea and the city. Seated at a loom was a young woman dressed in a long white gown. Her gleaming red-gold hair fell in a broad free cascade of color down her back. Her deep-green eyes looked boldly yet calmly at the dark figure which stood before her.

Ah, she does have the true beauty, the Master thought to himself, *beauty almost greater than gems and coins, her eyes than emeralds, her hair than gold, her love worth more almost than power.*

"How are you this morning, Princess?" rumbled the Master in his rocky, deep-sea voice as he pulled the door to behind him until its latch lock clicked closed.

"Indeed, General, I have been so fatigued by the constant stream of visitors," said the girl, "that I hope you will excuse me if I do not rise to greet you with the respect you deserve."

He ignored the irony as he limped toward the loom. "You look well enough, Princess. You were more courteous to your master in days past."

"You are not my master, nor will you or any other ever be," she replied with a mixture of calm amusement and indignation. "You can conceal me, you can keep me prisoner, you can even kill me, but you cannot command or corrupt me. Surely you must have learned that by now."

With warring emotions, he regarded the proud, beautiful figure whose hands shifted the shuttle rapidly through the warp and drew repeatedly the bar to her beautiful breast. He desperately craved this serene, wild soul to legitimize his rule, but he also wished to rip and crush her when she defied him. He felt he could as easily tear with his briary hands that beautiful skin as caress it.

Matters had gone past the point where he could merely release her and the king. She must capitulate, or she and her father must die. Why not just kill them and be rid of them? Indeed, why not! What was the necessity of a family connection between himself and Aleth Trealthweow? It was a weakness in him. He knew it, but his reign required it if he were to rule over people rather than stones. Ah, the people. How he wished he could do without them. It was their wretched regard for her that drove him to these compromises. Ach! The paradoxes of power. Such humiliation to have to court such a willful filly.

"All I have learned, my dear princess, is that my love for you grows stronger every day," he began smoothly. "It is only the frustration of that love which urges me to possessiveness. It is your own refusal you must blame for your treatment. If you will marry me forever, you will find no more equable a lover in the universe."

She looked up at him archly from her loom. "My 'dear' Juncata, Darkness Walking, have I not often told you that fair action is the only promise worth regarding? You may best court me by freeing my father and me. Then we will consider your proposal. You may yet have your chance at the riddle, and your wisdom may yet win me, but it is by that means alone you may succeed. My father will *not* entrust me to someone who cannot meet the test. And consent *cannot* be forced from me. You know all this, yet you persist in holding us."

"It has taken me years, Princess, to get where I am, and I do not intend to sacrifice any advantage now that I have. Consider your alternatives. It is either me, or virtually nothing, since that poor red-headed fool who stepped up to answer would surely have had no answer, and even if he had had one that satisfied you and your father and that inept, bumbling, mumbling RiddleMaster, would you really want to be matched with a farm boy who had never been out into the world, who had never even fought a battle in that laughable rusty armor he inherited?"

The shuttle and the bar paused. "He has fought one battle and emerged victorious too."

"That paltry skirmish? The boy's knighthood is a fraud. Clifford of the Rocks was only a king by his own designation."

"And yourself?" asked the princess.

The black electricity of anger spurted into his right hand, raising it upright and making it itch grievously to strike her. He took hold of it with his left and brought it back down and held it on his chest. "Princess, you really have no alternatives."

"You forget that there is always one alternative to the dishonor you are offering me."

"Honor, dishonor what is the difference? They are meaningless words," he spat out angrily. "What matters is wealth, pleasure, power, and progeny. You should not abandon your destiny for a mere word, an airy nothing of 'honor,' Princess. No one would, unless they were insane."

"You think honor is just a word?"

"Truly it is, Princess. The world cares nothing for it. Any sensible woman knows that."

"And so my captivity here is to help me come to my right senses? Is that it?"

Juncata smiled, showing a line of sharklike white teeth through the thick dark beard that covered his face and chin. The princess shuddered in spite of herself.

"You have hit it quite exactly," said the Master of Darkness. "You *will* eventually see the rightness of what I say."

"If that is so, then I know myself only slenderly," replied the princess, returning her attention to her weaving. She again began to sing in her high, clear voice, the same serene song the general had heard from outside the door, a random melody that started a small white flame of panic deep within him.

"Sing no more in my presence," he growled harshly. The princess stopped but continued her weaving. "You will come to see that my way is the way of stability and order for the people. What did I find here when I arrived? Anarchy! Mere anarchy! I brought order and discipline, and it is these benefits that you are denying *them* when you deny me. Between us, we could bring that order to the rest of the land and to the lands beyond. It is mere perversity that keeps you from recognizing it. It is a necessary and inevitable development and by your stiff-necked resistance you are merely delaying what will eventually come. Spare yourself and me further pain by acquiescing. Become my bride."

"Master Dark, if it is inevitable, you certainly don't need my help. And besides, what would your—what do we call her now—your 'sister' say?"

At this, Juncata stomped his foot in fury and pointing his left hand at the princess, cursed her witheringly. She gasped as her joints twisted with contorting pains and a sharp throbbing filled her head. She dropped the shuttle and rose from the loom to face the general.

Standing unsteadily as the pain increased, she said in a voice filled with mixed anger and anguish, "I will not give in, Dark. You cannot have me by force." And then as the pain spread into her muscles and finally her womb, she fainted and fell in a heap on the floor.

Juncata lowered his hand, turned in disgust, and, unlocking the door, left the room, leaving the princess lying twisted and unconscious by her loom. He relocked the door and then drew the beam across it and slammed it into place in the iron staples with a crash that shook the whole tower. Descending the tower staircase limpingly two steps at a time, Juncata snarled, "Out of my way," at Slug, whose drooling boy-head bobbed up and down in worshipful servility. Two soft, hurt eyes peered out through the tower door window, staring after the Master as he hobbled in rage back to the great hall. He crossed it to the north tower on the opposite side of the castle and climbed another flight of stairs until he came to a room partway up and knocked. A woman's voice, sounding like steel on slate called out, "Enter."

Juncata pushed open the door. Standing by an open window dressed in a slickly glittering black leather jacket and leather pants was a pale bony woman. She had one booted foot up on the window ledge and, with a file-surfaced dagger, was shaping her black nails into points. Her short black hair ruffled at her collar, but in a line down the middle of her part, at the roots, the hair was ghastly dead white. She turned to the door, showing a gaunt, shriveled, and lined face, the face of a crone. "Ah, brother," croaked the figure. "I have been wondering where you were."

"I have been talking to Aleth, and she has made me mad again."

"She always will. I wish you could see, brother, that you do not need her. All you wish, all you need, you can have without her. The king, however, I agree you must have."

"And how, dear sister, can I secure the king without securing the daughter?"

"Drink, drugs, and desire," she snapped out, "the downfall of royalty from the beginning of time."

"And if he shows no such interests?"

"Torture. Let *me* have him," she smiled cruelly, showing pointed black teeth.

"Perhaps it will yet come to that. But not yet. Sister, come with me on an inspection of the castle. I do not like the feel of things. There are no grumblings I know of, but in the concentration I have been making on affairs over the mountains, I don't wish to let things closer to home get out of hand."

"Very well, brother."

The two left the room and descended the tower staircase, two dark, hard, figures: Juncata the taller and thicker, walking swiftly even with his limp. Within the citadel, one guardsman was without his helmet, and Juncata ordered him to the brig for ten days. They made a circuit of the main courtyard, inspecting the gate and its defenses and found nothing untoward. Back inside the castle, they descended into its bowels where the dungeons and storerooms were. They came into a great barnlike room with a huge door in the floor that opened right out into empty space. A huge pulley mounted on a tetrangular frame straddled the opening. Below, moored to a large, square floating raft, they saw lighters loading a huge cargo net with bales and sacks and casks. In the gloom off to the side of the cavernous storeroom, a crew chief barked an order and eight prisoners in chains began clanking and tramping around a capstan whose rope ran to the pulley. Down below, the cargo net drew to a knot and slowly began to rise toward the opening. When it was within the opening, another crew grappled it aside on to the storeroom floor, emptied it quickly, and then sent it back down to the surface of the sea. Everything seemed to be in order. The storerooms were filled with enough food and drink to sustain the garrison for a year or more.

They descended further to the prison cells. The jailers were all awake, and all the prisoners were accounted for. At last they came to a double-locked room. Juncata withdrew from his shirt the cord chain on which he kept his key. His companion drew out a similar key, and using their two keys together, in two separate locks, they unlocked the door. Then, turning a large wheel on the door, they slowly drew back steel bolts as thick as a man's thigh and swung the heavy door open. Entering, they pulled the door shut and slid the bolts home with a parallel wheel on the inside. The small room was dimly lit by a pale-green glow which ascended from a round opening three feet in diameter in the floor of the room. Looking down, Juncata saw the surface of the ocean water trembling slightly and the sandy bottom of the bay. An occasional fish crossed his view.

Without a word, the woman stepped to the edge of the rock rim. She raised her arms straight above her head and uttered three jagged, guttural words. Then she stepped off the edge of the opening and dropped from view. A moment later a small sound of the parting of water rose up the shaft of the rock well. Sighing, Juncata imitated her gesture, words, and act, and he too disappeared into the depths.

Presently, Juncata was seen to emerge from the captain's cabin in the stern of his black ship, startling the deck watch, which had not been aware he was aboard. He spoke to his first mate, who disappeared below. A slim, dark-haired ensign almost immediately appeared and presented himself to Captain Juncata for instructions. Receiving them, he lowered a boat which pulled off swiftly across the bay with four oarsmen rowing and the ensign himself at the tiller. The afternoon waned, and eventually the boat that had left returned. A crow circled lazily in the sky above the ship as the ensign climbed the ladder, and the boat itself was hoisted back into its stays. After speaking briefly to Juncata, the ensign disappeared below. As the sun sank, Juncata finally left the deck in charge of the first mate. When the disk of the sun was fully beneath the horizon, two dark, squid-shaped shadows detached themselves from the stern of the black ship and shot swiftly back toward the castle. As they approached it, they melted into the shadows at the base of the citadel and were swallowed up by the black granite base of the rock itself.

Chapter 37

The Arena

Earlier that afternoon, in the crowded entrance passage under the arena seats, John, Palla Nad, and Yanibo waited in clown costumes for their cue. The band played a watery fanfare, Chauri bawled out a nearly incomprehensible welcome in the center ring, and then he blew his shiny whistle three times as the band struck up a wheezing march. The whole troupe of performers lurched into a quick-paced trot around the arena, the horses, the elephants, the two camels, balky and awkward, circling around to the noise of applause in the packed arena, with clowns interspersed among the animals. Yanibo did cartwheels on the sand. Palla Nad danced crazily while he played his flute, and John, with his red beard protruding from the white clown face and his shaved head glistening above, trotted along inside a costume horse with a skirt of cloth that hid his legs. He made the large-eyed, silly-faced horse caper and curvet and run forward and backward and sideways in deliberate mockery of the actual trained horses in Chauri's circus. He pulled back on the reins yet made the stuffed body of the horse go forward, so it seemed as if he really were a very big rider on a very small horse which had a decidedly independent mind of its own. He pranced close to the seats, and when there was a child in the front row, he offered to thumb wrestle with him, and, of course, the child always won against the circus strongman.

As he stopped in front of a small, black-haired girl who was just ready to offer her hand to him, something hit him on his forehead. Someone in the seats was throwing things at him. He was hit again, with an unshelled peanut, right on the top of his bald head. After the child had won, John cavorted away, turning about and trying to see who the barbarous citizen was who was pelting him with peanuts. In the front row, two sections to the right from where the little dark-haired girl sat, was a small gnome of a man with a long white beard, bushy protruding eyebrows, and a tall conical cap who was standing up between two very beautiful girls. The little old man was throwing peanuts at him. A wave of anger swept over John. Who did he think he was, this ancient delinquent, and why had he picked on John? Suddenly, his knees went weak. The girl to the old man's left was Illanna, the daughter of Hubert the Gardener. So she had succeeded in reaching the coast! But had she located L'Orka yet? And did she know that her beloved was working for the customs service?

He still did not understand why the old man was throwing peanuts at him, but his anger subsided with the discovery of Illanna. Here at least was one old friend who might be of some help. On his second circuit of the arena, John pranced his clown horse close to the wall so he could catch Illanna's eye. He did so, and he saw her say with her mouth, "After the performance." The old man was no longer throwing nuts at him but was smiling in a most strange way. *Well*, thought John, *I will certainly give him a lesson when I meet him.*

The show went off successfully. The animal trainer in the center ring did sufficiently daring tricks to satisfy the crowd. The acrobats flew gracefully and dangerously over both end rings, and even though Yanibo, John, and Palla Nad were not in the center ring, their juggling act went well, with John's steadiness and massive strength an effective contrast to the monkeylike agility of Yanibo. For their final trick, Yanibo stood on one hand on John's head and spun colored rings around both feet and his free hand so that he looked for a moment like an oscillating rainbow.

Chauri had recruited every member of the troupe, even the aerialists, to do double duty in order to fill the three rings. Even more so John and Yanibo and Palla Nad, who were all required to participate in several acts in the end rings. One of these was a stale old magic performance Palla Nad had put together out of decrepit equipment Chauri had given him. Palla Nad had dressed himself up like a jungle witch doctor and did one or two simple productions and then a fake firing of a ruff-necked pig from a cannon into a barrel suspended from the top of the arena. Everyone but the youngest children knew the frizzy-headed old man used two pigs, but the crowd laughed riotously anyway, especially when the pig suspended high over the arena in the barrel squealed loudly and urinated on Palla Nad. Another of the added acts involved a strongman routine, in which John stood on a platform and held six of the aerialists supported by a long bar while they spun on swivels. For a finale, he supported a small bridge on his back while various members of the menagerie, including an elephant, walked over it.

Finally, however, the performance was over, completed to warm, loud, and long applause; now Chauri had only to await the verdict of the general's Master of the Revels. Chauri knew he had performed miracles in the last three days, but even so, there was still a chance he would not be rewarded and retained but would be shipped back to Imbal in disgrace and poverty, or perhaps worse. As the audience members slowly left their seats, Chauri waited in the corridor beneath the arena, mopping his brow anxiously.

Presently, D'Orcade appeared at the performers' entrance with his two companions, entered the curving corridor beneath the arena, and picked his way fastidiously among the animals and people. Chauri rushed up to him, bowing and scraping with his usual bustling obsequiousness, a manner that both offended and pleased D'Orcade. He welcomed it because he knew Chauri was serious about it, yet it also offended him because it reminded him of his own behavior toward Juncata. *Ah, these tyrannies,* he thought. *When freedom is absent, façade is survival.* Behind him, a few other members of the audience were peeking through the wide doors into the performers' area.

"Well, Chauri, not bad at all," said D'Orcade. "Not the best, but the people seemed to like it, and that is what counts with the general. I plan to recommend that your engagement here be continued, but you must work to maintain quality and to expand variety. Too many of the acts are obviously new and not fully rehearsed. We will ignore the tastelessness of the one with the pig. And for the rest, you must increase the polish. The people see you now as a novelty, but the longer you stay, the better you must be. And you must keep looking for new acts."

"Most assuredly, Lord D'Orcade. Most assuredly, we will try to do our best. Thank you, thank you, thank you."

"You must do more than try, Cheeri, if you value your health. You must succeed," said D'Orcade, adopting his best tone of motivational menace, enjoying the torment of the greasy little man, even while acknowledging to himself that the two of them actually worked at the same trade. He even acknowledged fearfully to himself, mustering a certain spiritual courage to do so, that his own health depended as much on Chauri as Chauri's did on him. A funny, fat, unattractive little man, to be sure, but you had to hand it to him, he knew circus.

Having activated Chauri's fear sufficiently, D'Orcade then shifted to the role of amicable producer, saying, "If I can help you to secure people or *matériel*, please call on me. We are, after all, so to speak, somewhat in the same boat, are we not?"

"What you say, Meestaire D'Orcade, you want my boat? Of course, of course. As long as you need it. I send it to your house quick quick."

"No, Chauri. You do not understand. It's just a manner of speaking. It means our interests are the same."

"If you say so, sir, if you say so, it must be."

He does not understand, thought D'Orcade, *how serious a crisis we are really in. Well, maybe it will be the greedy, shallow fools like him who will survive, and the rest of us . . .* He shuddered. "And now, Chauri, I would like to give my personal congratulations to some of your performers, if you will conduct me. I particularly want to say a word to that amazing little juggler you have, the one I met on the ship. What a most remarkable find. What did you say his background was?"

Still sweating, Chauri said, "I will find him for Your Excellency, but really he is a most mischievous boy. He is not worthy of your attention."

"Mister Cheerry, please do not contradict me. You may at some point owe your own fortunes to such members of your troupe. Lead me to him directly."

Bowing backward, Chauri responded with a despairing, "Yes, sir," irked and frustrated that the most uncontrollable member of his troupe was finding favor in his employer's eyes rather than one of his old dependables whom he had totally under his thumb and whom he knew would make no trouble for him.

Meanwhile, others were also seeking clown alley. An old man, accompanied by two young women, slipped into the shadows inside the performers' door just as Chauri led D'Orcade and his friends off in search of Yanibo. Morduc, Marianna, and Illanna waited until the group had progressed some distance down the row of stalls, and then they sauntered after them. The elephants were being fed, as were the rest of the animals. The roustabouts were just finishing putting the arena back in shape for the next performance. The entire back area was relaxed and comfortable. As Morduc and the girls followed at a distance, they finally saw D'Orcade and Chauri come to one of the end stalls where the clowns put on and took off their makeup and their costumes. John and Palla Nad and Yanibo were deep within the stall removing their makeup and changing into their street clothes. Chauri called Yanibo out, who, when he saw who was there, grinned his broadest white smile and greeted D'Orcade easily.

"Hey, Play Boss. How you like me juggle?"

"Most excellent, dear boy," said D'Orcade, placing a hand on Yanibo's shoulder. "How would you like to earn some more of those gold coins that interest you so much?"

"Sure, boss, what I got to do?"

"I'm giving a small private party tonight, and I would like you to perform, if you are free. Even if you are not free, let me advise you to get free. Not many people receive such invitations, and I urge you to accept."

"Sure, boss. My friends like parties too. They come with me. OK?" he said, indicating John and the old wooly-headed Palla Nad back among the other disrobing clowns.

"Come by yourself, Yanibo. My invitation is only for you. Leave your friends at home for the evening. I assure you, you'll have a wonderful time."

"Strong man got to get some gold too. Old man got to eat too. You invite all three, boss. Old man very funny. Him got special stories. Animals do funny things to animals, animals to people, people to animals. Make you fall on floor laugh. Him do funny magic. Him play flute good, I sing. Him do pissing pig routine too."

"Exactly, dear boy, why you should come alone," said D'Orcade emphatically, but then one of his companions leaned over to him and spoke in his ear. After a moment D'Orcade said, "Tommy thinks it is charming to see such loyalty to old friends in one so young. It is too rare an instance in this wicked world. You may bring your friends, and there will be gold for all of you, but you must tell your grandfather to leave his porcine humor here."

"OK! Mister Play Boss Man. We do. Where we go? When?"

"Tonight, anytime after sundown, dear boy, at my villa by the sea," replied D'Orcade, squeezing Yanibo's shoulder and his upper arm. "Just ask anyone. You will hardly be able to miss it. All the torches will be lit."

"OK, boss. We be there. Everyone got good time."

D'Orcade turned and began walking away with Chauri but suddenly turned back. "By the way, Chauri, I have yet another idea. Tomorrow evening, an old street magician will be playing at the castle for General Juncata himself. What would you say to our presenting that old walking skeleton there, and his magic act as well, and making it into a kind of competition between the two magicians? The street magician is very, very good. I wouldn't expect yours to win, you understand, but presenting it as a contest might be amusing. What do you say?"

John's heart jumped in his breast, and Yanibo's eyes lit up. Being careful not to appear too eager, Yanibo said boldly to D'Orcade, "I take care old man's business. Grandfather very good magic man. How much you pay? Cost extra, go to castle."

"Of course he'll perform, and for free too," said Chauri waving his arms and half shouting.

D'Orcade laughed at Yanibo. "You little gold digger, you. Everything is pay, pay, pay with you. Is there anything you wouldn't do for money?"

"Not much, boss," leered Yanibo brightly.

With a bland smile, D'Orcade tousled the boy's straight black hair and looked into his bold eyes. "Don't worry, Yano. I will see to it that you and your grandfather are properly rewarded."

"OK, boss. I trust you. We go to big rock castle and make old magician look silly."

"Very well, then," said D'Orcade, much amused by the boy's confidence, even though it was obviously his grandfather's magic act that would look silly if he went up against that wily old street fakir. "I'll see you tonight," he continued. "I'll let you know then whether the Master will approve adding your grandfather to the program. If he does, let me emphasize that you must be on time to the castle. The performances will come first, and after they are over, the general is providing a sumptuous supper for his guests. Of course, you will not be required to stay for that." D'Orcade turned and began to saunter away.

"Gotcha, Party Boss," Yanibo called after him. "We do good show. Very funny. Princess laugh really hard."

D'Orcade stopped in his tracks and spun about. "Who said anything about a princess?" he hissed at Yanibo, narrowing his eyes and looking hard at him. The boy lost his smile, realizing he had said too much. In the back of the stall, John could hardly breathe from anxiety.

Yanibo recovered himself and looked at D'Orcade drolly. "What you talking about, boss? Piss-ness with pig very hard. You gotta pay extra for pissing pig part."

D'Orcade looked at him, hardly believing the boy's effrontery. "You are both tasteless and indiscreet. I can put up with one, but not the other. Do you understand?"

"Gotcha, boss. Yano good monkey. See, hear, say, know nothing . . ."

"Exactly," said D'Orcade. Then after a pause, he continued smoothly, "I think we can do without the pig part tomorrow night." John breathed a silent sigh of relief.

"Sure, boss. Do with mice, with doves, whatever you want."

"Just eliminate that part completely," said D'Orcade musingly, as he contemplated the boy. *What did he know?* he reflected inwardly. *Am I taking too much of a risk with so young a minion? But such a young and beautiful child. He's tractable. If I make his fortune, he may be grateful.* Finally he began to move back toward the door along the curving line of stalls, with the fussing and steaming Chauri dancing attendance on him. "Until tonight then, Yano," he said over his shoulder. "Do not fail me—in any way."

"Right, boss," called Yanibo after him.

As they strolled past the stalls back up to the door, Chauri introduced D'Orcade to other members of the troupe. He made inquiries of several about whether they would be willing to play at the castle at some time in the future. All who were asked were willing and delighted at the chance of making some extra money, and Chauri too was immensely satisfied that the circus had found favor. Although he continued to be worried about the insecurity of their position, just at that moment he saw visions of coins tumbling into the nearly empty strongbox under his desk in the boat-on-wheels ticket office parked in the murkiest recesses of the arena holding area.

As D'Orcade and his companions moved ever closer to the main door, Morduc slipped carefully out of the stall into which he had retreated and moved through the shadows toward the clowns' stall. Marianna and Illanna flowed closely behind. Morduc nodded to Illanna who went forward and called softly, "John."

John and Yanibo and Palla Nad were huddled together closely, whispering. Only one of the other clowns was left. At the sound of her voice, John raised his head and looked stupidly at her. He looked around fully and carefully and then slowly got up and came over to her.

"Illanna?" he said quietly.

"Yes," she replied.

"How did you get here?"

"It's a long story. Is it safe to talk here?"

"I'm not really sure any place in this city is safe to talk. What is it?"

"I have a friend of yours with me. Two friends, in fact."

"Who is it?" said John, unable to conceive of what she meant, but beginning nevertheless to give her his own news. "And I know, Illanna, there is alive a friend of yours as well, about whom you no doubt have worried mightily."

"Have you found L'Orka?" she gasped.

"I haven't talked to him, but I have seen him, and I know what work he does. What possible friend of mine could be with you?" Illanna took him by one of his huge hands and drew him slowly out of clown alley and into the adjoining stall. There in the shadows, he saw the strange little old man who had been throwing peanuts at him.

"So it's you," said John, growing angry again. "Why did you throw things at me, old man? I have half a mind to show you the consequences of your discourtesy."

At this, a slim figure slipped out of the shadows, a dark-haired girl with beautiful features and dark eyes. "If you think to try it, big man, you must deal with me first," she said, "and you will find me harder to deal with than I look."

From behind her, the old man cackled in laughter. "My daughter gets somewhat petulant when people threaten me. You're a pretty big egg, but she could crack you and cook you just as easily as I myself once cooked eggs for you when you were cracked, fried, and nearly scrambled yourself many long days and nights ago."

John started and looked carefully at the laughing green eyes. He looked all around him and saw none other but himself and the two girls and the old man before him. Softly he said, "Morduc?"

"None other, but be careful still . . ." Before Morduc could finish his sentence, John had jumped forward and put both his giant arms around the little old man and had given him a huge hug.

"At last!" John said. "I wondered if I would ever see you again, my friend. You give me hope once more that we will be able to . . ." Here Morduc interrupted John, putting his hand over his mouth.

"Ssh. Not aloud," he said. "And I am glad to see you too. When you disappeared in the river, I thought I might have to do . . . er . . . 'this job' alone. My hopes soar too to find you here and as sturdy as ever, and with new allies as well, even as I have, and with resolution, like your head, undulled."

John finally calmed down enough to be introduced to Marianna and to tell them briefly about Palla Nad and Yanibo.

"Well, John, we mustn't drag our feet. Sooner or later someone we need not name will get on to us. We really have only one chance. Do you have a plan?"

"None at all. I am actually lucky just to be here alive. Do you?"

"Not a plan, but a thought. To make that thought into not even a whole plan, but into just the major part of a plan requires someone to create a distraction, as it were. I don't quite see how I can do what I want without help, but if I had help—well, in short—I have a chance to get inside the castle tomorrow . . ."

"So do Yanibo and Palla Nad," said John, his heart leaping. "They are to be part of a contest against some magician. That fellow in velvet who just left wants Palla Nad to show his circus magic at the castle tomorrow night against some nasty old disreputable street magician who is in the pay of Juncata. If anyone could disrupt his performance, it would be Yanibo. I'm not part of it, but that's the closest I can come to getting inside, but it doesn't sound very promising to me."

"Indeed?" said Morduc, chuckling. "I think I know who their nasty opponent will be. He would be green with envy if your friend went up against him and won."

"Green?" said John, suddenly beginning to grasp the situation and smiling broadly. "Then they ought surely to talk sometime, my friends and this other magician. One wouldn't want to go about arranging the outcome of such a contest ahead of time, I suppose, especially, when the audience is so important a person as the He Whom We Will Not Name, but still something might come of it. What do you think?"

"I think I would rather have you there too, but then Our Mutual Friend might recognize you, in spite of your sliding your head hair down to your chin, but it may be the best we can do."

"Come and meet my friends then," said John eagerly. "You can tell them what you want done and what you plan to do." John moved toward the opening of the stall, but Morduc hung back in the shadows.

"Wait," he whispered. John turned back. "I think I should spare all of you the knowledge of what I shall try. Simply tell your young friend and the old man to prepare chaos and confusion. I will do the rest. Perhaps you, John, will be able to help at the right moment from outside."

"Very well, if you think that best. But it doesn't seem quite right. After all, she is my . . ." Morduc put his hand over John's mouth again to keep him from saying more.

"I also think that we must not ever be seen together, these friends of yours and myself. Suppositions are best dealt with by being prevented."

"Well thought again. I will carry the message and trust to the best. But one more thing. Yanibo and Palla Nad and I are supposed to go to a party tonight at the house of that orchid who hired them for tomorrow. Should we go?"

"I think I know of whom you speak. You should go. He may be of help to us in spite of himself. Our fisherman friend is likely to be somewhere in the city as well. I haven't seen or talked to him yet, but he will have some suggestion if we can find him before tomorrow night." Morduc held out his hand. John took it in his great paw and shook it. Then Morduc moved to the entrance of the stall where the two girls were on guard, and together all three moved quietly and unobtrusively up the barn and slipped out the door.

John waited a moment, then left the stall and sauntered back down toward the clowns' dressing room. When he got there, Yanibo was grinning broadly at him. "Now we gottum. Everybody here. We fix good."

John looked over the edge of the stall and around the empty barn quickly. "Ssh," he said, astonished at Yanibo's percipience. The clowns' makeup alley was now completely deserted except for the three. Yanibo grabbed the hands of both Palla Nad and John and started dancing around in a circle. In the dimly lit barn, the noise disturbed the animals, and they started squawking and roaring. A rough human voice yelled at them from the darkness near the main door, "Cut that, you fools."

Yanibo stopped his dance abruptly and mouthed the word silently, "Bolta?" John nodded. They had thought the barn was deserted. *Had he heard anything?* John wondered. *Had he seen anything?* The three finished changing into their street clothes. As they went off to dinner, they passed Bolta as they did so, curled up behind a hay bale, with a brown bottle cradled in his arms. As the three went off through the darkness, Bolta said to himself, "So the Ox is happy. Happy at being in the show while I'm still hauling logs. I'll fix him. I'll gore that Ox." He laughed to himself at his joke and took another sip of the bottle. A faint rustling came from the far end of the arena barn. A small flow of black oil came down over the gunwale of Chauri's houseboat and dropped into the straw on the barn floor. It flowed limpingly across the straw. It smelled pig. Bolta saw the small river of oil slither past him over the straw. He had had the horrors several times, but there had never been anything like this in them before. A blind head, with wounds festering a purplish gray moss, stuck its snout over the hay bale, behind which Bolta cowered, speechless and motionless. The head smelled the alcohol and backed away. Not pig. It went on down the barn. Bolta fainted dead away, the bottle in his hand falling on the floor and trickling almost empty.

CHAPTER 38

Night Beetle

When Morduc, Illanna, and Marianna got back to the Green Dragon from the circus and were about to go upstairs to their rooms, Mother Gump called to Morduc, who stopped while the others went on. Drawing him aside in the noisy, busy, smoke-filled room she said, "You have a visitor. Go into the cellar."

Morduc looked at her carefully. She returned his gaze steadily, almost as if she had not in fact asked him to do so unusual a thing.

Morduc inclined his head toward the open door through which the tapsters descended to the cellar where the barrels of beer and wine were kept in cool, dark dampness.

"There?" he said.

"Yes," she said quietly, looking away from him as she spoke. Morduc drifted as inconspicuously as he could toward the end of the bar, and then slipped past it, to an open door from which a flight of stone steps went down to the cellar. The steps were steep, and the cellar seemed very dark indeed. He reached the bottom and could smell a certain dankness mixed with the smell of wine and beer. There was a pale light burning behind some large casks, and he cautiously made his way toward it. He came around a large beer barrel and saw a small stub of candle set upright on the floor, in front of the earthen wall of the cellar. Morduc looked around him. There was no one about. He stepped closer to the candle and picked it up in its dish, not knowing what to do next. Suddenly he felt something like a cannon ball slam into the small of his back, propelling him toward the wall and extinguishing the candle in his hand all in the same moment. But instead of being smashed up against the dirt wall of the cellar, he hit nothing and found himself stumbling forward into emptiness for eight or ten feet in total darkness and falling face downward on damp dirt. What was happening? Had he misjudged the distance to the wall? He reached out ahead of him to see if he could touch it but encountered nothing. He spat out a few crumbs of dirt. Then, behind him, he heard a door swishing closed and a wooden bar dropping into place. No one assaulted him further, but he felt as if he were surrounded by a darkness that extended up and out from the floor where he lay millions and millions of miles into eternity. He smelled a faint fishy odor which he suddenly recognized. Then a match was struck and a candle lit in what was now clearly a room, though how large Morduc could not tell. Plummet's round face and large form emerged from the darkness in deep chiaroscuro.

"Well, Master Magician, we meet for the first time, ha, ha. You look like a little shriveled-up old bean of a man. But if we plant you, will you grow?"

"Well, just among us magicians," said Morduc from where he lay, much relieved but still a bit out of breath, "how did you do *that* trick?"

"Dum, tee, dum," hummed Plummet. "There is more to mastering darkness than even someone else who might think he knows all about it truly knows."

"I thought for a moment," said Morduc sitting up and brushing the dirt off his hand, "that Mother Gump had turned me in to the police."

"Never, never, never for a moment," said Plummet. "She is one of us, and as quick and clever as can be. And another one you can rely on is NightBeetle there behind you." Morduc turned his head but saw no one and turned back to Plummet.

"Jokes again?"

"No. Look again."

Morduc got to his knees and swiveled around. The shadows shifted, and there moved toward him on fingertips and toes the nearly prone figure of a lithe and muscular young man dressed completely in black. His skin too was inky black; black his hair and mustache, and most surprisingly, not only the pupils and the irises of his eyes were dark, but the eyeballs themselves were a deep gray, almost-black graphite color. The face smiled a narrow white grimacing smile of teeth all filed to sharp points. It nodded at Morduc but said nothing. Morduc shivered a bit.

"Yes," said Plummet. "He does somewhat inspire terror when you see him. But few ever do. Beetle is a creature of the night, of the undersides of docks, of secret tunnels. He carries messages and money from one place to another for me. He sleeps in small holes. And sometimes"—and here Plummet too gave a kind of involuntary shudder—"Beetle even bites if necessary."

Behind him in the darkness, Morduc heard a soft snickering and heard a faint scuttling of feet over the packed earth. Morduc remembered the sharpness of the thrust forward and his still-aching neck that had been snapped like a whip by the swiftness of the blow. Morduc stood up and went over to where the young man was stretched out against the wall and held out his hand, but Beetle merely scowled, shaking his head.

"Ah, Morduc," Plummet explained, "Beetle is reliable but not friendly. Just pretend he is not there."

Morduc rubbed his neck thoughtfully.

"Well now," said Plummet, taking his own advice, "what have you found out? Where are we in this project? At least I know you have arrived safely, and I must say you certainly look the part."

"There are two singular bits of news," said Morduc. "The best is that by accident I have found John."

Plummet snapped his head up, and his jaw dropped open. "Yes? And the Master's spies have not recognized him?"

"One cannot be sure," continued Morduc, "but only in the girth of his arms and thighs does he resemble his former self. Our friend Red John is now what might be called the Bald and Bearded John. He is with a circus and has two friends with him, an old man and a boy from the rain forest."

Plummet stared at Morduc, incredulous. He took off his hat, and ran his hand over his white hair. "Red John? Alive? *And* in the city? Well!" he chuckled, "We really are in luck then. We may not have to carve this roast all by ourselves after all. Well, what else?"

"The second is the most interesting. I am scheduled to perform for Juncata at the castle tomorrow evening."

Plummet turned completely around where he stood. "*Fandago?* You will actually be admitted *to* the castle?"

"I believe so," said Morduc. "Myself, certainly, and possibly Illanna and Marianna as well."

Plummet was silent for a minute or so, chewing on a braid of his beard. "Very well, then. You must bring me an exact description of the layout and the defenses." His eyes gleamed in the faint light of the candle, the flame of which wavered and shook in the still air whenever he moved. "We must also find a way to get a message to the princess so that she will be ready when the time comes to cooperate with our attempt to rescue her and her father. But how we are to do that without arousing the suspicions of the general, I do not know."

They sat in silence. Suddenly, Morduc had an idea. "If you can get me a frog before tomorrow morning, I think I can deliver the message."

Plummet looked at him strangely. "A frog, good Morduc? A frog?"

"Yes, Plummet. A frog. Just a frog. Any frog, not too young though. A fair-sized frog."

"Very well. Beetle? Will you see to that please?"

A faint twittering and clacking came from out of the darkness.

"He wants to know—alive or dead?" said Plummet.

Startled, Morduc said quickly, "Alive, if you please. Very much alive. Unfrightened, if possible."

With no more than a breathing in the shadows, he was gone. Somewhere, Morduc heard a whistle of wind for just a second, and then nothing. "My minions have also brought me some additional intelligence as well," continued Plummet. "Sometime tonight there will be a pirate raid, or at least a pseudo pirate raid. My guess is that Juncata is feeling insecure and that he has planned this raid in order to remind the people once again of his value to them. The pirates, so called, will attack, the alarm will be given, and his troops will rush to the defense. The pirates will be driven off, and a grateful populace will once again overlook his spying, his exactions, and his solitary control. But I hope to have a little surprise for the general. Through Beetle, I have made contact with someone in the customs service that some of us may know, one L'Orka by name. He has gathered a group of stout lads who are willing to try themselves to drive off the pirates without the aid of the regular troops. If the people discover that they can defend themselves, Juncata's hold will be that much weakened."

"I should like to be part of that action," said Morduc.

"That can be arranged," said Plummet, "but would it not be best to save yourself for the castle?"

"Are you suggesting that I might be killed? Some will be, you know," said Morduc, "perhaps even this cheerful person whose name begins with L and whose demise would make supremely uncheerful a certain person whom we both know."

"He and his friends know that, but they are intending to win their happiness now, in their youth, for a long, free life, rather than sneak and submit for a long life that is no life, where some other is master over them rather than they be masters over themselves. Some will die, but they prefer that to the fear and walking death they live now. They are willing to try to unseat Juncata. If he can be destroyed, they will be remembered as heroes."

"And if not?"

"Then undoubtedly all of us will be killed and, if Juncata has his way, forgotten rather than despised. He has been trying to extirpate all memory of a time when things were done differently, and he has almost succeeded. Yet even if he did, there would still be born some who would hate him with their souls just for what he is. That is his great weakness. He can never be loved, only feared."

The candle flickered. In a moment or two, Beetle materialized from the darkness with a fat frog in his hands. The frog squirmed and kicked, but Beetle held it firmly.

"That was quick," said Morduc.

There was a clicking and twittering in Beetle's throat behind the razor-toothed smile.

"What did he say?" asked Morduc.

"He said, 'Quick as death,'" replied Plummet. "To look at Beetle now, you wouldn't imagine that he once sang and danced and was happy in the light."

"Yes?" said Morduc carefully reaching out and taking the frog from Beetle.

"Yes," said Plummet. "But the general thought he sang too much, talked too much, laughed and showed his teeth too much."

Morduc shivered again but asked anyway, "And?"

"The general cut out his tongue and kicked him out of the castle door, naked and bleeding at the mouth. People did not speak as openly as they had after that."

The frog was struggling vigorously in Morduc's hands. Morduc turned his head down and made a few strange noises to it. The frog looked up in startlement, became motionless, and croaked back. "Yes, yes," said Morduc. "This frog and I will get along just fine. You have done well, Beetle."

Beetle looked first at the frog and then at Morduc. For the first time since Morduc had seen him, NightBeetle had an interested, respectful look on his face. He came over and stood before Morduc. With his right hand, Beetle first touched his own forehead and then his breast and then bowed to Morduc.

"Thank you," said Morduc, returning the gesture.

"Hmmmm," said Plummet. "You have learned a thing or two in your travels, I see."

"Yes," said Morduc, "at least one thing, perhaps even two."

"Very well, then, perhaps you will wish to stow your frog. If you do intend to fight with us tonight, you must obviously appear in a different guise than your present one, and further, Mother Gump needs to show you another secret of this inn. There are several entrances and exits besides the main one. When you change, I will instruct her to let you out into the city by another passage. I will leave Beetle here, and he can take you to our rendezvous. We can use every fighting hand we can get to drive off the pirates, or whoever it is that Juncata is paying to impersonate them."

"Good," said Morduc. "I will talk with the girls, have dinner, and then see you later tonight." Beetle put out the candle and unbarred the door into the inn cellar. They heard one of the tapsters come clumping down the stairs, draw a flagon of wine, and then stumble upstairs again. Softly Beetle opened the earth-covered door, and Morduc went into the cellar from which he went up the stairs and slipped back into the main room of the tavern just as if he had never been gone.

First he went upstairs to talk to Marianna and Illanna. Illanna agreed to stay in the inn for the evening to watch over their equipment and their new comrade, the frog, who was deposited in a covered basket. Marianna, however, wanted to join Morduc in the band that was to fight the pirates. Although Morduc did not wish to expose her to the danger, there was no denying her once she had her mind made up, and so it was agreed.

Next they went downstairs as the old magician Porteus Middock and his two daughters. They had dinner at a prominent table and were recognized by many. Morduc did one or two small table tricks to amuse the patrons and then announced loudly to Mother Gump that, old man as he was, he needed his rest and was therefore retiring for the night. The girls pretended they wished to remain in the tavern longer, but Morduc loudly required them to withdraw since he would not be there to chaperone them. They protested, but their old father insisted. The citizens in the room laughed good-naturedly, passing one or two sly winks among them.

Once upstairs, Morduc carefully removed his disguise, put on his usual suit of seventy times seven shades of green, and with Marianna in fighting clothes as well, they all three, along with Anga and the frog, sat waiting, locked in Morduc's room. Presently they heard a scraping in the wall, as if a mouse were scuttling along behind the panels. There was a soft knock, and a small invisible door only two feet square opened out into the room at the baseboard. Beetle's face appeared in the opening. He held out a cake of soot and made motions to Morduc and Marianna to put it on their faces and hands. When they had done so to Beetle's satisfaction, he put it back into a small pocket in his belt, beckoned to them, and disappeared into the opening. First Morduc and then Marianna squeezed through, and then the door closed silently. Illanna, extinguishing the candle, lay down on the bed and pulled a robe over her. Anga rested on the floor at the foot of the bed with his head on his paws. As Illanna drifted off to sleep, she heard the frog shifting and making low, but not unhappy, croaking sounds in its basket.

CHAPTER 39

The Party

After John, Palla Nad, and Yanibo had eaten their dinner at a small tavern close to the arena, they returned to clown alley to get ready for the party. All three washed. Palla Nad combed his iron-gray hair so it stood up straight on his head and tightened his rainbow belt around his long white tunic. Yanibo had found a long shirt to go on top of his leopard skin waist wrap. John made his sleeveless leather jerkin shine. Yanibo danced around the stall. "Woo woo. John got party clothes on! All ready?"

John nodded, but he felt incomplete without his sword and armor. It was supposed to be a party they were going to, but who knew what might happen? They were deep within the city of the Master of Darkness, his archenemy. At any moment they could be attacked, and he would have no weapon with which to defend himself.

"Why sad face?" asked Yanibo.

"I don't feel right without a weapon."

Yanibo tapped his head with his finger. "Here best weapon. You sharp there, you no need sharp anything else. Always find big knife."

John smiled at the boy. "Well, I haven't lost my head—yet. I guess I'm ready then."

Yanibo led the way in his white tunic, carrying his bag of juggling apparatus. Palla Nad, tall, thin, and brown, his flute tucked in his rainbow belt, followed. John brought up the rear, looking quite formidable with his bald brown head, the red-gold hair of his long beard, and his massive chest and shoulders nearly bursting the sleeveless leather jerkin.

By now Bolta had regained consciousness but had not moved from behind the hay bale. He eyed them enviously as they passed him on the way out. "All pretty for the party?" he sneered. "Some people have all the luck."

"Hey, Bolta," Yanibo said brightly. "I steal bottle big folks brandy for you. You like?"

Bolta paused a moment before he spoke. "You can keep your friggin' velvet pretty boy's brandy. I don't need no help from you to get what I want. Maybe I'll get some tonight, same as you."

"I steal you two bottles, Bolta. You have good time along us." Bolta grumbled but said no more as they passed. As they left the arena, all three pulled hooded brown cloaks about them. Bolta was too drunk to stand. He really wanted to be out of the barn going to their party with them but knew he could not. After that weird dream he had had of a large black snake facing him, he did not want to be alone, but he was. He had been too proud to ask. He was as good as they were, in spite of their fancy connections. But he'd show them, somehow. Maybe in the morning he'd just say something to one of the policemen. Then things would go back to the way they had been when everyone was afraid of him, even Chauri. He pulled the bales of hay closer around him and fell asleep.

John, Palla Nad, and Yanibo moved silently through the streets, still crowded with people, though stars-out time was approaching. As they walked northward across the peninsula toward the north shore, Yanibo inquired directions twice, and once they were stopped by a pair of the ubiquitous police, who laughed a hard, knowing laugh when Yanibo told them where they were going. Eventually the street they were on came to an end close to the shore, and they turned eastward along a broad divided boulevard lined with great walled estates fronting on the beach.

They could hear the ocean and occasionally see it through spaces between the walls. They continued their eastward progress for a mile or so. Occasionally a carriage would rattle up the street from behind and pass them. Eventually they saw several carriages pulling into a huge pink stuccoed house surrounded by a pink stone wall. Lamps were lit at the gate, and as the three on foot were approaching the gate house, yet another carriage flew past them full of laughing, costumed young men and women, all dressed in bright clothing and shining jewels. The guards checked their list of names and admitted the carriage and then did the same for the three on foot.

Inside the gate, they found a huge flagstone square surrounded by gardens with a small fountain playing in the middle, like a miniature town plaza. The carriages were drawn up around the edges, and the coachmen were lounging about under the trees, smoking, talking, and eating. Flaring yellow torches on poles cast a shifting light into the square. Opposite the gate, across the square, leading to the huge pink stucco house, was a broad flight of pink stone steps which swept up to a tall entryway with a stained-glass fanlight over it depicting a grape arbor. Its two red-lacquered, brass-bound doors stood wide open, disclosing a crowd of people in exotic dress milling about inside. John and Palla Nad and Yanibo ascended the stone steps and entered the high main hall. Straight ahead of them, spiraling up the sides of the hall, were two broad staircases leading to a railed landing from which corridors ran west and east into the second-floor wings of the house. Running under and between the two sweeping staircases was a broad passageway leading straight back to the ocean side of the house. To their left was a huge room lit by glittering chandeliers under which couples were dancing to the music of a small orchestra on a stage at the far end of the room. The large room to the right was filled with small, round white wire table sets with matching chairs; a long buffet loaded with food and drink ran along the inner wall.

John and Palla Nad and Yanibo went to the door of the dancing room and stood on its threshold, staring. All of the dancers were in costume. John noticed one woman clad only in a leopard skin and gold boots. Another floated by in a mist of diaphanous purple film which seemed at any moment ready to evaporate. For many of the dancing couples, he had difficulty telling which was the man and which the woman. Some couples seemed to be comprised of two of the same.

The host, Marivaux D'Orcade himself, sat in an orange velvet armchair raised above the level of the dancing floor on a small three-tiered dais set against the outside wall of the room between two of its long windows. He was wearing a pink velvet suit and held in one hand a tall glass filled with a pale-pink bubbly liquid. With the other, he waved a long pink cigarette holder. He greeted each of the arrivals effusively, at the same time talking loudly and animatedly to a flock of exotically costumed young men draped over the steps of the dais. D'Orcade looked up and saw the three standing in the doorway looking into the room, a crude and rough trio compared to the spangled fantasy of his other guests. With a little scream of delight, and holding his glass in his hand high above his head, he bounded down the three steps of the little platform and on his pink high heels streaked through the dancers, parting them like the petals of an orchid.

"I'm so glad you managed to find your way. We won't be ready for the entertainment for some time, however. Meanwhile, make yourselves at home, and Yano, I particularly want you to come and see some friends of mine. They're all dying to meet you, and they're such fun. You'll like them, and furthermore, they have just lots and lots of those gold coins you like so much. Leave your equipment with your friends there and come with me." Yanibo gave his bag of juggling paraphernalia to Palla Nad and allowed D'Orcade to pilot him back across the dance floor to the group he had just left and to perch him right on the gold velvet thronelike chair in which he had himself just been sitting.

"You are *my* king, tonight, Yano!" shrieked out D'Orcade in extravagant hilarity. John and Palla Nad saw D'Orcade and all his friends bowing to Yanibo, who stood up on the chair and took off his cloak so that he stood only in his leopard skin briefs, young, strong, brown, and slim. Laughing and joking with Yanibo, D'Orcade introduced him to each of his friends, for each of whom

Yanibo had a witticism which pleased the crowd of athletically molded and scantily clad young men.

Servants circulated about the floor with trays of tall glasses filled with the pale-pink bubbly liquid. One, slightly tipsy, stopped in front of John and Palla Nad and, offering the tray to them, said to John, "Wunnerful costume."

A bit taken aback, John replied evenly. "Not a costume. We're here to entertain."

"I thought you didn' look like one of these butterflies. What distric' you from? Y'remind me of my sister-in-law's secon' cousin. Make's him my wife's secon' cuzin too, right? Well, who cares? Drink up. H's a red beard too."

John debated what to answer. Finally he said, "I'm from cross river, in the country."

"Oh, that still makes you a local boy. Never mind. This is pretty good stuff. When D'Orky boy throws a party he goes aaaaaaalllllll out, and he don' mind if the he'p—you know—he'p—themselves." The waiter laughed uproariously at his joke. "'Ere, 'ave some."

Gravely, John and Palla Nad each took one of the tall glasses as the waiter himself quickly tipped up one of the glasses on the tray into his mouth, emptied it in three quick swallows, and put it back empty. The smiling waiter dodged off unsteadily among the mass of swirling dancers.

"I'm going to look around," said John in a low voice to Palla Nad. He went slowly back to the entrance hall of the house and then drifted beneath the curving wings of the stairs and down the large first-floor passageway running beneath them to the back. There were rooms off it to either side, and in them each, groups of men and women dressed in garish gold, or flowing silver, or smoldering red, or breathless purple were talking and laughing loudly. At the end of the corridor, a pair of paned glass doors had been thrown open to the night. Through them John could see that the party had spread out on to the lawn and beyond down to the water's edge. On the white beach beyond the grass, dark figures silhouetted against the shimmering moon-washed water chased each other, laughing back and forth across the sand. D'Orcade's villa was separated from the neighboring estates by bright pink walls running all the way to the water's edge.

After standing awhile on the terrace just outside the open glass doors, John drifted back into the house and back up the passageway to the main hall. From there, he slowly and deliberately went up one of the white-and-gold spiral staircases, while others passed him, running both up and down. When he got to the second-floor landing, John chose the westward-leading corridor and strolled toward the large window-door he saw at its end. He looked into several of the rooms that had open doors; in one he saw pink-and-white-striped satin walls, and a large wooden bed with purple sheets and orange blankets. Most of the doors were closed, and from behind some he heard muted laughter. At the end of the corridor, he opened the glass window doors and stepped out onto a small balcony.

From that height, he could see westward, down the long line of great villas on the shore all the way to the castle. To his left, on the other side of the shore boulevard, to the south, were a number of close-packed, modest houses of citizens, with wisps of smoke rising from their chimneys and the occasional glow of lamplight still in a few windows where the respectable members of the population were being kept awake by the sounds of D'Orcade's revelry. Far off down the peninsula to the west loomed the black mass of Juncata's castle rising on its rock. In one of the towers, the one to the south, like a very small star that had settled there, John saw a light. As he watched, it flickered, as if someone were passing to and fro in front of it. His heart leapt. *That could be Aleth*, he thought. His entire soul yearned to fly to that window, to see her, to talk to her again, to release her from her bondage, to restore her freedom. Then perhaps he would learn whether his answer had won him the quest. So much yet remained to be done before he could even begin to try to win her. First she must be freed, and then they must both forget that it was he who had freed her. He wondered indeed whether his strength and, more importantly, his patience would be equal to his desire.

Down below, the wild dance music of the orchestra had stopped and the guests had quieted. John heard Palla Nad's flute start to play. Above it rose Yanibo's high, clear, boyish voice. He was singing one of those entrancing songs of courtship and true love he had sung on their long trip down the river. The night was hushed. To the east, the moon was finally lifting free of the mountains' jagged edge.

As John returned his gaze to the light in the castle, so small and so far away, he caught, out of the corner of his right eye, a movement down on the beach. He turned and leaned out over the balcony, looking to seaward down the side of the villa. In the faint moonlight, he saw a small dark ship off the beach and four dark, silent boats rowing in. One had already touched the beach, and dark men were leaping out noiselessly. As John watched, he saw one of them approach two of the guests who were lying on the sand in an embrace. The lovers rolled apart just as the dark figure lifted a wide, curved sword above his head and, with one stroke, cut off the head of the man. The girl began screaming. The figure raised and let fall the sword again; her terrified shriek ended abruptly in a bubbling gurgle as her head too rolled seaward on the sand. By then, the other three boats had touched the beach with a soft scrunching. Over a hundred men with drawn swords were running up the beach toward the back door of the house.

Before John could move, he heard their running feet within the house, and almost immediately he heard most of them pass through and go out the front door. John leaned out over the balcony and looked southward toward the wide boulevard. The marauders who had passed out the front door, across the plaza, and out through the front gates into the boulevard crossed it and then systematically started kicking in the doors of the small houses lining it. A group would enter and then, a few minutes later, exit carrying bags of loot and then go on to the next. A few of the pirates remained in the little plaza before the house to cow the coachmen. Apparently someone in the houses across the avenue had gotten away out a back door because in the distance, John could hear an alarm bell ringing. Immediately after that, he saw crossing the boulevard and cutting through the yard of one of the villas west of him a different group of dark figures led by a fat man in a broad yellow hat. *Could it really be Plummet?* thought John in astonishment. *If he is here, leading a band, then perhaps . . .* They vanished among the trees. Presently there was a squirming motion atop the pink western wall of D'Orcade's estate. Dark figures began dropping to the ground just inside it.

One of the four guards left by the boats immediately blew an extremely loud whistle as members of the newly arrived band fell upon them and slew them all and began to hack at the boats. Now John could hear running feet coming back toward D'Orcade's house from eastward on the avenue.

John ran quickly back down the second-floor corridor to the stairs and peered over the rail of the landing. At the bottom of each staircase stood two heavily armed men, back to back, with vicious, cruel, and filthy faces and scimitars in each hand. *Four pirates and eight swords*, thought John. *How can I do this?* The guests in the two large main rooms of the house had all been herded into the ballroom where they were being systematically stripped of their jewels by three of the pirates.

If only I had Red Dragon, thought John. *Yanibo is not always right. The weapon has its place, both in order and disorder. But I must make do with what I have.*

Now clearly was his chance. The attention of the four pirates guarding the stairs was directed toward the front and back doors. Just as the members of Plummet's group burst in through the back and the pirates by the stairs turned to fight them, John gave a great yell and, leaping down the left-hand stairs five steps at a time, grabbed the neck of each of the surprised pirates at the bottom and knocked their heads together. As they dropped, he instantly caught up two of their cutlasses, one in each hand, and began to attack the boulevard-looting pirates who were beginning to surge back into the house through the front door.

He stabbed one in the back, severing his spine so that he crumpled like a piece of discarded rag. A second turned, and John slashed with his other sword, severing his head from his body in one blow. The body fell backward, and the head went bounding across the floor like a kicked ball splattering blood on the pink marble as it rolled down the steps into the ballroom and across its floor.

By now, the hall was filled with the men of Plummet's band coming in through the back passageway, cutting off the retreat of the pirates who were boiling in through the front door, trying to get to their boats.

In the ballroom, the guests shrank back against the stage on which the members of the orchestra were crouching behind their instruments. At the sides of the room, other guests were trying to open windows to climb out. John could see from the hall that several of the pirates were still menacing a group clustered around D'Orcade, within which was Yanibo and Palla Nad. Fighting furiously, both swords flashing around him like wheels, John gave a great yell and leaped rightward to the threshold of the ballroom. At his yell, the pirates in the ballroom turned. Yanibo reached out with one of his juggling clubs and knocked one of them on the head, dropping him to the marble floor like a piece of thread. Palla Nad, old as he was, grabbed up the fallen pirate's sword and stuck it in the side of another pirate. The remaining pirates swept past John out of the ballroom. He let them go and quickly crossed to Palla Nad and Yanibo.

As the intensity of the fighting increased in the hallway, the superior experience and discipline of the pirates began to tell. Slowly the citizens who had come in through the rear passageway were pushed back down the wide corridor, and more and more pirates were able to crowd into the main hall through the front door. Suddenly there was a wild yell from the back of the house. Some of the pirates had pulled the same trick on the citizens that the citizens had pulled on them. They had climbed over the walls of the adjoining houses and, from there, over the pink eastward wall of D'Orcade's estate to attack their attackers in the rear. Plummet's citizens rushed out the back door of the house through the wide open glass doors to help their comrades outside. The pirates coming through the front door were sucked after them with a great whoosh, like water going down a suddenly unclogged drain.

John waited until he saw that all the pirates were out of the hall and that the people in the ballroom were safe. Then, followed by Palla Nad and Yanibo, he ran after the pirates down the passageway to the back, his two swords at the ready, like the shining horns of a bull. The fighting was now all on the lawn and the beach. Instead of two lines facing each other, there was a tangle of individual fights on the grass and sand. As the moon rose higher in the east, illuminating the scene on the beach, John fought furiously in the center with Palla Nad beside him. Time and time again, the massive red-bearded warrior struck a pirate in the eye or hacked off an arm. The pirates as a group had broken through the citizens and were now retreating in good order toward their boats. Just as the last group was about to push off in the two boats that remained seaworthy, John gave a yell and rallied a group of the citizens. They dashed into the surf and each one pulled one more pirate out of each boat and slew him in the shallows, darkening with blood, the already-dark water. Finally, however, the pirates succeeded in disengaging. They rowed out onto the moonlit black slick of the sea just as the clattering hoof beats of Juncata's pirate guard troops could be heard arriving in the boulevard before D'Orcade's house.

The citizens and some of the guests together gave a great shout and hoisted John on their shoulders. "Hooray for the red beard. Hooray for Two Swords." They put him back down on the sand as the pirate guard came through the house, led by their captain, a tall man with a great long mustache and a drawn sword, but there was no longer anything for them to do except prod the dead bodies with the toes of their boots.

"Well," said the captain, smoothing his mustache, "you've done pretty well all by yourselves. Hardly anything left for us to do. The general will be very interested to know that a group of citizens fought off the pirates by themselves. Of course, he will be pleased, won't he?" Then, casting his eye around the group of citizens he inquired sharply, "Who's in charge of this posse?" The citizens began quickly to melt into the darkness and flow back up over the pink walls. In just a few moments, John was left standing alone with Palla Nad on the beach, holding two bloody cutlasses, surrounded by the bodies of the slain pirates.

The captain walked up to John and said, "So. Fine job you did leading this band."

"Me no lead," said John. "Me go party."

"What is your name?"

"Strongman in the circus. What my name, Yano?" said John, turning to the boy.

"Him Barbarossa, guard man," said Yanibo, almost beside himself with laughter. John's face lit up. "Yah! Bar-bar-os-sa. That all. Pirates come. I fight. I no leader."

"For your sake," muttered the captain under his breath, "I certainly hope not."

"Captain Goth," called a voice from the house. "I am sooooo glad to see you." It was D'Orcade, picking his way across the sandy lawn in his pink, spangled high-heeled shoes. "Those terrible pirates have made a shambles of my party. You came in the nick of time to save us."

"Why, no, D'Orcade!" said a voice from the shadows. "The pirates were driven off before he arrived. Your brawny-beef guest there won the day without their help. Do what you want in private, but at least don't lie in public."

Captain Goth turned to see if he could identify the speaker in the group of guests huddled against the wall. He stepped toward them, but the group slid away from him in the night like black quicksilver.

"Never mind, Goth," said D'Orcade in irritation and petulance. "I'm glad to see you anyway. At least you can assure me that there will be no further attacks tonight, something that these rag-tag citizens cannot."

Goth saluted and replied, "That I can, Lord D'Orcade. I will protect you against any further assaults tonight." A ripple of laughter ran through the faceless crowd of young men and women in the shadows.

"And I do hope you'll get these nasty bodies cleared away."

"Not my job, D'Orcade. I'm a soldier, not a garbage man."

"Well, someone's got to do it. You don't expect me to touch those beastly bodies, do you?"

"Get some of your guests to do it," said Goth gruffly.

"Captain Goth, you are a most distressing person. When the Master arranged this raid . . . oops," said D'Orcade, stopping abruptly.

"What did you say?" said Goth fiercely.

"Nothing, Captain, nothing. I'll get people to move the bodies, but at least go and commandeer four or five carriages, will you?"

Goth, with a baleful glance at D'Orcade, turned and went back into the house, through the passage into the main hallway, and out into the plaza. He looked for the five biggest coaches, pointed to their coachmen, and told them to form a line at the front door.

"Hearses they are now, men," said Goth, "and don't let me hear any complaints. Now go grab some bodies and load them up. *All of you!*" he shouted in a fuming rage. The coachmen scurried into the house, through it and out to the beach, and began the job of carrying the dead to the makeshift tumbrels.

Returning to D'Orcade, Goth grumbled, "It's being taken care of, Lord D'Orcade. But if your guests have weak stomachs, perhaps you had better send them home."

"*Quite* right, Captain. Quite right. It would have been such a lovely party," he said, dispirited. "It was going so well. Such sweet music, and, and . . ." Then brightening up, he continued, "But now we will have to have another one to make up for this one. I will invite you too, Captain. We'll have such a lovely time."

"Not bloody likely," muttered Goth to himself, turning his back and bawling out an order to his lieutenant. The soldiers went down to the beach to supervise the drivers and footmen in their collection of the dead. The corpses were carried from the beach and loaded into the coaches, piled one on top of another. John went down to the water's edge to wash off his hands and arms and the two captured cutlasses. He stuck the two swords in the sand, waded in up to his knees, and gathering up two handfuls of the cold water, splashed it over his head. His toe hit something under the water. He reached down and touched the shoulder of another dead body. At his touch, it turned in the water and rose to the surface face up. John stepped back and reached for one of the swords, but the form merely floated on the water in the moonlight. He lifted the body under its armpits and dragged it toward the beach. The pirate's wet head cloth came off in the water, and there suddenly shone in the moonlight a broad white streak of hair down the middle of the corpse's head. John stopped in the wash of the waves. Steingar? He put the body down into the water again and lifted its right wrist. There were several newly healed white scar marks, the marks Anga had made when he sank his teeth into Steingar's arm. It was he indeed, Illanna's jealous brother, dead before him in the shallow wash of the sea. By whatever means he had made it to the coast and by whatever means he had come to be in the pirate band, now, at least, he would neither persecute his sister nor disgrace his human form any longer. Illanna would be both saddened and relieved. John left the body in the wash and went back up the beach and spoke to Goth. "One more in shallow place."

Goth yelled out, "Hold the coaches! One more." He signaled to two of the now-blood-covered and sweating coachmen to retrieve the body. Finally it too was brought dripping through D'Orcade's marble-floored house, out the front door, down the steps, and tossed into the last carriage atop the pile of bodies. The coach drivers climbed up on their boxes, still with bloody hands, shook the reins, and the coaches began a slow silent walk out the pink gates of D'Orcade's villa, turned right on the boulevard, and proceeded westward in the direction of town.

Some of the guests had already departed, and the others did so as soon as they could get their coachmen to bring up their carriages or they could beg rides from the owners of uncomandeered coaches. Soon, all that were left in the house were the soldiers, D'Orcade and his servants and minions, and Yanibo, Palla Nad, and John. D'Orcade was filling Yanibo's bag with bottles and other delicacies left over from the party. As they were on their way out, the Master of the Revels alternated reiterated invitations to Yanibo with black looks at John. When Yanibo brought the clanking bag up to John, John stuck a cutlass in each side of his thick leather belt, took the bulging bag in his arms, and studiously ignored D'Orcade.

"Good party, Mr. Play Boss," said Yanibo brightly to mollify D'Orcade. "Circus people like gifts. You invite again. We come."

Captain Goth spat on the stones of the Plaza. D'Orcade ignored him and went up his pink steps into the house.

"*Mount up!*" roared Captain Goth to the pirate guard waiting by their horses in the plaza. "This party's over." The troop rode slowly out the gate in pairs and wheeled right. When all were in the boulevard, the column broke into a brisk trot toward town.

Finally the three companions walked out the gate and began the long trek back to the circus. At a fair distance behind them, two of Juncata's policemen strolled along slowly. As they walked down the boulevard in the moonlight, Yanibo nudged John with his elbow and whispered, "Good news."

"What?" said John.

"Play Boss say Palla Nad and Yanibo still go to castle tomorrow night. He very happy with me tonight. I sing good song. Is good, John?"

John stopped and looked at Yanibo, his heart racing.

"And?"

"Bad news too. You still not invited. Play master not happy with you, John," said Yanibo as they began walking again. "He want to be saved only by official soldiers."

John looked at Yanibo. "He knew?"

"He not scared," replied Yanibo simply, holding his hands out and shrugging his shoulders, as if the fact of D'Orcade's courage were proof enough.

They walked the rest of the way home in silence, John's heart heavy yet glad that at least Yanibo would be with Palla Nad to reconnoiter. The dark shadows of the policemen drifted along behind them, and when they entered the back door of the arena, the two policemen stayed opposite it, just standing and watching. At four o'clock in the morning, two others came and relieved them. These two likewise stood patiently in the shadows, watching and waiting.

Yanibo stopped John just inside the doors and took a bottle out of the bag John was carrying. "Bolta," the boy whispered. "I bring party drink." There was a slight rustle behind the hay bale and a single shaking hand lifted up into the air behind it. Yanibo put the bottle into the hand, which grasped it convulsively, waggled it back and forth, and then disappeared with it. With Yanibo dancing on down the corridor in front of John and Palla Nad, they arrived at their stall. John lay down on a hay bale, tired but satisfied, yet still wondering what the partial loss of his anonymity would mean for his plan to rescue the princess. Then he remembered that he had no plan. What was he, just a cylinder of muscle? Maybe his brain was muscle too. He seemed to drift from adventure to adventure, never taking control of anything. He had seen the police following behind him, and he knew they were waiting and watching outside the arena. What would come in the morning? So tired. Yes, all he could seem to do was endure and defend, never plan, execute, and control. Would that be enough to win the princess? But febore he would quin the pincress, he yawned, he had to escrue. Soooooo teered! He yawned again. Immediately he fell asleep on the hay.

Back toward the main door, Bolta nursed the brandy bottle Yanibo had brought him. It smelled of plums and burned like fire going down. He smeared a little on his face and hair. It stung one of his open sores. The little jungle rat was not so bad, maybe, he thought. He had finished half the bottle and had almost fallen into the dreamless stupor he sought every night but which was becoming harder and harder for him to find. This time, however, he had a dream stranger than the one before. He dreamed he heard a scraping and scuttling beneath him, as if a giant beetle were crawling through the ancient sewer beneath the arena. He dreamed that one of the old square sewer gratings within the stable slowly lifted and a long, dark figure crawled out, pulling a large bundle of rags after him. He dreamed that when the dark figure hoisted the bundle onto its back it made a single quiet but distinct clank. He dreamed that the figure slithered off down the corridor among the animals and sleeping roustabouts. First wounded snakes, and now walking beetles. He wondered if he were going to have the horrors again, worse than he had ever had them before. He tried to get up and follow the dream shadow but stumbled trying to climb over the hay bale behind which he had been lying. He sprawled face downward on the bale and went unconscious. Presently, the dark shadow returned, but without the bundle, slipped again into the sewer, replaced the grating, and disappeared underground. All was silent save for an occasional stomping or blowing of the animals or the frightened squealing of a pig and Bolta's tortured, labored snores.

CHAPTER 40

Strong Thumbs

By daybreak, the entire city had heard of the pirate attack and that it had been beaten back for the first time in twenty years by an unnamed group of citizens at whose head had fought a red-bearded youth from across the river, a local boy, who was presently working as a strongman in the circus. Maybe he was not quite as smart as one would have wished for a hero, but he was definitely one of the common people like themselves. They had heard how Captain Goth and his flying squad of soldiers in the pirate patrol had arrived too late to do anything but supervise the cleanup.

By morning, a small group of people had gathered at the door to the arena. When finally John did look out the door at the morning light, they gave a cheer for Barbarossa, the pirate fighter. As he walked in the town later, he was recognized on the street, and people came up to him and shook his hand and wished him well. In the performance that afternoon, the entire arena was filled. When John appeared, a great cheer went up. When he pranced in his clown-horse around the arena to thumb wrestle the children, there were more than ever who held their small hands over the front rail. Now when they won they could claim that they had beaten not just the circus strongman, named StrongThumbs BaldHead, but the great pirate fighter, Barbarossa TwinSwords. John had time to thumb wrestle any child who wanted to because part of Palla Nad's act was cut. When he had been getting ready for his routine, he found he had only one pig. The other had disappeared in the night. The door of the cage was open, but the second one had not run out. Even now it cowered in the back of the cage, frightened and stupefied, unable to perform.

Chauri was delighted at the increased attendance. Not only would it please D'Orcade, but it meant additional coin in his private coffers. On the other hand, he was worried that John's deeds and popularity might not be pleasing to the Master of Darkness and that the circus would suffer for it. After the performance had ended, John, Yanibo, and Palla Nad returned to their stall to find two of Juncata's policemen waiting for them. These were not, however, the ordinary uniformed street police; they wore dark slouch hats which they did not remove and dark unfashionable suits of heavy material, and they spoke with a heavy, stolid menace, as if they knew where the power really lay and were a part of it.

"Greetings, Brother Barbarossa," said the taller and heavier of the two, sitting down on a hay bale in the cluttered stall. "My name is Major Muckt. I am a personal representative of General Juncata. He has heard of your magnificent exploits and wishes to invite you to the castle this evening as one of his special guests." The major paused, waiting for a reaction. John just looked at him as if he had not understood. "There will be a magic competition as well as a sumptuous supper afterward. So important a hero of the people should be recognized, and the general's many important guests would like the opportunity to meet you. He plans to decorate you for your bravery against the pirates, who have been a scourge of great age in this city. And then perhaps, you might demonstrate one of your amazing feats of strength for the nobles. Will you be able to join us?"

"I no hero," said John, frowning and drooling. "I merely there. Anyone could done."

And that, my naive Barbarossa, thought Muckt to himself, *is just exactly the idea we do not wish to occur to others.* But in his reply to John he merely said, "Nonsense. The general feels you are special and that you should be given what you deserve. Will I be able to tell the general that you will attend this evening's dinner? I urge you to agree."

John bowed an awkward bow. "I happy boy. Glad famous General Juncata like me. He true great pirate fighter. Happy boy he think good of me. No reward. I just do my duty."

"Hey, boss," said Yanibo to the major. "Invite me, Old Nad too. We want eat after magic contest. Get good food at castle. Get us invite for dinner too." Major Muckt was slightly taken aback at this interjection into the conversation by the circus performer whom he had seen billed outside as the Monkey Boy, but he said nothing, only stared in astonishment. John knew this was his chance to enter the castle openly but knew he must not appear in the least bit eager.

"Major, I no noble. I eat dinner here. Friends here perform tonight for General. They do good show for General. I go if they stay dinner. I eat with circus people. No eat with higher people."

Major Muckt looked at the two brown jungle people beside John and considered. He knew his mission was to guarantee the strong youth's appearance in the castle that night, but he also knew the general's real purpose was either to recruit the strong-armed, weak-headed youth into his forces or to kill him before he gained any more renown. It would be best if he were without comrades to look out for him. Although the boy and the old man didn't look like they would make any trouble, still there would be two more bodies for him to dispose of. He could always give in if the big fool refused. He took the risk.

"Come, come, Barbarossa. Just you come to dinner for the recognition. We won't expect you to perform tonight. It is a great honor to be asked to sit down to dinner with the general. Let your two friends go home after they perform. You can tell them all about it when you return. After all, you're a local boy. You can't really rank yourself equal with jungle people."

John knew he had the major hooked. He puffed up his chest as if he were proud of himself and finally said, "Yah, Major. I come myself. After all, I am one who done best fighting. I tell my friends all what great lords and ladies say. Maybe I bring them some leftover food too from dinner. Yah. I stay by myself."

Inwardly disgusted by the big man's boorishness, Muckt reflected that large pride and little brains made weak men. Yanibo affected to be hurt by John's exclusion of him from the dinner invitation and retreated to the very back of the stall, where he sat down dejectedly on a large pile of rags. Palla Nad remained standing but turned his back on John in an excellent imitation of a grandfatherly sulk.

"Tell General for me, no money needed. Recognition for duty is good though," said John. "You tell?"

"Ha. Yes. Most exactly, Sir Barbarossa StrongThumbs TwoSwords. I will inform the general of your sentiments," said Muckt. With that, the two secret servicemen, thick and dangerous in their black suits and broad black hats, turned and made their way slowly through the small crowd of circus people who had gathered around to hear the invitation.

The man with the dog act came up to John. "A friend of the general already! Put in a good word for me, will you, if he wants to see some other acts. Don't forget your pals when you get up in the world. Maybe he'll give you one of those purses of gold he sometimes hands out."

John brooded on the thought that tonight would most likely have to be the night of his attempt and still he had no plan. He deliberated on how to answer the performer; that foolish man thought they all lived in a simple, stable world with no real evil, where narrow profit was all a man needed to consider. Well, John thought to himself, he had succeeded in gaining admittance to the castle and into the very presence of the Master of Darkness himself. Or, strictly speaking, he himself had achieved nothing, but somehow, the invisible powers of providence had placed him where he needed to be in order to fight for justice. For that, he gave thanks to Drefon. But what would he do when he got there? How would he rescue the princess and her father? It was all profoundly unclear to him still. He would have the chance, however. Morduc would be there as well, an ally unbeknown to Juncata, as were Yanibo and Palla Nad. Morduc had something in mind. He said create a diversion. A diversion, but not a rescue. After all, she was his love. Why should Morduc be the one to rescue her? He must rescue her himself, and she must know it . . . to be able to . . . give . . . him . . . proper . . . gratitude.

He suddenly bounded up from the bundle of rags. What was he thinking? He was disgusted with himself. He was letting desire drive him rather than disinterested service. How ignoble of him. So close to a rescue, yet so far from the proper mentality for one. He was letting lust for her beauty pervert his purity of motive. So hard it was though, to keep the two separated. So hard. Well, he had come this far with a high mind; he would go through to the end without hope, but with hope. Could it really be that virtue alone brought happiness? And what was virtue? Not despairing joylessness surely, more likely doing Drefon's good works. Drefon, the distant, the mysterious. But Drefon did care. He cared for him, and he cared for Aleth. Of that he was sure, and that was enough. Doing Drefon's works was happiness. Anything more was Drefon's gift, to be received joyfully if given, and if not, to be happy without. He and Aleth by themselves were nothing, mere man and woman, but with Drefon, they were all. He smiled to himself with renewed faith, faith that was better than hope.

He lay back on the straw to await the events of the night. Watched continually as he now was, he couldn't risk a message to Morduc to coordinate more fully. But even without a plan, at least Plummet had somehow managed to send him his armor. He would wear it tonight and along with it the red-steel sword of his father, shining Red Dragon, that flew so swiftly and bit so deeply. The scrap of paper pinned to the bundle had said merely, "A jacket and waders in case you go fishing. Provide your own hook, line, and bait."

CHAPTER 41

Frog Hoard

Just as Captain Goth came striding down to the beach from the back door of D'Orcade's villa, Plummet plucked Morduc by the sleeve, Morduc touched Marianna lightly on the shoulder, and they, all three, melted into the shadows under the trees by the wall. Quickly slipping down to the water, they turned D'Orcade's seawall by wading, and then two more until they reached the gap between villas by which they had arrived, went quickly out through it, and gained the boulevard some blocks down from where the soldiers were milling about in the street. They crossed the boulevard and, with others of their band, disappeared into the allies and lanes of the dark city. The three walked across the city until they reached what appeared to be a closed clock shop. Plummet spoke softly. "Beetle is within. He will take you back through passages to your room. I still have to see people at the docks. I will send a message before you go to the castle tomorrow evening." Then he knocked at the door twice and, after a pause, once again. The door opened, and Morduc and Marianna slipped in. Plummet bustled off down the street humming tunelessly under his breath as the door closed. Beetle led the two tired fighters through long dark narrow corridors that went high and then low and then high again. He stopped in one of them and made his peculiar clicking in his throat. He carefully and silently swung a panel outward, and Marianna and Morduc crawled into the room they had left many hours before. As quietly as he had opened it, Beetle closed the panel behind them and scuttled silently off down the passageway in the wall. Illanna was still asleep on the bed. The candle had burned low. Anga stood up, stretched, and came over to the returned adventurers, wagging furiously from head to tail. Marianna gently shook Illanna awake. She sat up quickly when she saw the red stains on both Marianna and Morduc and smelled the blood.

"Are you all right?" she asked Marianna.

"Yes. It was magnificent. We beat them before the guards arrived. Come. I need to clean up." They unlocked the door, and, Marianna, after giving Morduc a kiss, went with Illanna down the hall to their own room. Morduc locked his door again, stripped off his clothes, and fell into bed, exhausted but satisfied.

The next morning he heard loud cheers of "RedBeard!" and "StrongThumbs!" and "TwoSwords!" in the street beneath his window and the buzz of many voices below in the inn. He got up, much refreshed, washed himself, rubbed himself all down, and then stood contemplating his face in the mirror, that smooth, ever-youthful face. When he became fully mortal, it would begin to age as those of his now dearest friends would, as Plummet's and Mother Gump's already had. In many years it would be wrinkled, his knees would be weak, he would look like—yes—he would look like the old magician he was impersonating, but he would not then be able to remove the disguise. The mask of enfeebling old age would then be his until—until he died. And Marianna died. If he helped his friend rescue the princess, then he would be free, free to return home or free to stay with Marianna for the rest of their lives. A mortal life, not long by elf time, but perhaps long enough for such happiness as there was available either to elf or human. Yet he knew that he had already made his decision. He had told Marianna he loved her. He had not lied. He had told her truly his heart. But it was not completed yet and would not be until . . . they had become married lovers. Until then, he could still retrieve the infinite life of his elfin youth. Until then, still, he could.

He sat looking at his smooth, greenish face for some time; then slowly, and with extreme care, using hair cement, he began to put on the gray eyebrows and beard. He whitened his hair with a dye, increased the pallor of his skin, and drew in creases at the eyes with a black grease pencil. When he had finished dressing himself in his magician's robes, he looked at himself in the mirror again and saw an aged, wizened man—himself.

That night would be the performance of his life. On it would depend his entire future. Going to the boxes, he checked over his equipment. After that, from beneath his shirt he drew the pouch containing the stone the OWO had given him. He took it out and looked at it again. Deep within its pure blue depths, the white star hung as if in the sky itself. As he looked, he drew strength from it, harmonizing his soul, and purging himself of all confusions and fears. He held it up to the morning light by the window. Suddenly he began to hear the distant roaring he had heard in the forest after he had drunk from the cup. Quickly he lowered it, moved away from the window, and returned it to its pouch on his breast. What could the connection be? No time to puzzle it out now. Yet he longed to know. Finally, he sat down and wrote something on a slip of paper and rolled it into a ball and put it in one of the many invisible pockets in his robe. Now he was ready.

Picking up the basket which held the frog, he unlocked his door, went out, relocked it, and went down the corridor to the door of Marianna and Illanna's room. He knocked. The door was answered almost immediately. They too were nearly ready. Each had on the golden suit that had been made for them. And the face of each was also covered by the gold makeup that they wore for performances. Looking like strange, lithe cats or exotic birds, they descended the stairs with their wizard keeper, into an inn room that was buzzing with excitement.

"Oh, Magician, have ye heerd," called out one of the men.

"Have I heard what?" replied Morduc. Marianna and Illanna, like two creatures from another world, stood by him, shimmering and shifting in a way that would have distracted strangers, but by now the regular frequenters of the inn were so used to them that they neither noticed nor bothered them, considering them simply as appendages to the old magician.

"There was another pirate raid last night, and local boys beat 'em off before the guard got there. What do you think of that? *Local boys!*"

"What local boys?" asked Morduc.

"Eh, some from here, some from crost river. Leader of 'um's feller I used ter know. Red Beard we calls 'em, er StrongThumbs."

"Indeed," said Morduc. "Did you know him well?"

"Yessireebob. Just like that," said the man holding up two crossed fingers. "Had to go working in the circus fer a spell, 'cause there's no real work fer honest men any more round here. But he done some last night, awrightee. Heh, heh, heh."

"And you were there with him, this StrongThumbs, helping drive off the pirates?"

"As good as, old man."

"Most interesting," said Morduc, smiling to himself. "And what do you think will come of it?"

"Well, I suppose, if we done it once, we can do it again."

"And do you think that will make the general happy?" asked Morduc. The man opened his mouth to answer but then closed it without saying anything. He looked around him stupidly, furtively, and thoughtfully all at the same time, as if that were the first moment in his enthusiasm for what the local boys had done that the general's reaction had occurred to him.

"Hey, Magician. Whose side you on anyway?" said the man.

Morduc looked at him with a sharp swift glance and said, "Whose side are *you* on?"

The man got up and went back to his cronies, with a fearful glance backward at Morduc. They put their heads down together while Morduc and Marianna and Illanna sat at a corner table to eat breakfast. After they had been served and had eaten, they took their leave. Morduc nodded to Mother Gump and went out, the two girls following him like golden birds of a distant planet, mysterious creatures of another world, wandering in this one, sinuous, serene, and silent.

As they walked to the main avenue, all they heard on every side was talk of the events of the previous night.

"Barbarossa, that's our boy," said one.

"What will the general do?" asked another.

Everywhere as well the police could be seen passing through the noisy crowds surrounded by little circles of silence as they moved through the people. Morduc and Marianna and Illanna finally found a carriage to take them to the castle. As they rode down the avenue, people turned to watch them pass, two golden spirits with golden masks and golden faces, flanking a grizzled, bearded gnome wrapped in rainbow robes and topped by a tall conical hat. They stopped at the gate of the military camp while Morduc explained their business.

"You are on the list, but you aren't due till this evening, along with that there StrongThumbs fella and the WitchDoctor."

"WitchDoctor?" said Morduc, trying to hold his voice steady.

"Yeah. Just been added to the list. Circus magician. Ya got competition, old man."

"Indeed," said Morduc thoughtfully. "There will be more on the program than I thought."

"That's right. Ya ain't got the stage to yourself no more. Think ya can take it, pops?"

"I will be returning this evening. I do not wish to enter the castle now. I only wish to deliver a gift for the princess, the general's guest."

"Well, I'm not sure." The golden-faced girls smiled at the guard as they stretched their bodies on the seat and fixed him with their dark, serious eyes in deep-blue eye shadow and smiled faintly with their full red lips. "I'll send you on with a guard," he finally said. They rode through the camp, with a pair of soldiers riding on the back of the coach, and pulled up at the drawbridge. There they got out and presented themselves to the guard at the bridge gate. He permitted them to cross it on foot accompanied by their two guards. Morduc carried a small basket in his hands. When they arrived at the lowered portcullis, Morduc explained that he wanted to deliver the basket to the princess. The guard did not know what to do. He would consult Herr Sprok, the keeper of the wicket.

Eventually, they saw the pale, white-blond figure of Sprok walking across the courtyard in his black gown with the buttons down the front and his keys around his neck.

"What is it, old man?" he said as he eyed the two exotic figures in gold through the portcullis, flicking his tongue over his suddenly dry lips. "You are not due here until eight o'clock this evening. Why do you come at noon?"

"I have a gift for the princess. It is part of the performance. I need to give it to her now."

"The princess sees no one, old man. Surely you are aware of that?'

"Why no, I was not," replied Morduc innocently. "She sees you, doesn't she?"

Sprok glared at him. "What is this gift?" said Sprok suspiciously.

Morduc brought the basket close to one of the openings in the iron grate and lifted its cover. Inside Sprok saw a frog squatting stupidly on a red satin cloth. In front of the frog was a golden signet ring with a swan carved into it. Around the bottom of the basket, in the shadow of the rim, lay a ring of emeralds linked by a golden chain. Sprok's eyes widened when he saw the gems. His lips became even drier than when he had first seen the girls. He kept his voice steady. "What a disgusting treasure box, old man."

Morduc put the cover on the basket again. "Perhaps," he said in an even, noncommittal voice, "She would be more pleased by the pet than by the rest." Sprok himself had wondered often how the princess had borne the isolation of her captivity. The gems he would not dare to touch, but the ring looked old and solid and valuable. The wizard was speaking again. "After all, she is not expecting it, nor is the general. Can you see that she gets this pet?"

Sprok did not answer directly. The fiction was maintained that the princess and her father were the willing guests of the general, but it was in fact the practice of the general himself to check all packages, messages, and gifts that came to the princess from whatever source. None got through. The wizard droned on, "I am sure the gift will find favor with her, as I expect my performance will as well. If the general wishes to please Her Highness, let him put his trust in me to do it." Morduc looked significantly at Sprok. "Lord D'Orcade has not made a mistake in engaging me. I am sure that the princess's enjoyment of her stay will be increased if the general will permit me my little whimsy. Perhaps, the general would be so kind even as to convey my gift to the princess himself?"

"I will certainly see that your sentiments are conveyed to the general," said Sprok, reaching out and accepting the small basket through one of the square openings in the portcullis. "And now you must leave immediately. Your presence here is already quite irregular. Come tonight, and do not be late."

"You may be most assured that I would not miss this evening for anything. I will be on time, and everything will happen as it should. If it does not, well then, you must answer to the general, not to me."

"I am, perhaps, old magician, more aware of what answering to the general entails than you are," said Sprok, turning and starting back across the courtyard, holding the basket with distaste. "Now be gone with you." The guards who had been sent with Morduc and his assistants nudged them to turn and go back across the drawbridge. They retraced their steps across the high-slung span as Sprok returned across the courtyard with the basket under his arm. He resented being reduced to coming across the courtyard himself for the conference, but now there was perhaps something in it for him. The Master had very strange notions about pleasing the princess. He himself would have killed her and her father immediately. To secure their cooperation would never be possible, certainly not by simple amusements such as these paltry, insane conjurers. Yet it was not his decision to make. He mounted the steps to the great iron doors, went in through the one-person wicket and up the corridor through the semidarkness, stopping once, briefly, to shift the basket in his hands, as he went toward the main hall.

The general was, as usual, sitting on his ebony throne, brooding in rage, this time over the events of the previous night. The sinister sister was sitting next to him in her smaller ebony chair. They were turned away from each other, not talking, and seemed to have been arguing. Sprok coughed discreetly.

The dark, baleful face of the Master rotated toward Sprok, fixing him with his lifeless, foil-backed fish eyes in his ancient, bony, undersea face. "Yes. What is it?" he hissed malevolently.

"The old magician performing here tonight?"

"Yes, what of him?"

"He has sent a gift to the princess."

"A gift? That is ridiculous. A street entertainer sending gifts? Throw the rubbish out."

"If it please you, sir, it is not rubbish." He opened the basket. For a moment, all that Darkness saw was the frog sitting on its cloth.

"A frog? Are you trying to play some kind of indecent joke, Sprok? Because if you are, I am not in the mood. Have you gone mad?"

"Around the bottom of the basket, if you please, sir," said Sprok. The Master of Darkness and his sister both peered into the basket. The frog peered up at them, blinking stupidly from its nest and shifted a bit. The sister saw it first and with, a swift, deft movement, slipped the necklace of green gems out of the basket and held it up to the light.

"Frog Hoard," whispered the sister, hardly breathing.

"That's only an old rumor," said the Master carelessly for the benefit of Sprok, yet he was hardly able to tear his eyes away from the shining stones and the gleaming gold. He knew she was right, that he was at last beholding a genuine sample of that fabled treasure, that deep-lake hoard, which he had been sent to these very shores so many years ago to trace, to control, and to gain. How did this fake wizard come by this piece of it? If he could only discover where the rest of it was, that legendary mountain-high pyramid of green gems, he could simply take his soldiers inland, capture them, and sail back to Argusturia to the glory and comfort and power toward which he had been working all his life. Control of the regions beyond the mountains would not then be necessary. And, he thought in angry frustration, he would no longer have to continue this charade of courtship with her so Right Royal Pain in the Highness, Princess Aleth Trealthweow. He could rape her and kill her afterward, and her father too, and damn them all to DrefonDrear for opposing him for so long. "Arrrrugggh!" he shouted, making the rafters echo, as he pushed himself up from his throne.

The Dark Sister was speaking. "And why, my brother, do not such presents ever come to *me*, who is and should be acknowledged your true partner in government? Why is it always this wretched, feeble princess who occupies your attention?"

"You know, sister, the circumstances as well as I."

Sprok thought to himself, *If she's his sister then I'm that frog.*

"I want this," she said icily.

After a moment, the Master answered, "Very well. You may have it." Then turning to Sprok he said, "Is there anything else in the basket?"

"Nothing, Master. I have searched it."

"I was sure you had," said the Master, casting a mordant eye on Sprok. "Take it to her. Tell her I will visit her shortly myself with a word about this gift, and then return to your post immediately."

"Yes, Master," he said but did not move off in the direction of the tower door. He merely stood there waiting.

"*Yes?*" said the Master.

"If she will not open the door . . . ?" His voice trailed off.

"You fool," he hissed. "Leave the basket. I will take it myself."

The sister was suddenly alert. "Why can he not take it himself?" she asked. "Surely the princess is your prisoner still."

"It doesn't concern you, sister," said the Master. "Return to your post, Sprok, immediately."

"No, let him stay for a moment, brother," said the sister. "What does he need?"

Suddenly the sister divined the case. She gasped, and her pale face filled with blood, swelling it to blotchy redness. "You couldn't have," she hissed.

"We'll talk of this later," he snarled.

"We shall talk of it *now*," she said, drawing her key on its chain out from under her leather shirt and holding it out to Sprok. Before the Master could say or do anything, Sprok took it and went off toward the tower.

When he arrived at the tower door, he rapped. The window flew open and the bloated, soft face of Slug appeared.

"I am to take this to the princess," said Sprok. The bolt shot back and the door opened, but Slug blocked the way.

"What is it, you fool?" said Sprok. Slug nodded his head toward the basket. "That won't be necessary. The Master has already checked it." A dark cloud passed over the boy's face and his jaw set. "Well, search it then, if you're going to," spat out Sprok. When the boy saw the frog, he smiled. He felt around in the basket and satisfied himself that it contained no contraband for which he could be held accountable. The boy slobbered out a few words. "Bafket scleeen," he said. "Bin there 'fore me, afen't cheuw?"

Sprok said nothing but began climbing the stairs with a faint smile on his face. He thought to himself, *I wonder if there is anything to that notion about saint-seducing gold. If the Master should ever wish to dispose of the Princess . . . Well, I must not think such thoughts.*

As Sprok climbed upward, below in the hall, the Master of Darkness faced his irate sister.

"How could you use our key for the lock on *her* door?"

"Now, sister. It means nothing. After all, you have the emeralds."

"And," she lowered balefully at him, "I shall expect considerably more in compensation for this betrayal. I'll teach you a lesson you'll never forget. You've gone soft hearted over that disgusting girl. If I reported what you had done . . ."

A look of such vicious threat came into the Master's face that the sister took a step backward and said no more. When the shining hatred had somewhat passed from the Master's face, he began to speak slowly. "As we were saying when Herr Sprok interrupted us, you will go to the ship and send a message to instruct them to attack again tomorrow night and in greater force. By then I will have taken care of this fool StrongThumbs, and that will show these stupid people that they cannot do without me and my forces."

"Very well, brother. But you know my sentiments. Direct force, direct rule. They will never love you—as I do."

"They will. They will," he said, smashing his black gloved hand down on the throne arm.

"If you say so, brother," said the Dark Sister, fingering the green gems as they lay on the black of her leather shirt.

"Go then," he said.

"You forget, brother," she said sarcastically. "I must wait for the return of my key." They sat there in the large black room lit by the faint red light, waiting in seething silence.

As Sprok neared the top of the stairs, he heard the click of the shuttle in Aleth's loom and her soft, tuneless music. *How can she sing,* he thought, *when her days are numbered? She must know that the Master will finally become impatient with her intransigence.* He knocked.

"Enter," said the low, rich, thrilling voice, "if you can." Sprok moved the beam and then unlocked the door and entered.

"Herr Sprok," said the princess in surprise. "I had not thought any but the Master had a key to my chamber door."

"Who has a key is none of your concern."

"Oh, but it is. If the Master loans out his key to just anyone . . ."

"He did not give me the key."

"Then how do you come by it?"

Reluctantly Sprok said, "The Master's sister has a key too."

"The sister!" said the princess in astonishment. "Now that is news."

"Princess, what some have chosen to call a gift has come for you."

"Indeed, Sprok. It is not my birthday." Her sarcasm and her total composure unnerved him. He did not like to be in her presence.

"The magician sent it."

"What magician, may I inquire?" she said indifferently.

"There is to be another entertainment tonight, Your Majesty. A fine conjurer from the provinces, I believe. A real old-style wizard."

"He will be most welcome for his own sake, though what these performers will do to win approval from the general is most disgraceful. This is the first time I have received a gift from one of them. Does the general think he can win my gratitude this way?"

"Your Majesty should first examine the gift before you accuse anyone of attempting to earn your gratitude with it."

Setting down the shuttle and sliding off the loom bench, she came over to Sprok and took the basket from him and set it on a table. Opening it, she gave a little startled "Oh!" when she saw the frog, which promptly jumped out on to the table and turned this way and that. The princess put her hand gently on its back to keep it from leaping to the floor, as it seemed about ready to do.

"It is a most dignified frog," said the Princess, smiling. "It will divert me in my loneliness here. I know it comes from someone other than the general, since it shows real kindness, but you may tell the general that I am grateful for his permitting it to reach me. The wizard I will thank myself this evening."

"Very well," said Sprok. "The general himself will be up shortly to say something more to you about this gift. Now I will leave you."

The princess stroked the frog as Sprok's iron footsteps could be heard descending the stairs hollowly beyond the relocked and rebarred door. All of a sudden, the frog opened its mouth and a small ball of paper rolled out on to the princess's table.

When Sprok reappeared in the throne room and returned the key to the Dark Sister, the Master said nothing to him. Sprok returned to his post at the wicket, and General Juncata and his paramour went in the direction of the dungeon corridor. Presently he returned alone, limped across the hall to the door in the tower, was admitted, and himself ascended the tower to pay a visit to the princess. Though as cold and indifferent to him as ever, she made no objection to his disposition of the necklace that had come with the frog; he found her perfectly tractable and acquiescent in his suggestion that she concur in making it a gift to his sister. He was even more surprised when she made no protest concerning the existence of a second key to her sanctum.

CHAPTER 42

Levitations

Morduc, Marianna, and Illanna, all three still dressed in their gray-and-gold guises, sat in a corner of the Green Dragon Inn, eating a light supper. They knew that everything depended upon their evening's performance. Mother Gump bustled over and sat down at the table. Under her breath, she said to Morduc, "The fisherman says the hook is baited and he is ready for the cast."

"Good. Tell him I wish him a good catch."

When they were finished, they went upstairs to get their equipment. Morduc and the girls brought down the two boxes and set them by the door. Soon, Harry stumbled in and informed them that their coach was at the head of the alley. With the help of Harry and the footman, they carried the two long black boxes out the narrow alley and loaded them onto the front seat and then climbed in themselves opposite it. As the carriage rolled away into the gathering darkness, Harry tossed his cap in the air shouting, "Hooray for Middock the Magician!" The coach drove slowly through the darkening town toward the castle. Low in the west, thick clouds had begun to obscure the sinking sun.

Meanwhile, at the arena, John unrolled the bundle of rags he had received from the fisherman and took out the red-steel chain-mail byrnie and the sword, Red Dragon, from among the rest of the red-steel armor. He quickly put on the byrnie, slung the sword by his side, and covered both with a long, loose white tunic. On the outside of the tunic, he buckled a broad leather belt, into which he stuck the two famous cutlasses he had used to win his fight against the pirates. Then he rewrapped the rest of the armor and hid it back under the straw. Yanibo put Palla Nad's magic apparatus in a bag while the old man frizzed up his hair until it stood straight up from his head. He stuck his flute in his rainbow belt and was ready. All three put on their hooded brown cloaks and then stepped outside the arena door into the deepening dusk. They sniffed the wind that was blowing from the west.

"Rain?" said Palla Nad.

"Storm," replied John dourly.

They set off through the town in the direction of the castle. Yanibo danced ahead, eager for the encounter, while John trudged stolidly and silently beside Palla Nad. John turned up his hood and kept his head down and thus went through the streets mostly unrecognized by the citizens bustling toward their homes. As the three companions walked down the long avenue, stars began to appear in the sky directly above them, but far off to the west the clouds billowed up ominously in high ranks. Occasionally a jagged streak of silver lightning shot from beneath the dark-cloud mountains toward the surface of the sea.

Eventually they arrived at the outer gate of the guard camp. There the soldiers were delighted to see the famous pirate fighter and made much of him. They consulted their lists, found their names were on it, and checked them in. The three walked through the camp, which was illuminated at regular intervals by guard fires, and made their way to the sentry post and gate at the bridge. Here again their names were checked against a list before they were allowed on to the bridge itself. As they walked across, their feet just barely sounded above the wind, swirling and buffeting in the sea canyon below.

Halfway across, they heard behind them the rumbling of a carriage. They stepped to the side, and as it passed, John saw within its window the silhouetted face of the old magician flanked by two flashes of liquid gold. The magician turned his head briefly to look directly at John but gave no sign of recognition. The carriage passed the pedestrians, drew up at the castle entrance, and waited for the portcullis to be raised. The pedestrians reached the opening just as the carriage was passing through. John looked up as he walked under the great iron barrier and saw the long steel teeth which fitted into holes in the gatehouse floor. They begin their grinding descent. He was surprised at how quickly the portcullis could come down. It slammed behind them as they passed the soldiers working the great windlasses which raised and lowered it.

D'Orcade's carriage stood with many others to one side in the court of the castle, and D'Orcade himself, resplendent in blue velvet trimmed with gold, was waiting impatiently on the castle steps to greet them. "Hurry, hurry, hurry. You're almost late."

John stood looking up and up at the tall castle and was shaken and surprised to see its walls covered with large ropy strands of the same black briars that had bound him long ago in the King of Time's castle. Now he was here voluntarily, about to enter the stronghold of their planter and propagator. He shuddered, but he did not hesitate. He understood his goal clearly enough. He would rescue his true love or die trying. He would answer the riddle or not. He would fulfill the quest or not. If she would have him, he would be hers and she his, and their children theirs together, and if not, not, but whichever way those discrete events went, his continuous and perpetual mission in life was to cut those evil binding fibers of tyranny from the world and destroy them forever. Even in the growing darkness, he could see the huge, black, hook-shaped thorns under the leaves of the ivylike trunks and tendrils snaking their way up the jagged stone walls of the edifice. These were not just bonds of the body, but briars of the soul.

While Morduc and the girls were taking the equipment boxes out of the carriage, John, Palla Nad, and Yanibo presented themselves at the narrow iron grate. Instead of Sprok, however, it was now being guarded by the skull-faced man who had originally recruited them in Imbal. He looked at them without emotion, barring the way through the wicket. "And where do you think you're going?" he said.

"This hero Barbarossa," said Yanibo brightly.

"And I am Skrulldan, recently appointed keeper of the wicket, and I say you do not enter."

"General give feast in his honor tonight. Then grandfather here compete in magic with old fakir there," said Yanibo, pointing in the direction of the carriage where Morduc and the girls were still struggling with the boxes.

"Yah," said John, smiling idiotically, holding out his hand to Skrulldan. "Wrestle thumbs?"

"What do you take me for?" said Skrulldan drawing back in disgust. "I'm not one of those spoiled children who attend your stupid circus."

A puzzled look came over John's face. "No thumbs?" said John in a disappointed tone.

"No thumbs!" said Skrulldan decisively. "And you'll have to give up your swords too, hero or not."

"Invitation not say that," said John, as a dark cloud passed over his face.

Yanibo went up closer to Skrulldan and said in his ear, "Strong in arm, weak in head. I fix." Then turning to John, Yanibo said, "Big swords scare ladies at dinner, Barbarossa. Leave with Skrulldan here."

With seeming reluctance, John drew the two cutlasses out of his belt. "Do I get back after dinner?" he asked Skrulldan.

"Yes, Barbarossa," said Skrulldan, smiling a faint, ghastly smile, "you get swords after dinner." He examined John's face closely for a moment as he came up to take the swords and then nodded curtly, saying, "You are expected." Skrulldan was well aware that the Master intended either to entice this hero of the people to work for him or, if he refused, to kill him. Otherwise his master would not have bothered with such fools. As Skrulldan opened the narrow iron grate and permitted them to enter one at a time, he added with faint irony to Yanibo as he went past, "Strong in arm, weak in head, easy to lead. Yes, I see."

As the three walked down the hall, Skrulldan heard John's slow voice saying to Yanibo, "What he mean, weak head. My head strong too. Thick head. Thick head break boards. Head break even stones. Me show."

"Yes, Barbarossa, yes," came back Yanibo's voice. "You break bricks with noggin. You break any grip."

"Yah," Skrulldan heard John say with a deep, childlike satisfaction. "I break grip of anything."

Skrulldan turned his attention to the old magician and his two assistants who were struggling up the steps with their gear. "Hurry, hurry, hurry, you laggards!" bleated D'Orcade. "The Master is already in his chair. We are keeping him waiting!"

"Perhaps," said the old magician, "a little help with the equipment would . . ."

"Oh, please, please, please hurry," twittered D'Orcade, running up and down the steps. Skrulldan made a signal to four of the guards standing by the door. Each took an end of a box, lifting it by the handle there, and went up the steps. The boxes were just a bit too large to fit through the wicket. They tried them flat and they tried them sideways, but they would not go through.

"Open, open, *open!*" screamed the agitated D'Orcade. "We'll be late."

Skrulldan did not like the thought of opening even one of the two great iron doors which blocked access to the main passage of the hall. He turned to the magician. "Take your equipment out of the boxes."

For answer, Morduc simply turned around and began walking back toward the portcullis. Marianna and Illanna glided gracefully after him, like two shimmering birds. Inside, in the darkness of the hall, John held his breath.

"You fool," spat out D'Orcade. "We'll both lose our heads for this. You can follow Sprok if you want to, but I do not wish to displease the Master. Open these doors immediately. Open, open, open, open!" he screamed in a whisper. Skrulldan looked at the retreating figures of the magician and his assistants. The soldiers at the portcullis windlasses had gotten up from their benches and had begun to arrange themselves by the spokes.

When Morduc was almost to the portcullis and the grate had begun to rise, Skrulldan called out loudly, "Stop, Magician. Stop!" The three figures stopped but did not turn.

"One leaf. One leaf only, and for five seconds only!" shouted Skrulldan. Morduc turned and began walking back across the courtyard to the steps, followed by his two golden shadows. Skrulldan nodded to the guards. The four who had been carrying the chests set them down and entered by the small iron port. Inside, by the light of a torch, the four guards each took one of the peg handles of the beam and struggled together to heave the huge oak bar far enough into its receiving hole in the wall so that one of the doors could be opened. Then they went out through the port again, picked up the boxes, and waited. Skrulldan stepped to the left leaf, inserted the huge key which hung around his neck into the lock, and turned it. The internal claw lifted, and he swung the leaf open. "Quickly, quickly," he hissed as the four soldiers moved the boxes through the opening. But as Morduc and the others stepped forward to follow them, Skrulldan held up his hand and shouted, "No! You must go through the wicket." He banged the door closed in their faces. The spring lock's tongue clicked into place in the opposite leaf. On the other side of the door, they heard the grinding of the bar as the soldiers pushed it into place.

"Such a fuss," hissed D'Orcade to Skrulldan as he slipped through the portal, followed by the magician and his two golden assistants.

Inside they saw John and Palla Nad and Yanibo walking slowly far ahead of them in the torch-lit passage. "Hurry up," snapped D'Orcade as he led the way, followed by Morduc, Marianna, and Illanna, and the four soldiers carrying the two long, broad black boxes.

As they walked up the hall they heard a loud buzz of conversation coming through the arched opening leading into the main hall. D'Orcade had caught up with John, Yanibo, and Palla Nad. "I will go first," D'Orcade hissed.

"OK, Party Boss," whispered Yanibo.

They all stopped at the arch and D'Orcade gave a signal. A fanfare of trumpets sounded. The hall was filled with men and women of the town, notables of the wealthier citizenry, who supported and profited from General Juncata's rule. The whole assembly of guests within the hall turned toward the arch to look at the line of figures crossing the stone floor of the high-ceilinged room. D'Orcade went first, followed by the old wizard with a shimmering assistant on each side. The crowd sighed as they saw the golden-suited girls. Palla Nad, as the official competitor, followed, with Yanibo in his jaguar pelt loin wrap on one side and John on the other. In spite of the exotic appearance of Yanibo and Palla Nad, it was to John that all eyes were drawn. His shaven head shone in the red light above his red beard, which flowed down over the front of his long white gown. Murmurs of admiration went through the crowd. "It's Barbarossa."

"How strong he looks!"

"No wonder he beat the pirates."

Hearing these remarks, the Master of Darkness flashed out a look of irritation across the room from where he was sitting upright in his high, dark chair on the dais. He was dressed in a black jeweled suit. His great sword with the black diamond in its hilt hung by his side. To his left and lower sat his sister, also in black, her head high in the air, aloof, cold, and contemptuous of all the shows which her brother thought necessary. Around her neck gleamed the ring of green gems. On her left middle finger was the massive golden ring Sprok had pilfered from the basket.

To the Master's right, in a white gown, sat the princess, with a guardsman on either side of her. Next to her, on the same level, sat her father, similarly guarded. John noticed that the King of Time looked older and more tired than John had remembered him. Ahead of him, John saw the old magician and his assistants being presented to the Master by D'Orcade, who had on his best blue velvet coat, blue velvet knickers, and vertically striped blue-and-white stockings. All bowed low to the Master. As Morduc bowed, he caught sight of the green gems around the neck of the general's sister and anxiously stole a look out of the side of his eyes at the Princess Aleth. She sat serenely looking at no one, but in her lap she held her new pet frog, stroking its back. Much relieved, he retired with Marianna and Illanna to the left side, closest to where the princess sat.

Palla Nad, John, and Yanibo in their turn advanced to the dais. John bowed gravely, as did Palla Nad. The Master looked carefully at John. He seemed faintly familiar. The brown red-gold beard and the mustache he had never seen before, surely. He would have remembered them, but there was something in the eyes, which he had been told were the eyes of an idiot, that disturbed him. Where had he seen those eyes before? Just as he thought it would come to him, Yanibo stepped brashly up on the first step of the dais, as if to say something to the Master, and was ready to advance to the second when the guards standing next to the Master's chair instantly lowered their pikes, crossing them in front of the throne.

Yanibo retreated cheerily, giving a wave to the Master of Darkness and grinning broadly with his strong white teeth, his eyes shining from under the black bowl of his hair. Then he abruptly flipped up on his hands, and with his legs curved in the air over his head, he walked around nimbly in front of everyone. Laughter and light applause rippled through the crowd, and even the Master seemed to smile in a forced and strained grimace.

"Not now, you silly fool," hissed D'Orcade from the side and made a grab for him. Yanibo flipped back over on to his feet, evaded him, and did a little mocking jig. More laughter followed. D'Orcade finally pushed him off to the right side, and John and Palla Nad followed him to the three chairs set there for them.

Morduc and Marianna and Illanna on the right of the Master faced John and Palla Nad and Yanibo across a square open space in front of the figures on the dais. The Master looked out across the open space to ranks of chairs on all three sides in which his guests were seated. Behind both the guests and the performers stood several lines of soldiers. Behind them, servants crowded in to see the great pirate fighter and the two new magicians.

The Master rose and signaled for silence. Yanibo wiggled in his chair and seemed to whisper to John. The Master gave him a stern look mixed with feigned strained benevolence, welcoming the opportunity to exhibit to his agents, supporters, and dependents the mixture of severity and favor he thought best calculated to control them. Yanibo shrank back in his seat, playing the chastened little boy with deep, disarming craft.

The Master began to speak in his loud voice, as of great stones clacking on each other in the roil of the sea. "Welcome friends, supporters, and subjects. I have invited you here once again to witness, to note, and to celebrate one of the personages who are currently contributing to the happiness, the peace, and the order which our protectorship has brought to this city, this coast, and this region. Even though you may not have condescended to go to the arena of the common people to see the circus or have had time to stop in the square yourselves to look at, see, and inspect the recently famed old magician, you are still entitled to enjoy under comfortable, pleasant, and convenient circumstances the best of my many servants, helpers, and entertainers, both as a token of our gratitude for your contributions throughout the many hard days, months, and years of bringing peace to this region and as a way of understanding the mood, the mind, and the manner of the great mass of people whom we rule and through whom we hope to extend our benevolent control even further into this continent. By this, I mean Porteus Middock the Magician."

Morduc stood and bowed to scattered applause and then sat down again. "He will be competing against the magician who has recently arrived with the Chauri Circus in town." Palla Nad arose and, holding up his hand and rotating it for a wave, as if he were royalty, slowly turned completely around, greeting the crowd with a foolish and nearly toothless smile. A scattering of laughter rippled around the room. The Master held up his hand for silence. When he had it, he said, "You, the citizens of Kerballa, will decide, determine, and declare who is the winner by your vote." There was silence. No one in Kerballa had voted on anything for eighteen years, and the people did not know how the Master intended the word to be responded to. Years ago, people who had talked too loudly of voting had mysteriously disappeared. D'Orcade started applauding wildly, and the rest in the room nervously but quickly joined in.

When there was quiet again, the Master spoke. "I have also invited here this evening Barbarossa, of whom you have no doubt all heard, the great pirate fighter, whom I wish to distinguish for his help in defending the city, and in particular the person of Lord D'Orcade, whose life he saved, a life we tender very dearly." D'Orcade preened fatuously in his seat, nodding left and right.

"Thus, oh Barbarossa, so aptly named, it is a pleasure to have you among us. Perhaps you would say a word or two."

John arose gravely and bowed to the Master of Darkness. There was loud applause until everyone noticed that the Master had a genuinely displeased look on his face, at which silence fell through the people as quickly as a bucket of pebbles dumped in a pool fall through water. John remained standing, and when there was quiet, said, "Lord General. I very happy. I like fight pirates," and here he let fall a syrupy drool of saliva out of his mouth, at which a tittering in the crowd began until the general looked sternly in its direction, which extinguished it like a candle flame blown out at night. John chewed his lip. He slapped himself on the top of his head with both hands quickly. He struggled to formulate his words. He took in a deep breath and blurted out, "Pirates no good. General good. I got no more to say." And then he sat down, seemingly highly embarrassed at having made even such a speech as this.

"I am glad to see that you feel that way," continued the general. "Let me publicly say here, Barbarossa, that I would like you to leave the circus and join my pirate guard so that we will have the benefit of your strength and integrity always. You owe it to your fellow citizens to serve to protect them."

John pretended to know only that the general was speaking to him and stood up in apparent confusion. He turned to Yanibo. Yanibo skipped up the stairs and said in a loud whisper that could be heard by everyone, "Big man not understand you, General." Laughter flickered around the circle of plump matrons and well-bellied burghers who were now beginning to realize that the Barbarossa they had heard so much of was a good deal less than had they expected. The Master was immensely pleased. He was having just the effect he wished. Everyone would know by tomorrow of what quality this reputed Barbarossa was and would turn back to their daily tasks with the renewed conviction that once more, no local savior had appeared and that only the Master could be relied upon to protect them.

"Barbarossa," said the Master to him. "Do you want to be one of my guards? Good pay. Regular work. Fight pirates all the time."

"Ah," said John, a beatific light spreading over his entire face. "Fight pirates all time? That not work! Fight is fun. I do for you, Master."

"Wonderful, Barbarossa. Do you all understand, ladies and gentlemen? Barbarossa has agreed to join the pirate guard." *And,* thought the Master to himself, *he will join the ever-missing when tomorrow night's raid dispatches him to dead and moldering oblivion and his bones and blood feed my black roses.* "And my first order to you, Barbarossa, is that following the performance of the magician, that you give my guests a little demonstration of your skill and strength."

"I do for you, Master," said John and sat down. Polite applause scattered through the audience. The princess too was applauding politely, the Master saw out of the corner of his eye. *What does that mean?* he thought. *Is she coming around? Perhaps I will give her a chance to save her looks, her honor, and her life after all.*

Turning toward the princess and the king, the Master continued. "And let me recommend to the notice too of our guests, the King of Time and his lovely daughter Aleth, how all the most noble champions are joining me in my efforts to bring prosperity, civilization, and order to this part of the world. I hope in the near future to also hear that you too wish to unite your power, strength, and command to mine. If you wish to make such an announcement at this moment, I am sure all present would be delighted to hear it."

The Dark Sister leaned toward the general. "What are you doing?" she whispered. "We have not discussed this."

The general shot a quick baleful look at her but said nothing.

Meanwhile the princess had inclined her head toward the Master and was speaking. "I thank Your Grace for the honor he does me. After the performances are over, I will have an announcement. For the moment, I neither refuse nor assent. You are aware of the complications attendant on my marriage. My father has determined I shall not marry any save the one who answers the riddle. Until today, I have always maintained that until you wished to rejoin us at my father's castle to deliver your answer, I was required most respectfully to decline to give my own answer. But perhaps that trip will not be necessary after all." Here the king looked at his daughter in barely concealed astonishment but said nothing. She continued, "So I merely ask your indulgence for a slight additional postponement. If on the other hand, you wish at this moment to appoint a time at our own castle to give your answer to the riddle, we will proceed immediately to our father's kingdom and trouble your hospitality no more. It lies solely within your own choice."

Indeed it does, thought the Master to himself. *You are close to a perpetual postponement, though you know it not. Why do I submit myself to these public humiliations? Why do I continue to hope she will see that she* must *assent, as this poor muscle-bound fool has? This is her final chance. Perhaps Sister is correct. Perhaps I can extend my power without even the pretense of legitimacy. Perhaps in tomorrow's pirate raid, both of them . . . Hmn. Now, that is a thought. We shall see.*

Returning his attention to the princess, he replied, "Dear Princess, let me urge you and your father to remain with us for just a day or two longer."

"As you wish," replied the princess, stroking the frog in her lap.

"And I await with eagerness your announcement following the entertainments," answered the Master. She inclined her head toward him but said nothing more. The Master now signaled D'Orcade, who stood up and strutted to the center of the cleared space.

"His High Graciousness, the Master of this castle, city, and region has provided a most special entertainment for you all this evening, after which he has asked me to announce that there will be a delicious supper for you in the side hall." Yanibo stood up and cheered. D'Orcade glared at him, and he dropped back into his seat grinning foolishly. The audience smiled indulgently. "You have perhaps heard of a new magician in town," D'Orcade continued. "I have myself seen him, and he is extraordinary. But there are two new magicians in town. Both are here with us this evening to entertain the princess and her father, and you yourselves, of course, who, the Master wishes you to know, deserve the very best that our fair country can offer. Therefore, without further ado"—here a voice from the back yelled out, "Too much ado already!"—"I present to you the Master Magician of the Road, the Great Porteus Middock, as he calls himself, I believe." He extended his arm toward Morduc and sat down.

Morduc and Marianna and Illanna stood up simultaneously, the two girls casting off with one motion their gray cloaks, disclosing their shimmering golden-clad forms, their golden-masked faces, and their red lips spangled with gold flecks. A gasp went up from the audience. Marianna had a small harp which she began to strum, and the two girls began a slow ballet around the old magician as he shuffled to the middle of the space. He clapped his hands sharply, and the girls, still moving gracefully as if in a dance, by small steps, moved the two black boxes together into the middle of the space to form a small, black, bare, raised wooden stage. Then they continued their dance around the old magician as he stepped up onto the platform created by the boxes.

Raising his hands and showing them empty all around, he cupped them together. Slowly out of the space between them, there began to flow a soft cascade of silk squares—blue, red, gold, green—one after another flowing out of the small space within his hands as if they would never stop. As the mound on his hands grew larger and larger, some of them fell to the surface of the boxes until he was ringed by the silks of many colors. The girls moved around the boxes, gathering up the fallen silks. As the flow of silks from his hands came to an end, the girls returned those they had picked up to him. Gathering them all together into a ball in his hand, he threw them high into the air above his head. At the top of the arc, they suddenly slid into each other. When they fell back to Morduc's hands, he spread out for all to see a single huge, swirling, varicolored rectangle of silk. Each of the girls caught a corner and spread it out until the shimmering rainbow silk stretched nearly from one side of the square open space to the other. The girls came together, folding it in half and then folded it a second time, draping it over Morduc's left arm, where it hung halfway to the platform.

Reaching under the draped rainbow silk, he suddenly began withdrawing what looked like immense roses of every color. These he flung at the top of the black boxes on which he stood and there they stuck upright, each with a decided thump. In a few short moments, Morduc was standing in a garden thick with brilliant-hued roses. The last flower the old magician produced from the silk was a black rose. This Illanna took from Morduc, and with a low bow, presented it to the Master of Darkness.

The Master started, seeing in his hand a full black rose, such as he had been trying to breed for years in his own private castle garden but so far had failed to achieve. What secret did the old magician have? First the gems from the Frog Hoard and now this! He recognized the old magician's bid for his patronage. Perhaps he would be useful. This scouring of the world for embodied concentrations of knowledge of the powers of life was finally beginning to pay off. His sister was wrong. He would yet find the secret of ruling with absolute power and yet be loved for it. The fools of the masses did not really want freedom and independence. They wanted a powerful, strict, but wealthy parent who could give them everything. Applause rang round the room. The Master held up the black rose in his gloved hand, motioning for silence.

"Master Magician Porteus, I thank you for this token. You know your craft well."

"Do you wish to see more?"

The Master hesitated. So far, everything had gone well. He was anxious for the entertainments to be over and to hear what the princess had to say, yet he was intrigued by what additional marvels might be forthcoming.

"Master Magician. I can see that you have only begun. Play on."

Morduc then reached under the draped silk rainbow over his arm and brought forth a clear glass bowl of water nearly overflowing, in which were swimming a number of small, varicolored fish: some gold, some brown, some shining red, one or two black, all the colors of the silks and the flowers. More applause spattered through the high hall. Morduc waved his hand over the water in the bowl, and it instantly grew cloudy, dark, and opaque. He waved his hand again and the clouds began to disperse, and within it glowed a bright light shining out through the clear, deep-blue water. As he held the bowl, the light within the water grew in intensity. One of the golden assistants came and took the bowl from him and walked around the square cleared space, exhibiting the floating, shining gem to the crowd. Morduc clapped his hands, and D'Orcade signaled to the servants. All around the hall, lights were extinguished until the square was in darkness, lit only by the light floating within the water in the bowl.

The other golden assistant took the cloth from Morduc's arms while the first returned to him the bowl with the light shimmering in its depths. Together, the two assistants threw the multicolored silk over the lighted bowl in his hands. The light glowed through the sheen of silk. Slowly the lighted shape under the silk began to rise from the old magician's hands. The light seemed to become brighter. It rose to the height of his head and then slowly above his outstretched hands. There was a profound hush in the hall as each spectator was stirred in his heart by this symbol of the invisible hopes in their own hearts, once shining so brightly but now bleared by tyranny, earth, and age.

In the far distance, beyond the roof, faint rumblings from the approaching storm could be heard, but no one in the hall paid any attention to them, so entranced were they by the suspended light. As the shining object under the silken varicolored cloth rose higher, lifting itself free from the bowl of water, it increased in brightness and seemed to begin to strain at the fabric to escape. It crept closer and closer to the fabric's edge and then emerged like a brilliant star riding on the top edge of the silk, filling the hall with a bright white light shining out from within a transparent oval blue gem.

The audience gasped and started to talk to one another. The closest ones shielded their eyes. The general's sister leaned toward him with her hand on his arm, speaking excitedly in his ear. Marianna and Illanna deftly retrieved the now-dark bowl from under the rainbow silk.

Juncata stood up and spoke in a choking, agonized voice, "Magician, this is your most wonderful trick. That stone. I must have it. I will pay whatever you wish."

"General, there are more wonders to come. This is not my best. As for the stone, your highness, it is not for sale, but I do intend to present it to the princess, if you will have the patience to bear with me. When it is hers, of course, she may do with it whatever she wishes. It would not be an inappropriate dowry for any husband," he added noncommittally. "Indeed, with your permission, I would like to ask the princess to come forward now to accept it from me."

The Master of Darkness stood transfixed, struggling and trembling. The princess stood up, placed the frog on her chair, and started to step forward, but her guards blocked her by crossing their pikes in front of her, waiting for a sign from the general. The princess placed her hands on the pikes and tried to separate them gently, but the guards held firm. The sister was clawing at her brother's arm. "Get the stone," she cawed hoarsely. "It is an Eye Stone." The stone hung above their heads, bobbing ever so slightly, seeming indeed to lift clear of the edge of the rainbow waterfall of scarf.

Finally, Juncata made a gesture of assent with his hand and the two guards parted their pikes, and the princess stepped gravely and slowly down the three steps of the dais and, as if in a dream, crossed the level space to the black boxes. With one hand continually extended toward the stone, the magician waved his other at the princess, who stiffened and fell backward, to be deftly caught at the neck and feet by Marianna and Illanna. They lifted her gently and swiftly into the garden of flowers on top of the boxes and nestled her among them, quickly covering her with the bottom edge of the huge rainbow silk. Motioning toward the stone as if to gather it in, the magician brought it closer and closer to him.

From the dais, the harsh whisper of the sister's voice could be heard saying, "Take it, you fool. Take it now!" But no one moved as the stone came down and down and settled on the chest of the silken-covered figure of the princess.

"Princess," said Morduc. "I want you to take in your hands the stone that is resting on you. If you can hear me, do so now." Two hands from under the silk closed around the stone through the thin, sheer fabric. The light still radiated upward. Morduc gestured. Slowly the body of the princess began to rise with the stone still clasped in her hands. Slowly the draped body rose from the garden of magically made roses. All eyes were on the shining stone, illuminating the length of the silk under which floated the body of the princess.

Outside, the sound of thunder again rolled over the roof of the castle, and then another sound, which, in the intensity of the moment, barely penetrated the minds of those in the hall. It was the distant ringing from far off over the city of the pirate alarm bells. All of a sudden, soldiers who had been standing in the hall, mute at the beauty and wonder of the suspended, shining princess, began to push through the crowd of servants to report to their stations. A panting messenger came rushing through the hall shouting, "General, General!"

"What is it?" shouted the general from his seat.

"Pirate attacks."

"What?" said the Master, turning to his sister. "Did you not . . . ?" He stopped but turned instantly back to the messenger, "*What did you say?*"

"Attacks, General. In three places."

"*Three places!*" thundered the general. He stood up. "Call out the guard immediately." More soldiers began to run toward the main gate as the guests stood up and began to mill about in confusion.

"Magician," said the Master in a level but deadly voice. "This performance is ended. Lower the princess, and give me that stone immediately." As he said this, he drew his sword and began to descend from the dais. Before he had reached the bottom step, however, the old magician had snatched the stone from the hands beneath the silk that had held it. He retreated from the suspended shape, stepping down off the small stage so that the floating figure of the princess was between himself and the Master of Darkness.

"*Stop,*" he called. "The stone is for the princess alone. Return to your chair. Let me complete the performance."

The Master looked about him. Off to his left he saw his new recruit, the thick-armed idiot, Barbarossa, standing between his two circus-performer companions, still looking on in drooling wonder at the floating princess. He called to him. "You! Barbarossa!" John slowly turned his eyes to the Master. "Yes! I mean you, idiot. Pinion that old magician. Hold him for me. Do not let him escape."

"Yes, Master," said John, quickly moving behind Morduc and putting his massive arms around the small, wizened figure. "I have him."

"Get that stone," hissed the Master's sister beside him. Another peal of thunder rolled over the castle. The Master came down the last two steps from the dais and strode rapidly with his drawn sword toward the shape of silk suspended above the flower-topped black boxes.

The old magician struggled in the Barbarossa's arms and called out in a voice louder than one would have expected from so small and ancient a man. "Do not touch the princess. You will break the spell. I cannot be responsible."

The Master stepped to the boxes and waved his sword in the empty space beneath the suspended shape. The shape wobbled a bit in the air but did not fall.

"Stop," said Morduc. "You will harm the princess."

"Then be damned to the princess, you old fakir," said the Master as he turned the edge of his sword upright and, with a mighty motion, swung it upward in a great arc.

The King of Time rose from his chair and gave an agonized cry. But the sword met no resistance save the silk, which it severed, and its two halves drifted softly and noiselessly to the stone floor of the hall to reveal floating above the black boxes in the empty air—nothing, nothing at all.

"Where is the princess?" roared the Master.

"I don't know, sir," the old magician whined from within the gripping circle of Barbarossa's arms. "You interrupted the spell, and now I have lost her."

"Thieves and charlatans!" the Master roared. The rumble of more thunder came from high above the castle. More soldiers crossed the hall in the direction of the main door mingling with guests streaming toward the gate. Three slim figures in gray cloaks that made them nearly invisible slipped along with the crowd toward the door.

"Light! More light!" screamed the general.

"You weak, doting, trusting child," snarled the Sister as she drew a silver dagger from a sheath on her back and began to descend the dais. Suddenly there was an intense flash of lightning outside the high windows followed by a clap of thunder that shook the roof. From outside, the sounds of fighting could be heard, and over it all floated the high, horn-call-like sounds of a fragmented, tuneless battle song.

"You old fool," howled the general, jumping across the small black stage in the center of the cleared space and leveling his sword at Morduc's throat. "You will pay for your crimes—hold him, Barbarossa—you will pay for your crimes, *now!*" Just as he lunged, John turned, thrusting Morduc to the side.

"Nay, Master. Thee woulds't ha' done for me too with that stroke," said John.

"Be it as you wish, then," said the Master, raising his sword and beginning to direct a flurry of blows toward John, who swiftly drew from beneath his tunic his red-steel sword and parried the enraged rain of blows. *First Sprok, and now Skrulldan has failed me*, the Master thought to himself as he drove John leftward back around the stage toward the dais. One of his cuts stripped the white tunic from John, and the red-steel byrnie now shone through.

"You?" said the Master in astonishment, recognizing the armor. "I thought you were bound for death long ago."

"Well, I am unbound now," said John, "and have come to claim the princess. But if you have lost her, I shall require her at your hand. If her life be lost, I shall take yours in return."

Suddenly it became clear to the Master. "You and that old magician are working together!" At the top of his lungs, he screamed out to the remaining guards in the hall, "Kill the magician and Barbarossa!"

The King of Time's two guards rushed down from the dais to carry out the order. Morduc threw off his cloak and hat and from under his robe drew his green-bladed sword and stood ready to defend himself, with the blue-white stone still shining in his left hand. The King of Time, seeing his chance, quickly followed the two guards down from the dais, tripping one of them to crash on the floor, where Morduc immediately dispatched him with a thrust through the throat. As the second guard was maneuvering to drive his pike into Morduc's side, the King of Time wrenched backward on the end of the leveled pike, and Morduc drove forward into the soldier's lower belly with his blade. Gripping his bowels in both hands, the soldier fell to his knees and then onto his face. The King of Time kept the released pike. Fighting furiously with the captured pike and, with Morduc's sword flashing, the two managed to join forces and stand back to back on the hall side of the black boxes.

Meanwhile, the Master of Darkness had driven John leftward around the black boxes in the direction of the dais. The Dark Sister had been waiting her chance to cross the cleared space to kill Morduc and take the gem. But as John passed by her, she made ready to thrust at him instead. Just as she was about to do so, Yanibo threw one of the severed halves of the rainbow silk over her head and tripped her, tying the silk around her. Then he and Palla Nad armed themselves quickly from the bodies of the fallen guards and joined Morduc and the King of Time to make a four-sided knot of bristling steel.

The Master of Darkness had driven John backward up the dais. where he was trapped in front of the black throne. The Dark Sister disentangled herself from the folds of the cloth and joined her brother in attacking John. The sword blows of the two dark figures rained down on the red-bearded young man. He parried desperately. The sweat ran down his face, and his breath began to come in great gasps. He climbed up on the ebony chair. With an immense thrust, the Master sought to pin him to the wood by his groin, but he leapt above it just in time. The Master's sword stuck in the dense black wood of the throne. John jumped down to the Master's right and brought the blade of his sword down on the elbow of the Master. The gauntleted hand, still holding the sword, separated from the arm and fell with the sword, clattering to the stone steps.

A scream like that of a dying reptile rang though the hall. John turned an instant too late to parry a stroke from the Sister's silver sword. He felt its ice-cold metal enter his thigh flesh just below the hem of his byrnie. Then he struck her sword from her hand. It fell clattering behind her. She turned and ran, but instead of pursuing her, John jumped bleeding across the cleared spot to join his friends and the King of Time. Slowly the five began to inch their way toward the arch, which marked the entrance to the passage that led to the main doors.

From that direction came the sound of increasing tumult. The Master saw the backs of his soldiers engaging a somewhat rag-tag group of young men bursting through the arch led by a snarling gray dog, followed by a broad figure in a large yellow straw hat. In spite of his bulk, the old man slashed and thrust nimbly and parried with his round shield, and every now and then, the dog would dash forward and bite a soldier on the leg.

As the fat old man saw John and Morduc and the other three, the King of Time, Palla Nad, and Yanibo, at the upper end of the hall, beset by guards and fighting for their lives, he raised a high cry, "Tally-ho, me hearties. There is the quarry." A great shout went up from the fighters, and with a charge, they broke through the line of soldiers before them. They swept up the hall, running toward the knot of their five beleaguered companions. When the other soldiers saw them coming, they retreated around behind the spiky knot in the direction of the dais, so that very quickly John, Morduc, the King of Time, Palla Nad, and Yanibo were absorbed into the group led by the large man and the dog. Then, slowly, ever so slowly, harassed at the edges by the Master's soldiers, the entire large body of fighters began to move back down the hall, through the arch, and toward the huge open iron doors through which they had entered.

By now the Master had bound his stump with the other half of the silk and had picked up his sword in his left hand. With the Dark Sister, who had retrieved her sword, he moved down the hall to direct the counterattack. He passed under the arch and saw to his astonishment that the main doors were standing wide open.

"Close those doors!" roared the Master of Darkness. Some of the soldiers behind Plummet's group began to push the iron leaves shut before the circle of fighters could reach them. Plummet's men went as fast as they could down the hall, but they were not in time to get through the doors before the huge leaves clanged shut and the lock latch clicked. The soldiers at the door drew the bar from its wall hole into the brackets.

"We have them now!" screamed the Master. "Attack, guards, attack. Kill them all." The circle of Plummet's fighters drove off the soldiers at the door but were themselves driven up against the closed doors. One tried to get out the wicket, but castle soldiers on the other side drove him back.   Limping quickly down the hall and still thrusting furiously, the Master killed first one of Plummet's men and then another, driving the group ever more closely in upon itself, pinning them against the locked and barred door.

"John," called Plummet. "Push that bar back." John allowed himself to be squeezed back within the group to the door. He sheathed his sword and, taking two of the four peg handles, one in each hand, braced himself in the moiling cluster of men. With a mighty heave, he slid the bar back into its slot. A shout went up from Plummet's men by the door. John pushed on the leaves, but the latch would not give. In the very center of the group, Morduc still clutched the star stone. In the dark, he held it up as high over his head as he could. Its bright rays shot out in every direction lighting up the hall like a prism in sunlight.

The sister screamed out, "There it is. The star stone. A thousand pieces of gold to the man who gets it!" The castle soldiers pressed forward. The light in the stone sent a glare over the dark heads and bodies of the struggling men, making gigantic shadows on the walls and reflecting off the flashing blades. As Morduc held it up, the light coming from the stone began to grow brighter and brighter until it filled the hall with a nearly blinding shimmering effulgence, reaching into every corner of the high, timber-roofed hall.

Suddenly, a gigantic lightning bolt sliced through the doors to the stone, springing open the lock. Morduc screamed as the bolt filled the stone and crackled around it. The doors flew open, and all the people pressing against them tumbled outward down the steps, followed by the Master of Darkness and his remaining soldiers.

At the foot of the steps, Plummet and his men scrambled to their feet and regrouped about John, the king, and Morduc. Fighting furiously at the head of his guards, the Master of Darkness pursued the group into the courtyard. Morduc stopped again to hold the stone up in the air as high as he could. Again it began to grow brighter and brighter. Out of the dark, rainy sky, another crashing bolt snaked down jaggedly toward the stone, knocking all those around it to the ground. This time, Morduc could not hold on to the stone. It jumped out of his hand and skittered along the flags of the courtyard underfoot, shining brightly, its rays flashing out among the feet of the furiously fighting men in the dark courtyard.

The Dark Sister took her silver sword in both hands and, laying about her with a supernatural energy, cut her way through both the Master's own soldiers and Plummet's men until she reached the stone, its light streaming up, spinning and rocking on the slate. She dived for it, and as her hand closed over it, she rose up yelling, "I have it, I have it!" and she began retreating toward the castle steps. Another lightning bolt flashed down out of the stormy, rainy sky, landing beside her and cracking the steps as she ran up them. She passed her brother and disappeared within the open black maw of the castle doorway.

Plummet's men regrouped and pushed back to where the Master continued to fight alone on the steps. As they came closer, he too now turned and followed his sister back inside the door of the castle and disappeared into the darkness of the passageway. As Morduc lifted his face to the beginning rain, another lightning bolt hit the north tower of the castle, and it began to fall in upon itself. Another and another and another jagged shining sword of light hit the roof of the castle as the roar of collapsing stone grew louder and louder. Pieces of roof tile began to slide down and crash into the courtyard. In the light of one of the flashes, Morduc saw the upturned, crushed face of Skrulldan on the steps, where he had fallen when the great doors had been flung back against him.

With the castle crashing behind them as more lightning bolts struck it, the fighting turned into a flight of both soldier and citizen across the drawbridge. The portcullis shivered above them as they poured beneath it. Plummet came up to John and Morduc and said urgently, "We must leave immediately." Reluctantly, John and Morduc turned and, with Anga and Plummet, followed the crowd running across the bridge. As they were on it, it shook and trembled. They felt it shift sideways. Behind their backs, lightning bolts continued to spear the castle in a fury of giant jagged strokes. The huge trunks of briar ivy that clung to the stone walls writhed in agony every time the lightning hit.

The crowd pushed and shoved to get across the bridge. The bridge continued to heave and grind as the great suspension chains shook and vibrated from the rumbling and shaking of the granite island. Several of the rushing people who tried to shove ahead of others were pushed off the edges of the bridge and fell screaming to the black waves below.

Finally, the great mass of people had passed over and surged off the land end of the bridge. Just as John and Palla Nad set foot on the headland, another large lightning bolt hit the right suspension chain and severed one of the links. The bridge shivered and began to tilt slowly down into the gulf and, with a wrenching sound, pulled the two massive gate towers and the portcullis machinery down the face of the granite cliff. The huge mass fell silently for several seconds until out of the deep darkness below arose a gigantic crashing and splash.

On the end of the peninsula, the remainder of the Master's soldiers and Plummet's band all stood together in the rain, watching bolt after bolt of lightning fall on the castle, shattering its second tall tower and its roofs, rooms, and halls into hissing, smoking rubble. The briar ivy writhed torturously. Pieces broke off and slithered down the sides of the granite island and dropped into the sea. Lightning bolts continued to rain down on the sea-surrounded stone, illuminating the hundreds of upturned faces on the headland watching the disintegration of the castle and the plans of the Master of Darkness.

Suddenly, a huge jagged flash of lightning struck not at the top of the rock, but at its base on the ocean side, exploding it upward, sending a spray of rocks and granite flakes raining down on the headland. The people turned their backs and shielded their eyes. When they turned back, what had been the granite cylinder of the island was breaking up and sinking into the sea, sending great waves against the base of the headland cliff.

The people stood in the rain, listening and waiting. Now all they heard was the howl of the wind and the heavy splatter of the rain at their feet. The rain continued to fall heavily and steadily, hissing down through the air, pelting the earth. The violent center of the storm had passed over them, speeding on eastward toward the mountains. No more lightning darted out of the clouds. The crowd stood drenched and exhausted on the headland.

Although they were soaked and their feet clodded, they were alive. In the darkness, Plummet's men talked to the soldiers of the fort. Without any further struggle, the attackers allowed the soldiers and all the others who had escaped across the bridge to the headland to leave and move down into the town. Plummet himself was talking to several figures standing next to a coach which had become mired in the road and then tipped out of the way when it would no longer move. Plummet brought them over to where John and Morduc were standing. One of the four was dressed in D'Orcade's clothes, which were sodden and soaked, but he had short, close-cropped black hair. He looked like a shorn, bedraggled peacock. The figure was in fact D'Orcade, but it was the first time any of them had ever seen him without his wig. He was saying imploringly to Plummet, "Now be sure to remember what I did. Tell them how I helped.

Without my putting them in my carriage, they would never have gotten across the bridge. I do hope everyone understands that. I never really liked that man, or fish, or whatever he was anyway, with his nasty scaly hands. You can be sure I am on the side of the new government, whatever or whoever that may be. If you don't mind, I'd just as soon be going. Will that be all right?"

"That will be fine, Mr. D'Orcade," they heard Plummet saying.

"Good. I am so pleased. Now can you get someone to right my coach?"

"Come now, Mr. D'Orcade," said Plummet grimly. "Be grateful you're alive. Walk it along with everyone else tonight."

"Oh, I suppose so, if I must," he said, looking down at his mud-caked, spangled, high-heeled purple shoes. Painfully, awkwardly, he began to pick his way down the road. After a few steps, he reached down and took off his platform shoes and then moved forward in his muddy-stockinged, soon-to-be-bare feet.

Plummet brought over to John, to Morduc, and to the King of Time the remaining three huddled figures from the coach, all in gray cloaks that made them almost invisible in the dark. Marianna flung back her hood and leapt to Morduc and gave him a big hug. He winced. She unclasped him to see what the difficulty was. Suddenly she saw his blackened, twisted left hand dangling by his side. Immediately she tore a strip off her cloak and made a sling for it. Then she said to him mockingly, "Well, injuries will happen if you insist on playing with fire."

"But I thought I was only playing with you," he said.

"Verily the same thing," she replied, smiling, as she opened her cloak to allow Morduc under it with her. "We do make the sparks fly, do we not?"

"We do and will," he said, accepting her invitation and huddling under the cloak with her, with his right arm around her waist.

By this time, the other two figures had thrown back their hoods to disclose the streaked, golden-covered face of Illanna, and for the first time any of them had ever seen her in that mood, the face of the princess beaming with joy and laughter. Even the King of Time was smiling, his white teeth showing behind his black beard. He stepped to his daughter, hugged her, and kissed her on the forehead. "For a moment there," he said in his hoarse whisper, "I thought we had been parted."

His daughter looked at him with a keen gleam in her eye and replied, "Father, I nearly was." Then she turned to where John was standing, the rain running down his bald head, his beard, and his red-steel byrnie, stained with still-fresh blood, and placed her hands on his shoulders. He took her elbows in his arms as they looked at each other, wordlessly, for a full minute.

"It has been a long time coming, this meeting," said John finally.

"And I have waited long for it," replied the princess, her smile and red-gold hair almost rivaling the brightness of the star stone. "I thank you, for myself and for my father. I am glad to discover you are much more man than the

Master thought you were. He might have done well by you if you had thought to join him."

"Wise and beautiful lady," said John gravely, "surely you understand he could never have given me anything I cared for, which is only you. I think and do for myself now."

"I am glad to hear it," she replied, still smiling at him. "No less will do." She paused for a moment and then continued, "Not only are you less tongue-tied than when I first saw you, but I also hear you fared better in the fight against the Master than when you went up against him the previous time."

"Indeed, my princess," said John, allowing himself a small smile for the first time since he had left the King of Time's castle, "I would like to say that he succumbed to my disarming charms." The princess looked at him archly sideways while Plummet, standing beside them, laughed aloud in the raining darkness.

"Well," continued John, "in any case, he is finished."

"And you, I suspect, have only just begun," said the princess, moving a step closer to him so that his arms joined around her and he could feel her soft full body against him even through his byrnie as she kissed him, open mouth to open mouth, deeply.

When the kiss was finished, John's face beamed. Then it fell again into seriousness as he considered a second possible meaning to her remark. "The quest, do you mean?"

"Not exactly. The matter of the riddle must be cleared up, of course, but if you did answer correctly, some might say that you have already completed the quest by showing the kind of character that the quest was designed to test. You simply put the quest before the question," said the princess, smiling mischievously directly into the serious face of Red John.

"And who might say such a thing?" said John.

"I might say so, and I doubt not that my father will see it in the same way."

"I pray that it may so be," said John.

"Are you as good for life as you are for one night?" asked the princess.

Taking her elbows in his palms again, Red John looked at the princess and said, "Better. Infinitely better. And better every day of it too."

"Such a bold claim," said Aleth, still smiling.

"Try me," said John.

"I will, Red John. I will. If you are truly worthy of me, you will have me, but that is all I can say for now."

"My most dear and admired Aleth, it is enough," replied Red John, smiling in spite of his soaked clothes and tired and cold body and his stiffening wound.

The princess then drew John with her as she returned to her father's side, and taking his arm as well, the three, with Aleth in the center, began to walk together down from the headland into the city. At one point, the trio stopped as Aleth noticed John limping. She tore a strip from her dress, knelt in the mud, and bound up the wound in John's thigh. Then the three resumed their progress toward town.

Watching them depart, Illanna stood forlornly by Plummet when one of his men, dressed partly in the uniform of the customs service and with a large, blood-soaked bandage on his head, came limping up and saluted him.

"All secure, Chief," he said. Illanna stared at him. He looked directly back at her with warm brown eyes in a warm brown face at her golden one and up and down her golden-clad body but gave no sign of recognition. Illanna stared at the wet, stained face. "L'Orka?"

"Yes, my name is L'Orka. And who are you, golden girl?" But suddenly he recognized the voice. "Illanna? Is it you?"

For answer, she flew to him and kissed and hugged him so hard that she knocked him over into the mud as she kissed and kissed again his handsome dark-brown face. When she finally lifted her head, he had streaks and smudges of gold all over his laughing dark face.

"Yea, that's my farm girl all right, but by the looks of things, you've taken up another line of work."

"I promised you," broke in Plummet, "that you would see him again, did I not? Without him, and a goodly number of his comrades, we would not have succeeded tonight. He is all in one piece, I guess, if a bit gashed."

"Indeed, but even though worse for wear as I am, Illanna," said L'Orka from the mud, "my love, will you give up whatever golden work this is that you are doing and be a sailor's wife?"

"Kiss me back first," she said, "before I answer." And he did, rolling over on top of her in the mud.

At their feet, Anga barked once and then nodded his head up and down and drew a stroke in the rain-dimpled mud.

"Not *too* much the worse for wear that I can tell," said Illanna, smiling and breathless, as she came up for air. "You sailor boys do know how to submerge a girl. And whatever strength you may lack now, I will nurse you back to having. Henceforth I will live with you here on the coast. Agreed?"

"Agreed, girl, if we can stay out of the sight of your brother. You may have to put to sea with me, though, for I have heard that he is in the city and inquiring for you."

Illanna's face filled with alarm.

Plummet stepped closer to them and said gently, "You do not need to worry ever again about Steingar." The look of fear was replaced by one of anguish.

"How do you know?" she asked hesitantly.

"When we are warm and dry," he said, "I will tell you all of what I have heard and seen, which, in short, is a man with a white streak through his black hair dead in the shallows of the sea."

Illanna gasped and began to cry, lying there in the mud. L'Orka, next to her, put his arm around her. "I may be a sailor by trade, but I like not so much of this water now. Let me comfort you in this storm. Let's go somewhere and get out of this beastly rain." Plummet helped L'Orka to his feet. He in turn drew Illanna upright. With arms about each other's muddy clothes, the two of them started for town.

After conferring with Plummet, the highest-ranking officer of the guards left alive agreed to garrison the headland fort with equal numbers of each party.

"What about the pirates?" said one of the guards.

"We were the pirates," replied Plummet. "No danger from them tonight. We will meet tomorrow to discuss what sort of government the city wishes, but tonight, it will be enough simply to perform the regular watches. Is that agreed? My men, who are assuredly not pirates, but rather your fellow citizens, will be about the city. Most of Juncata's secret police have fled. Those that remain are no doubt in hiding but may be willing to submit to the new civil authority we must establish. I think the city will be at peace for the night when the news of the general's death in the destruction of the castle is known."

"What makes you so sure that he was destroyed?" said Morduc, his blackened left hand continuing to ache and tingle.

"I had surely thought," said Plummet, "that no one could survive a disaster like that, but now that you mention it, the general is no regular person, and perhaps we have not seen the last of him. But I am sure that he cannot bother us tonight."

"I think I agree with that," said Morduc.

Finally all but the joint garrison left the headland of the peninsula and, in a straggling line, trudged back toward town in the dark, wet night. Talking of these matters, they wended their way through the rain-drenched city, bone weary, many with wounds, and all, from the highest of rank and greatest in wealth to the lowest, wet equally by the steady rain falling. Among all the great crowds of mingled citizens and soldiers, there was not a single instance of disorder or mistreatment, one of the other. It is true that as they came through the plaza, the people with one voice agreed to topple the general's statue. A cable was brought from the shipyard, and a daring sailor scaled the tower in the rain. Then all the people put a hand to it, and with a great cry, the statue and column came crashing down on the rain-wet plaza.

Though they did not know what would happen in the morning, for the moment, the oppressive tyranny that had loomed over them for so many years had been thrown off. The release from that tension set some to wish to sing, and sing they did, in the dark of the night rain, a strong anthem of joy and freedom, an ancient song that all knew but which had not been heard for many years in that city.

Those who had not been at the battle of the castle heard the song and its singers coming through the streets and were glad in their hearts and opened their windows, letting light from inside the houses out into the wet streets. Mother Gump heard it as it approached the Green Dragon Inn. She bustled to throw open her doors. Morduc and Marianna, John, the princess, and the King of Time, Illanna and L'Orka, and Plummet and the dog Anga came down the alley to her gate. As they entered the main inn room, the one patron still there that late, turned and looked incredulously at the broad smiles and streaked faces under matted hair and above muddy clothes, from which water still dripped on the floor.

Mother Gump began to laugh, saying, "Come in, come in. You look like orphans of war. Come in, even with all that mud on your feet, come in and rest and eat and drink something warming after your struggles."

The dog Anga pushed in between their legs toward the fire and, feeling himself at last out of the rain, stood on the hearth and shook and shook and shook himself, spraying everyone and then, with the utmost contentment, lay down and turned his long gray head in the direction of the tired, ecstatic group at the door. As they laughed, the dog raised one of his eyebrows and looked at them with the fond, amused expression that so many of them, and Morduc especially, knew so well.

CHAPTER 43

Morning and Marriages

The morning broke clear and blue. The city had been rinsed clean by the previous evening's downpour. From the dark, jumbled mound of granite rubble that had been the fortress island and castle of the Master of Darkness a small, thin spiral of white smoke rose up. The black bark was gone—whether sunk or sailed, none knew. The white-capped blue water sparkled under the sun as it broke against the granite blocks on the shore of the island.

In the serene early light, Plummet tramped the town, going from guard post to guard post, scotching rumors and negotiating harmony between the sailors and the police. He stood finally at the head of the peninsula, looking across the chasm between it and the shattered granite on which the castle had stood. *Good riddance to him,* he thought to himself, *but holding the city and region together now will be no easy task. The real struggle has only just begun.* Having inspected this ultimate post and having satisfied himself of its quiet and order, he turned his steps back toward the center of town.

In the Green Dragon, Anga, sleeping at the foot of Morduc's bed, lifted his head and sniffed the air as light came in through the shutters. He got up and stretched, first his back legs and then his front. He yawned. Then he went over to the bed and rested his long triangular head on the covers and waited. When nothing happened, he started to whine and sing a little bit. Eventually Morduc's hand groped its way toward the large gray head and scratched behind the ears. Anga wagged his upcurled tail furiously and smiled in amused and playful delight.

In other rooms of the inn, others too were waking: Marianna and Illanna, the king, the princess, and in a small back room, the only one Mother Gump had had left, Red John himself, now called LimbLopper and LightBringer and TyrantToppler for his defeat of the Master of Darkness. He tossed and turned his muscular bulk in the bed that was too narrow and too short for him. A knock came at the door. John started awake and reached for his sword but then realized where he was.

"Who is it?" he called out.

"Morduc," came the quiet reply.

"Come in," he said. The door opened and Morduc entered, no longer gray bearded and gray browed, but dressed once again in his suit of seventy times seven shades of green and looking much as he did when they had first set out on their journey, save for his lightning-seared left hand where the green had mixed with charcoal.

"Well, you great slug-a-bed," said Morduc. "How can you sleep on a morning of victory? Aren't you burning to see your bride?"

John sat up abruptly. "I am," he said, flushing suddenly so that his face was nearly as red as his beard. "I was having dreams as if I were locked in a box and drowned in the ocean. It's this cursed bed. It's not big enough for a child."

"Then out of it. I am sure, somewhere in this town we can find you a bigger bed." And he added with a big grin, "We are both going to need one, you know. No more lonely nights for either of us."

"Indeed," said John with a serious look, "you are closer to needing such a bed than I, though I have every hope. But you are right. I must be up and stirring. I have slept too long, even for a victor. I must see the king, I must answer the riddle, and we must help Plummet restore liberty and self-government to this city if it is not to fall prey once again to some tyrant who would govern it for his own purposes. Indeed, there is much to do. It is noble work, and I hope joyous, and I look forward to it all."

By the time John had dressed and come down to the main room of the inn, the king and the princess, Morduc and Marianna, and Illanna and Anga had already left. He grabbed a muffin from the bar top and went running out into the street, where people were hurrying toward the square. The sun shone down on John's red-gold beard. It glinted off his red-steel byrnie. If one squinted one's eyes until John was a blur, he could be taken for a tall, solid, walking flame, so brightly shone he in the clear morning light.

Everyone in the street recognized him. StrongThumbs the Circus Performer, who became Barbarossa the Pirate Fighter, and who now was revealed as LimbLopper and LightBringer, who, by control over himself, had returned to the people of the city control over themselves. People in the street called to him and wanted to stop him to shake his huge hand or just to touch him. Without being discourteous, he hurried along through the crowd, looking splendid and massive in his red-steel mail shirt, with his red-gold beard spread out over his chest and his sword at his side.

By the time he arrived in the square, a great crowd had gathered before a platform on which the king and the princess were seated and on which Plummet, in his straw hat, was standing, looking out over the crowd. When he saw John approaching, he called out, "Make way! Make way for StrongThumbs DarkDriver." The crowd cheered and parted happily, opening a path for him as he strode through, strong and eager, yet still a little nervous to be the focus of such a great throng of people. At the foot of the platform, he found assembled a large number of the leading citizens of the city, the old wise men and women, the merchants and the marketers, the judges and teachers, the chiefs of the men's and the women's guilds, and the mayor of the city himself, as well as the heads of all the civil departments.

Finally, Plummet raised his arms for silence, and the crowd slowly became quiet. He spoke. "Citizens, no longer subjects, it has been a momentous and hard-fought night. Red John, Barbarossa, LightBringer, has fought the Master of Darkness and has won. He has freed the city and the country from that oppressive presence. I have called you here today to consider, if consider we can in so large a group, how to arrange matters for the future. Perhaps we have learned a lesson from the Master about giving up our rights for the sake of safety, yet in doing so, we lost them both. On the other hand, we still know that there must be order for there to be, safety, justice, and rights. I have walked the town this night, seeing to a temporary order. All those to whom I have spoken have shown cooperation and self-restraint in the immediate need. But now it is time to search out ways of perpetuating this temporary and provisional harmony and order, of staying free without falling into anarchy, of securing order without falling into tyranny. What is your wish?"

Various voices from several parts of the crowd began shouting out such phrases as, "King Plummet!" or "No king, no government, all for oneself!" or "StrongThumbs, StrongThumbs, StrongThumbs!" More and more took up the chant of "StrongThumbs," until its noise drowned out the others and filled the square. Plummet again held up his arms for silence.

When the crowd had quieted he spoke again. "Citizens, I agree that StrongThumbs has proven himself capable of defending your safety. He would make a fine captain, but do you want to replace one captain with another? Who is to govern the captain? Here beside me is your former king, whose rightful rule you threw off for the Master of Darkness. Should you not resubmit yourselves to him?"

At this, the mayor of the city ascended the platform. "Citizen Plummet," he said in a loud voice. "We welcome you back from your exile. We ever knew you to be an honest and upright man. We thank you also for your role in this night's fight for freedom. But we need hardly remind you that our problem many years ago was that the king beyond the mountains did not watch over us, did not help us when we needed him, did not have the strength to do what a good king must. We fell into the hands of the Master through that king's neglect . . ." Here a warning murmur ran through the crowd. The mayor held up his hand for quiet. "And I do acknowledge it, yes, through our own folly and weakness. It cannot be denied. Still, if we were to again become a city of the king, would this same thing not happen again? Would he not go back beyond the mountains? Would he not still be weak? Now, if the king were to live here with us, then perhaps we could accept him again as our lord and leader."

An even louder murmur of dissent ran through the crowd. When it had passed, the mayor resumed, "I have talked to many of you this morning, and you have counseled me never to use the word 'lord' again, and so I shall say merely, perhaps we could accept the king again as our leader if he were to live with us and for us and share our fate as well as our fortune. But if he is to go again beyond the mountains, we must respectfully decline to resubmit ourselves to the King of Time."

"Friend, Mayor," returned Plummet, "Time is your Lord whether you will or no, but I do understand your thirst for safety and justice and your need for a guardian of it who will live among you and thus immediately share in the fate or fortune of the decisions he makes. Have you then, in consultation with the members of your council, some suggestion of your own, some way to provide for the visible government, for that which is or should be the image of justice in every citizen's soul?"

The mayor drew up his short, plump bulk and replied, "Old Plummet, and Your Honor the king, we do have a suggestion. May we put it as delicately as possible? If StrongThumbs and the princess were to . . . and then . . . ." Here he let his voice fall off as the crowd caught the idea and began calling out, "StrongThumbs, Aleth, Red John, Princess, Just Strength, wise truth, govern self, govern best." As these and similar cries ran through the crowd standing in the sunny open air of the plaza across which the dark shadow of Juncata's column no longer fell, the king slowly rose from his seat on the platform.

Beside him, the princess sat quietly in her white gown, her red-gold hair flowing in braided flame down her back. The king waited for silence, his large dark eyes looking out over the crowd from under his thick black eyebrows. His crown sat upon his dark hair like stars in the blackness of the night. His black beard and mustache flecked with gray framed his lips. Finally the noise in the crowd was stilled. He began to speak in that hoarse, whispered voice so difficult to understand that it seemed as if he spoke a foreign language. As the people in the crowd concentrated, however, they began to understand the words and the meanings as he spoke a form of their language that carried the accent of ancient ages.

"Men and women of the coast. Your mind is in accordance with my own. It was my intention from the beginning to give you your own leadership, yet when I left you unsupervised many years ago to create it among yourselves, you did not do so but broke up into your village thought, assuming that because the sun would always shine, peace was free. When the attacks came, you blindly and cravenly threw yourselves into the arms of the attacker. You paid heavily for your short thinking." Angry murmurs grew in the crowd but were hushed by other voices, saying, "It is true. You know it is true." The king waited patiently.

"I saw then that you would not free yourselves and must have a leader to embody your best wishes, to give you heart, to encourage you, to help you, and yes, to deny you. But where was such a leader to be found? To find this leader, I posed a question to all the world. The answerer of it, I deemed, would be strong enough to free you and wise and good enough to maintain justice on the coast once freed. To that end, I promised my daughter to such a knight, if, first answering the riddle, he then came on quest to the coast to relieve your distress under the Master of Darkness.

"But before I could bring my plans to completion, the Master himself, in a bold stroke, appeared among the suitors for the hand of my daughter, corrupted the RiddleMaster, and then made her and me captive before the riddle was judged. Made captive because he correctly divined that a young man of promise had been identified and that he seemed right fair to give the correct answer to the riddle. That man was he whom you now call StrongThumbs, DarkDriver, Barbarossa. If you agree, I propose to go forward with the original plan. If John StrongThumbs can answer the question he was about to answer before the interference of the Master of Darkness, I will give him my daughter in marriage, and I will then give them both to you as the focus of your self-preservation. He has already, to my judgment, successfully performed the quest he would have been asked to undertake after answering the riddle, but by my oath, I may not give him my daughter unless the riddle be correctly answered."

The crowd cheered. "Where is StrongThumbs? Bring StrongThumbs forth." The crowd pushed him forward, in fact lifted him, carrying him to the platform and setting him upon it. "Answer, John," cried the crowd. "Answer the riddle. And you will be our king and the princess will be our queen."

John stood waiting in the sunlight for quiet.

"People, King, Princess, Plummet," he began. This was the first time most had heard him speak, and they approved his grave tone and the terms of his address. "Before the one riddling question is asked me, I must ask the people, the king, and the princess each to answer a question of their own."

"What question? What question?" shouted the crowd.

"Of the princess, first. Are you willing to be given in this way, for without free consent, there can be no true compact." The princess arose and stepped to the edge of the platform. A sigh went through the crowd as her bright beauty washed over them. When they had quieted, she touched John on the red steel of his shoulder and said with a smile both serious and mischievous, "Inasmuch as this knight Red John has sought for me and fought for me, has fed me and freed me, and has been ready to give up his life for me, and inasmuch as I have seen his good heart in his deeds even more than in his words, I do stand willing to join myself to him. Moreover, though his head is as bald as a baby's with only a sparse furze of red fuzz growing on it, his person also pleases me greatly. I will make do with his beard until his head has hair again. Yes. I will have him, and freely. May his loyalty and justice and defense of me be an image and promise of his loyalty and justice toward you and defense of the city." With that, she stood on her tip toes and kissed Red John on the cheek. He turned as red as his beard again but had the presence of mind to turn to Aleth, take her hands in his, and return a kiss on her cheek.

The crowd cheered and laughed loudly at the same time. "Hurrah for Aleth. Pert princess. Spunky girl. That's tellin' 'im." She returned to her seat. John's gaze followed her filled with amazement and admiration, wondering in the back of his mind, however, when he had fed her, and then, with a shock, he remembered Morduc's supposition that she herself had been the red-gold-pelted squirrel who had visited him. What was this princess whom he might win? Ever an enigma inside a surprise. Well, no time for his courage to fail him now. He went on.

"Of the king, I must ask this question. The RiddleMaster was slain by the Master of Darkness. Who will now judge the rightness of my answer?" There was silence. In the crowd were mutters of "A hard question that," "It can't be himself, surely, nor the princess, since she is partial." No voices were raised with an answer. The crowd grew restless. "Well," John said again. "Who can be the judge? This I must know, for who judges me now judges all my life. How if I say right but am judged wrong? I lose all I wish and risked and fought for. Moreover, I seek a judge who will judge me every day and ever again in this land, one who will judge my disposition of the riddles of government. Who is master of the riddles here?"

Silence continued still. Then a voice called out, "Judge the rightness yourself, StrongThumbs." The crowd took up the chant, "Judge yourself. Judge yourself." John remained impassive. When silence had settled again, he spoke.

"Nay," he said, "That was the late general's way. It is not fitting. I refuse to judge myself. I show good judgment in refusing to judge, but in so refusing, I cannot then be judge of the answer to the riddle. How do we escape this paradox? We must think again."

"Let the people judge," called out another voice.

"They always do judge in the end, Time and the people," said John, "but how are the people to speak with one voice? You have heard yourselves here today. You do not agree. We must think again."

"Let the King of Time judge. It is his daughter," called a voice.

"Aye, Time is always the judge of truth, but will he remain here to judge? Can you wait for his judgment?"

"Well, what is it to be? There is no answer then," came a voice from the crowd. "Here is a riddle before a riddle," said another. "How is it to be solved?" said a third.

At this point, Morduc stepped up on to the platform. "Who is that?" ran round the crowd. "The old magician," said one. "But he doesn't look old." "Is he really a magician? Let him do a trick now. Good! Some entertainment. This thinking is too hard work. Let's forget it all until tomorrow." But Morduc performed no trick; he merely stood waiting. When the crowd finally quieted, he spoke.

"Once, when I was traveling in a certain realm, the people, or perhaps I should say the citizens of that realm used to appeal to their Old Wise One. Have you not somewhere in this city someone who has thought deeply about many things, one who knows the ancient traditions and has heard all the arguments so often that he knows the difference between novelty and truth, one who knows a clear statement from an unclear one? Someone who loves wisdom and knowledge before power?"

The mayor of the city spoke up. "There is such a one here among us who has proved his wisdom and his courage. The one you now call the fisherman, old Plummet."

There was no wild clapping, no noisy support, but everyone turned to look at Plummet where he stood out of the way on the platform. John looked at him too, and the princess, and the King.

"Come forward, Plummet, and be examined," said John.

Plummet stepped to the front of the stage wearily.

"Would you agree to judge my answer, Plummet, who have already done so much to free this city?"

"I had hoped," said Plummet, "to cease my labors and to return to my fishing. But I see there is a kind of impasse here that must be resolved. The people cannot agree. You cannot judge your own case, nor may the others because they all have an interest. I too have an interest, but of a different sort from John and from the princess. My interest is more like that of each good and true man here, to possess his peace in purity if he can, in courage if he must. I do agree to judge, but only if *all* here will accept me. If one, even one, does not accept, then I will not judge."

John turned to the crowd and said in a loud voice, "I declare I am satisfied to have Plummet judge my answer, now, and if need be, in the future."

Turning to the princess, he asked, "Will you accept Plummet as the judge?"

"I will," she said, "and happily."

To the king he asked the same question, to which he replied that he would. Turning again to the people, he called out, "You have seen how all of us will abide by the judgment of Plummet, be it for our happiness or otherwise. Will you too accept his judgment, without grumbling or revolt, whether you agree in each case or not? Think carefully on this. You bind me and you bind yourselves to have him forever meddling in your affairs. You will be giving up some of your newfound, hard-wrought freedom, and freedom won at such cost and at such pain is sore to relinquish for short odds. How speak you?"

"He speaks well," said one in the crowd. "Was this the idiot we saw in the circus?" said another. "A smart idiot," said a third.

"Well," said John, "Are we ready to hear how you determine?" But before he could ask them to give their assent in voice, Plummet raised his hand for silence.

"Friends, if you are to confirm me in this role, I would ask that it be done so none can impeach me later, saying they did not agree. I ask that you give your assent one by one, and in secrecy, for the secrecy of that declaring is the image of the secrecy of your own heart. I will refuse to serve save that each man's body be secret when he declare the secret counsel of his heart. Bring ye each a token on the morrow and place it, in a tent set here, in a great jar if ye would have me judge. He who agrees may drop in a white bean. He who disagrees may drop in a black bean. Under no other condition will I serve."

"He judges well already," cried a voice. "Let it be so," cried another. "Let it be done on the morrow." And so it was. Each one in the crowd went home, discussing the vote to be held the next day on Plummet as judge of the riddle. Each discussed it with all in his household. And each found their bean.

The second morning dawned no less clear than the previous, and every resident of the city came to the square during the course of the day and entered the tent set up there. Within the tent, each woman and each man was alone with a jar made by the master potter, its lid sealed save for a hole just large enough for a bean to be dropped in. All that day, the citizens filed through the tent. At sundown, the master potter came and sealed the opening with clay, and those who were to watch over the urn that night pressed their seals into the wet clay. All the night following, the jar sat in the tent, guarded by the mayor and his men, by L'Orka, by the chief of the guards, and by a representative of each of the groups in the city.

On the third day, a huge white canvas was spread out in the plaza in front of the platform. On the platform again stood the king, the princess, Plummet, and John. The tent was taken down. Each guard declared to all that the urn had been untouched and that the sign of sealing for each warder on its now-dry top was his own and had not been tampered with. At a signal from Plummet, Red John descended from the platform and gave his sword to the mayor. Carefully, the mayor took the blade and inserted it midway between the leaves of a huge leather-bound book containing the ancient laws of their city along with an equal number of completely new and unwritten-on pages. Then, the mayor swung, hitting the jar with the hilt of John's red sword, and smashed the clay vessel. All its contents spilled out on to the white canvas. Men and women with rakes spread the beans over the white cloth, spread, and spread, and spread, until the layer of beans was only one bean thick and all the beans could be seen. Everyone in the square looked and looked and looked, but among the vast expanse of white beans, there was not a single black one to be found.

The mayor announced the result, inviting all to inspect the canvas. The people crowded around, but none challenged the mayor's declaration. For the new beginning, then, all were in agreement. It was unanimous. The mayor and all his informal council wrote their names on a new leaf of the book of laws. When all in the crowd who wished to look had looked their fill, the mayor stood on the platform and said in a loud voice, "Then, Plummet shall judge the answer. It is decided. His answer will be the answer of the people of Kerballa." A great shout went up from the crowd.

"Indeed, it is decided," said Plummet. "For now I too agree to serve because the people have agreed. Red John, are you ready to stand the test?"

John came forward, reascended the platform, and said, "Oh justicing judge, I am ready to abide the test."

Then Plummet said, "I ask the king to conduct the examination."

"Very well," replied the king. "Red John, do you remember the riddling question?"

"Yes," replied John.

"Then repeat it, please," said the king.

In his strong, loud voice, John repeated the verse he had first heard from the crazed lips of the RiddleMaster:

"Swiftest and most slow

Above and then below,

Beauty's best

In shadow's show.

Mind me, find me, bind me."

"That is correct," said the king. "And do you remember, Red John, the answers that have already been given?"

"I do," said John.

"Repeat them, please," said the King.

"The Blonde Knight answered 'the stars,' but the RiddleMaster did not approve the answer because no quest can bring back the stars."

"That is correct," said the king. "And what was the next?"

"The next answer was given by Otto the Squat, the large knight in the ridged armor. His answer was 'the sea,' and this too the RiddleMaster did not approve because the sea has no speed nor could it be brought back from the quest."

"Yes, indeed," said the king. "And what do you think of this answer?"

"It too seems to me to be a most ingenious and careful answer, yet true it is that the ocean no more than the stars can be brought back from a quest."

"Very well," said the king. "Before we come to your own answer, were there any other answers that should be rejected?"

"The Master of Darkness too gave an answer."

"What was that?"

"That dark prince," said John, shuddering a bit at the memory, "claimed that the answer was a black stone rose. But whether the RiddleMaster would have disqualified it or not or why, I do not know because it was at that point that the Master made his attack."

"But what do you say now," asked the king, "to the logic of the Master of Darkness? Was his answer a fair answer?"

"That, of course, is truly for the judge to determine, but frankly, oh king, I find no logic in the answer at all and see it as a most perverse and impetuous answer quite characteristic of the Master of Darkness. The black stone rose does not satisfy the conditions of the riddle simultaneously as a true answer must. A rose passes swiftly, but a stone rose would never blossom at all nor would it be subject to death either. The answer is no answer at all, sustained only by purely specious identities. A black stone rose might be sought on a quest, yet it could as easily be made, so it is no quest at all but a sculptor's problem."

"You speak most judiciously," said the king, smiling. The princess too smiled encouragingly at John, as she had many months before, a true but serious smile, since he was staking his all on a single answer, and her fate and wish now too depended on his wisdom.

"Then, Sir John, if I may call you that," continued the king, "are you now ready to yourself try an answer to this puzzling riddle? Not only your own happiness depends on it, but that of my daughter, and as well the security and happiness of this city, this coast, and this region. If you answer it, you will marry the princess and undertake the responsibilities of governing this portion of the realm. If not, you will be no more than a circus strongman, a mere wanderer in shows, a curiosity. 'StrongThumbs, who lost the princess,' they will call you. Or perhaps 'Beef wit in beef body.' It is a grave hazard. If you wish, I can postpone the time of answering, giving you a year and a day to travel the world searching out answers before you hazard. Think well before you decide."

John went down the steps of the platform. Morduc and Marianna came to his side, and Yanibo and Palla Nad. By him too stood L'Orka and Illanna. They formed a circle around John as he consulted with them, speaking in a low voice. The dog Anga pushed his nose between their legs into the center of the group. As the group opened up again to face the platform, the dog drew a single stroke on the ground in front of John.

"Most noble and august king," said John, reascending the steps to the platform and turning and facing the crowd. "I am ready to answer now, with no further delay." A hush fell over the square. In a tense voice, John spoke:

"Swiftest and most slow,

Above and then below,

Beauty's best

In shadow's show.

Find me, mind me, bind me.

"The word which came out of my mouth during my first questioning, that was spoken in bafflement and confusion, that word which leapt out of me born of desperate intuition and deep desire, was the correct answer then as it is now. The saving word is 'I.' I myself am the answer."

The king sat pondering the answer, as did the princess, and Plummet too, giving sign neither of assent nor of disapproval. Finally the king said, "I do not yet understand. Explain your answer further."

"I am myself the answer," said John, pausing. "I or any individual man or woman. In thought, most swift, going in an instant to and beyond the stars, but in gait most slow, and slower yet on my way into the grave's shadow, stopped altogether when buried, yet I or any human most utterly beautiful in supreme when fulfilling my true nature, though death shadow's slave nevertheless. So am I or the princess, and so are we all, everyone in this square, this city, this country, this all-where. Recognition of this alone founds justice securely on the rock of mortal equality and equal mortality. If this be not the answer, I know no other, and on this I take my stand. I call for judgment."

The king continued to sit in silence, pondering the answer. The huge crowd breathed so quietly in the sunlit square that they seemed to be holding their breaths. The moment of suspension prolonged itself. Then Plummet arose and went to the princess. He held out his hand. She put hers within it and stood up. She allowed herself to be drawn to the front of the platform where John still stood in silence, his eyes closed, facing the crowd. Now Plummet lifted John's hand and placed that of the princess within it and said in a sober, level voice,

"Red John, I adjudge your answer correct. The Princess Aleth will be the bride of Red John, Barbarossa, StrongThumbs, DarkDriver, LightBringer, Master of the Master of Darkness. May you rule yourselves in happiness and bring happiness of rule to this city."

The crowd still did not dare to let out its breath, waiting, waiting, waiting. Then the Princess Aleth spoke to John, saying it so all could hear, "John, I too approve the heart of your answer with all my heart. I commit my individual self and soul that has endured kidnap and capture to your individual self and soul that has discovered its meaning in your quest to free me. I am yours as you are mine."

The dog Anga began barking, and the crowd erupted in shouts of joy. John now took her other hand in his and faced her as the crowd cried, "Hooray!" "Hooray!" and "Hooray!" again. Although the riddle had been answered correctly, the king remained sitting. The noise eventually died away, and people began to look doubtfully at him. What problem could remain? When there was complete silence in the square again, he arose and asked in his voice that was so quiet that it seemed to be coming from within each person and thus strangely to fill the sky.

"A most excellent answer, young John, but incomplete. You have won the right to the quest, but how now can you go on quest for yourself? How can one go on a quest for the soul of man or woman and bring it back when it is always here, and to whom can you present it? The quest for man seems to be no more capable of success than for the stars or the sea. What do you say to that?"

"Noble king. I have already answered that. I am, myself, the answer. I have brought myself here, I have recognized evil for what it is, I have fought it and conquered it, both within and without myself, and, in so doing, I find myself. I discover, recognize, and know my true self. I am, in my own person, now and always both the end and the beginning of the quest, and by continuous virtue and courage and self-knowledge, I am worthy to be Aleth's husband and your son. I deliver myself to you both, to respect Time and to love Truth. This is the end of man and of woman, and of myself and of all. There can be no other. On this, I risk all."

Then to the degree that so august a personage as the king could smile at all, he did so, a slight upturning of lips in the dark, stern, bearded face. In his deep voice, he said, "You have answered well. I am pleased. It will be done with my blessing as well as by consent of the city. You are correct. I declare the quest to have been accomplished with the discovery of the wisdom within the answer. Let your marriage be tomorrow." And taking both of the young people in his arms, he hugged them strongly.

Seeing this, the square burst into even louder cheering than before. People threw their caps in the air and began singing and dancing. John and the princess and Plummet and the king descended the steps and began to walk through the crowd. Morduc and Marianna and L'Orka and Illanna came to them first to shake their hands. As they did so, Morduc and L'Orka spoke to John in his ear. John listened attentively and then nodded his head. Then he spoke to the king and to Plummet and to the mayor, and they too listened and then nodded their heads in agreement, up and down. The crowd milled around John and Aleth as they walked hand in hand in the direction of the Green Dragon. The citizens, each one, wished to call out his own best wishes and greeting, but finally they began to stream homeward with the news of the morrow's marriage.

Before each one left, he or she took a bean from the great Cloth of Counting, treasuring it, and later planting it in their gardens in memory of the new foundation of their city. And when the square was empty, the mayor and his men signed the cloth and then took it up and folded it and placed it in the town's archives. And Plummet, well satisfied with his morning's work, sat down briefly on a bench under the trees of the park opposite the square. From a tavern door that faced on the green, a young waiter brought him a beaker of beer and slab of bread with some cheese on it.

"What is this?" asked Plummet.

"Compliments of the house, sir," said the boy brightly.

"And whose house is it?" asked Plummet.

"My new master's," said the boy. "He just bought it from my old master and kept me on. He says he knows you. That you are old friends."

"And what is your master's name?" asked Plummet, puzzled but smiling.

"That's the strange of it," said the boy, suddenly voluble. "'E's that tall, short-haired fella standing in the door there with the apron on, but he calls himself MarCade. Strange name, don't you think, sir?"

Plummet looked where the boy was pointing and saw a figure he just barely recognized without his finery standing at the door of a hole in the wall bar, in between a butcher's store and a fishmonger's. *He's landed on his feet again*, thought Plummet to himself, *and in short order too*. Plummet took off his hat and waved it. In response, the figure snatched a towel from his shoulder and waved it side to side in the air.

"Tell your new master," said Plummet, "that I am grateful for his gift, but now that I am a judge, I must always pay for my meals." He paid the boy for the bread and cheese and beer with a small coin, and then he slipped another one ten times its value into the boy's hand, saying, "Here's something for yourself as well. Just for you, not for your master. Perhaps you can buy your own bar one day too if you save up, and then you'll be the master."

"Yes, *sir*," said the boy, saluting smartly. "I'd like that a great deal."

"And finally," said Plummet, putting an even larger coin in the boy's hand, "Tell your master that I wish to order twenty thousand times as much bread, cheese, and beer as he has just sent me for tomorrow noon."

"*Twenty thousand* times as much?" said the boy, his eyes widening. "Can you really eat that much, sir?"

Plummet laughed so loud, he shook all over.

"No boy. There will be wedding feasts tomorrow, and all must have enough."

"Yes, sir," said the boy suddenly understanding and running off toward the bar door at top speed.

As Plummet rested and ate, he watched the people passing happily and without fear on their business to and fro across the open, sunlit space, the air washed by the freely playing water of the spouting fountain.

When the innkeepers and the caterers, the bakers and the cooks, all heard the news of the royal marriage and the orders began to arrive, they set to work frantically. Why did it have to be tomorrow? They would have to work all night. And what? There were to be not just one marriage, but three marriages! Red John and the princess and some unknown friends of StrongThumbs were to be married simultaneously? What a party it would be! What festivities, what dancing, what music! The entire city would turn out for the occasion, and all the roasters of meats and bakers of pies would have to be busy all the afternoon and all the evening to be ready.

The musicians arranged times to rehearse. People began to look into their closets to see what they possessed to wear. Wives complained to their husbands that they needed a new dress, and the husbands pointed out that there was no time. It was tomorrow, tomorrow, only twenty-four hours away, less than twenty-four hours, really. Women called to their maids to get ready to do their hair. The barbers did a brisk trade as young gallants arrived to be shaved and tonsured for the morrow. The stable boys began brushing the horses, and polishing the harnesses, and making the coaches ready for the marriage procession. The children pleaded to be allowed to attend, and the mothers, finally relenting, began to fuss over them; they too had to have something special to wear.

And deep in the city, Plummet had taken the princess, Marianna, and Illanna to a dressmaker of his acquaintance and told her what was expected of her and by when. The old woman, with her three helpers cowering behind her, had put her hand to her brow and said in a strong accent, "It iss im*poss*ible," but then began to look at the three girls, to turn them this way and that, to murmur, "How beootiful she iss." And then, in a flurry, she set to work, taking their measurements and shouting orders to the other women in the shop.

After her dress had been ordered, the princess went back to the government guesthouse with John and, there, in the privacy of its parlor, talked a long afternoon about their new responsibilities. They discovered each other to be as wise and prudent and mutually passionate about justice as they found each other handsome and beautiful. Illanna, dressed as a sailor, accompanied L'Orka around the city. Everywhere they went, they were cheered by the soldiers and sailors at the guard posts, and especially on the wharves. But Plummet led Morduc and Marianna, followed by Anga, through twisting streets until they came to a small stone archway at the back of a large building. The arch led into a small garden with a blue pool at its center. The pool was ringed with three concentric beds of roses of every color. Here and there, as in a maze, narrow strips of green grass divided the beds so visitors could walk among the roses. Ivy grew up the stone walls and ran along their tops. Under a pine tree growing against the wall opposite the arch was a gray bench. In the center of the garden, the blue pool reflected the sun. Morduc stared. He had seen that light in that color before. Why here? Why now? Was it Drefon's message for him?

Plummet led the way across the garden and knocked on a heavy wooden door recessed in an arched portal in the wall of the large building. There was no answer. Plummet knocked again. After a long wait, they heard slow steps coming along the hall. The door was opened by a very old, slightly stooped man with long white hair and a long white beard. He was dressed in a long, shimmering robe. As he stood there in the doorway, he looked at them with piercing, serene, and kindly eyes.

"Well, yes. I am here."

"It is Plummet. I have brought some friends to speak with you. They have a request."

"Is it really you, Plummet? I seem to remember you as more chestnut in the leaf and leaner in the twig than you are now. Does the world give you so much pleasure that you enjoy swimming in a sea of flesh, old Plummet?"

"Ah, AppleGnarle, we all swim in a sea, and us of time. These friends are young. Say, will you talk to them and listen to their request?"

"Of course, Plummet. Of course. Come in, come in. For our youth together and comradeship's memory alone I would admit you, and for many another virtue as well would I listen to your friends' request and satisfy it too, if it is proper and within my power, but chiefly because they are young and have a certain twinkle in their eyes that I remember well and well approve."

The old man held open the door, and they entered a hall. He closed the door behind them, and the hall darkened to deep reds and blues and yellows warming the darkness from small windows filled with pictures worked in stained glass high in the corridor. The old man led them down a long hall and into a small study lit by a single large round window in one wall. Books filled shelves on the other three walls. More books were piled on a large table in the center of the room and on all the several chairs. There were even piles of books on the floor. AppleGnarle lifted some volumes off a chair for Plummet and indicated a leather bench for Morduc and Marianna. He himself sat on a stool before the only neat space in the room, a broad tilted desk by the window, on which a large leather-bound volume written in a strange character lay open.

"Now then," said AppleGnarle, "what can a poor, drab scholar such as I do for you?"

"You do yourself an injustice," said Plummet. "You were and are, first of all, a most holy man, the best in the city to bless a marriage. It is in that capacity that we seek you out. In your second, as a reader of lost languages, for that too we have sought you."

"Indeed," said AppleGnarle, giving them a quizzical sidelong glance. "And with the fall of the Master, is there so soon a rush to reopen the locked and shuttered fanes? He did not dare to kill me, but he isolated me because I would not grace any part of his graceless reign, by word, symbol, or act. Thus I have held no services nor performed any marriages nor buried any during his time. For my own safety, I cared not, but I did not want to jeopardize the people."

"Let me introduce my friends. This young man is Morduc, son of the elf king of the groves beyond the highest mountains. His companion is Lord Ballan's daughter. They wish to be married."

"Ah, they wish to be coupled," said AppleGnarle.

"No, sir," answered Morduc. "Coupling is for those who anticipate uncoupling. We wish rather to be married in the old meaning, and we wish you to perform the blessing and to guide our ceremony. Would you be willing to do it?"

"Indeed," said the old man, without answering the question, "And is our great dog to be left out?"

"Of the marriages?" said Morduc in astonishment.

"Of the introductions," said AppleGnarle, reaching out his ancient thin hand to the great gray head.

"The dog's name," said Morduc, "is Anga."

"And by the look of him," said AppleGnarle, "he understands us well enough. Am I right?"

"You are right indeed," said Morduc, "but how could you know?"

"I also know something about you as well," said the old man, gazing into Morduc's green eyes. "You have injured your hand in your friend's war, and you have lost a jewel of great power. And now you wish to lose something for which all here seek. Am I not right?"

Breathing deeply, gasping almost, Morduc answered him, "Yes, you are right."

"Then what did you bring me to read?" he said, completely confusing Morduc. Morduc looked at Plummet for guidance. Plummet merely nodded. Morduc removed the folded paper from the pouch hung about his neck. On it were the rubbings he had made of the strange characters that circled the forest cup. He handed it to the old priest. With his ancient but untrembling hands, AppleGnarle unfolded it. Morduc explained the circumstances under which he had found the cup, the curiosity of its construction, and the consequences of drinking from it.

"Can you read it, sir? It is a most strange script," said Morduc.

AppleGnarle laid aside the paper with trembling hands. A tear fell from his eye. There was silence in the small, book-lined room. "Will you remain in this city long?" he said.

Morduc and Marianna looked at each other. They had no answer for him. After another silence, AppleGnarle resumed his former subject, seemingly as if the discussion of the mysterious script had never occurred.

"Then let me counsel you carefully, my young friend. If you do this thing, you will not be able to return home. If you try, if you go there, you will find nothing when you arrive, and nothing here when you return. Did you know that?"

Morduc was silent for a long time. Then he finally said slowly, "This I was not told. That I would sacrifice myself I was aware, but that I could never see my father and friends again I was not. Is it truly so?"

"Yes, it is truly so. If you take your bride home to visit with your loveds, you will find there nothing but leaf mold at the foot of the trees. The world in which you were raised will be closed to you. And then if you return here after that trip, you will find all that you loved and left behind likewise gone, changed, disintegrated. Even your children. By marrying a mortal, you lose that much."

Morduc thought silently. Marianna slipped her arm into his. Finally he spoke. "It is a grief," he said simply, "that I must bear."

"Very well, then," said AppleGnarle. "When?"

"Tomorrow," said Morduc and Marianna together.

"Indeed," said AppleGnarle, his eyebrows shooting up. "I can do it then for you, since I am always ready, but Plummet, can the church be opened and cleaned in that time? I am here by myself."

"There is a complication," said Plummet. "There are two other couples, and moreover, the entire city should witness it. Can you do it in the square?"

"In the square?" said AppleGnarle leaning back on his stool and looking out the round window into the sunlight. "In the square!" he marveled. "Well, things have changed if the city would make a precinct of its market. That would be thought on." He sat very still, relaxed yet upright, looking now not outward but inward. Finally he returned to them, swung round on his stool, and stood up. "Yes," he said. "I will do it, and in the square. I will need help, but, yes, yes, I know who to get. I will certainly do it for you two," he said, speaking to Morduc and Marianna, "but these others. Who are they? I would like to talk with them too. These are no easy oaths I offer."

Plummet explained to AppleGnarle the identity of the other two couples, their origins, their commitment, their sponsors, until finally the ancient priest agreed to include all three couples in the ceremony.

"Then at noon, tomorrow, AppleGnarle, in the square," said Plummet.

"At noon tomorrow, Morduc, Marianna, Plummet. And good-bye to thee too, dog Anga," he said as he led them back down the dark corridor of colored light to the small arched door. AppleGnarle opened it to the sunlight and let them out into the garden. After he had closed the door behind them and they had heard the latch fall and his feet retreating down the passageway, Morduc suddenly said, "He didn't tell me the message of the cup," and turned as if to knock once again on the door.

"Patience," said Marianna, taking his hand and holding him. They lingered a while in the garden, looking at the flowers, walking hand in hand. They paused by the pool and looked in. The sun had passed over and no longer shone in the blue water. As they watched, a small dry leaf carried by the breeze dropped on to the surface of the water and a circle of rings radiated out from it. Morduc put his arm around Marianna's shoulders, and she slipped hers around his waist.

Eventually, Plummet said, "Come. We should not linger here longer. Let us to supper." Leaving the garden, they returned through the narrow alleys and streets until they once again gained the main avenue. Crossing it, they made westward and southward in the direction of the Green Dragon. That evening by the fireside of that inn, there sat down together Morduc and John, Plummet and Yanibo, and Palla Nad and L'Orka. The king and the princess had invited Marianna and Illanna to dinner at the government guesthouse where the three brides to be were to lodge that night. The comrades in arms at the Green Dragon ate and drank well but not excessively. They sat long over their wine, recalling the stories of their journeys together, filling in the spaces of their separations, and discussing the seemingly more mundane but still real challenges of their futures. Though they joyously anticipated their new lives, there was the grief too of the loss of the comradeship of war. Even Beetle came up out of the cellar briefly to wish well to John and Morduc, and then he disappeared again into his tunnels, though they urged him to stay with them. Finally the dinner broke up, and each retired to rest up for the morning.

Before he went to bed, Morduc opened the shutters of his window and looked up into the clear night air. High in the sky he saw the bright star of love, Caracanta, that had guided him from his native forest and which had shone on his meeting with Marianna. At the government guesthouse, Marianna too looked out her window, up into the serene darkness, and saw the same star. Both watched for many minutes before going to bed. What would it be like, Marianna wondered, when her inner light had become completely merged with Morduc's soul flame into one light, fused and inseparable? Would she be a different person? Would he be a different person? Would the two of them become a single flame, or two lights glowing side by side? What would married love feel like? She decided that there would not be twin lights, but a single lumination, a single flame, a single sun, as if two stars had merged into one. What had been differentiated energy centers would no longer be so. They would still seem to the eyes of their friends to be two, but, in fact, they would be one. She knew she would like that, loving Morduc as she did, but would he like it? Would he not regret the loss of himself, his former immortal self? Could she be sufficient compensation? It troubled her. Perhaps she should slip out, go to the Green Dragon, and discuss it with him before . . . before it was too late for him to change his mind. She looked up at Caracanta. Should she go? Then, as if the star were a mirror reflecting his thought to her from a great distance, she felt Morduc's mind within her, entering through her eyes. *He is watching this star too, at this very moment,* she said to herself. She opened herself to the flow of Morduc's thought as it went up to the star and back down into her. He, in his turn, felt her question as he stood at the window of his solitary room in the Green Dragon. He did not have to say anything to communicate with her. No words could be sufficiently clear, correct, and strong enough to reassure and comfort her. Words left out too much. He let the star draw his spirit wordlessly flowing to her, to join hers, smiling, joyous, comforting, putting her doubts to rest by joining, interpenetrating hers in a momentary precursor of the union which their marriage would make eternal. She felt Morduc within her, steady, bright, and at one with her own spirit. She relaxed, finding their spirits had become a single flame. She was suddenly surprised to become aware of a third unknown flame dwelling next to yet within their own single flame. She smiled, satisfied, closed the shutters, and went to bed secure, finally, in the rightness of their love.

The star continued its slow progress across the heavens but did not sink below the horizon even with the coming of dawn. As the dark velvet sky became faintly purple in the east and the birds began to chirp fretfully, it continued to shine brightly until in the gold-and-pink eastern sky the sun finally appeared and outshone the star's distant serene light.

Down below in the still dark city of Kerballa, there were more than a hundred pinpoints of yellow light marking preparations for the festivities. Bakers' boys were loading wagons. Vintners were rolling casks up on to carts. Caterers of meats were getting the roasts out of their ovens. The musicians of the various bands and orchestras were tuning their pipes and testing their drums. Up in the cathedral, AppleGnarle was saying his morning prayers. And rattling toward the government guesthouse came a carriage carrying Madame Merrisou and her three helpers. She struggled out of the carriage, bustled toward the large carved door, and knocked imperiously. "Open zis tur immedeeately. Vee will be late!" A sleepy servant opened it wide, spilling light into the predawn street. Madame Merrisou and her three apprentices swept in. She climbed the stairs laboriously, carrying her bag of needles, threads, and pins, while her apprentices staggered up the stairs behind her, each carrying a huge dress box.

The princess, Marianna, and Illanna were all awake. They had taken nought but hot lemon water for breakfast. On this solemn yet joyous day, they would wait until after their marriages to break their fast. They had put on all new white undergarments and had assembled in the large room of the princess where the three best hairdressers in Kerballa, Billtum, Adorolfo, and Rammone, had been assembled to create the hairdos of the three brides. Although Illanna, the princess, and Marianna had all protested that they could do their own hair, the King of Time had arranged for it, and to indulge him, they endured good-humoredly the competition among the three "artistes of the glory." Madame Merrisou knocked with her cane on the door with a crack loud enough to startle the dead, yelling at the top of her lungs, "Vee haf not a moment to lose. Get these feelthy hair boys out of my way!" But as the three brides stood up and turned from their mirrors and looked at Madame Merrisou and she looked back at them, she was struck dumb by their beauty. Marianna's dark hair was lifted and piled high on her head and pinned there, showing her beautiful ears and the elegant line of her neck. Aleth's long golden-red hair shone even brighter than usual, and part of it had been cut in bangs over her forehead so that she looked fetching and flirtatious. Yet it was Illanna who proved to be the crowning beauty of them all, whose light brown hair had always been bound up messily on her head under a scarf or hood. Her hairdresser had braided her hair all over her head, interlacing the braids with golden and purple threads and beads and flowers.

Madame Merrisou began to cry. "Ach. You are the three moooost beeeeyoutiful girls I haf evair in my life seen. For once, I must say to you hair boyses, you are geniuses. *Gene yus es*! I apologize for *evair* having had a hardt t'ought about you in my entire layfe." Billtum and Adorolfo and Rammone bowed deeply to the doyen of wedding organizers in Kerballa, and after mumbling a quiet "Thank you, thank you, madame. It is the greatest tribute we have ever had," they bowed again deeply and backed out of the room.

"*Now*," said Madame Merrisou, recovering her imperiousness and clapping her hands at her assistants nearly buried beneath their huge boxes, "*Eet* is time to *dress*! Bring the camisole of the princess!" She began to dress the princess while the others looked on in quiet joy.

In the naval barracks, L'Orka had risen and washed and dressed himself in his best uniform, parrying the spirited jokes of his fellow officers about boarding and cargo and harbors. At the Green Dragon, John and Morduc had also awakened. John's armor had been polished until it gleamed like a red-steel mirror and Morduc's seventy times seven shaded suit of green had been washed under the careful eye of Mother Gump until it resembled the colors of country fields in springtime. When both were dressed, they descended and, like their brides-to-be, ate nothing but drank only some hot lemon water.

"We have come a long journey," said John to Morduc.

"Indeed we have," said the elf. "Though, in a sense, mine is only beginning."

"And truly, mine as well," replied Red John. "As I serve the city, those responsibilities will be a journey within myself. But I am ready. What will you and Marianna do? Would you consider remaining here to advise me and friend me?"

"I will always friend you," said Morduc, "but Marianna has her astronomical studies, which she can pursue best at home. And I, I have so much to learn there as well and to provide, since Marianna's brother . . ." His voice trailed off. "I owe Lord Ballan so much that I would like to provide what comfort I can to him. Marianna and I will visit, so our children and yours will know each other as cousins."

"That would be the delight of my life," said John.

"And mine as well," said Morduc.

"Well," said John, "are we ready then?"

"I believe we are," said Morduc.

Outside, the mixed music of two different walking bands could be heard, one composed of strings and pipes and the other of horns and drums. As the two bridegrooms stepped out of the Green Dragon's door, a small crowd waiting in the narrow alley began to cheer. John had never looked stronger or more massive in his red-steel armor and his gold-red beard. He smiled at the crowd, which yelled, "Long live StrongThumbs." Morduc, shorter and slimmer, stood beside him in his suit of seventy times seven shades of green. He had a new green feather in his hat. His bow was on his back, and the light-green glow of his dagger was scarcely concealed within its scabbard. The scorched hand did not hurt and worked reasonably well, only occasionally twitching and itching as the burned, blacked flesh healed and scarred over. As they strode forward, the horns and drums fell in before them and the strings and pipes behind. The two musical groups finally broke free of their exploratory cacophony into the same tempo and tune, and the entire crowd marched northward on the cross street until they reached the avenue where people lined both sides waiting to see them.

Flags flew along the main avenue and pennons waved from the housetop flagpoles. With Anga trotting a pace behind, the red-and-green comrades marched down the avenue in the clear golden sunlight, and as they marched, they could see where the long, broad street widened in the distance into the plaza on the left and the park full of trees on the right. From the distance ahead came the sound of cheering as they approached.

As they walked toward the square, a crowd of sailors with L'Orka at its center erupted from one of the harbor-side cross streets. He joined Morduc and John. John strode in the middle, glinting in his red-steel armor with L'Orka on his left in his bright white-and-brass-buttoned uniform, and Morduc to his right in his shining, shifting green.

As they approached the square, they saw that the platform upon which the test of the riddle had been conducted was now draped in white, and atop it stood AppleGnarle in a glistening pale-blue-and-silver robe. His long white hair was combed smooth and streamed down his back while his white beard, combed and brushed as well, flowed smoothly down his chest. Below his beard hung a shining silver disk encrusted with diamonds. He held his arms up to the sun, singing raptly, though the music of the bands drowned out his prayer. From the other direction came an open carriage drawn by six pairs of horses, each pair containing one white and one black horse, alternating one behind the other. The carriage was followed by the music of a walking string orchestra. As the three bridegrooms attained the eastern edge of the square, the golden carriage entered the western. In it, the king and the princess sat on the seat facing forward. Opposite them sat Illanna and Marianna.

The princess's red-gold hair shone in the sunlight as it streamed down her back under a chaplet of small white flowers which kept her veil in place. The flowers surmounting Marianna's veil were blue, and those topping Illanna's were yellow. The carriage reached the center of the square opposite the platform. The king descended first and gave his hand to the princess. As she descended, John stepped toward the king and received her right hand in the crook of his left arm. She carried a small bouquet of white flowers in her left hand. Together they stepped onto a long blue carpet which led to the steps of the platform. Marianna then stepped down from the carriage, her face veiled and her dark hair crowned with blue flowers. Morduc stepped to her, and she placed her right hand within his left arm. Morduc had such a broad smile on his face that she had to put her blue bouquet to her face to cover her blush. Finally the brown-haired, yellow-chapleted Illanna came down the carriage step to the ground and was joined by L'Orka, who could not resist a mischievous wink at her even in the solemnity of the occasion.

The coach pulled away, leaving the three couples standing one behind the other on the long blue pathway to the platform. Lining it on both sides stood two rows of alternating men and women, dressed in long, pale, shimmering blue robes just like AppleGnarle's. Each held a tall unlighted torch. At the head of the steps up on to the platform stood AppleGnarle, holding a small silver bowl which flamed waveringly in the slightly moving air. At a signal from him, the person in each of the lines closest to the platform lit his or her torch from the bowl and then passed the flame to the man or woman next to him. Marianna squeezed Morduc's arm as the flame came toward them along each of the lines. The crowd, which now pressed in behind them, filling the square, cheered as the last torch was lit to make a flaming corridor to the platform. AppleGnarle, standing at the top of the steps with two female priestly assistants, one on each side, beckoned John and Aleth to come forward. They approached the platform on the long blue carpet laid over the stones of the square. The other two couples followed.

When John and Aleth reached the steps, they slowly climbed them. John and the princess took their places directly in front of AppleGnarle, facing him, their backs to the crowd. Morduc and Marianna climbed the steps and moved to John and Aleth's right. L'Orka and Illanna stepped to the left when they reached the top of the stairs. The blue-robed deacons who had held the torches along the blue carpet now gathered around the platform, ringing it. In that rectangle of fire, on the white platform, AppleGnarle reached out his hands, placing one on John's shoulder and one on the shoulder of the princess, and under that light pressure, they both knelt before him. Morduc and Marianna and L'Orka and Illanna did the same. The crowd grew silent except for the rustling of feet, and then, as AppleGnarle waited with his hands uplifted, even that ceased.

Standing straighter than anyone had seen him able to do in many years, and in a strong, clear voice that the entire city had nearly forgotten, AppleGnarle began to sing the service of marriage in an ancient language whose words were nevertheless strangely comfortable and familiar, especially to the ears of those who had come to maturity before the tyranny of the Master of Darkness.

As AppleGnarle continued to sing, stopping at the appropriate places for the three couples to make their answers to the questions he put to them, a peace and joy came into the hearts of all the witnesses in the great square. They heard in the open air the simple, dignified, and significant words of their ancient custom. Each of the three couples drank a sip from a golden cup and ate a morsel from a golden plate. Presently it was ended. AppleGnarle struck a silver bell three times. Each of the couples rose. John lifted the veil of the princess and, leaning into her, kissed her on her lips. Morduc did the same. Illanna lifted the veil herself and gave L'Orka so strong a kiss, they nearly fell over on the platform. The crowd laughed. Now AppleGnarle chanted a final benediction, and as he finished it, he flung his arms wide. All the bands in the square began to play an ancient, deep-throbbing air of dance such that the music seemed to rise up out of the earth and simultaneously to descend from the heavens. The three couples turned to the crowd, standing a little unsteadily, almost in a daze, smiled at each other, and kissed again.

The crowd cheered three times loudly above the music. As John and Aleth came down the steps of the platform, a group of young people formed around them and began a skipping, running, circling dance. Around that circle formed a larger one, but moving in the opposite direction. Around these two counterrunning circles formed yet another, but running in the direction of the innermost circle and then another around that reversing direction again. At the center, John and Aleth circled too, their foreheads touching, her hands on his shoulders and his on her waist.

Morduc and Marianna were likewise snatched from the foot of the stairs by a circle of boys and girls in bright outfits with ribbons flying and then surrounded by a second circle, and then a third. So too were L'Orka and Illanna drawn into the crowd, until the entire plaza was filled with dancing circles within circles within circles, all going in different directions, celebrating freedom, celebrating love, celebrating the freedom to love.

Those who stood on the sides of the plaza filled the air with clouds of small white beans thrown heavenward. After the circles of dancers with the new couples in them had danced for many minutes, they began to break apart and made their way to the great park opposite the plaza, under whose trees long trestle tables had been set up loaded with bread and meat and drink and cake. John and the princess were led to a table at the outer edge of the grove, facing the plaza, and were each given a cup of wine, followed by a piece cut from the biggest white cake there. Another cheer went up from the people, who then themselves also fell to drinking and eating with gusto.

Throughout the plaza now, clowns began to appear and play jokes on the people in the crowd. A tall, thin, frizzy-headed clown and a short half-naked boy were among the most industrious in the joking. The three newly married couples looked on from their table with indulgence and good humor. Even the king, from his place next to Morduc and Marianna where he sat with Plummet, condescended to smile from time to time at the antics of the merrymakers in the plaza before him. The entire city seemed to vibrate with laughter during the entire long afternoon.

Finally, the celebration began to play itself out. In the avenue traversing the square, three painted open carriages pulled up. L'Orka and Illanna got into the first, a bright sea blue, and were driven away as if in a rattling race toward their new quarters in the navy yard. A group of cheering sailors bearing torches and clanging gongs and cymbals followed the carriage, running all the way to the river. John and the princess got into the second, a bright crimson, pulled by RedFire himself and a white mare both in breeching harness, and they in their turn, but at a more sedate pace, were conveyed westward surrounded by a crowd of singing and cheering young men and women toward the government guesthouse where John and the princess would now live. The King of Time remained behind with Plummet and AppleGnarle, who would later escort him to AppleGnarle's cloister from which on the morrow he would set out for home with a body of cavalry provided from the city's garrison by Plummet.

After playing the most tricks of anyone, Yanibo and Palla Nad began to trudge homeward toward the circus, passing as they did so parties all over the city at which the citizens continued the celebration of their new freedom and of the marriages of John and Aleth, L'Orka and Illanna, and Morduc and Marianna.

Finally, of those married that day, only Morduc and Marianna were left at the plaza, and with them Anga. They walked to their coach, painted a brilliant green, and climbed in. The dog jumped in with them. Surrounded by a group of boys carrying torches and clanging gongs and tooting whistles, they were escorted at a happy walk back to the Green Dragon. Mother Gump met them at the door. Morduc and Marianna followed her up the stairs to the best bedroom in the house. In the room was a shaded candle sitting on a small table, on which stood a bottle of wine, a loaf of bread, and a small, round cheese.

"Mother Gump," said Morduc, "you are extremely thoughtful."

"It is my pleasure," she replied. "You are my children now. May you sleep well. I will leave you and give this great dog of yours some dinner too." She left the room, with Anga trotting after her, his toenails clicking on the ancient plank floors of the narrow hallway. Closing the heavy door behind the retreating figures, Morduc put the bar in place. He approached Marianna and carefully took the delicate ring of flowers from her hair and placed it on the table. Then, carefully and slowly, one by one he took out the long shell pins from her piled-up hair, until it finally hung down long and straight as when he first had met her. He took her elbows in his hands, and then, moving closer, he circled the lithe slimness of her waist with his fingers and, putting his lips to hers, kissed her deeply and passionately, and she put her slim arms around his neck and replied to him with equal desire.

Suddenly, outside their window in the street, they heard an outbreak of bells and gongs and whistles. Morduc and Marianna, hand in hand, stepped to the shutters and opened them. As they looked out, a cheer went up from the torchbearers below, among them Yanibo and Palla Nad, their upturned faces clear among the flames. Morduc waved. The boys cheered again, giving one long last rattle of their cattle bells, and a last banging of their gongs, and a last shrilling of their flutes.

As the group began to break up and then to drift away by ones and twos, the shutters closed, and after a while the faint candlelight behind them went out too. Except for an occasional passerby, the street was empty and quiet. The city was at peace. In the moonless sky above, Caracanta shone bright and clear, guiding us then as now toward the happiness of beauty, truth, and love.

CPSIA information can be obtained at www.ICGtesting.com
Printed in the USA
LVOW07*1015050914

402619LV00001B/10/P